SHADOWBORN'S TERROR

Book IV of 'The Magician's Brother' Series

HDA Roberts

Cover by Warren Design

CONTENTS

CHAPTER 1

I was bored.

So very, very bored.

It was actually a nice change from scared, wounded and angry, but still... politics were so, so dull!

After being presented to the Conclave as the fifth Archon, in what was actually a very nice ceremony, I was expected to take my Seat for the important sessions, agonising though that was. This particular one was the opening of the Conclave for the Summer Session. Once it was over, I wouldn't have to come back for a while, but I was making up for it that day. Good grief, how could the others stand the never-ending babble?

As it was a full assembly, the entire place was packed from floor to ceiling with Magicians, observers, diplomats and various creatures. Between them, they hadn't stopped talking for *four hours*, and I'd really needed to pee for the last two.

The Grand Conclave Chamber was built like an amphitheatre, with a set of large wooden doors built into the west wall, opposite which was an open space containing the Seats of the Archons. Mine was far left, as I was the most junior. Hopkins was next to me, with Kron in the centre as High Seat for this session (we rotate on a decade-basis, it wouldn't be my turn for a while, thank God), then Killian and finally Palmyra. The rest of the chamber was organised into three tiers of seats, stretching up towards the domed roof, each tier containing various rows of (relatively comfortable) chairs, with the more important people closer to the front of each tier.

The councillors representing British Magicians occupied the lowest rows, closest to the Archons; above them were representatives from other countries and groups as well as the press and even a block for non-magical observers from Her Majesty's Government (who could never resist sticking their noses or fingers into other people's pies). Above *them* were the country's non-political Mages, sorted by power level, and generally just there to get stuck into a good argument, should one turn up (and with this many Magicians in one place, one usually did, just not on Opening Day).

Every country with a significant magical population had their own Conclave, along with their own Seats (though the names for these varied from place to place, naturally). As a result, the Archons were normally a little more spread out; Palmyra, for example, liked to make her home at the French Conclave in Paris. But because they'd just returned from their self-imposed exile a few months earlier, the decision had been made to re-establish the power base in a single Conclave there before spreading back out to their old territories. The one in Stonebridge had been chosen for a number of reasons, not the least of which was because this had been their... *our* official capital since the fall of the Roman Empire, and it was a necessary symbolic act to reclaim it first (that, and Great Britain was home to the largest concentration of Sorcerers in the world; it was best not to snub them).

My fellow Archons also wanted to have a good yell at the Magicians who thought that they could fold up our political power without our say-so. There had been a very brief debate in the Conclave (in which Killian, Lord Death, had expressed his displeasure at their presumption) before a swift repeal of those acts. Only two other Conclaves had even *tried* to put legislation like that into effect, and both of them had recanted before close of business that same day (Lord Death was scary when he wanted to be. The rest of the time he was a horrific prankster with an evil sense of humour; but a word of advice: *never* piss him off. He could *literally* kill with a look).

I contained a yawn with an effort, flicking a piece of lint

off my jacket. I was dressed in a navy blue suit with a dark tie, white shirt and highly polished shoes, over which I had a set of black academic robes and the enchanted hood which concealed my face from prying eyes (I was still trying to keep a low profile). The others were dressed similarly, and formally, in business suits of one sort or another, though theirs were considerably more expensive and better tailored than mine. Kron, who was never one for modern trends, wore her own version of formal attire, which amounted to an ornate suit of gold-chased black armour; to complete the look, she had a heavy-headed war-hammer next to her seat within easy snatching distance.

Councillor... Something-or-other was droning on about... some-such. I think it was about closer ties with... someone, I couldn't tell you for sure; it was far from important. He'd been talking for twenty minutes, and even the glacially patient Kron was starting to look like she was bored.

Then, just as I was considering something Magically drastic to relieve the pressure in my bladder, someone came in through one of the side doors, a tiny fellow I recognised as one of Arianna Hellstrom's lackeys. He darted straight over to her.

Hellstrom was the new Domestic Minister, a post she'd inherited when she beat the living snot out of her predecessor, Balthazar Thorne (now serving six consecutive life sentences at the Farm, and good riddance to him). Hellstrom was now the power behind the *Primus inter pares*, called the Primus for ease of conversation (that means 'first among equals', sort of our Prime Minister). The Primus was a watery man called Aiden Foltre; he sat in the front row, near the Seats, and largely did what he was told. I'd thought that Hellstrom would have taken the spot for herself, but she wasn't the sort to stand in the limelight.

Hellstrom was blonde and attractive, appearing to be in her early thirties, but was in fact far older. She wore a simple dress which should have looked silly under a robe, with her Imperial-purple Sorcerer's hood draped around the shoulders, but somehow she made it look stylish. The various symbols and metal badges on the front of her hood marked her out as a woman of wide interests and not inconsiderable skill (as I'd learned the hard way).

Hellstrom's lackey bent over and whispered something in her ear. She turned and whispered something back. He nodded and left again. I thought that was it for a moment and my heart sank, but then she stood, meaning she wanted the chance to speak, raising her hand to indicate urgency.

"The Seat recognises Duchess Hellstrom," Kron said, with almost indecent haste.

Councillor Boring-me-to-death sat down with an irate look on his face, after a moment where his mouth continued moving without any words coming out.

"Lady Namia Sutton of the Peace Legion requests a moment of our time," Hellstrom said, looking towards Kron, "I think it would be best to see her. She says that she has news of a threat to us all."

Lady who of the what? I sent, Telepathically, to Hopkins.

Ever since we'd joined our wells and minds for a rather nasty little fight a couple of months earlier, it had been very easy to link with her and talk like this (it also made it less embarrassing to ask questions in the middle of Conclave).

Namia Sutton, she replied (the same way), *one of our best and most loyal allies. She's what you might call a scout, looking out for threats to Magical society. The Peace Legion is her group; Magicians and Magical creatures that work together and help out where they can. They keep people safe; keep the peace.*

Sounds like a great idea to me, does she come into Conclave often?

Rarely. Normally she can deal with any issues herself. If she's here then there must be something badly wrong.

"Bring her in," Kron said while we were 'talking'.

The big doors at the other end of the room opened, and in marched a woman, a man at her side in cuffs. He was older and dishevelled, with a heavily lined face, wearing a wrinkled grey suit that was stained in the armpits and groin. His eyes were blank, like he was almost dead.

She... she was something else entirely.

Namia Sutton was the kind of beautiful you only read about. Tall and strong-looking, graceful and athletic, but not so much as to take from an appearance of soft femininity. Her face looked kind and sweet, framed by long, flowing, golden hair that curled around her cheeks. Her lips were red and generous, her eyes a startling blue. She wore a conservative outfit, a blue jacket over long skirt. In short, she looked like the sort of cute girl-next-door you'd love on sight and treasure for your whole life.

And one look was all it took for that woman to terrify me to my very core.

I don't know if you've ever been scared. Not scared of something in a movie, or by someone jumping from the shadows to frighten you, I mean truly *terrified* of something that could have ended your life, the kind of fear that comes from being in the presence of something that is going to do you immense harm.

I took one look at her, and *that* feeling of utter, horrible dread came over me. Terror seared through my mind, making my hands shake and my bladder control waver dangerously. I could feel my Shadows at the edge of my perception perk up at my reaction, trying to come for me and offer comfort. It was an immense effort to push them back and away.

I saw Palmyra looking around the others at me. She was a Life Mage, sometimes called a White Magician, and so an Empath. She was able to feel my fear like it was her own. Hopkins noticed too, she took my hand and squeezed the fingers.

What is it? she sent.

I don't know, I replied, my heart pounding as Sutton approached the Seats.

Do you want to adjourn?

No, that's okay. I'll manage.

I breathed carefully, controlling my emotions, watching

intently as the woman stopped and bowed to the Seat.

"My Lords and Ladies," she said; her voice was high and musical, very gentle. It should have been soothing, but instead it sent shivers down my spine and I broke into a cold sweat, "I apologise for interrupting, but something terrible has been brought to my attention."

She paused to pull something out of her pocket; it was a clear plastic pouch that fit comfortably in the palm of her hand, a thimbleful's worth of miniscule red crystals in the bottom.

"This is Source," she said, holding it up, "It is a drug; manufactured by this man and his associates in great quantity. We don't know what it's made from, but we *do* know is that it greatly enhances the innate powers of a Magician. It is even possible to give a normal human being, a Pureborn, the powers of an Acolyte, even an Adept if he takes enough of it."

She paused for a moment, looking around, her eyes earnest and respectful.

I didn't believe a word of it. It might have been the terror talking, but something wasn't right with this, I was certain.

"I'm here because I need help. The *Legion* needs help to stop this epidemic before it can get any worse. Already thousands of men and women have used it, and the power is addictive. Imagine a Wizard taking a dose of this, or even a Sorcerer. Imagine the kind of power he'd have!"

This whole thing smelled funny to me. The way she was talking... she sounded more like a salesman than a crusader.

I took a tight rein on my fear and stood, walking towards Sutton and the man. She stopped talking at my approach. There was muttering (there's usually muttering when I do things, I try not to take it personally).

"Lord Shadow?" Kron said from behind me.

Matty, what are you doing? Hopkins sent.

Something's wrong, I'm taking a look, I replied.

The man was just standing there as I approached, his eyes glazed over. He didn't even seem to register my presence.

"Sir?" I said, standing in front of him. He flinched a very little bit, "Can you hear me?"

He nodded slowly.

"You have questions for my prisoner, my lord?" Sutton said, her voice making my skin crawl, though her tone was reasonable and utterly respectful.

I nodded.

"Sir, you have no reason to be afraid here," I said quietly.

He nodded, though nothing in his eyes showed understanding of what I'd said.

"I'd like to touch your mind. Would you allow that, Sir?"

His lip trembled, but he nodded.

"I'm not sure that's wise, Milord, this man was a killer. You might be better off keeping out," Sutton said, her voice filled with concern. She sounded genuine; my heart told me she wasn't.

So I ignored her and sent in a Telepathic probe...

And very nearly got my mind peeled apart by a neural shredder. If I hadn't been moving carefully, I'd have lost a chunk of memory, or something even more important. I dodged it and moved around his headspace even more cautiously. I felt my way in deeper and saw the shredder as a chunk of foreign power in his mind. It took some time to dismantle it and pull away the pieces.

Whoever had put it in there had been both competent and vicious. It would have left both me and the prisoner a vegetable if it had been triggered. If that wasn't enough, the poor man's memories had been extensively altered; carefully, meticulously, but still recognisably if you knew what to look for. I could feel the edges of the false engrams, where they were just the tiniest fraction out of sync with the rest of his mind.

I took a closer look at those. There were memories of him making something very complicated, drugs, presumably; more of him selling them to people whose faces he couldn't remember. The memories felt discordant, out of balance. It was like... his mind was a train, and his memories were the tracks.

It was as if he were forced into a cycle of falseness that ground his real personality against the implants, fraying them both away. There was only a little damage so far, but it wouldn't be long before his mind was a broken thing, driven into total insanity.

Whoever had done this was simultaneously very competent and yet also quite sloppy. I guessed that they hadn't expected him to come under Telepathic scrutiny, or that if he did, then the shredder would take care of the problem. I set to work fixing the damage, being as gentle as I could, excising the falsehoods one by one. There were quite a few, and each time I had to reconnect the empty sections with the rest of his mind.

The actual memories buried under the false ones were gone; there would be no recovering them. Nor could I find any evidence of who'd done this to him aside from the very vague impression of a Magical signature I could feel within the implanted memories.

The last six months or so of memory was where the damage was at its worst. Beyond that, everything seemed to be more or less stable. I wasn't really practiced at this sort of reconstructive work, but I did a passable job. The human mind was a very robust thing; it could heal most damage on its own as long as everything was more or less in the right place.

The man's eyes cleared as I finished snipping out the last false memory. He looked around, a dazed look on his face.

"Where am I?" he asked, moving about a little before he realised he was cuffed, "What is this?"

"Don't worry, Mister...?" I asked calmly, waving at the cuffs, which fell away into a heap at his feet.

"Clayton. Andrew Clayton. Where am I?" he asked again, looking around.

"In the Conclave building in Stonebridge," I said, "You've been falsely accused of a crime and have had your memory altered. I've repaired the damage, but I'm afraid you've lost a few months of time."

There was further muttering, much of it angry, from

around me.

Sutton looked shocked and confused. She threw her hand over her chest and her eyes were suddenly wet.

"Stonebridge?" Clayton said, his eyes wide, "And what crime? I've never committed a crime in my life! Who said I did?"

"*That* is a very good question," I said, turning towards Sutton.

"I had no idea..." she said, looking mortified. She dropped to a knee, "I will accept any punishment my Lords decide I deserve. I have brought shame on myself and my Legion. I am nothing, nothing but a worthless fool."

Kron was at the cowering woman's side in an instant, glaring daggers at me as I stood between Sutton and the man she'd abused. Well, that someone had abused, anyway. I couldn't help but think it was her, in spite of her current theatrics. Oh, I didn't think she'd done it *herself*; the Telepath's Magical signature just didn't mesh with Sutton, so it wasn't her. But I just *knew* that she was responsible *somehow*.

Kron helped Sutton to her feet.

"No, my Lady, I have erred horribly, I must pay recompense," Sutton said, trying to drop to her knees again.

"That is ludicrous," Kron said, "You were sold a bill of goods. It's hardly your fault."

"Really?" I asked, letting a little incredulous doubt enter my voice, "That man was the victim of a terrible abuse. Do you really mean to tell me that she couldn't spot something like that over the course of an interrogation, when I managed to see it in seconds *without* Magic?"

Kron turned and gave me a look of such vehement hate that I actually took an involuntary step backwards. The only person I wished to piss off even less than Killian was Kron, and it seemed that I'd managed to do precisely that.

"Lady Namia has been a trusted confidant and friend of this Conclave and your brother Archons for hundreds of years before you were born," Kron spat, glaring at me, "you will show her the respect she's due."

That dismissive attitude rankled at me a little, making me defensive and perhaps a little unnecessarily tactless...

"There are currently two potential explanations on the table," I said, staring Lady Time down while the other Archons approached, no doubt hoping to diffuse the situation, "Either she didn't notice, in which case she's incompetent and negligent in the face of inhuman suffering; or she *did*, and she's complicit in severe mental abuse. Which theory deserves the most respect?"

Kron's face went white with rage while Sutton cried onto her shoulder. I thought for a long moment that I'd made a terrible mistake, but then I saw one of Sutton's eyes open and look right at me.

There wasn't just hatred in that look; there was a complete and utter *loathing*; disgust coupled with a destructive, total contempt.

It was a look I saw mirrored in Kron's eyes, but it wasn't nearly as intense as Sutton's.

"We will adjourn now," Lady Time said, her voice trembling in fury, "When we return, you will be elsewhere, understand?"

"What about Mister Clayton?" I asked.

"He'll be taken care of, now get out!" Kron hissed.

I stood for a moment, shocked by what she'd said, but I nodded, turning on my heel and walking out, heading straight for the big doors. I was disappointed; the other Archons were supposed to be the ones who believed me when crap like this came up, for heaven's sake! They're supposed to be on my side, even when nobody else is. I should have known that would be an empty promise.

I walked through the doors and took a hard left, heading towards the Archons' offices where I could change and get the hell out of there.

"Matty!" Hopkins called. I turned and saw her, hot on my heels, "What the hell was that?"

"That was apparently me getting ejected from the Conclave for telling the truth," I said as Captain Cassandra Vaillancourt came out of nowhere and fell in at my side, her right hand resting on the pommel of her gladius.

"What did he do now?" my Warden asked Hopkins in a long-suffering voice that really wasn't warranted... this time.

"He..." Hopkins started, "I don't know. What happened back there?"

I sighed as we went through the doors leading to our rooms, on either side of which there were guards that saluted as we passed. I explained how Sutton had made me feel, and then what I'd found in Clayton's head.

"Ah," Hopkins said, "Look, Matty, you can't just go after Sutton like that. She's one of the best people I know. She's like a daughter to Kron. If there was a mistake made, it wasn't by her."

"And the sheer, God-awful terror I felt at the very sight of her?"

"She is a Light Mage. The strongest Light Mage in the world, actually. Maybe your Shadows sensed that?" Hopkins suggested.

"I've never been afraid of Light Magic before. This was something else. It felt like... like I was meeting the person who'd destroy me," I said, shivering, "Like she'd be the thing that ended me."

Hopkins shuddered slightly as well. I got to my office, which wasn't much, just a desk, a chair and a lot of empty shelves. There was a small nook with a cupboard in it; I stored my hood and robes in there before pulling out my satchel and hooking it over my shoulder.

"She couldn't, Matty," Hopkins said, putting her hand on my shoulder, "she's the Commander of the Peace Legion. She wouldn't hurt anyone, much less an Archon."

"If you say so," I said, just wanting out of there, "You know where I'll be if you need me."

She nodded, "Kron will calm down. She's just protective

of Namia. She'll be alright in a few days, you'll see."

"She loves that girl," I said, shaking my head, "I recognise the look on her face. She's going to be mad for a while."

I turned to leave, but just couldn't let it be, "Watch your backs around that woman. She's up to something with that drug."

Hopkins frowned, "Namia Sutton's word is above reproach, Mathew," she said, her tone now a little angry, "She has never lied to us before, and she's saved us from threats we'd never have seen coming otherwise. You can't conceive of the things she's done for all of us."

I rubbed my forehead, "When this goes belly-up, don't say I didn't warn you."

I walked around her and out the door, Cassandra right next to me.

"Matty?" Hopkins said, I turned around, "The others owe Sutton. So do I. Don't push this, please?"

"None of my business, Miss Hopkins. I'm not S.C.A., and drugs are their problem," I said, rather hurt that even Hopkins was taking Sutton's side.

I knew that I shouldn't be. The others had only known me for a few months, Hopkins just a little more, a bit over a year. I couldn't blame them, really, I was a relative stranger and they'd known Sutton for centuries. I knew all that *intellectually*, but I couldn't quite put the bad feeling to one side. It felt like a betrayal.

"Alright," she said, "We'll smooth this over with Sutton. You'll see in time that she's a truly wonderful person."

"I'm sure," I said.

Cassandra snorted, recognising my tone even though I'd done my very best to sound sincere.

"If I don't see you before then, I'll see you next week at school," Hopkins said.

I nodded and walked out with Cassandra, who followed me into the April sunshine. She'd been my Warden (personal guard) ever since that day I'd been to see Hellstrom in her house. She went most places with me; lived with me, more or less. I had no idea how she ended up with that job, but she seemed to be happy with it, and goodness knows she made my work considerably easier. She was, apart from everything else she meant to me, an indispensable source of advice.

"So, on a scale of one to ten, just how pissed off are you?" she asked, nudging me with her elbow as we walked towards a nearby taxi rank.

"Eleven," I said, smiling at my friend, "I know it's unfair to expect it, but they're supposed to be the ones that I don't have to fight against, does that make sense?"

"Of course. You think of them as family, you expect them to act like it. And they would; you know they'd go right to the end for you, Matty. But that woman is a famous good guy, and you..."

"Yes, I know. I'm a sneaky, mean-spirited Shadowborn who hasn't proven anything yet. I certainly don't compare well to one of those hero types."

"I didn't mean it like that. You just don't have the history that they do, that's all."

I smiled, patting her shoulder, "It'll be fine. It's not like I'm unused to being a pariah."

Cassandra snorted and we hopped into a cab, "Five, Lord's Way, please," she said, sitting back with me as the car pulled away.

"You know, we'd save a lot of money if you'd just let me fly us," I pointed out.

"I am not Princess Jasmine, you're not Aladdin, and your flying carpet is made of horrors, no thank you," she said, glaring, the hint of a smile on her face ruining the effect.

"You loved it the last time," I said, nudging her.

"Did not!" she complained, blushing.

Cassandra didn't like Shadow Magic, and no matter how fond of me she might be, she still had to fight that contradiction every time I did something like a Shadowborn.

So I smiled and stared out the window, knowing that

to press my advantage was to get punched in the arm until I stopped.

CHAPTER 2

Stonebridge was a grand old city. It brimmed over with history, ancient buildings sharing the city limits with newer glass towers, cramped warrens of alleyways a few blocks away from modern thoroughfares. Old and new, beautiful and grotesque, everything had a place there. It was home to one of the oldest Universities in the country, which filled the city with youth and vigour. It also had the largest per capita Magical population of any settlement in Europe, making the whole place seem to thrum with hidden power.

My official residence went by the slightly dramatic name of Blackhold Manor, and was located in the Old Quarter. The property had been passed down from the previous First Shadow as part of the trust, and had been empty for the last nineteen years; ever since the *last* First Shadow went insane, used the Black, and had to be brought down by the other Archons.

It sat on its own plot, deep in the most ancient part of the city. It was closer to a palace than a house, with four wings, three of which I had no use for. I say wings; that's what the staff called them. They were actually the four massive sides of the rough square that made up the house. The stone was a light brown, the roof slate grey, and it was Magically warded like nothing else I'd ever seen, surrounded by a tall stone wall with a reinforced steel gate. There was a bit of lawn around the buildings, and a beautiful little garden nestled inside the square made up of the house's 'wings', where there was grass, some bushes, flowers and a couple of trees, including an old oak I was very fond of. Beyond the house was a long, low set of buildings where the staff made their homes.

I used the 'wing' closest to the gates, which would have made a comfortable palace just on its own, if you ask me. Each wing was made up of four floors, with less space on each ascending storey, giving the inside of the square a tiered appearance, sort of like a colossal cross between an ancient Roman villa and a square amphitheatre. Each inner floor had a balcony covered in yet more plants, which I liked.

Personally, I thought the place was far too big for me. I would have preferred to stay at home, even if it was a hundred miles away, but this was the First Shadow's official residence, and it helped to have somewhere close to the Conclave.

In the South Wing (mine), there were seven bedrooms, about that many bathrooms, a huge reception room, library (where I spent most of my time), sitting rooms, a colossal kitchen, a dining room, a breakfast room and a small conservatory. Apparently, Magicians, particularly Archons, tended to accumulate wives (yes plural, and concurrent) and... girlfriends over the centuries, which tended to result in big families, needing big houses. My predecessor hadn't bothered with either, being more concerned with some light genocide and world domination.

Cassandra had moved herself in, of course; and taken the biggest room, too. Mine was more comfortable, though, with a terrific bathroom and a cosy fireplace. I hadn't redecorated anything, not really feeling at home yet (and having precisely *no* taste, besides).

The cab pulled up to the gates and we hopped out. I paid the man and he drove off. Money had ceased to be a problem once I'd gotten hold of my part of the Archon's combined trust, in addition to the pile that was the First Shadow's individual trust.

I had no idea what to do with that, either, but that's what my meeting tonight was all about. Cassandra followed me to the front door, where Case Webb, the Major-domo, had come out to greet us (he preferred to be called the Butler, and wore coat and tails at all times).

He was a fatherly looking man, middle aged with grey-ing hair and a friendly smile; his family had been managing Blackhold for four hundred years and ten generations. He'd been perfectly formal with me when we'd first met, not know-ing what to expect. When I told him that I wasn't planning to interfere with his running of the place, he warmed up a little, and after four months, he was even willing to smile from time to time.

"Welcome home, Sir," he said, "You've returned earlier than expected."

"My presence was no longer required," I said, smiling sadly, "All well here?"

"Of course, Sir. Shall I have Miss Jenkins prepare a light lunch?"

"Oh, yes please," I said, with a more happy smile, "break-fast room in say half an hour or so?"

"I'll see to it," he said, giving a small bow, "Will the lady be joining you as usual?"

"Where there's food, there's Cassandra," I said before taking the hit to my arm I knew was coming.

Webb nodded and went off, passing by the two guards on the front doors. They were both Cassandra's people. She had taken over the house's security and brought in half a dozen of her people from the Archive to act as Wardens. They were all highly trained, both Magically and martially, all wore ar-mour and carried firearms at all times. That reassured me; it meant that even if the Wards on that place *didn't* strip hostile Magicians of their power and physically injure anyone acting with hostile intent, then these women would still be more than enough to take on anything short of an Archon and come through far better than the poor idiot who tried attacking my home.

I nodded to them and they nodded back. I knew them all by name, and liked most of them. One of them hated my guts for some reason or another, but Cassandra didn't seem to think that was a flaw in a bodyguard...

Cassandra went off to store her sword while I changed into something more comfortable. It was just after two in the afternoon; the day was warm and quiet, the sun shining. I was already in a better mood by the time I made my way to the breakfast room, where Cassandra was waiting impatiently, back in her usual jeans-shirt-jumper combination, her gun at the small of her back and a series of smaller blades concealed about her person (she produced them from time to time, practicing her quick-draws).

Miss Connie Jenkins came bustling in, supervising a young valet who carefully placed a number of trays and dishes on the table before bustling right back out again with a smile on her round and pleasant face. She was one of the reasons why I was willing to live at Blackhold so much. She was the chef, and she was just... terrific. She was an older woman, with a warm smile and a perpetual desire to feed me up. She wasn't a Magician, but that didn't stop her from weaving *some* sort of Magic on the food. She could do things with pastry that would make you think you'd died and gone to gastro-heaven. That day there was soup, freshly baked bread and a selection of cold meat and cheese.

Cassandra all but dove into her meal, and I nearly lost a finger claiming some bread and soup before she could get to it.

"Not hungry?" she asked as I picked at my lunch. She'd already demolished everything else and was wiping the last of her soup up with the last crust of bread.

"Not really," I said, thinking on the Conclave, and the sudden, jarring, estrangement between me and the others.

"Then are you going to finish that?" she asked ruthlessly, pointing at my soup.

I grinned and slid it over, along with the last of my bread, which she set to as well.

"You want me to come with you tonight?" she asked after failing to conceal a very un-ladylike belch (which earned me a punch when I giggled at it).

"Nah, that's okay. It's only dinner, and I know you have plans."

Theatre with an old friend. Planned for months in advance; there was no way I was interrupting that. She'd be in a snit for weeks.

"I can send one of the girls with you."

"And have them disapproving their way through the whole thing?" I asked, which made her laugh.

"Just be careful, you know she's been getting more aggressive lately," Cassandra said with a leer. I glared, but it didn't seem to discourage her.

Amico Cucina was a nice little Italian place in the more modern part of Stonebridge.

My companion for the evening was waiting in a booth at the far end of the packed restaurant and smiled when I approached. I grinned back and went over to her, making my way past the wealthy clientele and their dates. It was dimly lit; the tables were round and small enough to be intimate, covered in pristine white tablecloths and set with real silverware. I was dressed in another suit, but with a more cheerful tie than earlier.

Tethys was stunning as always, clothed in a red, form-hugging dress that drew attention to her curves. She had deep violet eyes, which always seemed to dance with mischief, long black hair and lips that were difficult not to kiss. She pulled me into a warm hug that I returned before sitting next to her in the booth.

This was her favourite restaurant. Not that she *needed* food, you understand, but she could still enjoy eating it. She also had a favourite diner, wine bar, sushi place... a favourite everything, really. She was a Succubus, after all, and she seemed to take a certain warped pride in indulging in every form of hedonism known to man (and a few that weren't. Don't ask, you don't want to know).

She was temptation in the flesh, and one of my very best

friends.

"Long time, no see," she said, shifting in closer to me, looping her arm through mine.

"We had lunch four days ago," I replied, grinning at her. That was one of my favourite things about Tethys; she always made me smile.

"An eternity," she said with that smirk I liked so much, kissing me gently on the cheek, "you have no idea of the *depraved* things Kandi has to do to distract me when you're away that long."

"Oh yes I do, you keep sending me pictures, and would you stop that? Cathy found some of those."

"So you're keeping them? Interesting."

Walked right into that one, I must admit. I gave her a look, but she just laughed, leaning against me.

"How are things going lately?" I asked, "Busy?"

"Quiet, actually. Consolidating. I'm happy to sit on my laurels awhile."

We chatted for a bit, catching up. We were comfortable enough with each other that talking was easy and arguments non-existent. She told me about some of Kandi's recent misadventures trying to find out who was stealing outfits from the Purple Pussycat and I laughed. I told her about the latest Conclave nonsense and she sympathised. It was a pleasant dinner, I relaxed and so did she. She also kept trying to grope me, but that's par for the course with her.

"So, I was wondering if you might be willing to do me a favour?" I asked as the waiter took our dessert things away.

"Is it sexual?" she asked, suddenly very close, her nose on my neck, "because absolutely."

I smiled, squeezing her shoulders.

"No, I need advice, business advice, actually."

"Less fun, but still interesting," she said, running her nose up and down a little, making me shiver.

I took a moment to re-gather my thoughts from where Tethys had scattered them. One could see why she was a minor business mogul, none of her opponents could remember their negotiating position...

"As you know, I've come into a bit of money. Well, it's a lot more than I thought it was."

I pulled a small diary out of my pocket, where I'd scribbled some basic notes, passing it to her.

"I have absolutely no idea what to do with any of it," I said.

She sucked in a breath as she looked over the summary page.

"Damn, Matty," she said as she flipped through the little book, "You'd need a team of people just to keep up with the paperwork."

"There *are* teams of people; one with the Archons' combined trust and another with my individual one. I don't know any of them, and I don't know what's best for anything. You are the smartest businesswoman I know, and I trust you; can you help?"

"This is a lot of work, Mathew," she said, "Full time work, as a matter of fact."

"It goes without saying that you'd get a cut."

She turned her eyes on me, smirking just a little, "What sort of a cut?"

"What's standard?"

"For a business this extensive? About ten percent of the annual profits and incomes. That's after taxes and all the rest of the expenses and so forth," she said, a twinkle in her eye.

"Take twenty."

She blinked. Hard.

"Matty, I was kidding. People get five percent, and that's if they're good."

"Take twenty," I repeated, "That still leaves me with crap-loads more money than I could ever spend. And you'll be able to run and grow your own holdings while you're growing mine. I know that it's a lot to ask of you, especially when you're trying to build your own business, but there's no one else I'd trust with this."

"Matty, if I did this, I'd make more money in a year than I'd see in the next thirty on my own, and that's a conservative estimate. It is not a lot to ask, it's a lot to *give*. Are you sure you want to give it to me?"

I nodded, "I wouldn't give it to anyone else."

She leant back in her seat, tapping at the little book, thinking hard.

"This will take some time to set up. I'll need to vet staff, set up premises somewhere and make arrangements to get someone to take over the day to day management of my holdings so I can focus on the bigger picture for both of us."

"I may be able to help with one of those," I said with a smile, "Is that a yes?"

She smiled widely, wrapping her arms around my neck, "Oh yes," she said, flushed, "do you have any idea what I'm going to be able to do with these resources? If you thought I was good at getting information before, just imagine what I'll be able to do now."

I smiled back at my friend.

"Thanks you, Tethys," I said, hugging her, "I can't tell you what this means."

"You just gave me everything I've been working for on a platter, Matty. You don't thank me for this. And that you're trusting me with all of that... it means a lot to me, too."

I smiled as she held me a bit tighter.

"Cassandra's going to be pissed. She has no idea what I came here for."

"Oh, can I tell her? Please, please?!" she said, bouncing up and down.

"Just wait until I'm out of the room."

"And what was the thing you thought you'd be able to help with?" she asked.

I smiled even wider.

"Premises," I said.

She raised an eyebrow.

"Oh yes," Tethys said as we came out of the sky into the front drive of the House, "This will do very nicely."

"I use a tiny portion of this thing," I said, "The rest is yours, if you want it."

She went towards the door, and the guards glared at her as she walked up the steps. They knew who she was and they didn't approve. Cassandra didn't either, but (as you know) she was conveniently elsewhere, almost as if someone had planned it that way...

Tethys was grinning like a kid in a toy store as she walked into the reception hall and took in the marble floor and mahogany staircase.

Webb was off after six, but one of the valets took Tethys' wrap and my overcoat.

"You've been holding out on me," she said, rounding on me, suddenly very close again.

"Hardly," I said, "I told you I had a place."

"You didn't tell me that you had a *palace*."

"Well, it's one of the most heavily defended homes in the country, if not the world. Even another Archon would be hard pressed to do anyone a mischief in here. There's space for any-one or anything you might want to bring in. Hell, you can have your own wing, if you want."

"First you ask me to run your business, now you're ask-ing me to move in with you," she said with a sultry look in her eye, "Aren't we moving fast tonight?"

She grinned, sliding past me, brushing her back against my front.

"I'm saying that the space is yours, if you don't think this will be a good fit, that's up to you of course."

She gave me a look, half glare, half pity, "I'll want Kandi to come with me."

"Like I say, up to you."

"What's the catch?" she asked, "I'm looking for the catch, there has to be one somewhere. Nobody just comes out of the blue and drops this in your lap for nothing."

"It's not like I'm not getting something in return," I replied, "What you'll be doing for me is invaluable; that you are someone I can completely rely on is priceless. From my perspective, I'm getting the better end of this deal."

She smiled, moving to put her arms around my chest, "So," she said, her eyes locking with mine, "Where's your room?"

"Have you no shame?"

"Not really, but I figured you'd be wanting me to take a look at this place. The decor is going to need work, and I know for a fact that your tastes run more towards 'modern comfort' than 'turn of the century splendour'."

"Please don't bankrupt me remodelling," I begged.

She grinned evilly, "No promises."

I showed her around the place, and I laid out the few things I knew I wanted. Mostly I intended to just leave her to it. She laid claim to the suite right next door to mine and informed me that she wouldn't be sleeping in there too much. She smiled in a certain way that made her actual intentions ambiguous, but I chose to take that as meaning she'd be working.

"You sure you want to up-sticks just like that? I know you're a nester and you told me how much you love your place," I asked as the tour was winding down.

"Let me see, sub-basement adjacent to strip club," she said, "or a suite in my own palace. It's a tough one."

"I have a lawyer, he'll draw up any paperwork you might need," I said, "Just let me know if there's anything not covered under a Power of Attorney."

That startled her, "You're really serious about this, aren't you? You really trust me that much?"

I nodded.

"You realise that with that sort of power, I could thoroughly rip you off."

"I know you could," I said, walking her towards the garden.

"And that doesn't worry you?"

"Nope."

"You realise that men who trust succubae tend to come to bad ends, right?"

"Maybe, but one could also say that spending time with a Shadowborn is bad for your health, and yet here you are."

"I love you, what's your excuse?"

"Same thing, really," I replied with a smile and a little blush.

Just to clarify, it wasn't *that* sort of relationship. We did love one another, but it wasn't in a romantic way. Well, not entirely. Ours was a friendship, based on trust and respect. The fact that she occasionally tried to trick me into a physical relationship kept me on my toes, and the outrageous flirting was fun. I missed her when she wasn't around.

Yes, I realise how deluded that all sounds, but I really did think of Tethys as a friend (a very attractive, flirty friend), and besides which I was still head over heels in love with Cathy, and there was nothing that could change that. But that didn't mean that I wouldn't do just about anything for Tethys. She really was one of my very favourite people.

"You realise that when this becomes physical, our business relationship may be affected?" she said.

"Well, I guess we'll just have to keep it from getting physical," I replied with a smile.

"You're less fun when you're on your game. I miss the days when a statement like that would make you blush like a novice nun and clam up tighter than a mussel," she said, squeezing my hand.

"You know very well just how easily you make me blush," I said as we emerged into the garden square, lit by dim lamps which cast a soothing glow over the plants. We sat on a small bench, her close to me.

"Told you I'd end up living with you," she said after a

quiet minute in the cool evening.

"And far ahead of your estimate, too."

She held my hand, "I won't let you down. I wanted you to know that."

"I already know that. Just remember that this is a big thing. If you need help with something, ask for it. That's what the money's there for. There are no judgements with me, you know that."

She smiled evilly, looking up at the stars. There was a subtle enchantment built into the square that blocked out the lights of the city and let the stars shine brightly. Normally you'd need to go to the desert to get a view like that.

"I'm going to turn this place into a new Caligula's Palace, you realise that?" she said, turning back to me.

I shook my head, "Well, I wasn't expecting you to turn it into a convent."

She snorted, leaning her head against my shoulder, "Oh, this is going to be so much fun!"

We sat like that for a while, just enjoying each other's company.

Naturally someone had to come and ruin it...

"I see the half-breed's attempts to seduce you have finally born fruit," said a familiar voice from right behind us.

I turned to glare at the two interlopers, Tethys turned too, but her face was suddenly pale with fear.

There were two beautiful women, both about the same height with perfect, pale skin. There, the similarities ended; one was a delicate redhead with soft eyes, wearing a calf-length white dress which left her arms and feet bare; the other was curvaceous, radiating sensuality, with black hair and red eyes. Her clothing was all black and tight, with a plunging neckline, revealing a bare midriff.

Rose and Gabrielle. An angel and a demon, my liaisons.

"You know, I'd just about persuaded myself I'd imagined them," I said to Tethys as I stood to greet them.

"Me too," she replied, taking my hand again. Gabrielle

scared Tethys, and that made me edgy.

"Good evening, Mathew," Rose said with a beaming smile that soothed me, "and to you too, Miss Smyth."

I replied in kind, trying to be polite, "To what do we owe the pleasure?" I asked.

Gabrielle snorted; I wasn't a fan of hers.

"Something funny?" I asked the demon.

"The way you say 'pleasure'," she replied, "It interests me."

I felt power then, coming from Gabrielle. It radiated off her like a wave and slammed smack into a Telepathic shield I'd put around Tethys and myself, just in case. Even so, I felt a tingle of desire. That was worrying, if I could feel it through a shield that strong, I could only imagine I'd have been a gibbering wreck if I'd got the full blast. Tethys squeezed my hand tighter, moving in closer to me, protectively.

Gabrielle smiled nastily as she felt her gambit fail, licking her lips slowly before turning her attention back to Tethys.

"Relax, half-breed. If I wanted to play with your toy, I'd have done it and thrown away the broken pieces long since," the demon said, looking Tethys in the eyes. Tethys looked away and moved behind me; her go to move whenever something nasty came around.

"Isn't that sweet? She thinks he can protect her. He can't, but I can. Come to me little girl, I'll show you things you've never imagined," Gabrielle said, reaching forward.

"Touch her, and there won't be enough of you left for the devil himself to scrape back together," I said softly, and all the more menacingly for it.

Gabrielle turned her attention back to me, and her mental attack redoubled. It made me wince slightly, but that was about it.

"Enough!" Rose said, smacking Gabrielle's arm, "You know the rules, and you know what happens if you break them!"

The demon sighed, and her attack ceased, she blew me a

kiss and stepped back a little.

"Again, I apologise for my associate. She's not known for playing well with others," Rose said.

"Evidently," I said, "What can I do for you?"

"You learned today about something called Source," Rose said.

I went pale.

"Yes?" I replied warily.

"You need to deal with that. Quickly. It's not what people think it is," Rose said.

"And what is it?" I asked.

"Can't tell you that," she replied, "You wouldn't go anywhere near it. And you have to. We can't intervene in this. It's in human hands, a human needs to deal with it."

"Or as close to human as a Shadowborn and a half-breed can get, anyway," Gabrielle chimed in unpleasantly.

"Don't you have a goat you can be fondling?" I snapped at the demon.

Rose hid a smile and Gabrielle scowled.

"A word of warning," Rose said, "One you *must* pay attention to."

The way she said it had me paying *very* close attention, not that words out of an angel's mouth were easily ignored, bearing in mind my hopes for a pleasant afterlife.

"Do not use any magic on Namia Sutton before the end. No, don't ask why or when that is. Just know that if you do, the chances of a positive outcome drop to very near zero. Do you understand me? No magic that would strike her, or even touch her. Nothing, not even something positive."

I nodded carefully.

"And if I don't deal with the problem, or I'm unable to?" I asked.

"Bad things happen. Very, very bad things," Rose replied.

"Any time-frame?" I asked with a resigned sigh.

"Months, not very many of them, so don't dawdle," Gabrielle said.

"Isn't this really the sort of thing the S.C.A. should be dealing with?" I asked, clutching at straws.

"If it were that simple, do you think we'd be here watching you dance around your gal-pal?" Gabrielle said.

"Alright," I said, scratching my head, "Can I take it from your warning that Sutton is involved in this somehow?"

"That's not for me to say," Rose said, stepping away from us, "just remember what we said. We'll be watching."

"Couldn't you at least tell me where to start loo-" I began. They vanished.

"I hate it when people do that," I said to Tethys, who was still hiding behind me.

She peeked over my shoulder and let out a sigh of relief, "Don't antagonise Gabrielle, Matty. She's not to be trifled with."

"Neither am I," I replied confidently.

"Mathew, I may be described as a Succubus, but I'm not, not really. I'm only descended from a creature very much like *her*. I'm the diluted version. She's the original."

"Please, you'd need ten of her just to make a dent. She tried tonight, made exactly no progress," I said, rubbing her arms in what I hoped was a comforting gesture. She went even paler.

"She made a move?" she asked, her voice a strangled squeak, "On you?"

"Eggs against concrete, Tethys, she's no threat to me."

"Matty, you know that I'm attached to you, and I hate to tell you this, but that started because I tried for you and *failed*. There's nothing more attractive to something like me than being rejected, because it doesn't happen very often. Or at all, really. Less so for someone like her."

"So you're saying that if we ever... then you'd lose interest?"

She smiled, cupping my face gently before planting a little kiss on my lips.

"Not anymore," she said softly, "Now we're rather stuck with each other. You may well be the best friend I ever had. I love you for that far more than I'm attracted to the challenge you represent. And when we do end up together, *when*, not if, then you and I are going to share an eternity of debauchery that will leave us both repeatedly begging for mercy. Over and over and over."

I shivered, and she wrapped herself around me in a warm hug that made me feel safe and loved. That girl made my head spin something vicious...

"So, we're together, thick and thin, all that crap. True friends, confidants, occasional sleeping partners. Sound good to you?" she asked, whispering in my ear.

That's sleeping as in snoring, not sleeping as it anything else, just so you know.

"Sounds great," I said, holding her tightly to me.

"Good. Then it looks as if I have my first task as your Spymaster," she said with a grin.

"That seems like a very unsubtle job title. Who's going to tell anything to someone called a 'Spymaster'?" I asked.

She snorted and rolled her eyes, "We don't *tell* people that, you nit. And besides, I have lackeys for that sort of thing. They just know me as the person who pays their snooping fees."

"Snooping fees? Aren't you just a font of official jargon."

"Shut up," she said, returning my smile, "I'll start getting everything set up tomorrow. Tonight, I have some things to do back at the 'Cat."

I escorted her to the gate, where she called a cab and I put her in it.

"See you tomorrow," she said.

"Looking forward to it," I replied, still smiling broadly.

She drove away and I went back indoors, relieved and also a little nervous. This whole Angels and Demons crap was *not* in the small print when I learned I was an Archon. Probably for the best, I'd have given the ring back.

CHAPTER 3

"Why is that woman in my house?" Cassandra said, waking me up the next morning, looming over my bed as I blinked sleep out of my eyes.

"What?" I asked.

"Your Succubus. What is she doing here, and why does she have bags?"

"You know how you were telling me to get a handle on all the paperwork, the responsibilities and the administrative mess?" I asked.

"Yes," she replied slowly, her eyes narrowing.

"She's here to do all that," I said, rolling over, determined to get back to sleep.

"Mathew Graves, I will not have that woman living here! She's a danger!"

"If that's what you're worried about, then this is the safest place she could possibly be, seeing as how it's physically impossible for anyone to do me harm within these grounds."

Her mouth opened and shut a few times as she digested my argument.

"This isn't over," she said before disappearing.

Heh, not bad for a man who hadn't had his breakfast.

I went back to sleep.

"Webb wants to know how long she'll be staying," Cassandra said a while later, waking me up again.

"Cassie, I'm trying to sleep," I complained.

"I want to know, too," she said, dropping onto the bed next to me, dislodging me enough to wake me all the way up.

"Alright," I said with a yawn, dragging myself up against the headboard, "Tethys has agreed to handle my financial business, as well as my... intelligence activities. To do that, she needs a workspace, and I just so happen to have a whole pile of free rooms."

"So, a while?" she said with a glare.

"Permanently, in fact."

"And you didn't think to ask me, first?"

"Of course I did," I replied, "But here's the thing, you're smarter than I am, and a far better strategist. If I'd given you even the tiniest bit of warning, you'd have either talked me out of it or blocked me completely, somehow."

She preened a little at that, smiling at the compliment.

"I wanted to get her in and make you think. To help you see what she brings to the table. I know you don't like her much; I'm not expecting you two to be friends. But I trust her, and I've made it clear to her that when it comes to security, or the safety of anyone under your care, including me and her, your word is law."

"And she bought that?" Cassandra asked.

"She did. She knows that in your field, you are unmatched, and that you have my best interests at heart. Just like she does."

She grunted, twitching her pretty nose.

"Alright, fine," she said with a sigh, "I can hardly refuse now that she's agreed to be so reasonable. But don't think this means I'm not mad at you."

I hopped out of the bed and pulled a wrapped box out of a drawer, handing it to her.

"In anticipation of your wrath, I took the liberty of arranging a little peace offering," I said.

She gave me another evil look as she pulled the paper away and opened the box.

"Oh, Matty, is this what I think it is?" she asked in a reverent whisper, pulling a silver revolver from the package.

"It is. Prewitt and Kass, special issue, fitted for dispel," I explained.

Prewitt and Kass made magical items. Generally staves, rods, wands, armour, that sort of things. I had to pay them an *astronomical* amount of money to make a firearm, much less a pistol. Only her status as a head-of-state's private bodyguard allowed Cassandra to carry one in public. The gun was a special order. Like a staff or a wand, she could channel energy into the gun's enchantments, which then transferred a specific spell to the bullets as they passed through the barrel. In this case, a dispel. That gun would tear Mage Shields to shreds.

She smiled, pulling the custom holster from within the box.

"That's the nicest gift anyone's ever given me," she said, "This must have taken ages to make. How long have you been planning to bring Tethys in?"

She glared again, the effect ruined by the almost child-like grin on her face.

"I knew I'd do something to piss you off eventually, I figured I'd need something around," I said with a smile, sitting down again.

"And you decided to give me something I could use to shoot you as a way of dealing with me in a bad mood? Didn't really think that one through, did you?" she said, smiling broadly as she pulled off her jacket and strapped the shoulder holster under her right arm, her left already had an automatic pistol under it. She loaded the gun with quick, professional movements, pulling bullets from the case faster than I could really follow, before holstering it.

She pulled her jacket back on, yanked me into a hug and kissed my cheek, "Alright, she can stay," she said, "but you owe me."

"Yes, Ma'am."

"Now get dressed. I'm hungry and they're waiting to feed you."

"Can't I just go back to sleep for a few more minutes?" I asked, rubbing my eyes.

"It's seven-thirty, you've had quite enough sleep; you're making a pig of yourself!"

"Seven th-?!" I asked, aghast, dropping back into bed and pulling the covers over myself, "What kind of monster are you?"

"Matty, your butler won't tell me where anything is, and *her* security won't let my tech people into the study," Tethys said, appearing out of nowhere and startling Cassandra.

"Cassie, please play nicely with Tethys, and would you mind awfully smoothing things over with Mister Webb while I get dressed?" I asked.

I'd left a note with the valet on duty last night to make sure that precisely this *didn't* happen...

"Fine," Cassandra said, hopping up, "Come on, I'll introduce you properly to the staff. And I suppose I can let your people in."

"No, stop, I can't take the gushing acceptance," Tethys said, deadpan, flashing me a wink as she followed Cassandra out the door.

Suckers. No way I was getting up before nine in a school holiday. I made exceptions when Cathy was within groping distance, but that's it, thank you. I flopped back down and closed my eyes, drifting back to sleep.

You see where this is going?

Kandi next.

She was a vivacious little redhead, smart and beautiful with an adorable spread of freckles over her nose. She was the best chess player I knew; even able to beat Cathy with almost contemptible ease, and my girlfriend was no slouch. I could beat her from time to time, but I wasn't certain she didn't let me win (strip chess; don't ask, I'm not going to tell you).

It took me longer than I'm comfortable admitting to realise that the arms and leg snaking themselves around me were Kandi's. I was not a force to be reckoned with first thing in the morning...

"Mm, warm in here," she whispered into my ear, burrowing her nose into the back of my neck.

"Morning Kandi," I said groggily.

"You are in so much trouble. Captain Vaillancourt thinks you've drowned in the loo or something, you said you were getting dressed an hour ago."

"Can't talk, need my beauty sleep."

"Tethys told me that if you don't get up on your own, then I should start doing things to you until you cooperate," she said into my ear, raising all sorts of goosebumps.

"Or, you could stay right there and enjoy a little nap," I said, "It is all warm in here, and these are clean sheets."

"Tethys will bend me over her knee if I do that," she said, but she was already snuggling in tighter and I could feel her relaxing behind me.

"Then it's good that you enjoy that sort of thing, isn't it?"

"If you want me to nap, then don't get me all riled up," she replied.

She yawned and I heard her breathing slow.

Hee hee! Tethys may have the monopoly on inducing lust, but she doesn't hold a candle to my powers over sloth.

"Oh! For heaven's sake!" Cassandra said loudly, startling me and Kandi out of sleep yet again.

"Wha?" I said, again articulate.

"I sent you to empty the bed, not add to its occupants," Cassandra said to Kandi, who sniggered.

"Yeah, never send Kandi to get Mathew to do something," Tethys said, "He snaps his fingers in just the right way and she'll do things to him that would make *me* blush."

"She's not kidding, Matty," Kandi whispered, "That's *all* it would take."

"What could you people possibly want right now?" I asked in a put-upon tone.

"There's someone here to see you," Tethys said.

"Tell them I'm dead."

"It's Lady Kron," Cassandra said.

"Definitely tell her I'm dead," I replied.

"Graves!" Kron barked, making me bolt upright, dislodge Kandi, who squeaked, at which point I fell out of bed and banged my knee on the floor.

"Can you come by every morning?" Cassandra said to my sister Archon, "Getting him up is a nightmare, and you seem to have the knack."

I pulled myself up on the edge of the bed and looked at Kron, who was standing in the doorway, dressed in a dark and perfectly tailored suit, the gold signet with the hourglass sigil on her finger rather prominent. All the signets were different in colour and style, mine was black (surprise) and simple; hers was big and ornate.

"What can I do for you today?" I asked politely after I'd come to.

"You can get dressed for starters, I'm not having this conversation with someone in their pyjamas," she said before turning on her heel and stomping out.

"All I can say is thank God I wasn't wearing my Star Wars set today," I said, which made Kandi burst out laughing.

After one of the quickest changes of my life, I darted into the drawing room, where I found Kron sipping coffee from a china cup. It was a large, not especially comfortable room with hard furnishings and a wide fireplace. It really needed to be redone; I imagined it was already on Tethys' to-do list...

I sat down in an armchair, and Kron ignored me.

I let her. She may well have invented awkward silences, but I perfected them. I sat back and relaxed while she took her immense time finishing her coffee and eating one of the biscuits she had on her saucer.

"I am now ready to hear your apology," she said once she was done with her little performance piece.

"Alright, I'm sorry," I said.

She blinked. I could almost see the conversational and argumentative web she'd prepared dissolve behind her eyes. It made me happy.

"What?" she said, still on the back foot.

"I said I'm sorry. Completely in the wrong. My fault, no doubt," I lied.

I heard a very distinctive (and very Tethys) snigger from around the corner. I think Kron was too surprised by my sudden cooperation to notice.

"You'll say that to Lady Sutton?" she asked.

"Not in a million years. She terrifies me, I'm not going anywhere near her," I said firmly.

"Hopkins mentioned that, what do you mean, 'she terrifies you'?" she asked, her eyes narrowing, but in concentration rather than fury.

"I don't know how to explain it. The second I saw her, I just felt a deep, awful dread; like I was suddenly staring at my murderer. It was *that* strong."

Kron leant back, tapping her jaw with an index finger as she thought about it.

"That could mean any number of things," she said finally, suddenly seeming very uncomfortable.

"What's it most likely to mean?" I asked, deliberately meeting her eyes.

"It's not that. That's impossible."

"Alright. If a stranger came to you and described what I just had about another stranger, what would you tell them it meant?"

She sighed, rubbing her eyes, "Commonly, that reaction would tend to indicate an action so traumatic, so *horrific*, to you that it resonated through your soul from the point of cause, back and forward in time. It's rare, and only applies in cases where the action was... truly monstrous, soul-rendingly bad. In Shadowborn, this reaction can be associated with the person who causes them to... to use the Black."

My heart rate tripled at that, and I felt sick to my stomach. No wonder I'd had such a reaction.

"Or it could be that she's to become very close to you, and her death is what causes the trauma, or any number of potential things. There's just no way to know for sure."

That didn't help. Kron was supposed to be quite good at this whole predictive, Time Magic thing.

"Well, if it's all the same to you, I'm going to keep away from her," I said, "Good or bad cause, trauma isn't fun."

I said that to make her feel better. I knew in my bones that the reason wasn't good. I'd seen the look in Sutton's eyes. There was real *evil* there, I knew it like I knew how to breathe. Whatever future event inspired my terror, it wasn't because I was fond of the animal.

"That... might be for the best," she replied, "She hasn't had the best luck with men, and I don't want your obvious dislike to hurt her."

I bristled a little at that, but let it go, I didn't want to start another fight with Kron, and she might be willing to tell me something useful, if I was nice.

"What do you mean?" I asked.

She cleared her throat, wringing her hands.

"She was born to a very poor family, back in the fourteenth century. She was sold to a Magician when her powers came out, at which point she was forbidden to as much as *look* at a man. Back then, in that part of the world, it was believed that a Sorceress' powers would be diminished if she were to ever... 'take a husband'. Drivel, of course, but it was the Stupid Ages.

"So, the man who bought her kept her among other female practitioners, each of whom impressed upon her, sometimes violently, the evils that other men represented. She was able to sneak away from time to time, women with that much power can't be contained forever, after all, and after some time and a few missteps, she found a man. She fell in love, but promptly lost him when her master discovered their affair.

"She was punished, very thoroughly. And when this was

finished, he exposed her to the very worst of mankind, made her watch as more than fifty particularly vile criminals were forced to confess and describe their crimes in detail before she was then in turn forced to slay them. When Bjorn was done, Namia couldn't even look at a man without hating him intensely, seeing every one of you as a representation both of the man who'd taken her capacity for love, and the monsters she'd been exposed to.

"I met her when she was presented to the Italian Conclave in fourteen-ten. She was a scared, cowering, little thing, afraid of her own shadow and practically radiating hatred for every man she met or who tried to talk to her."

She paused for a moment and I poured her another cup of coffee, which she accepted with a nod.

"I talked to her, and she told me her story. I challenged Bjorn to a duel on the spot and beat him like a mule. I took Namia with me and made her my apprentice. It took me a century to begin to undo the damage Bjorn had done. And almost another fifty years after that before she began looking at men and not seeing monsters. Even so, she never found someone to love again. Her Legion of Peace is eight-tenths female, you know. But for all that, she is the kindest, most decent, sweetest girl I ever met. I hated you for making her cry. I almost hit you back there, because I *know* Namia Sutton. She'd never hurt you. Not for anything. She's like you, in many ways, she doesn't believe that magic should be used to harm people."

I leant back in my chair, thinking over what she'd said. She watched me carefully.

"I will keep an open mind," I finally said, "But she's a Sorceress with a Light Affinity. Essentially, to me, she's the most dangerous person on the face of the earth who isn't an Archon."

"Granted," she agreed stonily.

"I'll keep away from her, and pray to God that I'm simply allowing my cowardly nature to get the better of me. But I can't pretend that your response yesterday didn't hurt me. It did. I know that I'm... new, but I shouldn't have to feel like an outsider, not with you."

She had the good grace to look chagrined and avert her eyes.

"Palmyra told me how you felt. I didn't listen. I was too angry, too protective of Namia. She's like one of my daughters, Mathew, I hope you understand. You of all people know what it's like to be protective of family."

"I do," I said, "How many daughters do you have?"

"Twelve," she said with a smile, her face lighting up in a way I hadn't seen before, (we didn't really talk much, I was much closer to Palmyra and Hopkins than Killian and Kron), "and nine sons, thirty-six grandchildren, three times that many great-grandchildren and a more than a thousand in succeeding generations from two wonderful husbands."

I smiled, she was over a thousand years old (*well* over), and damn if she hadn't used that time productively...

"That's... wonderful," I said. If I had to pick a fate for myself, that's the one I'd choose. A vast swathe of children and grandchildren, a family I could never lose.

"My family, both by blood and by bond, has always been the most precious thing in my life," she said, "They bring me more joy than I can easily describe."

"I'm sorry I acted like I did," I said, actually meaning it for a change, "If I'd known ahead of time who she was to you... I'd have handled it differently."

"No. You are my brother as much as Namia is my daughter. More, even. That you had something to say should have been enough. And it will be from now on, alright? Goodness knows you've done enough to earn you the benefit of the doubt. I won't forget that again."

I smiled and nodded, "Thank you."

"Alright. Now that girly bollocks is out the way, there is an item of business that needs discussion," she said, her tone all business again.

Oh, what fresh hell is this?

"Okay," I replied carefully.

"After you had your little hissy fit and stormed out of Conclave," I remembered it slightly differently, but I wasn't going to start another fight... yet, "We were approached by a representative of the Seelie Queen."

"Elora?" I asked, "What does she want?"

"A conference. With us and the Conclave, to discuss the resumption of proper diplomatic exchanges. As you know, ever since we had our little hiatus, things became somewhat strained between the Newtonian World and the Fae. It would appear as if Elora wants to normalise things; presumably to ensure that something like the Crooked House doesn't happen again."

The Newtonian World referred to the human world, and our Magic, which was surprisingly scientific, hence Newtonian. Fae Magic worked differently, it was all emotion and intention and purity of purpose; confusing and messy. I never touched the stuff myself, not that I could, even if I wanted to. Crooked House was what the Seelie (the nice Fairies) called an abomination of a laboratory where a particularly monstrous Magician was harvesting Fairy creatures to make Black Magic. I was informed from time to time about how his 'correction' was progressing.

He screamed a lot, apparently. Still does to this day as far as I know, the Unseelie (Evil-ish Fairies) were feared for a reason. I must say that I found that knowledge quite satisfying. If you'd seen what he did, you would too.

"Sounds like a good idea," I said.

"Yes. Here's the thing..." Kron said, looking away.

"Yes?"

"She wants to use your colony as the meeting site."

My eyebrows raised and I sat back in my seat.

"It's not mine. I can't make that sort of decision."

"That place is under the protection provided by *your* Place of Power and *your* offer of Sanctuary. If anything in this world is yours, that Grotto is it," she replied a little testily.

I sighed, "Elora's harmless enough, I suppose. I'll head home today and ask them. I owe them a conversation at the very least; it's their home, after all. When do you want this thing to happen?"

"Sunday."

"As in the day after tomorrow? That's a little soon to make preparations for a royal visit."

"Elora will take care of the details, as soon as she has permission, she won't go anywhere near the place without it. Nobody will. You wouldn't believe how well that place is protected. It's a true merging of Fairy and Human Magic. I've never seen anything like it. How did you manage that, by the way? I've been meaning to ask."

"I didn't, all I did was tell them they could move in," I replied truthfully, "a Centaur called Lunson did the actual work."

"Fairy Magic," she said with a disgusted expression, "You never can tell what's going to work spectacularly and what's going to fizzle."

"Beats me, that's for sure," I agreed.

Kron rolled her eyes, "What doesn't?"

I smiled at my curmudgeonly sister. I knew she was better disposed towards me when the insults started flowing again.

We chatted a little more and then I walked her out, promising to call after I'd spoken to Lunson, who ran the Grotto, for all intents and purposes. She patted my shoulder, giving me a tight smile, and vanished into a Teleportation Spell.

I sighed, relieved that things were better, but now far more worried about Sutton than ever. If she was smart enough to fool *Kron* for centuries, then she was even more dangerous than I'd feared. Lady Time was, by no means, an idiot.

"Feeling better?" Tethys said, coming up beside me and leaning her head against my shoulder. She'd certainly been listening to the whole thing. She did that a lot.

"Much. Except now I have four hours in the car with an

uncomfortable conversation in the middle."

"You're never happy are you?" she asked, nudging me gently.

I snorted. I guess she has a point.

CHAPTER 4

In the two days before that wretched conference, Tethys and Kandi moved into Blackhold, and as far as I could tell, changed *everything*. I could only imagine the sheer amount of money Tethys spent to have it all done so quickly! I have to say that she did do a fantastic job. She managed to combine more modern comforts and technology with the older fixtures and fittings in a way that was impressively elegant.

She turned my library into a nirvana for someone with my particular passions (in other words, she filled it with technology, comfortable seats and a very discreet fridge); and she took over one of the larger reception rooms as her office. She redecorated her own suite in a way that Kandi described as 'delightfully naughty' and brought in half a dozen men and women (mostly women) to run a small office space. She told me that she was planning to open up the West Wing in a few weeks and put the South back as a pure residence, but she wanted to take her time with that, find her feet and sort out what she'd need.

My conversation with Lunson had been brief. The idea of having his Queen visit the Grotto had sent him into a near fit of activity before I'd even finished asking him if it was alright.

My three favourite Fairies, the Pixies Melody, Jewel and Meadow, were perched on my shoulders and head during this conversation, after what had been a very enthusiastic hello. I'd missed those three a lot while I was away.

I wasn't there long, but even after so short a time, leaving them was a wrench. They bawled like nobody else I'd ever seen, which always made me cry, despite my best efforts to preserve some semblance of manliness (which some might argue had been a lost cause even before the arrival of Fairies into my life). Said manly tears then made *them* cry even more in a vicious cycle of tears, wailing and snot that left all parties a wreck at the end, and my dignity in horrific tatters.

I really hated those partings, and always felt that it was a shame that they didn't do well in the city, or I'd have brought them with me to Blackhold. Alas, they needed greenery and the Magic of Home or they'd get sick after a short while.

When Sunday came around, I was at home, my real home, not Blackhold. I was alone, as my parents were off in Central America again. They had intended to spend the holidays at home with me, but they'd made the mistake of leaving their dig site in the care of their research assistant and (long story short) a ziggurat had fallen down. Naturally the Mexican authorities were not happy, and my parents had been forced to do some pretty fast talking and grovelling to avoid their entire team, and anyone even remotely associated with them, being violently hurled from the country and banned for life.

I woke up in my own bed, three Pixies curled up in a small heap up against my chest, snoring quietly. They were all of a type, about two feet tall and heavier than you'd think, with beautiful, delicate features, ears slightly pointed and big, expressive eyes that can give you the kind of guilt treatment a whole litter of puppies couldn't pull off. They wore little sleeping clothes my mother had sown for them herself; each had a whole wardrobe of such things in bright colours, all safely stored in one of my drawers (they considered my room their personal domain).

I stirred and slid out of bed, tucking the duvet around them. I smiled as I pulled a stack of clothes from the chair and headed for the bathroom. It was early enough that Burglar (my colossal Newfoundland not-a-guard dog) and Grommit (the red and horned Warp-cat that now rules the household with a slightly disinterested fist) hadn't woken up yet.

I ran a bath and looked in the mirror, something I normally avoided, but I didn't want to look scruffy for the meeting. I looked as pale as ever, my hair slightly darker than it had been the last time I'd looked at my reflection; there was a certain amount of facial hair- enough that I'd need to shave. My eyes were as horrific as always, a dark red sclera with a deep black pupil (magical accident) and the scars in the shape of a shaky pentagram on my left cheek hadn't faded any. I snorted disgustedly, it wasn't a pretty picture. I had good bone structure and a strong chin, and might have passed for moderately attractive at one time, before the eyes and the scars. Cathy said I looked dangerous, I thought I looked like an Ebola victim who'd stuck his cheek into a bear trap.

Another reason I avoided mirrors was that looking in them reminded me of Desmond; now an inmate at the Farm's Wing for the Criminally Insane, where he wasn't getting any better. My Magic broke his mind, and his using the Black squished the pieces. All he wanted to do now was kill, and hurt people (especially me). I shaved quickly and brushed my teeth before hopping into the warm water. I leant back and relaxed, closing my eyes, allowing myself to drift off a little.

I woke up to whoops of joy followed by splashes as Pixies hit water. I had given specific instructions regarding the sacrosanct nature of my bath time, or just about anything involving the bathroom, but they just ignored me. It was a nightmare even getting them to let do my business in peace. Thankfully their noses were too sensitive to let them intrude on *that* too often.

Bath time, though... that, they'd happily interrupt. They started splashing each other, giggling and squealing happily. Completely naked, by the way, they had no modesty around people they liked. I put a flannel over my bits and just left them to it, it was the easiest way. There was no getting rid of them without ending up on the receiving end of a full blast of their puppy-dog eyes, and I didn't want to embarrass myself that early in the morning.

At that point, it occurred to me just how much power the women in my life had over me, and I thanked God that they were all people I could trust. I shook my head with a smile and leant back again as they made a ruckus and got water *everywhere*.

Eventually I felt them slide up onto my chest and fall back to sleep, half in the water. Cathy walked in on us like this once and she thought it was the cutest thing she'd ever seen... until she realised that there were three naked and very attractive women sleeping on me, at which point the internal conflict between cute and outrageous seemed to send her into a spiral.

She solved the conflict by hopping into the tub with us, just so you know. That made the Fairies fly away pretty fast, let me tell you. Even they had a line.

"Girls, I've got to go," I said.

"Ten more minutes," Meadow said sleepily.

"I already gave you ten more minutes," I replied, tickling her ear, which made her swat at my finger even as she giggled.

They took off, their butterfly-like wings appearing out of nowhere and allowing them to dart away and disappear. I stretched and dressed, fed the dog, the cat and the Pixies and put on comfortable outdoor clothes, along with a light jacket and wellington boots. Wearing the full suit-robe-hood combination in the woods seemed ridiculous to me. I did wear my signet ring, though I generally did in those days, so I couldn't claim credit for making an effort to appear official.

I took a last look in the mirror and headed out towards the Grotto. The Pixies came along, Meadow and Jewel on my shoulders and Melody sitting perched on my head, her feet just above my eyebrows.

"You three look nice today," I said. Their dresses were freshly made of young leaves and they had tiny wildflowers in their hair.

They smiled and blushed at the compliment.

"You look exactly the same as you always do when you

go for a walk, you could have put in the effort," Jewel replied. I reached up and tickled her until she squealed.

"Who wears a suit in the woods?" I asked.

As it turned out, *everybody* else.

The Grotto was a circular area of enchanted woodland, about a mile in diameter, centred on an island in the middle of a small lake. There were over thirty Fairy creatures living within that border; gnomes, centaurs, sprites, water nymphs, talking otters, Pixies of course, and even a pair of strange acid-puking frogs I was quite fond of. There was a wide, steep hill to the east where the centaurs had built their home right into the hillside.

Inside the circle, it was always summer, the flowers and trees in full leaf and bloom. It was always warm and the water in the lake was always the perfect temperature for swimming. I spent as much time there as I could; it was a place where I could feel completely relaxed and at peace.

As Kron mentioned, it was my Place of Power. These are generally Magical areas with which a Magician has managed to establish a link or bond, capable of providing safety and power to the Magician. My family's land wasn't especially Magical to start with, but it had been my home since birth and I loved it enough to attach me to it in a vague sort of way. The Fairies showing up and creating their colony had changed the very nature of the place. Given enough time and exposure to me, it likely would have changed on its own into a true Place of Power, but Lunson was able to greatly speed the process along, blending my Magic with the inherent power of the Fae to create a Sanctuary.

Lunson had prepared a meeting area close to the house, in a decently sized clearing. A large wooden table had been placed in the centre with wooden chairs on either side, each was simple, but looked strangely comfortable (even without cushions). Flowers had been strung around the clearing, making it look festive.

The other four Archons where already there (an hour early, I might add). They each had a clutch of people with them. Kron's entourage was the largest, and I recognised her features amongst them, a chin here, her eyes there, parts of her extended family, perhaps? Killian had three beautiful women with him, each tall and severely attractive with dark hair and piercing eyes, all armed with swords and guns, wearing heavily enchanted, form-hugging leather armour.

Hopkins had a studious looking fellow with her in addition to two burly bodyguards. Their forms bulged with 'concealed' weaponry. Palmyra was surrounded by hooded nun-looking women, all of whom were tall and strong. Everyone there was a Magician of some sort, ranging in strength from weak acolytes to strong Sorcerers. The three women with Killian were the most dangerous, Sorceresses and Death Mages all, but nobody there looked like a slouch. Everyone was dressed immaculately and looked impressive, a credit to their masters and their Conclave.

And then there was me... dressed in a cotton shirt and fleece with wellington boots on my feet and three Pixies as my escort. Cassandra had told me that she'd wanted to come but I'd waved her off. She'd have been bored to tears, and I saw no reason to inflict that on *both* of us. Still, maybe I should have brought her? I looked rather out of place.

No, I was my own sort of Archon, and that was my home. I didn't have anything to prove.

"Morning," I said cheerfully, moving out of the woods.

One of Killian's women had a sword out and swinging for my neck so fast I didn't have a chance to react. It didn't help her much, mind. The steel didn't get within a foot of me before there was a whine, a flash of light, and she was flung back and up, spinning as she flew over the others and into a tree with a great crunch and a greater deal of swearing.

I was too stunned to do anything more than stand there like a lemon as the other two drew weapons and came right at me, all this over the course of less than a *second*. The Pixies were suddenly behind my back, cowering like sensible people. I'd have done that too, but there wasn't a convenient back within diving distance.

"Stand down!" Killian barked as the women got within a step of a still-stunned me.

Their obedience was instant. They halted, staring at me, their weapons poised to continue the strike. I saw over their shoulders that the other bodyguards were in the process of getting ready to kill me too.

I tried to remain calm, but I was fairly pissed off. If it wasn't for (what I was assuming were) the protections built into those woods, I would even now be missing a head, and even I can't fix *that*!

"What the hell?!" I shouted, glaring at the women.

"Get back from the Lord Shadow," Killian growled. The women obeyed, sheathing their weapons as they stepped away from me, their eyes boring into me as they retreated.

Killian and the others came forward, "God, Kid, I'm sorry," he said, "You alright?"

"No, I need new underwear!" I replied, which made Palmyra snigger and Kron glare at my outfit now that I'd drawn attention to it.

"They reacted that way because we couldn't sense you coming. How did you do that, by the way?" Killian asked.

"I didn't do anything," I replied, "I was just walking!"

Kron's eyebrow inched up and she shared a look with Hopkins.

"What?" I asked the pair.

Kron shrugged.

"The part of the enchantment that keeps the Fae out of sight in these woods shouldn't work on a human," Hopkins answered, "It never has before, anyway."

"Meaning?" I asked.

"That you're away with the Fairies like I always said you were," Hopkins replied with an evil grin.

"Very droll," I said as the Pixies resumed their spots,

glaring at the Death-Amazons. The third one of them had finally managed to fall out of the tree she'd been flung into and was looking a little dazed, but still seemed quite prepared to follow the other two's example and glare at me.

"Well, exhibits A through C sitting on you as we speak," Hopkins said.

"He's comfy," Jewel said in a small voice, hiding her face behind my ear.

"So the Succubae tell us," Palmyra muttered.

"I heard that," I said.

She stuck her tongue out at me.

"I swear, Graves turns up and you people lose IQ points," Kron said, stomping back towards the table.

"Hey!" I complained; the Pixies just giggled happily.

I walked past the various bodyguards, following behind Hopkins and Palmyra, who introduced me to their various hangers-on. Killian did the same with his three lunatics; Demise, Scarlet and Raven, all of whom continued giving me the stink-eye (and no, that's not a typo, her name was actually Demise, with an 'm'. As in 'he suffered a tragic demise', as in death). The Archons went back to chatting about this and that, but I tuned it out, making my way towards the woods where I saw Lunson.

"Everything alright?" I asked him.

"Yes, Lo- Mathew," he said with a grin. It had been a nightmare getting these people to use my name instead of a title, and they still slipped from time to time, "Her Majesty should be quite comfortable."

"Hey! Who are you talking to?" I turned to see Demise standing next to me, her hand resting lazily on the pommel of her sword (it was she who'd ended up kissing tree).

You really shouldn't feed me open ended questions like that. It makes me want to be mischievous. However, she'd already tried to kill me once, so it was better not to annoy her too much.

"A friend of mine," I replied evenly.

"She can't see me, Mathew," Lunson said.

Oh. Well, in that case I probably looked insane (well, more insane than usual).

"Where?" she asked acidly, "Who?"

I sighed and cast an Illusion, making myself and the Pixies invisible. She drew her sword and backed away, her eyes darting to and fro.

"You do something with your Magic, Matty?" Meadow asked, "It doesn't smell as bad as usual."

"Thanks?" I said.

"Are you still there?" Lunson asked.

I adjusted the Illusion so it was open at the end pointing towards the centaur.

"Ah!" he said, "Her Majesty should be here shortly, do you need anything?"

"No thanks," I replied, "I just wanted to say thanks for letting us use the space, I know it must be an inconvenience."

"That is the most ridiculous thing I've heard you say, and you've come up with a few good ones. We're still laughing about that time you said the world was a great big spinning ball of rock! But this is your home, Lord. You must be willing to treat it as such."

"It's your home too," I replied.

He smiled, "You really are a very peculiar human."

"Strangely enough, that's the nicest thing anyone's said to me today," I said, which made the Pixies titter.

Lunson snorted and cocked his head for a moment. His eyes went wide.

"You didn't tell me *she* was coming!" he said, his voice suddenly high and worried.

"Who?" I asked, dropping my Glamour (the technical term. I didn't like it).

Lunson was looking over my shoulder at someone or something, fear crossing his features as he bowed low. I turned.

"Me," said Adriata. *Queen* Adriata of the *Unseelie*.

She was tall and statuesque, sharply beautiful. She wore black, matching her hair. Her eyes were dark and intelligent. She was also dangerous as hell. And if I was seeing *her*, I couldn't believe that Evelina was too far away.

"Beloved," said a soft voice from behind me, right on bloody cue.

I turned to Evelina. She was a little shorter than her mother, her features a little less sharp, her figure not as rounded, but she was still lovely, astonishing beautiful in fact. She was also under the distinct (and mistaken) impression that we were soul mates. It was a Fairy thing; don't ask me how that worked. I did have to admit that I felt... better when she touched me, even something as simple as holding my hand. From the look in her eyes when she did it, I was fairly certain she felt the same way. Which is why I avoided touching her, it wasn't fair to Cathy. Even that limited contact with Evelina felt like a betrayal of the girl I loved, and I simply wouldn't have that. I would not do anything that would bring Cathy pain, not for any reason.

"Hi Evi," I said with a smile. All that emotional stuff aside, I was quite fond of the Machiavellian Fairy.

She scowled, "I have told you my opinion about contracting my name," she said, crossing her arms.

And she'd also told me that she was alright with it when I told her it meant I was comfortable with her. But then I saw her eyes dart briefly to her mother and I understood. Evelina was the heir to Unseelie. Familiarity such as that could not be tolerated in a subject, even a Beloved, in public. Another reason I wanted to keep away from that mess, royal politics...

"Apologies, Princess Evelina," I said with a short bow and a neutral tone.

"Putting her need before your pride... interesting," Adriata said.

Evelina blinked and then blushed. Adriata gestured to her daughter and walked towards the gathered Archons, the younger Sidhe in tow. Unseelie bodyguards came out of the woods after them. They wore black armour and carried swords and shields. Every one radiated a lethal grace. The gathered Wardens watched them carefully as they approached.

"Your majesty," Kron said with a bow. I was still at the edge of the clearing, not wanting to interfere, "We weren't informed that you were coming."

"A meeting between the rulers of this pitiful dimension and my greatest rival and you thought I wouldn't be present? You're slipping Vanessa."

I rolled my eyes at the melodrama and settled down on an outstretched branch while Kron assured the evil queen that she was quite welcome and so forth. Melody quickly became bored and settled herself into the crook of my arm where she promptly fell asleep.

After a few minutes, a breeze rustled through the trees, carrying the scent of wild flowers and the warmth of the deep summer. The Pixies immediately perked up, looking in the direction the wind had come from. And just like that, Elora was there, walking gracefully along a small track in the woods. There were a number of Seelie guards with her, their armour gold and heavy, women in hoods and long flowing white dresses gliding along behind them.

She was as tall as Adriata, but her hair was golden blonde, her features delicate and yet soft, with just a hint of sharpness. She wore a white, comfortably modest dress that dragged on the floor and yet remained completely unstained. It was inlaid with pearls and diamonds and she wore a simple circlet of platinum around her forehead.

She came right up to me, smiling warmly. I stood to welcome her.

"Summer Shade, I thank you for welcoming me into your home," she said.

"It's my honour, your majesty," I replied, bowing.

Summer Shade was what the Seelie called me after that Crooked House thing. It was better than 'Rat-eyes' or 'Shadow-born-freak' as far as nicknames went...

"I've been looking forward to seeing you again, that I might thank you properly for what you did. You have friends among the Seelie, should you ever need them."

She took my hand in hers and bowed her head slightly over it, making me blush.

"I did only what my conscience dictated," I said truthfully.

"That makes it more impressive, not less. We haven't known many humans who act like that. Not after they've been exposed to the world's ugliness," she said, tracing her fingers gently along the scars on my left cheek, a flash of empathetic pain crossing her eyes.

"You'd be surprised," I said, "For every monster humanity has made, there's twice as many good men willing to do the right thing."

She smiled; it was warm and kind, indulgent almost. It told me that I was far too young to know what I was talking about. Compared to her, she was probably right.

"I believed that once. Sometimes I can even bring myself to remember it. People like you help with that."

She stepped back. I noticed that the Magicians and the Unseelie had been watching this interaction very carefully. Adriata didn't look pleased.

Elora moved towards the table, followed by her people. The ones in the armour ignored me completely; the women looked at me sideways as they passed me by. All except one, who took one look at me and went rigid. I barely noticed, following the queen.

I yawned slightly, it was just after ten in the morning, but I was ready for a nap and another breakfast; and I was feeling guilty for not walking Burglar. The groundskeeper couldn't either; he had specific instructions to stay indoors today, as did the housekeeper, in case there was a screw-up and spells started flying about the place.

"Excuse m- Ah!" said a musical voice from behind me; I turned and was immediately tackled to the ground by a white and gold blur. Pixies darted away with tiny squeaks, barely avoiding the impact. Goodness knows how Melody woke up in time...

We landed with a thump, her hands grabbing my shirt sleeves by reflex. Everyone froze as the girl started apologising profusely. She was flat on me, her legs tangled with mine. It looked like she'd tripped. I'd never seen a Sidhe trip before. Her hood flopped back over her head and my breath caught in my throat.

She had to be the most adorable looking person I'd ever seen in my life. She looked about my age, maybe a little younger, her face was heart-shaped and soft, her eyes big and bright blue. She had a dainty nose, full lips and cute cheeks; like one of the Pixies writ large. Her hair was curly, not overly long, but a dark gold that seemed to suit her. She was quite lovely.

She stopped talking as our eyes met. Her hand released my arm and she placed the palm over my heart. I was very aware of her, her warmth, her gentility. I felt her heart beat speed up and suddenly it was beating in time to mine.

Just like what happens with Evelina...

"Uh oh," I whispered, the words just tumbling out almost on their own.

"I've been looking for you," the girl whispered, tears in those lovely eyes as she smiled at me.

Guards were suddenly above us, they quickly pulled her up and drew weapons to point at me.

"No!" the girl all but screamed, and suddenly the guards were flying through the air to land none too gently in the shrubbery (which was certainly taking a beating from flying imbeciles today).

She stood between me and the other guards, who'd also drawn weapons.

"You leave him alone!" she said, her tone commanding and strong. Quite impressive actually; more than a little attractive...

Focus, damn it!

"Gwendolyn, do calm down," Elora said indulgently, waving at her guards, who sheathed their weapons, "that is Mathew Graves. And the Lord Shadow is certainly the person in the very least danger here."

She squeaked, it was a very 'Cathy' thing and it made me smile as she turned around, looking down.

"I'm sorry Milord," she said, "I was presumptuous... and, and, and... foolish."

"Not at all," I said, standing up and dusting myself off, "I appreciate you standing up for me. You weren't to know otherwise; you just stood between a stranger and harm. That's nothing to apologise for, nothing at all. It's impressive."

She blushed from her chin to her forehead and seemed to lose all ability to speak. I looked around, hoping to find someone to help me. I didn't really have the necessary social skills to deal with situations like that.

Elora smiled and walked up to the girl.

"This is my youngest, Gwendolyn," she said to me, putting her hand on the girl's shoulder, "Gwendolyn, this is Mathew."

She extended her hand automatically, still looking down, and I took it, bending over to kiss the back as etiquette demanded. She blushed even harder if that was possible.

"Come on, Little One," Elora said. She led her daughter to the other side of the table while the guards Gwendolyn had tossed like they were confetti got to their feet. She tugged on her mother's sleeve and Elora leant towards her daughter.

Whatever Gwendolyn said couldn't have been good, because Elora tensed.

"Are you sure?" the Queen asked as I walked over to stand with Hopkins.

"The women just literally fall all over you, don't they?" my sister asked, nudging my ribs.

"Oh, ha de ha," I said, glaring, "I think she broke my coccyx."

Hopkins snorted.

"Adriata," Elora said, beckoning the Unseelie queen.

"What?" The Unseelie asked, her arms crossed, impatient as she stomped over to her counterpart.

Elora whispered to Adriata, I might have listened in, but I was feeling courteous for once.

"Any idea about that? This isn't normal," Palmyra said.

"How would I know?" I asked.

"You live with Fairies," Hopkins pointed out as the girls resumed their spots.

"Not *those* ones, they scare the crap out of me," I replied.

"What doesn't these days?" Palmyra asked sweetly.

"That's not very nice."

"True, though," she said, grinning mischievously.

"I'll set the Pixies on you," I threatened.

"I'm an Archon," Palmyra said with a smile, "Do your worst, Shadowborn."

This was all in good fun, Palmyra liked to talk big. I was rather fond of it.

"You asked for it, Girls, would you?"

"I don't know Matty," Meadow said, "That seems a little harsh, has she really earned that sort of punishment?"

Palmyra grinned at the girls.

"I think so," I said.

"Alright," the little Fairy replied.

I stepped forward and the little Pixies stood on their various perches, looking at Palmyra, and simply burst into tears.

Completely false, they used just the *threat* of this tactic to make me give them my sweets and dessert all the time. It was completely devastating, even knowing it was faked.

"Oh God!" Palmyra said, darting forward, "I'm sorry, I'm sorry! I promise I'll never do it again!"

Jewel wailed convincingly, turning away so she could cry into my hair.

"God, Matty, make them stop!" Palmyra begged, trying to

pat Melody's shoulder.

"Okay, Girls, I think she gets it," I said.

Immediate cessation, like flicking a switch. They all grinned evilly as they wiped away their crocodile tears.

"You're supposed to be Seelie, how can you be this *evil*?" Palmyra said.

"Don't say that," Jewel said in a tiny voice, "We were only trying to help."

Her tiny lip trembled.

"Crap," Palmyra said, "I didn't mean it! I think you're lovely! Please don't cry again!"

I chuckled and Meadow sniggered evilly behind my ear. Jewel took a great, theatrical sniff and subsided onto her perch.

"Graves, you have thoroughly corrupted these innocent beings with your mean-spirited trickery. Shame on you," Palmyra said, grinning despite herself.

"I did not!" I complained.

"So they did this before they met you?" Hopkins asked.

"I only know of it because they do it to me!" I said.

"Graves!" Adriata hissed, making me jump, "Come here."

I looked to Hopkins, who shrugged and Palmyra, who did the same.

"Girls, maybe wait here?" I suggested.

They nodded and darted up before flying over to perch on the back of one of the chairs.

I walked around the table to where Adriata was waiting with Elora, Gwendolyn and Evelina.

"Yes?" I said.

"Put up your hands," Adriata commanded.

"Am I under arrest?" I asked.

"Please, Mathew," Elora said gently, "Put your hands out in front of you."

I sighed and obeyed. The queens gestured their daughters forward. Neither would look at me. Each took an outstretched hand in one of theirs.

I can't adequately describe what that felt like.

It felt... good isn't the right word. It felt like... the best way to describe it would be as 'coming home'. There was energy; it came from them to me, merged with my own and went back out to them. I saw their eyes close as they felt it too. It was warm and comforting like the feeling you get when you're wrapped up in your favourite blanket in front of a fire on a cold day, a bowl of soup in your lap made by someone who cares for you... times a thousand.

I let them go and stepped back, banging into the table, shaking my head. I was breathing hard, and I swallowed, getting my emotions in check.

"Damn," Elora said.

"What was that?" I asked.

"Nothing," Adriata snapped.

"You know better," Elora said, "They are both bonded to him."

Like hell they are! Cathy was going to kill me! It was bad enough when there was just the *one* princess...

"Soul mates don't come in threes!" Adriata hissed.

"True," Elora replied, which brought her counterpart up short, "He is a soul-mate to each of them. Not them to each other. They benefit from the two bonds *he* has, but do not share them. They each have only the one."

I was backing away at this point, as surreptitiously as I could.

"Well, what do you propose we do about this, then?!" Adriata asked, sounding seriously miffed, not that I could blame her.

"Nothing right now," Elora replied, "I think that we can both agree we need to handle this better than our great-grandmothers handled the *last* one. And that requires time. He's only human, he doesn't understand, and he's clearly in love with someone already."

Gwendolyn sniffed, cuffing at her eye. That broke my heart on the spot. She was the sort of person who made you feel like you'd be willing to move a mountain to protect her (an actual possibility when you're talking about an Archon). I wanted to hug that pain away, and that thought didn't belong in my head...

"That problem is being dealt with," Adriata continued, waving her hand dismissively.

"What?" I asked, "What's that supposed to mean?"

The queens turned to me, Elora's eyes went wide.

"He heard us," she said.

Ardiata cocked her head, "Impossible. He simply heard speech and asked what we were talking about."

"Did you understand us, Mathew?" Elora asked.

"Of course, you're speaking English not three feet from me."

"No we're not," Elora said.

"Yes you are."

"We're not speaking English *now*, you half-wit," Adriata said, "Look at our lips."

"You shouldn't be able to understand our speech, Mathew," Elora said, and indeed her mouth didn't match the words coming out of it.

"Leaving that aside, you didn't answer my question," I said to Adriata, "What do you mean 'That problem is being dealt with'?"

"Only that my daughter met your little concubine. She's going to break your heart. And I'm going to enjoy watching your pain," Adriata said, her voice dripping with venom.

I took a step forward, my Shadows leaping from every crevice, great waves and tendrils of blackness that surrounded me protectively as I glared at the Fairy queen. I knew that my eyes would be completely black with my power, making my glare even more intimidating.

"I do my very best to be polite to you for Evelina's sake," I said, my voice a low and sinister whisper that made Adriata step away from me, "but it would be unwise for you to forget where you are or who you're talking to. And if you do anything to Cathy I will redefine what you think of as *wrath*, do you understand me?"

Surprisingly, Adriata smiled, "My child said you had spine. You have nothing to fear from me, Lord Shadow. Your actions in the face of people attacking those under your care are well known. Not even I would tempt that sort of response. But just because I won't be solving my daughter's problem doesn't mean it won't get solved just fine on its own."

I glared hard at her and felt my brother and sisters nearby, their powers close at hand. It wouldn't take much for this whole thing to degenerate into a colossal mess.

"You've made your point, Graves," Adriata said, "Evelina already told me that you won't attack unless provoked in kind, this posturing is meaningless."

I grunted, but released my Shadows, they went slithering back to where they'd came from.

"Why doesn't it taste foul?" Gwendolyn asked her mother in a small voice, "The others reek from all the way over there, why doesn't he?"

"I don't know, Little One," Elora said, squeezing her daughter's shoulders, "Once this conference is over, you can ask him."

"He scares me, Mother," she said, her voice even frailer, "That magic of his, it looks horrible."

"You don't scare *me*, Beloved," Evelina said from right next to me.

"More's the pity," I replied, turning to smile at her. She replied with a glare and a stuck-out tongue that inspired a great many none-too-wholesome thoughts and made me blush again.

Gwendolyn heard Evelina and she turned back towards me, something much stronger in her eyes as she looked at the pair of us. She looked me up and down, as if trying to burn a picture of me into her mind. It was a tad unsettling.

"I have questions," she said finally, her voice a little stronger, "May I ask? When the conference is over?"

"Oh... alright," I said, "I can't promise good answers."

She nodded, giving me a tiny smile.

That made me happy. Not good. I could already foresee having *immense* trouble saying no to that girl. And I was going to have to; Cathy was nobody's consolation prize. She was the girl of my dreams, and I loved her more than I could easily describe.

I would not lose sight of that.

I moved off back to the Magician side of the table.

Can we please get this over with? I sent to Hopkins, *This is going to give me an ulcer!*

She snorted, *What the hell was that? There was all sorts of strange energy flowing.*

I explained the situation. She started laughing.

I felt a mental tap and Hopkins opened up her mind to let Killian join the conversation.

What we thinking about? he asked, his mental voice light, *Something dirty?*

Just Mathew's upcoming bigamy, nothing serious, Hopkins replied.

Damn, Jen, be cool! I complained.

I occasionally slipped on her name when we talked that way. Generally I called her Miss Hopkins, because that's how I'd known her when we'd first met.

Killian chuckled as the Fairies came to their end of the table, where a whole new set of chairs had appeared out of nowhere to accommodate Adriata and her band of emo-twits.

"Shall we begin?" Elora said.

Kron nodded and everyone took their seats, including the Pixies, who sat on the table in front of me, where they mischievously attacked my fingers as the opening drivel took place. I smiled and played with them while Palmyra tried not to grin and Hopkins silently despaired.

They mentioned things about allowing our ambassadors back into Seelie and Unseelie, though, naturally, the Fae had never left *our* world. They talked about resuming trade (Fairy artefacts were colossally valuable and impossible to produce outside their realms). Naturally there were restrictions, but those had been in place forever anyway and were simply resumed with a few additions I didn't pay attention to.

Three hours of this later, they started talking about some sort of security arrangements. I was having trouble staying awake, and the Pixies had tuckered themselves out and were sleeping curled up in my arms. I'd caught Gwendolyn staring more than once; she'd smiled as she watched the Pixies playing with me, her expression was even warmer now that she could see that they trusted me enough to sleep on me. I knew that there weren't a lot of friendships like ours; Fairies and humans hadn't got on well, historically.

"Who would you recommend for the post? One of your S.C.A. lapdogs?" Adriata said. Kron had done the talking for our side; I didn't even know why the rest of us were there.

"Of course. They are the most experienced in dealing with problems like the one you had in Seelie last year. They are also the best Battle Mages we have available, experienced in a wide variety of supernatural crime."

"I will want someone not quite so inclined to burn first and ask questions of whatever's left," Adriata replied.

"Let me guess, you have someone in mind?" Kron said.

Jewel took that opportunity to let out an adorable little sneeze, which startled me, dislodged the other two, and forced me to whisper soothing things to put them back to sleep before they could wake up in a snit with me for disturbing them.

Everyone was suddenly looking at me.

"What?" I asked.

"The obvious answer to our current predicament would be to provide our friends with access to a Magician with a firm understanding of Fairies and their culture," Kron said, "Where do you think we could find someone like that, Lord Shadow?"

"Hm," I said, stroking Melody's hair as she stirred, settling her back down, "I can't imagine what poor idiot could possibly qualify, I mean, does any Magician have regular contact with Fairies? I mean other than me-"

My eyes went wide. I should have been paying attention. Hopkins couldn't help but snort and Palmyra looked like she was holding in the laughter only with a very great deal of effort.

"Oh no," I said, "Not after last time. And *this* time. And what's this about?"

"If you hadn't gotten involved before, where would they be now?" Elora said, looking at the sleeping Pixies.

I sagged, letting out a breath as the queens and princesses looked at me, more than one of them looking smug. Wretched guilt-tripping Sidhe...

"What was it that needed doing, exactly?" I asked, resigned.

"Nothing right now, but if something like the Crooked House ever came up again, we would come to you to fix that," Elora said.

"It was only sheer dumb luck that I managed to come out of there without anybody dying horribly," I said, "If that ever came up again, I'd recommend asking one of these four rather than me."

"Unacceptable," Adriata said, "For all your irritating personality quirks, we can trust your good intentions towards the People. These four are only concerned with humans."

"I'm also concerned with humans," I pointed out.

"But you make no distinction between our people and yours," Elora said, "To you, a person is a person, an innocent is an innocent. Guilty is guilty. I mean no offence when I say that your brother and sisters would not have allowed us to take that monster. They would have put the welfare of a fellow human ahead of justice for us. You did not."

"That's only because what we would have done to him wouldn't have hurt enough," I said, looking down at the sleeping Pixies in my arms. He'd taken their wings. I'd rebuilt them, but he'd still been willing and able to do it. Damnation wasn't a bad enough fate for that man.

"And that's our point. To most Magicians, he would have

been worthy of protection because he was like them, and we are not," Elora said, "Am I wrong, honoured Archons?"

"I would have made the same choice as my brother," Palmyra said, looking at the Pixies, "But I would have insisted on a trial first."

"We all would, I see your point," Kron said.

"Wait, you're telling me I was supposed to go against two fairy queens, find a way to drag that idiot back here for a trial before somebody else dragged him right back to Seelie?" I asked.

The others looked shifty.

"Well...," Palmyra said.

"It's a legal grey area," Hopkins said, "but technically every Magician is supposed to have the right to a trial before their Conclave."

"Even when he isn't on the planet?" I asked.

"Again, grey area," Hopkins said.

"I'm just a terrible Archon, aren't I?" I asked.

"Yes, but your heart's in the right place," Hopkins said with a smile, patting my arm.

I shook my head.

I regretted nothing. That man deserved *exactly* what he got, and then some.

"Knowing then what you do now, would you have done anything differently?" Elora asked.

"No," I replied instantly, looking down again.

"He'll do," Adriata said in a tone that implied the conversation was over.

"Alright," I said, "I'll do my best."

Crap. I just knew that was going to cut into my napping time.

"Of course, we reserve the right to send representatives to talk to our... security liaison," Adriata said, her eyes alight with cunning again. I'd have found it attractive if it didn't mean trouble for me in the near future.

And then it hit me. They didn't want an official liaison.

They didn't even need it, they knew damn well that if anything like that ever came up again, all they'd have to do was ask and I'd do what was necessary (after a considerable amount of whining and / or complaining, but I'd still do it). They just wanted official permission to periodically drop a princess in my lap.

"What sort of representatives?" Kron asked suspiciously.

"Whoever we wish, that's our business," Adriata replied brusquely, confirming my theory.

"The usual diplomatic terms?"

"Of course. We're not savages."

Kron nodded, "Accepted. Any other business?"

I could have expressed my concerns, but truth be told, I wasn't even that worried, and I didn't want to slow them down now that it looked like we were *finally* getting to the end.

Nobody spoke up.

"Good," Kron said before standing, "a pleasure doing business with you."

CHAPTER 5

A wide table covered with food appeared out of nowhere as we all stood up. The Pixies immediately awoke and flew towards it with every sign of glee on their faces; for such tiny creatures, they could really pack away the food...

There were fruits of every description, bread, honey, raw vegetables, fresh milk and cream as well as freshly squeezed fruit juices (no meat, though, many Sidhe didn't eat it on principle). I knew that Lunson and the rest of the Grotto's inhabitants had worked hard on that spread, and the effort really showed. Hopkins had explained that the post-negotiation meal was one of the most important parts of the process. The meeting was where the official things happened, but it was lunches like ours that created the real understanding in a less formal setting.

I nibbled on fruit and drank some of the milk. I wasn't really that hungry, but I didn't want to be rude to Lunson. I was just desperate to get back to the house and switch off after what had been a *complicated* morning. And I could still feel *their* eyes on me. Gwendolyn and Evi. I could even tell you where they were, and I couldn't do that before. Both were close, Gwendolyn coming closer. I actually felt her trip again and turned on instinct to catch her before she could fall.

The feeling of calm started to come over me again as our eyes met.

"We have to stop meeting like this," I said as I straightened her up. She blushed.

"Thank you, Lord Shadow," she said in a small voice, looking away as she got back to her feet.

"Mathew," I said.

She looked up, smiling again.

"I'm sorry I said I was scared of you," she said, "I only just realised that you must have understood me when I said that, and it wasn't fair of me."

"It's alright. I'm used to it; a lot of people are scared of Shadowborn."

She blushed even harder and her lip started to tremble.

"That's even worse!" she said, "You don't deserve that from anyone, and I did it too!"

"Really, it's alright," I said, almost desperately. I did not want her to cry, and that lip was wobbling dangerously.

"No, it's not. My mother told me about you. She told me what you did for our people. I can feel your connection to this place, to our power, and still I let my own prejudice hurt you. I'm sorry Mathew."

"Oh relax," Evelina said, sidling up to us, "He understands, already, stop gushing and try to act like a Sidhe, for Goddess' sake."

Gwendolyn looked away, tears filling her eyes. I put my hand on her shoulder, just a gentle squeeze.

"Look, I don't begrudge people their first impressions. Even I know that I don't have the most comforting appearance, and my Magic doesn't look that friendly, either. It's only a problem if your first impression is the only one you keep, and I'm sure you won't do that, will you?"

"Oh no, I promise!" she said, perking up immediately, "I already know how wrong I was. I saw you with the Pixies, you see. They're a great judge of character, and they obviously love you. I didn't want you to think that I thought badly of you just because you have Dark Magic."

I smiled back, "It's really alright."

She stood there, looking bashful and adorable while Evelina stood right next to me, cool and slightly aloof. They were such a contrast; completely different women, yet both strong in their individual ways, and each with a certain vulnerability that made me instantly protective of them both, though more so of Gwendolyn, who was so utterly sweet and sincere. I just wanted to wrap her up in a hug and not let her go. I had similar ideas regarding Evelina, but with far less wholesome desires behind them...

It was like being trapped between a soothing rain and a burning dessert, but in that two-way tug I felt a looming satisfaction that was hard to put aside.

"May I... may I ask about this?" Gwendolyn said, touching my left cheek gently, "Does it mean something?"

Evelina snorted, "It means he's easily fooled. He heard the cries of a damsel in distress and let his manhood drag him straight into a trap. Idiot."

Gwendolyn looked at me, worry on her face.

"I wouldn't have put it quite like that," I said, glaring at the Unseelie, who just grinned back, "but that's essentially correct. I heard a girl crying, went to have a look, and it turns out that she was the bait in a trap laid by fanatics. They jumped me and cut this into my face."

Gwendolyn burst into tears.

"Please don't cry!" I said, panicking, "Everything turned out just fine."

"I'm sorry," she said, still weeping openly.

Okay, no more sad stories, the good Fairy can't take them.

"Bloody hells, if she reacts like this to *that*, what's she going to be like when she hears about your brother?" Evelina said nastily.

"What happened to your brother?" Gwendolyn asked in a voice that was suddenly very high and trembling.

"Nothing, nothing at all," I said, glaring at Evelina again who just kept up that evil (and slightly sexy) smile.

Gwendolyn kept crying, I had no idea what to do, so I moved across and pulled her into a hug.

"Oh, that crafty bitch!" Evelina muttered, looking on.

Gwendolyn slowly calmed down, leaning her head on

my shoulder. Having her in my arms... it felt good, right. She smelled of wild flowers and the forest after a storm. It relaxed me. She stopped crying at last and I offered her a hanky, which she used to dry her tears.

"Sorry," she said.

"Please, she did that on purpose," Evelina said, "She's manipulating you!"

Which was a bit rich, coming from her, but one problem at a time...

Gwendolyn's eyes flashed with anger, and she was suddenly glaring *hard* at Evelina.

"That's a lie!" she said, "Why do you have to ruin everything!"

"Because he's mine, and you're trying to take him from me!" Evelina hissed.

Oh, bloody hell. I stepped away from Gwendolyn, looking around. The conversations had stopped and everyone was looking in our direction.

"You think I chose this?" Gwendolyn replied, just as acidly, "Do you think I wanted to find my Beloved, only to discover that, not only is he already taken, but if he ever is free to love me then I have to share him with *you*?"

Well, I think we can all agree that I'd thoroughly bungled that. Don't hug one princess while the other's within shouting distance, good tip. Should have figured that out earlier, but we're not dwelling...

"Please stop this," I said.

"And you!" Evelina said, rounding on me, "I don't even know why I'm mad at you, but I am. This is all your fault, somehow!"

Yes, right on schedule, the crap thoroughly hits the fan.

"You know what? I just realised something," I said.

"And what would that be?" Evelina asked in a biting tone.

"I can leave! It was nice to meet you, Gwendolyn," I said, bowing to both princesses.

Gwendolyn offered me a little smile, while Evelina glared even harder. I vanished under a glamour and moved quickly into the woods. I heard Hopkins and Palmyra sniggering.

I'm getting out of here before I start a riot, I sent to Hopkins, *if any of you are interested, I have soup and things with refined sugars and caffeine when you're done.*

Oh, bless you! We'll be along in a bit. I can already feel Lucille itching for something a little less organic, she sent back.

I'll have it ready.

I called my Shadows and they carried me home at some speed.

I let Burglar out and he darted off into the woods (in the opposite direction to the conference) to do his business before trotting back for a belly rub and some dog biscuits. After making sure that the house was still in one piece (one never can be too careful with Magicians in the vicinity), I put a couple of pots of my father's home-made soup on the stove, switched on the coffee maker, boiled the kettle, and put out the various cakes and snacks I'd bought yesterday.

An hour later, Palmyra and Hopkins walked through my back door to the barks of Burglar and the indifference of Grommit, the warp-cat, who hadn't moved from his basket since I'd fed him.

Palmyra made a fuss of the dog while Hopkins came in and poured herself a big black coffee, throwing two donuts down her gullet before she spoke.

"Well, that was a mess and a half, Kron and Killian send their regrets, by the way, they had to get home." she said.

"You don't chuckle," Palmyra replied, "both princesses are now in a state. Both wanted to come after you, but their mothers forbade it, which led to a row, magic was readied, harsh words exchanged and now those princesses are in trouble not only for causing a rift between two dimensions but also between themselves and one of the five Archons."

I sighed and offered them soup, which they accepted and both ate a great quantity of while we went over what had happened. Burglar knew Palmyra to be an easy mark from her previous visits and wasn't disappointed this time as she surreptitiously dropped bits of meat for him.

"Anyway, when we left, the two queens were deep in negotiations, and I'm fairly certain it was about you," Hopkins said after polishing off her fifth bowl and half a loaf of bread.

"Oh joy," I said sarcastically, rubbing my aching forehead.

"Most men would be rather flattered to have the attention of a Fairy princess, much less two," Palmyra teased.

"Most men don't have a girlfriend that's already had to put up with a lot of their crap without adding another bucketful," I replied.

Palmyra snorted and went back to the hob for more soup.

"What do you think Adriata meant about that whole 'break your heart' thing?" Hopkins asked.

"No idea, probably just messing with my head," I said (hopefully).

"Maybe," Hopkins replied, tapping her lip.

They finished up and left with reassurances that everything would be fine. I didn't believe them, but it was nice of them to lie. I cleared up and spent the rest of the day relaxing. I Skyped Cathy and told her what had happened; she laughed her arse off for a solid ten minutes. She really was great, and knew me well enough to realise that I was immensely uncomfortable with the whole mess.

Knowing that Cathy wasn't bothered let me relax, and even start to forget about the whole thing; I went to bed that night in as good a state as I could expect, with the Pixies asleep next to me.

Naturally I couldn't get off *that* easily...

I woke up in a sea of darkness.

Sort of.

My Leviathan was there, I could feel him in the Shadows below me, a comforting presence.

Welcome, I heard him say into my mind. Like every other Elemental, he didn't speak with words, but with a complex combination of emotion and intent. Generally, it took an affinity with the Element in question, or some pretty powerful Empathy, to make heads or tails of anything one of them 'said' (I had both).

I was perking up; this wasn't like the last time I'd ended up in that place (I was pretty sure *that* time was a dream). This time I was definitely awake, and things were more defined; I could even feel a sort of floor beneath me. I was in an exact copy of my room, right down to the paperclips on my desk, only everything was made of Shadows. I was lying on the floor next to my bed.

"Where am I?" I asked, sitting up.

Home.

Home? His home would be the Shadow Realm. Which was... amazing, and yet a little worrying, as I'd been warned not to play around with other dimensions until I knew what I was doing.

There had been shockingly little literature on the nature and specifics of the Shadow Realm, for the simple reason that most Shadowborn who got there tended to be monsters bent on slaughter and dominion, and the rest simply didn't want to share.

The Shadow Codex I'd pinched from Lord Faust (yet another idiot who'd ended up at the Farm) had chapters on it, but I hadn't fully translated them yet. To put it simply (because I didn't understand the complicated version), the Shadow Realm existed as a 'mirror' to our own, an exact copy made of Shadow, the only exception being living things, which had no presence there. And, as you might expect, the shadows from the real world had their own mirrors, too, only they looked like banks of fog to me (though I wasn't really 'seeing', per se, that was just the best way to describe the sense).

"How did I get here?" I asked.

There were spells in the Shadow Codex that could open a gateway, but I wasn't even half done translating them.

It was time. I brought you.

"Why? Not that I'm complaining, you understand."

There was a deep rumble that resonated through the very fabric of the place, I think he was laughing.

Danger comes. Darkness we can't explain, evil we don't recognise. You must know of Home. It can keep you safe. You must survive.

Well, now my enjoyment was tinged with a bit of terror. I tried asking him about what he was afraid of, but he just repeated himself.

Darkness we can't explain, evil we don't recognise.

So I pushed past it. Knowing my luck, whatever it was would eventually end up trying to eat me, so there was no point in going looking for the thing...

Instead, I looked at this new and wonderful Realm I'd been exposed to. And it was astonishing! I'd never felt such connection to a place, my senses could feel every shadow like I'd conjured it; I had to pull my perceptions back so that I didn't get overwhelmed.

It really was a perfect copy of the real world! Even my pillow had the impression of my head in it, and the covers moved minutely as the Pixies breathed and snored... which I could hear! I leaned in and found that the sound was coming through the 'fog', which I remembered from my reading acted as the connection between the Newtonian World and the dimensional plane where the Shadow Realm existed.

Now that I was listening, it was like every shadow was the thread in a web, and I was the spider at the centre. I heard a gentle susurrus of sound from every direction; Burglar snoring in the kitchen overlapped with the flap of wings in the sky outside and the rush of the river about a hundred metres from our front door... a hundred other tiny sounds that I couldn't recognise.

The implications of such a place were enormous. Even aside from the fact that I could listen in on any conversation within hearing distance of a shadow, this place connected with every shadow... *everywhere*. In theory, I could step through any shadow large enough to admit me and come and go as I pleased; and because it was the Shadow Realm, distance was only an idea...

You feel it, the Leviathan rumbled.

I nodded.

Open the gateway.

"I don't know how," I said.

Of course you do. You simply don't know that you know. See the door, turn the handle, pull it open. Try.

The communication came with layers of intent and thought, explaining how to do what he suggested. It was difficult to grasp, and nothing like what I'd begun translating from the Codex. The Leviathan's method was relatively simple in theory, just focus on one of the shadows (the fog as I could perceive it at that moment) and push deeper into the very fabric of it until you could feel your destination at the other end (the shadows were contiguous with their real-world counterpart), at which point you sort of... pulled that place to you.

Simple to conceptualise, very hard to do for the first time; certainly impossible for anyone without a very, *very* strong Shadow Affinity.

It took me a *long* time. Hours, in fact, to get into a mental place where I could open a gate. But once I'd done it, I felt so idiotic for not being able to do it before! It was so simple once I'd got my head around it. It was like I'd forgotten how to use a limb, but had suddenly remembered.

I stepped through my first gateway and back into my bedroom, where the Pixies were still fast asleep. The gate snapped shut behind me. I grinned like an idiot.

Excellent progress.

Thanks, I sent back through the Shadows.

Come back. There is more you must learn.

I repeated the opening in reverse and stepped back into the Realm (much quicker this time).

Think of somewhere close, somewhere you would wish to go. Focus on where it is in relation to here.

I thought of the Grotto, the little island at its centre.

Find it, bring it to you.

"How do I do that?" I asked.

This place is of you. It is only as solid as you wish it to be. Distance is only what you will it to be.

That was a complicated thought. Theoretically, it should be just as simple to use the stuff of the Shadow Realm as it would to use any conjured Shadow, but should I really be messing with an entire plane of existence? If anyone could sneeze and accidentally wreck a universe, it was probably me...

Well, if the Leviathan didn't mind, and they were basically the bosses of the Shadow Realm, then it shouldn't be too much of a problem. And besides which, I couldn't really resist.

I sat carefully on the shade of my bed, wrapped up in the fog. The snoring of the Pixies soothed me and helped me centre myself and concentrate. I looked in the direction of the Grotto. I could see every shadow, and yet also *through* all of them, which again boggled my brain a little. I focussed, feeling my link to the Shadows expand in the right direction...

I reached out and pulled that place to me... and I tumbled into the Shadow Realm version of a river bed, about five *miles* away from where I meant to go. The water was flowing mist, not solid darkness, which I found odd until I thought about it. Things that allowed light through them also allowed Shadows to exist in them, hence water would look like fog in there.

I looked towards the forest, though of course there were no trees, just fog. Though now that I was looking carefully, I could see empty patches, where neither the stuff of the Shadow Realm, nor the fog could be found. Tree-sized empty patches. Well, that was certainly interesting, I couldn't see creatures, but I could see their absence (that thought made my head hurt as I tried to wrap an over-used brain around it).

That rumble again.

Focus, the chuckling Elemental reminded me.

I tried again. I ended up three miles to the east of where I wanted to go and tumbled down a hill, thankfully everything in the Shadow Realm was almost a part of me, so I always got a soft landing. My third attempt dropped me two miles north of the Grotto, at the edge of a ditch, which I then fell into.

After that, I took it slower, taking my time. I knew this land. It was my home. I knew where everything was. And besides, it was my Place of Power...

Damn, why didn't I think of that earlier?

I knew why, because *everything* in there felt like my power. It was hard to distinguish the beacon that the Grotto had at its heart from all the rest. But I knew the vague direction it was in, so I looked carefully. It took me a while, but I found it, a gentle hum against the background energy, poking through the Shadows.

I latched onto it... and I was suddenly standing on the island.

I jumped up and down like a little kid, laughing madly.

This is the first lesson. And the last I can teach you for a time. I must return to the deep, my friend. My brothers and sisters are calling me, and we must make ready for what's coming.

"What's coming?" I asked.

We don't know. But we shall be ready. Call if you need us. We will come if we can. The little ones will answer your call for now.

"Thank you for this," I said, looking down at his form deep in the Shade below me, "It would have taken me years on my own. I never even suspected that this was what it was like."

Life for the One. Goodbye, Friend.

"Goodbye," I said.

He dove deep into the Shade, his form receding until I couldn't feel him anymore. I opened a gate and emerged into the warm night, safe at the centre of the Grotto. I smiled as I padded down to the water's edge, before sitting in-between the larger roots of a willow tree, whose lowest branches touched the water. I settled my feet into the warm pond and closed my eyes.

I was eager to try more, but I wanted to be rested first. That was not an experience to rush; it needed to be done carefully. I got lost at the drop of a hat, after all. With my luck, I'd come out in China and have all sorts of explaining to do...

I fell asleep in the safest place I knew, warm and comfortable.

I woke up in the grips of three women. Their skin was a sky blue, their hair the colour of the deep sea. Nymphs. They wore white dresses that clung to attractive figures. Their eyes were blue as well, gentle and friendly. They had their feet in the water, curled around mine. I felt warm and safe as I came back to consciousness.

I felt no particular reason to move, but they must have felt me stir, because they woke up as well, smiling at me. They weren't big talkers, Nymphs, but they were still very expressive people. They each planted little kisses on my lips before giggling and darting into the water. I sat up and stretched, feeling rested. I was about to stand when four hands grabbed my feet and I was unceremoniously dragged into the water.

I came up spluttering as the Nymphs stuck their heads above the surface, giggling and smiling mischievously at me.

I glared and darted after them. They squealed and swam away. It was a game we played, and it was more or less the only exercise I got that didn't involve Cathy. I caught each in turn and tickled them for all I was worth, making them laugh and squeak until they transformed into a stream of water to slither away, only to reform and start the chase again. I loved swimming with those three; they were just so gentle and fun.

After an hour of this, I was exhausted, and I hugged the Nymphs goodbye before they used their magic to dry me off. I thanked Lunson again for everything he'd done the day before and had a few words with some of the others before flying home.

I spoke to the housekeeper, walked Burglar and endured a wrenching goodbye from the Pixies before finding a deep patch of Shadow and opening a gate.

It took... longer than I'm comfortable admitting to get back to Stonebridge. I overshot *repeatedly*. I was so badly disoriented once, that I had to open a gate and check my phone's map before resuming my journey. Somehow I'd ended up in North London, about three *hundred* miles away from where I'd meant to be...

Even so, using the Realm still took me less time than flying would have, and much less than driving. Eventually I found Stonebridge and from there it was easy to find Blackhold, as I could feel its power pulsing in my mind when I got within a few miles. I stood in the reflection of my home away from home and heard the sounds of a bustling house through the Shadows as my people went to and fro.

"...you have to be joking!" Cassandra's voice, coming from the ground floor where Tethys had taken over the study (she'd moved from her reception room). I focussed and snapped there (that part, at least, was getting easier!). The room didn't have much shadow-mist in it, as it was daytime, and there were wide windows, but there were always patches; under the desk, under sofas, behind books and shelves. There were always shadows.

"Nope, the idiot didn't even think, just swatted her head off and stood between me and what was left like it was nothing. He knew who she was, too; I'd told him. He still didn't hesitate," Tethys said.

Oh... I was hoping she wouldn't tell Cassandra that story. She'd lecture me for a solid hour.

"He has that Neanderthal streak, 'protect the women' and all that," Cassandra said, "He's old fashioned that way. It's actually quite endearing, and don't ever tell him I said that!"

Tethys chuckled in that throaty way I liked so much.

"He told me once that you were the strongest person he knew, if that helps at all," Tethys replied, "Not woman; person."

"It doesn't. He's too protective, it's going to get him killed one of these days!"

"Doubt it," Tethys replied, "Matty may be God's own fool when it comes to women, but he's a survivor, and he's smart with it."

Alright, enough is enough, now I was just eavesdropping.

"Tethys!" I shouted into the nearest mist, focussing on it carefully, "Can you hear me?!"

I heard surprised shouts and the sound of things falling. Maybe I was a little loud...

"Matty?!" Tethys said, "Where the hell are you? You scared the crap out of me!"

"That's a little hard to describe, would you shut the curtains?" I asked.

"Mathew Graves, are you in the Shadow Realm? Because if you are, you'd be better off staying there; otherwise I'm going to do you a mischief!" Cassandra said.

"Okay, maybe don't shut the curtains."

I heard Tethys snigger, and then the curtains shut and the empty room filled with deeper mist. I picked a patch and it shimmered with energy as I opened the gate and stepped out, letting it snap closed behind me.

Cassandra looked miffed, Tethys looked gleeful.

"How much did you hear?" Cassandra asked with a glare.

"I heard Tethys say someone was 'smart with something', does that mean anything?" I said, lying glibly, "I only just got here."

Cassandra glared, but I think she decided to believe me (thank God. Nobody wanted Cassandra in a snit).

"Doesn't mean anything," she said, "Now, what the hell were you doing in there?"

Tethys took that opportunity to hug me hello before

retaking her seat. The room had been thoroughly done over. There was now a wide desk with a trio of monitors on it, the shelves had been replaced with secure file cabinets, and there was a heavy duty wall safe. The furniture was new and tasteful, but also looked comfortable. Tethys had always had a gift for combining comfort, fashion and function.

"The Leviathan had to go away for a while. Showing me how the place worked was sort of a going away present," I replied before telling them all about it.

"How long did it take you to get home?" Tethys asked with a smirk, knowing how easily I got lost.

"Not long," I said, looking away.

"Half an hour?" Cassandra asked.

"Something like that."

"Matty, tell the truth or I'll sic Kandi on you," Tethys said.

"Seventy minutes," I admitted, they both sniggered.

"By the way," Tethys said, looking smug, "My sources have been saying all sorts of interesting things about that little conference of yours. Something about a second Sidhe princess? Care to fill in the blanks?"

"Not even a little," I said, walking towards the door.

Tethys was on me in a flash and lifted me up by the waist.

"No, bad Tethys, put me down!" I complained while Cassandra roared with laughter and I blushed.

She carried me back and deposited me in a comfortable chair in front of her desk, where she then sat on my lap.

"Tell your Tethys," she said softly into my ear.

"Isn't this the sort of thing you should be protecting me from?" I asked my bodyguard, who was still making like a hyena.

"You moved her in, she's your problem now," Cassandra said.

"Am I going to have to persuade you, Mathew?" Tethys purred into my ear, pressing herself closer to me, "I have ways of making you talk."

She bit my ear just a little.

"Alright, alright!" I said before she could increase my blood pressure enough to blow the top off my skull.

I spilled the beans. My two closest advisors and two of my best friends... the cows couldn't stop laughing.

"I hate you both," I said as Tethys finally detached herself from me with a peck on the cheek.

"Sure, *we're* the bad guys," Cassandra said, "*You're* the one who's leading two innocent princesses on."

"Oh, don't say that, I already feel like such a bastard," I replied, heading in the direction of the kitchens in search of lunch.

They followed me, naturally.

"It's the Seelie one, isn't it?" Tethys asked, "She got to you with all the tears and the cute, didn't she?"

"No," I insisted.

They sniggered.

"Oh, just shut up."

They laughed harder. I get no respect. Not that I deserved it, I did feel thoroughly like a prick.

CHAPTER 6

"Alright, I've got something," Tethys said, startling me out of my nap.

It was the following Wednesday, after what had been a quiet few days, thank goodness. I was dozing in my library, and Tethys really had done a fantastic job in there. It was a large, L-shaped room on the first floor, filled with books. She'd converted one big section into an entertainment centre, and filled the floor space with comfortable furniture. I loved it in there.

I'd spent the last few days practicing my new skills, which my Codex called Shadow-Walking. I was now competent enough to make the journey between home and Blackhold in about ten to twenty minutes, depending on how well I was concentrating.

"Regarding?" I asked, sitting up so she could drop down next to me on the sofa. She had a folder with her and spread the contents on the coffee table in front of us.

"Our sources tell me that there are three suppliers of Source in the country, North, Middle and South. Through bribery and sheer stubborn trickery I've managed to track their manufacturing back to somewhere on the Isle of Wight. Nobody knows exactly where, or who makes it, but the shipments come through Gosport. So I'd have to guess somewhere in Gardenia."

That last word said with a certain lustful dread that caught my attention.

"Gardenia?" I asked, "Never heard of it, should I have?"

"You're kidding," she said, "How have you not heard of Gardenia?"

"I don't know everything Tethys."

She sighed, "We really need to go through your knowledge and make sure that there aren't any more holes this big. Gardenia is to Las Vegas as Las Vegas is to Vatican City."

"What? It's the Isle of Wight, how can there be another Las Vegas on the Isle of Wight and I don't know about it?"

She sighed again, as if her very breath was calling me ignorant.

"When your people first came out to the world, there was a group of Magicians who didn't like it very much. They were certain that the government was going to descend on them with pitchforks and torches, so they bought up a whole bunch of land on the Isle of Wight and they fortified it against all comers."

"Survivalist Magicians... well, it takes all sorts, I guess," I replied.

"It didn't end there, though. There were a whole bunch of creatures and people thinking much the same way, and so they figured Gardenia was the best place to be; safety in numbers and all that. So one community became two then four then *ten*. They started building, bribing anyone they needed to keep themselves anonymous and threatening the rest. The dozen or so small villages became a town, and over the last fifteen years, it's become a city, right in the middle of the island."

I nodded along, this was certainly news to me. When I thought of the Isle of Wight at all (and that wasn't very often), I thought of farms, coasts and holiday resorts, not... *this*!

"It's... not a good place, Mathew. It's where you go when you want excess. Every sort of vice is available there. The police is in the Council's pocket, and not all of their officers are human. It's always dark there, there's an enchantment that draws in thick cloud that leaves it in perpetual night. It's got the largest population of Vampires and Ghouls *anywhere*; there are Shadowborn around every corner, Ogres under the bridges. And that's just the *least* dangerous threats.

"And I don't have anyone there, not really. I have a guy

who owes me a favour or two, and of course Karina lives there, but I don't have any real resources. We're blind."

"We won't ask Karina, that's a terrible idea and I won't have your family put in danger. Who's your guy?" I asked.

"A Detective Inspector. He moonlights as an enforcer. Again, not a great guy, nobody there is."

"Can you arrange a meeting?" I asked.

"Absolutely not! You will not go to Gardenia, Mathew, understand me? They don't call it Gomorrah for nothing!"

"I'll be fine," I said breezily.

"No, I won't have it," she said, "It's simply not happening."

"Tethys, you know I can take care of myself, I'll be fine, and this needs sorting a.s.a.p.. We're looking at some pretty bad consequences if we don't, remember?"

"Matty, people die in Gomorrah, a *lot* of people. Even Magicians," she said, gripping my arm.

I squeezed her hand, "From the way our *friends* were talking, not dealing with this would be far worse for me than a little trip to a bad neighbourhood. Their sort don't draw attention to *little* problems, Tethys."

She grunted unhappily.

"Besides, I'm far from defenceless," I said, "and I can blend in."

"God, Matty, I don't like this!"

"Don't like what?" Cassandra asked, coming into the room at *just* the wrong moment. I swear that woman had something in her head that let her know when I was about to do stupid things.

"I need to take a trip," I said as casually as possible, "Gardenia."

Cassandra blinked.

"Out of the question," she said *very* finally.

"And I have to go alone," I added.

"Already said it's out of the question," Cassandra said, "I'm not changing my mind because you said something even more stupid."

"Cassie-" I began.

"Don't 'Cassie' me, Graves!" she said, stomping over to glare in my face, "I wouldn't let you into Gardenia with all the other Archons and half the S.C.A. standing next to you! You sure as hell aren't going alone!"

"Pineapple," I said.

"No, Mathew. You don't get to pull that crap on me. Not over this!"

I should explain that. I'd sat her down shortly after she became my Warden. I'd told her that there were certain things that I would have to do that she wouldn't normally let me do. I'd explained in as vague a way as I could that implied Rose and Gabrielle without confirming them (because certain knowledge of the afterlife is a no-no, apparently). We established that if a situation like *that* came up, I would simply say 'Pineapple' and she'd leave it alone.

"My plan is to go in during the day. From what Tethys tells me, they don't really have full daylight, but you can't really dampen non-human nature. They'll be less active during the day, when it will certainly be a bit brighter. I'll talk to Tethys' contact and follow up as quickly as possible. I'll be indoors at sunset, and that's where I'll stay until sunrise the next morning. The risk will be minimal. Once we have more information, we can take it from there. But I will take exactly no risks whatsoever, I promise."

"And I can't come because?" she asked.

"Because if I need to run, I'll be Shadow-Walking. Are you willing to do that?"

She shuddered, "For you, of course," she said, but her voice was shaky.

"My preferred Magic is Illusions and Shadows," I continued, "If I go alone, it's easier to do what I need to do. Nobody is going to notice another kid in a hoodie in a dodgy town. They will notice you."

"She could go to the hotel with you, that shouldn't be a

problem. So she'd be close by if you needed her," Tethys said, tapping her bottom lip.

"Hotel?" I asked.

"Where else would you hole up during the night?" she said, "I'll book you adjoining suites under an assumed name, nobody will be any the wiser!"

"I might be willing to tolerate that," Cassandra said, daring me to argue.

Truth be told, I was relieved. I'd gotten used to having Cassandra close by. She kept me safe.

"If you're alright with me going out on my own, then that's fine with me," I said, letting out some of the tension I'd been holding in.

"Do I detect a little relief in your aura, Graves?" Cassandra asked, smirking at me, "Didn't want to go on your own, did you?"

"Shut up," I said, looking away, my cheeks colouring.

"You big girl," Cassandra said, patting my shoulder affectionately.

"I don't travel well, is all," I complained.

She smirked. Cassandra was a Life Mage. She could sense emotions; she knew exactly how I felt, and so she knew I was scared. But then I usually was.

My friends laughed at my discomfort. I wondered how many other Archons get laughed at that much...

Tethys made a few calls and arranged for her friend (whose name was Harrich) to meet us the following day. She laid on a car and driver for us, and we drove down to Gosport, which took about an hour and a half. Cassandra was dressed casually, in a suit and blouse, with sensible shoes. I knew she was loaded down with her usual weapons, but I couldn't see a sign of them.

I wore a blazer, shirt, jumper and black shoes. There was an Illusion covering my scars and eyes, tiny things, really, but they'd keep me anonymous. Tethys was wearing my Signet, so that if anyone asked, she was acting in my name while I was away. I had to put it on her myself and she giggled all the while, blushing hard (the Signet belonged to the First Shadow, and only the First Shadow could put it on a different person's finger).

We'd packed light, a flight bag each. Cassandra suggested taking a helicopter, but that would hardly fit a low profile, so we'd be taking a hovercraft from Gosport to Newport. I wasn't looking forward to that. You see, I wasn't lying before, I *really* didn't travel well...

And yep, the hovercraft was a *nightmare*.

I spent the forty minute ride throwing up over the side with my Warden simultaneously rubbing my back and laughing her arse off.

Finally, I stumbled off that infernal machine and onto a pier in Newport, which didn't look like a happy place. It was only about three in the afternoon, but it was already dark. I could taste the spell far up in the air, drawing clouds to it, blanketing the whole island in a sort of gloomy twilight.

The few people we saw outside of the private terminal looked edgy, like they were expecting something to leap out at them. The terminal itself was clean and well maintained, with people falling over themselves to help us with our bags.

There was another car waiting for us, as promised, and we drove off through the decaying town and into the countryside.

"The human population of the island drops every year," Cassandra said, "the only ones not fair game to the predators are the ones working for someone in the city."

"Why hasn't anyone done something?" I asked, disgusted.

"Like who?" she replied, "It's a city full of monsters, you'd need an army."

"Or an Archon," I muttered.

She pulled my head around by the chin so she could look in my eyes.

"Not your fight," she said deliberately, "I mean it Mathew. You may be the First Shadow, but you're still so young. You're not ready."

"And how many people die while I wait until I am?"

She smiled at me, a little sadly, "Figures, I'd get the only Shadowborn with a conscience. No crusades, I will sit on you if I have to, and no you shouldn't use that as an opening for a crude joke."

Damn, she knew me too well...

I squeezed her spare hand. I didn't think that I could promise her I'd keep my nose out of that place's business, so I just kept quiet.

"Just remember, Matty, if something happens to you, it means that I died trying to stop it and failed. You understand that, right? Any risk you take risks me, and I'm not an Archon."

"That's just mean, you know I can't take a guilt trip."

"That's part of my point. This is not a city that treats that kind of decency well. The people here come at you side-ways, and it's always ugly, Matty. You are alive as long as you are worth something to someone. The richer you are, the longer you last."

"I want to go home," I said, only half-joking.

"Then let's go," she said softly.

"What am I worth if I do that?" I asked, "If the *idea* of a place can drive me off? What sort of a man am I?"

"Not everyone is cut out for this life, Matty. You are a truly good person. I don't want this place getting its hooks into you."

"It'll be alright," I said, taking a breath as we drove into Gardenia proper.

The city limits were marked by an artificial river over which there were wide bridges. The one we drove over was higher than the others and offered a commanding view. Tall buildings, dozens of stories high, dominated the centre of the city, a dozen miles away, with incrementally smaller ones, getting less shiny and attractive as you approached the limits.

There were some smaller plots with larger houses on them, all were walled and looked almost like strongholds.

The darkening spell was thickening as we approached the centre of the urban area; the sun was already barely visible. Horribly enough, that made the place more comfortable to something like me.

We soon dipped back into street level and the driver sped up a little. The roads were lined with shops offering a wide variety of rather extreme services. I won't repeat them, I wasn't happy knowing that such places existed. Suffice to say, any perversion or abomination you could imagine was available openly, or some close approximation of it.

I could see normal shops and restaurants, but not one major brand. That spoke volumes and worried me even further. Men and women wandered the streets, many scantily clad, many looking shifty. They seemed to be mostly normal people, just going about their business. But they all moved quickly, always looking around, like prey animals who knew that predators were nearby.

As we got closer to the centre, it became cleaner; more vibrant, less seedy. Euphemisms and ambiguity covered exactly the same services offered closer to the outside. The places looked more classy, the decor was more elegant; the men and women walking the streets became more attractive. The atmosphere was more relaxed and it didn't smell so much of desperation; the people seemed less afraid.

There was more Magic too, meaning that there had to be a sizable number of Magicians around, which rather infuriated me. I kept my power to myself, pulling my energy in close; no need to attract attention. I saw policemen in black uniforms, red bands around their arms, all carrying firearms, which was a shock.

Tethys had booked us rooms at the Hemmingway Hotel. It was one of the taller buildings, wide and silver, faintly glimmering in the half-light. There was a set of wide marble steps at the front and the car pulled up to them. The driver came around and opened the door. I stepped out and offered my hand to Cassandra. She took it, gripping hard enough to make me wince and provide a reminder of who wears the pants in my house. It reassured me, though, which was the idea.

I gave the driver a tip and he nodded his thanks before he drove away (at speed). I led us in and up to the reception desk, where there was an overly cheerful young man waiting for us.

"Hello!" he said, smiling wide enough to show all his teeth, "Welcome to the Hemmingway, how may I help you?"

"Reservations for Stone?" I said.

Grave-Stone, Tethys' little joke. I even had a slush fund in that name, with working cards and ID and everything.

"Lord and Lady Stone," he said, "Welcome. Your suites are ready, here are your keys."

"Two copies for the Red Suite," Cassandra said.

That was my room.

"You're already planning to steal my dinner, aren't you?" I asked, narrowing my eyes.

She blushed.

"No," she said, "It's for your own safety!"

"My breakfast, too, huh?" I said with a raised eyebrow.

She smacked my arm as the man got the extra key for her and we headed up.

Cassandra's suite was next door to mine, the Gold Suite, the bigger one, she informed me. The Red Suite was rather more opulent than was my normal taste. There was a big sitting room with a small dining table, sofa, recliners and tasteful art on the wall. At either end were two connected bedrooms, a huge bathroom and a balcony that commanded an amazing view of the city. I unpacked the few things I'd brought and sat on the sofa, looking through various brochures for local businesses.

There were casinos, gentlemen's clubs, companion bars (brothels, Tethys told me, wish she hadn't), Houses of the Senses (Sin-central, indulge all seven of the big ones and come out not quite the same as you went in; again, Tethys) and a whole bunch of other things from the relatively innocent to the downright disturbing.

Cassandra came right in and flopped down next to me.

"I have to admit, this isn't such a bad way to spend a few days," she said.

"Right? Seen these yet?"

She looked through the brochures, "You perv!" she said with a grin.

"I was thinking casino, what were you looking at?"

"Nothing," she said with a grin, "Casino, eh? You any good?"

"If I can use Magic? Unbeatable. On my own? I can play Blackjack pretty well."

I counted cards. It wasn't even hard, Cathy taught me.

"They may not like cheats in this town," she warned.

"It's not cheating, it's remembering."

She rolled her eyes.

In the end, she talked me into taking in a show instead. There were a couple of theatres close by, and the one we went to was actually quite good. We ate dinner companionably in the hotel's quite impressive restaurant before we left and ordered breakfast for the following morning. It really wasn't so bad.

It started out *so* well...

The next day dawned (well, dawn may be a stretch. It got slightly less dark), and Cassandra fussed over me before I left, reminding me over and over to keep in touch and not to talk to strangers. I promised I'd be careful before dressing casually in dark trousers, hoodie, sunglasses and heavy walking shoes.

I stepped out of the hotel and into the gloom, hailing a taxi which I directed to somewhere called Hellion Plaza.

Tethys had told me I'd need money, so I had quite a bit of the stuff in my satchel, which made me even more paranoid about just wandering the streets. I thought I was carrying too much; I'd never seen that much money in one place before. But Tethys said that bribes in Gardenia were pricy, and that was that. Wonderfully enough, it didn't even put a tiny dent in the vast pile of cash Tethys was playing with.

Hellion Plaza was a wide open space in the middle of one of the more upscale districts, home to a moderately sized police station and some small businesses. The office building next to the station was where I'd be meeting Harrich.

I paid the cabbie and went up to the door, which was made of thick glass. I pressed the button for office four and waited.

"Who is it?" a gruff voice said.

"Mathew Stone," I replied, "Tethys sent me."

A grunt, then a buzz. I pushed the door open and followed the sign for the first floor. The place was clean and well maintained and it smelled like it was cared for. I found the office door, which was made of wood and looked a little worn. There was a plaque that said 'J.S.N Harrich, Private Security' in black on gold.

I knocked and was told to enter.

It didn't smell quite so fragrant in *there*...

It reeked of stale booze and cigarette smoke. There was a wide desk next to the window, covered in papers, a laptop, a clutter of stationary and what looked like a sawn-off shotgun within reach of Harrich's meaty right hand.

The man himself was standing next to his desk; he was tall, going slightly to fat, but with broad, strong shoulders. He wore a white shirt, stained with sweat, a dark tie at half-mast and dirty grey trousers. His eyes were unremarkable, brown and watery, his features might have been handsome, but there was too much stress in his features and posture. He looked weighed down by something, not that one could blame him for that, living in Gardenia.

"Detective Inspector Harrich?" I asked politely.

"Do I look like a copper to you, Kid?" he asked, his voice

deep and gravelly.

"Looks can be deceiving, Sir," I replied evenly.

"The force and I parted ways. What do you want?"

Straight to the point, I could deal with that.

"How much did Tethys tell you?"

"That you'd pay cash and that I should treat you right."

I shrugged, not much, then.

"I need information. I'm looking for the people that manufacture a drug called Source. I need to find them very quickly."

He sat down and leant back, scratching his head. A few hairs drifted out of the thinning patch.

"And why would a nice young man like you be looking for that sort of thing?" he asked.

"That's my concern."

He snorted.

"Take some advice, Kid, go home to your Mummy and Daddy, and forget all about this place. You'll be better off; you've got no business sticking your nose into these people's affairs."

"I know what I'm doing, Mister Harrich. I'd like your help and I'm willing to pay for it, but if you are unwilling or unable, then let me know now, so that I don't waste any more of my time."

"I loved her once, you know?" he said, resting his hand on the handle of his shotgun, "I would have given everything I had, and everything else I could get my hands on to get a fraction of the concern for me that she showed for you in just a few words."

Tethys...

Oh dear.

"And now she's calling in her favours... for you," he said with a sneer on his face, "What makes you so special."

"You won't like finding out, Mister Harrich," I said acidly, my tone making him blink, I didn't like the way he was fondling that gun of his and it was making me testy, "I am not here to play games with you. Information. Now, or I'll walk."

He had the gun up and pointed at my head in less time that it took me to blink. Not that it mattered, I'd been shielded since I'd left the hotel.

"You arrogant little prick!" he hissed, "You come into my town, *my office*, you stand there with your toff manners and your polite bullshit and you give me orders?"

He racked the slide, chambering a shell.

"Put that down," I said quietly, "Now."

He aimed at my head.

"Hand over any money you have, maybe I'll leave you with one or two working limbs."

I shook my head and called my Will. The trigger bent and splintered, flying away and slashing at Harrich's fingers on the way out. He bellowed in sudden pain and I lashed out again, little more than a mental swat, really. He fell back into his chair, which smacked into the wall behind him with a thump.

"Bloody Magicians!" he shouted, thrashing against my mental grip, grasping at his torn fingers.

"Oh, do be quiet," I replied.

It took him a second to calm down.

"I'll kill you," he said menacingly.

"Look, either you can tell me what I need to know or I can crack open your mind and drink the knowledge right out. Makes no difference to me, but I'd imagine you have a preference."

He glared, I kept up a steady pressure as he thought it over.

"Fine," he said.

I let him go.

"Ten grand, right now or you get nothing."

"Five. I don't like being threatened."

"Seven-five," he countered.

"Six."

"Done."

I pulled six small cylinders of fifties out of my satchel and tossed them to him. He caught them one by one and pulled the rubber bands off to count the money. He took his time; I think just to annoy me.

"Vivian Price. She runs the Red Carpet, one-eight-six King's Road. She'll know what you're looking for. She is to Gomorrah what Tethys is to everywhere else. She'll want payment, a lot of it, for the information you need."

"Can you set up a meeting?"

"You're rich, you're male and you're easily parted from thousands of pounds. Show up after sunset, she'll see you," he said with a smirk.

"If this turns out to be a false lead or a trap, then I'll be back," I said quietly.

"Leave town quick, Stone. Your kind don't do well here. If you had what it takes to live here, I'd be dead right now."

"I'll sent Tethys your regards," I said, perhaps a little mean-spirited of me, but I didn't like it when people pointed weapons at my one and only head.

He snorted again, but there was no amusement in the sound this time.

I stood and dropped the Asimov I'd been working on into his head. It was a discreet series of enchantments that would prevent him from willingly harming another sentient being, which seemed to be something of a necessity for a man willing to shoot an unarmed kid. I left him just about capable self defence, but hurting people had just become very difficult for Mister Harrich. I grinned nastily as I walked out of his building and back into the street.

Well, that was a waste of six grand. I should have just taken the knowledge directly from his mind, but that set a bad precedent, and I didn't want to start down what was a *very* slippery slope.

Now what? Sunset wasn't for... eight hours? What was I supposed to do until then?

"Well, well, well, lads, what have we here?" said a voice

from behind me. I turned to see three policemen, all immaculate, all *armed*. They were men, tall and strong-looking with dark hair and predatory eyes. I still had my shields up, and I reinforced them just to be safe. Gardenia wasn't the sort of place where policemen could be instantly trusted.

"Looks like scum up where he doesn't belong," said one.

"What you doing in decent places, Scum?" said another.

I snorted, which probably didn't help, but this place was just so... nasty. I mean, I wasn't wearing a Seville Row suit or anything, but I wasn't dressed *that* badly; certainly not enough for *this* reaction. Had Harrich tipped them off? I wouldn't put it past him, even if that meant he'd have had to arrange for this *before* our meeting (making him a bit of a turd and a prime candidate for a Magical neutering).

"Something funny?" the middle one asked, his eyes narrowing dangerously and giving him the look of an irate warthog.

"Idiocy in action," I replied, in no way intimidated. I'd already cast Mage Sight and knew that they didn't have a Spelleater Amulet with them; they were essentially harmless to me.

"What did you sa-"

They fell over. Sleep Hex. The trio dropped to the ground with satisfying thumps. It wasn't an especially strong version of that Hex, but the force of the Spell would keep them out for fifteen minutes or so. It was actually rather a complicated bit of Magic, and I'd had to sacrifice longevity for area of effect. Sleep spells, any Telepathy, really, generally required a very specific type of Magic construct, which didn't lend itself to multiple recipients. Modifying it as I had made it more easy to resist, if you knew how (not that they did, apparently).

I used Will to drag them into a nearby alley and then walked away. I didn't normally go around knocking out coppers, just so you know, but this seemed simpler at the time, and they didn't seem like particularly nice people.

I walked out of the plaza and onto a wide and busy

street, but I didn't make it far before I heard shouting.

"There he is!" one voice said, "Oy! Armed Police! Hands on your head!"

I turned around.

Six men, all aiming guns at me. Two Spelleaters. I'll say this for the Gardenia Police, they reacted quickly.

They opened fire before I'd even had the chance to follow their instructions. Bullets bounced off my shields by the dozen, ricocheting around as the two constables with Spelleaters sprinted for me from either side. There were screams all around as people made a break for it, trying to escape the gunfire.

Poor idiots...

Here's one of the perks of being an Archon, Spelleaters can knock out most Magicians' powers without any problems, but I could throw out enough power per spell to get through them without much more than an extra effort. Not that I was going to bother with *that*, too flashy.

No, I simply conjured a pair of heavy orbs made of Shadow, making them solid with an extra jolt of energy, using a specific spell from the Shadow Codex. That spell changed them from insubstantial constructs into actual, physical objects, not dependent on Magic to exist. They were still made of Shadows, but now the Shadows were actually *matter*. A tiny effort, and the orbs smashed into the Spelleater carrying policemen, knocking them down hard. The ones firing on me were reloading and I cast more sleep hexes.

More police were coming, dozens more from the station, all toting guns, many with Spelleaters. I should probably have been running.

But these people... they just opened fire without taking into account collateral damage, without even trying to stop me peacefully. They fully intended to do their very best to murder me, right there in the street.

I didn't want to run from people like that.

But I couldn't just knock the lot of them out with a

wide-angle Sleeping Hex; there were too many Spelleaters in amongst the onrushing mob which would easily disrupt anything big enough to put that many people down (without killing most of them, anyway. If I'd been *that* desperate, I could always have pulled a building down on them, Spelleaters didn't work on several thousand tons of rubble, but that was a little excessive).

Spelleaters were so dangerous because they stripped the Magic right out of a spell, leaving the energy to dissipate back into the world. This could still be quite dangerous, as spells could carry a lot of energy, which was why anyone trained in the use of Spelleaters knew to get close to the Mage as quickly as possible, thereby choking off spells at the source, rather than having to dismantle incoming weapons as they were coming at your face.

Now, with that in mind, the best response *against* a Spelleater is a Magical effect without the need of a spell to transfer that effect, like the solid shadows I'd thrown earlier. Simple physics did that job.

In the seconds I had until I had to do something drastic (and probably permanent), I called up a well practiced spell I'd learned for precisely this situation. I drew in light and sonic energy, not my two favourite energy types, but they were essential for the spell.

The air around my hand seemed to shimmer as I raised it, re-casting Mage Sight as I closed my eyes. The Air exploded with light and directed sound. I watched through my Magical senses, as upwards of thirty policemen staggered to a halt, clutching at their heads as they slowly but surely keeled over, first one at a time, and then more and more until they were all unconscious, some twitching uncontrollably as their brains took the strain and misfired.

Sensory overload. A very useful, if somewhat ugly, spell. A word of caution if you ever find yourself using it; practice first. The first time I tried it, I messed up the directional component and spent the next hour throwing up. Cassandra thought it was hilarious.

I went among the fallen police, pulling their Spelleaters off and stuffing them in my pocket, which was easy now, as the wearers needed to be conscious for the enchantments to work. It was a safety mechanism to avoid the amulets draining someone to death; they were powered by the wearers' life force, after all. A couple more police came out, I glared at them and they retreated in short order, no doubt calling for even more backup. I got the last amulet and looked for a suitable patch of shadow. I found one just as the first police cars showed up, sirens blaring.

By the time the first man got out, I was gone.

In my defence, I was in a strange city, and I'd just declared war on the police, so it's perfectly natural that I'd get a little bit lost, alright?

Anyway it took me an hour to get back into the hotel room, where I found Cassandra stress-eating her way through what looked like the entire room service menu.

"What the hell took so long?" she asked, coming over to inspect me for damage (with grease-covered fingers, I might add) and not very gently.

"Got lost coming back," I said sheepishly.

"You reek of guilt, what did you do? Not just guilt, either, vindictive satisfaction."

"I've got to start shielding again," I muttered before sitting down and stripping off my jacket.

I told her what happened.

"You brought the amulets with you?!" she almost shouted, "Matty, they can track those!"

"Please, how stupid do you think I am?" I asked, "I left them in the sewer."

"Why were you in the sewer?"

"I told you I got lost..." I said. She shook her head sadly.

"Worst Shadowborn ever," she said, nudging me gently.

I snorted, "So, what's good?" I asked, looking at the detritus of her meals.

I ordered some lunch and we spent a leisurely day enjoying some of the more wholesome attractions. We went to a couple of casinos and I managed to walk out with a small profit while Cassandra *stomped* out in a huff after losing three hundred quid on the roulette tables.

We took in a show, I called homes and friends various to check in, it wasn't so bad.

Getting Cassandra to let me go talk to Vivian Price after dark wasn't as easy, but I got it done.

CHAPTER 7

It was about half past eight when the car pulled up to a pair of wrought iron gates set into a massively thick brick wall with spikes built into the top. The gates had a guard on them, a huge man wearing dark clothes and glasses. I stepped out of the car and into the man's glower, slightly more elegantly dressed, this time, in shirt, trousers and blazer, with illusions in place to cover my various scars (I hadn't let them lapse since I'd arrived in Gardenia, actually).

The guard looked me over and frisked me before nodding and letting me through. The house was wide and brightly lit, made of grey stone with a dark slate roof. Most of the windows were covered with thick curtains. There were more guards on the front door, which one opened for me.

I'd cast Mage Sight as I approached, and there were a lot of people in that place, and less than a quarter were human. Most of them were Vampires, but there were also a few Ghouls, some Lycanthropes and a few other things I didn't recognise by aura. The smell hit me almost like a physical thing, a thick perfume, heady enough to disorientate; the effect multiplied by low and strangely coloured lights and soft music. A greeter came forward, a middle aged woman wearing a dark green suit.

"Good evening, Sir, welcome to the Red Carpet," she said, "I'm Bianca, the hostess."

Her voice was soft and comforting, her posture relaxed and non-threatening.

"Good evening," I replied politely, "I'm here to see Ms. Price, I was told that she had certain items for sale that I might be interested in?"

Tethys told me that subtlety and discretion went a long way with information brokers. It was often unwise to just come out and declare you're looking for information, it made you look crass.

Bianca smiled widely, "But of course, Sir. Ms. Price is seeing another client at the moment, but I'd be happy to take you to her office, if you wouldn't mind waiting?"

"That would be fine," I said.

"Would you care to enjoy a little entertainment while you wait?"

"What sort of entertainment do you offer? The gentleman who recommended you didn't say what sort of establishment this was," I said, genuinely curious.

Bianca let out a surprisingly young-sounding giggle, "We offer companionship, Sir. For an hour or an evening, at your discretion of course. A wide variety of interesting young ladies for every taste."

"Oh," I said, my face growing bright red on the spot.

I was in a brothel. Oh God, what would my mother say if she ever found out about this?! She'd pitch a fit!

"You don't really frequent our kind of establishment, do you?" she asked.

"That obvious?" I replied.

"You're blushing. Most of our customers don't blush."

I cleared my throat and Bianca smiled.

"We have a number of young ladies who specialise in first timers," she said, "You'll fit right in, I assure you."

"Thank you, but I have a girlfriend," I said lamely, so far out of my comfort zone it wasn't funny.

"If you have a picture, I'm sure we can come up with something. We have a couple of fairly good shape-shifters on staff."

Good grief...

"I prefer the original," I said, trying not to squeak in sheer embarrassment.

"Shine's still on it, eh? Fair enough. How about a conversationalist then, someone to chat with while you wait? Can be as clean as you like."

"You charge for conversation?"

"We charge for *time*, what you do with it is up to you. Some just want to be held, some like a little role play. Anything that causes injury costs extra, though, and we'll have to insist that you use a girl capable of regeneration."

"People deliberately hurt your girls?" I asked, aghast, "And you let them?"

"Only the girls that like it," she replied as if it were the most natural thing in the world.

Bloody hell! I just didn't need to know any of this! That last bit actually made me feel a little queasy.

We moved deeper into the house, and the sounds started to become less wholesome, if you know what I mean. She took me through a reception area with half a dozen scantily clad and ridiculously attractive women in it, all of whom smiled at me. After that, we had to have passed ten closed doors with little red lights over the handle and some three or four with green lights. I didn't know the significance, but I could guess from the sounds. Red = occupied.

I suppressed a shudder.

She took me up a flight of stairs, more doors and women, very few humans except in the rooms with the red lights. I didn't look too closely at those. At long last she brought me to a small waiting room with a handsome receptionist sitting at a tiny desk, tapping away at a computer.

"Are you sure I can't tempt you?" Bianca said.

"No, thank you," I said politely, my mind screaming at me to run the hell away from this whole mess and go home to Stonebridge where things weren't like *this* (I hoped).

"Francois will take care of you," she said before making her way back the way she'd come.

I walked over to the man and gave my fake name. His accent was vaguely French, and his attitude snooty, so I decided to ignore him. I sat down in a comfortable armchair to wait.

I didn't have to wait very long, the door opened and a weasely looking man darted out, his eyes downcast, his suit in disarray.

Francois stood and walked into the office after a brief knock. He came out again and gestured for me to go in.

Vivian Price's office was lavishly decorated, with expensive paintings on the wall and rich furnishings in silk and gold. Her desk was an antique, wide and impressive. She stood as I entered, smiling widely, showing fang (vampire, in case you hadn't guessed). She was a strikingly beautiful woman, tall and toned with a spectacular figure and a mischievous smile.

"Milord Shadow," she said with an elegant curtsey, "How may I be of service?"

I blinked hard.

If I'd had any doubts as to her effectiveness as an information gatherer, they were gone right then and there. She knew me on *sight*. That was bloody impressive.

"Excuse my surprise," I said at last, "I'm obviously nowhere near as sneaky as I thought I was."

She smiled and waved me towards a seat, "Don't feel too bad, I make it my business to know the people in power. You were harder to discover than most, if that's any consolation."

"A little."

"So, what can I do for you?" she asked.

"I need to know where Source comes from," I said without preamble.

Her expression became very calm.

"That is... not a good idea, my lord. With the greatest respect, there are some people whom you simply do not bother."

"These people..." I replied, and then stopped.

I felt something... odd. I still had Mage Sight cast and I looked towards the source of the mystical disturbance. Walls didn't mean an awful lot to someone who could cast Mage Sight, so I could see what was coming just fine. I must say that I was a little surprised (and more than a little terrified, but mostly surprised).

"Any particular reason why there would be an eighteen foot tall Frankenstein's minotaur coming this way at a great rate of knots?" I asked.

"What?" she asked, her voice going a little wobbly.

I stood, casting shields.

"You may want to get behind me," I suggested as the creature smashed into the side of the house.

Price was no slouch. She put me between her and the sudden ragged hole in the wall faster than I could blink. The creature on the other side of the hole was clearly dead and had been for quite some time. Well, bits of it. It was a patchwork of things. I would imagine that a lot of it was ogre. I could see crude stitching and a massive animating spell. It was clearly after Price; its red eyes (in a bull's head) were locked on her.

And it wasn't alone, though at least the others were smaller, but no less gruesome for that; combinations of dead animal and human parts, revolting constructs that made me want to start throwing fire.

They were all leaping for the hole in the wall. Price reached for a panel and flipped a switch. Alarms started blaring and I felt people start running. I called my Shadows and punched them straight through the big one's face as it tried to reach for Price. I expanded the coil and the monster's skull exploded messily, spilling necrotic brain all over the place and nearly making me throw up from the sheer, awful stench.

"If you have a safe place, I suggest you run there," I said over my shoulder.

"I'd rather not, if it's all the same."

I shrugged and started smashing the dead things as they jumped for us, scrambling up the wall on torn nails and claws. I opened a hole in my shields behind me.

"Come close and stay at my back," I said. She obeyed and I felt strong hands on my jacket.

"What the hell are these things?" I asked.

"The Hyde," she replied, "Monster makers; murder for

hire."

"You have such a lovely town," I said as another wave of the smaller ones were crushed under my Shadows, the animating power destroyed after so much damage.

These weren't true Necromantic constructs, not really. Real Necromancy involved spirits and possessions, really ugly stuff that needn't detain us right this minute. What I was seeing was Fleshcraft, the combining of disparate parts into a whole greater than the sum, reanimated by Flesh Magic, not Death. That made them less robust, but more versatile. I suppose, in the end, a zombie is a zombie, but these ones were more disgusting than the ones I'd dealt with before.

I stepped to the hole, letting my Shadows flow out and attack incoming creatures. There were dozens more of them, including two more of the big ones. A force that size would have made a mess of the Red Carpet.

But it was laughably inadequate for the purposes of dealing with *me*...

I let my Shadows spread far and wide, enveloping every last one of them, focusing hard as I sent them out. And then I clenched my fists, and the Shadows compressed, hard and sharp. There was a rolling wet crack, and suddenly there was nothing left of the Hyde's creatures but a vast pile of mangled (and very smelly) meat.

I looked around carefully, but there weren't any more of them. I saw a smashed sewer grate on the street opposite me; there was blood and fur on it. Maybe that's where they came from?

Something still seemed off. There was active magic around somewhere...

"What's going on?" Price asked.

"I'm not sure yet."

There!

A portal opened and a man stepped out. This one was quite alive, but his aura was all wrong, like it was decaying before my eyes. He wore dark robes and his face was hooded. I saw sharp teeth, and flickers of Space Magic.

He seemed to stare right at me for a long moment. Then he lifted his hand and a ball of Space Magic came right at us. I recalled my Shadows and a wall intercepted the attack. I felt a wrench as a whole mess of my constructs were compressed through a field and torn apart. That would not have been pleasant if it had hit us, I'd seen Hopkins use something similar to pull someone's brains out of their skull...

I retaliated, drawing in Force while my Shadows went for him. They arrived and he popped out of existence. I felt his Magic reappear behind me, far too close. I spun and half my shields were ripped away as another of those attack spells hit them. Another pop and he was gone again, reappearing on the lawn, where he took a face full of force.

It wasn't a very strong spell, I'd thrown a wave of Force in the hopes of catching some part of him, but it was enough to disorient him, and allow my Shadows to catch him. They hit hard enough to break bones, lots of bones. He screamed once, briefly, and then he was out like a light. The malignant power seemed to drain away now that he was down, and I allowed myself to relax a little.

"I think we're good," I said, releasing my shields and letting Price step away from me. I reached out with my Shadows and grabbed the downed Space Mage by the torso, dragging him up through the hole in the wall. I set him down on the carpet and nearly threw up again.

"Bloody hell, what's wrong with his face?!" I asked.

The entire thing was perfectly smooth grey flesh but for a wide and gaping mouth filled with needle-sharp teeth.

"Hyde-Prime," Price said with distaste, "They make them from Magicians, to control the others. They're not supposed to fight. They must really have wanted me dead."

"Bloody hell," I repeated, pulling the hood back into place before dropping a coma-hex into its head, "That's just not right."

"Welcome to Gomorrah," she said slyly, "Would you

mind waiting here a moment? I need to check on my people."

"Sure," I said, taking a few steps away from the faceless thing.

"Thank you," she said, and then she was gone, moving with awful speed.

I strolled about a bit, looking at the artwork, trying to calm down. Minotaur zombies? Faceless assassins? God, what a town!

"Hello?" said a small voice, breaking into my reverie, "is anyone there?"

"Hello?" I answered back, walking in the direction of the voice.

"Can you help? I'm stuck!" she said.

The door was smacked open, and the room was dark, not that that's a problem for yours truly...

The girl was stunning. They all were in that place, but she was something else. She had light blonde hair that was long and curly, a wonderful face with full lips. She was a vampire, with pale blue eyes and short, rather cute, fangs. She was also naked and strapped to a bed in a very compromising position.

It took me a moment to restore my wits and move to lend her a hand. The shackles were heavy metal and bound her to the headboard; both the hand-set and the feet-set if you catch my drift. Certainly the young lady was very flexible.

"Is there a key, Miss?" I asked, trying to keep my blush under control.

"On the bedside table," she said. I put a convenient dressing gown over her... everything as I went rummaging. The key had fallen behind the bed.

I undid the shackles and nearly got a foot to the face as she was released.

"Sorry!" she said as I went around the other side and repeated the action.

"Quite alright. Are you hurt?" I asked, not knowing what else to say.

"Pulled muscle," she said with a coquettish smile on her red lips, "part of the job, I'm afraid, it's already healing."

"Good," I said, "You got left behind?"

"Mm hm," she said, standing, slipping the robe I'd provided over herself and moving to a pile of lingerie, which she pulled on while I turned my back and left the room.

Oh, I was learning far too much on this outing...

"Never seeing that guy again. It's one thing to chain me up, quite another to leave me that way when bad things are happening. I'm Crystal, by the way," she said, coming into the corridor and extending her hand.

"Mathew," I replied, shaking it gently.

"What brings you by, Mathew?" she said with another naughty smile.

"A chat with the lady of the house," I said, indicating the nearby office, "We were interrupted."

"So I see. By Hydes? Oh dear."

"Not a nice bunch," I agreed, heading back that way.

"You see what happened?" she asked as she peeked out the hole in the wall, her cute nose wrinkling at the smell.

"Magician of some sort, I think," I replied, "Splat, problem solved."

"Magicians? Bleuch," she said, waving her hand, "Can't trust the bastards. I mean, they're creepy guys, always cursing this or fire-balling that. Creep me out. Useful in a pinch, I suppose, but can you trust someone who can get into your brain?"

I smiled and flopped down in a comfortable seat, stretching out.

"Aren't Vampires Telepathic?" I asked.

"That's different," she said, sitting next to me.

"How?"

"Well..." she started and then stopped, "It just is."

"If you say so."

"You ever come here before?" she asked, laying her hand gently on my own.

"No, not really my scene. My girlfriend wouldn't approve," I said pointedly.

Didn't faze her at all.

"Girlfriends can be a drag that way. They don't want big, strong men to have the fun they deserve," she said, her voice low and throaty.

I snorted.

"Crystal, I am neither big nor strong, and as for what I deserve... I would deserve nothing more than what those creatures outside got if I was willing to trade the feelings of the girl I love for a few moments' pleasure."

"Hours, Darling. *Hours* of pleasure," she purred, her hand stroking mine now.

"Crystal, stop trying to get into my head, it's not nice," I said as I felt her brush up against my defences.

She blinked.

"Ah, so when you said 'some sort of Magician'... you meant you. Now who's not being nice? Letting me carry on like that!"

She swatted my arm playfully before tracing the line of my jaw with a finger, which disturbed the Illusion over my cheek and eyes, making her recoil as she saw my real appearance.

Illusions couldn't be maintained if someone other than the caster touched them; it was a conflict of Auras and Will, which caused the Illusion to shatter.

"My God! What happened to you?!"

I winced at her reaction, quickly recasting the Illusion.

"Bad people," I replied.

"Sorry. I was surprised."

"You're not the first. Hence the Illusion."

"I've seen worse," she said, "I once had a man, he carved himself up from forehead to toe and made sure the cuts scarred. Weird fellow."

I chuckled again.

"The red eyes are new for me though. Make you look a little dangerous. I like that," she said, now rubbing my shoulder.

I was saved from needing a response when Price came back. I stood (manners you know).

"Would you come with me?" she asked politely, "This office is a little draughty."

I laughed a little and followed her, Crystal hot on my heels for some reason.

"Crystal, dear, why don't you go make yourself useful?" Price said.

"I thought that Mathew might get lonely," she said, her voice high and sensuous (and distracting).

"He'll be just fine," Price said.

Crystal sighed.

"Come back soon, Mathew," she said, leaning up to plant a kiss on my cheek, "I'll give you the friends and family discount."

"Shoo, Crystal," Price said indulgently and the girl bounced away with a smile.

We resumed our walk through the house, which was now refilling with girls and irritated looking men (and some women) being led by the hand back to rooms.

"She likes you," Price said, "Perhaps you'd be willing to let her spend a little time with you? As my way of saying thank you?"

"Really not my thing," I said blushing again.

She snorted, "You have a Y-chromosome, she's your thing. Even gay men like Crystal."

"I mean that I'm attached."

I'd had that conversation at least three times since I got there; did everyone in that building assume that I was some sort of rutting monkey? Having said that, I would imagine that a lot of their clientele is of that basic persuasion, so I couldn't really blame them, even if it creeped me out no bloody end.

"If you say so," she said, leading me into another office and closing the door behind me, "so, before we were interrupted, you useful man, you, we were talking about Source."

"I need to know where it's being made, with as much detail as you feel you can safely gather, but that as a bare minimum," I replied.

She bit her lip, tapping her fingers on the table.

"That may not be simple. The trade in that is managed by a select few dealers in the High-rises with the Magicians, even getting to one will be difficult. It will take time, money and effort to cultivate the sort of contacts that provide that information."

"I have limited time. I was informed that there would be a large-scale negative consequence if the sale of Source is allowed to continue. I was given months as a time frame, probably no more than four, I would guess."

"'Large-scale negative consequence'? What does that mean?"

"Given my source, apocalyptic would be my guess."

She tapped her chin again.

"Would you let me see your mind?"

"Why?" I asked, wary.

"If I am to do as you ask, it will be dangerous. I need to know that what you're saying is true. I need to know that you believe it."

I thought about it.

"Alright," I said, "but if you stray off topic, I'll know. And I'll be annoyed."

She nodded and I lowered my shields and thought of Rose and Gabrielle's instructions, making sure to keep any details about them fuzzy.

I felt her mind slide gently into mine. I'd been mind-prodded by a Vampire before, but she was far more gentle about it, and she kept her probe where it was supposed to be.

Who are these two? she asked.

You don't want to know. Do you believe me?

I do, she replied, *God only knows why.*

"You must do nothing to provoke or startle them," I said aloud once she'd pulled away from my mind, "We can't risk them vanishing on us."

"I understand the stakes, Lord Shadow," she said, "Now, let's talk terms."

"Alright," I said, leaning back.

We talked money for a while. In the end, I was going to have to part with a *lot* of it.

"I can be here rapidly if required," I said, handing contact details to her on a slip of paper.

"I'll work as fast as I can, but don't expect anything instantly."

"Okay," I replied, "Are you going to be alright? Hyde-wise, I mean."

"I have a few favours of my own to call in now that I know they're after me. I'm just lucky you happened to be here when they came."

"Rather convenient, wasn't it?"

"Meaning?" she replied.

"Nothing in particular, just wondering if someone's playing a game here. Or if someone wanted to prevent your helping me."

"Well, if they are, it's going to be a very costly mistake," she said, her eyes suddenly sharp and flinty, "I do *not* intimidate."

I decided I quite liked Vivian Price.

We shook hands and she offered me a complimentary anything I wanted, which I politely declined before opening a Gate and making my way back to the hotel.

I fell out of the Shadow Realm and into Cassandra's bathroom, where I tripped over her bath mat and went face first into her loo, barely avoiding the water while swearing profusely, only to discover that she wasn't even there. I went to my room and found her tense and irate, the remains of three dinners on the dining table.

"What took you so long?" she snapped.

I explained, and she calmed down once I told her that

we could get the hell out of town first thing in the morning. I offered to Shadow-Walk us home, but she hit me and told me that I wasn't to even suggest that again. So I resigned myself to car-hovercraft (vomit)-car.

I'd been quiet throughout the return trip, thinking back on the sort of place Gomorrah was. Simply, it was a hell-hole. People were suffering there, locked into lives of pain and degradation. Even the police tried to kill strangers.

Cassie held my hand, understanding what I was going through. I was going to have to do something, and I couldn't do it alone. I'd need my brother and sisters, but would they help? Could they?

Bah. One problem at a time. Deal with the drugs first, clean up an entire city later.

Tethys was glad to see us and wrapped me in a hug I desperately needed after three days in that heap. I didn't let her go for a while and she just stayed there, making me feel better.

"Told you you'd hate it," she whispered in my ear.

CHAPTER 8

What little remained of that week passed quickly, and I allowed myself to drift back into what I considered normal; away from thoughts of *that* place. So, when Sunday came around I was more than ready to go back to school, where it was more... innocent, and I could pretend, at least for a while, that there wasn't a world outside where things like Gardenia existed.

Cassandra didn't especially like the idea of my going off alone, and to a place where people had already tried to kill me (repeatedly), but I managed to persuade her not to come with me, under the proviso that I checked in with her regularly. I promised to do one better and meet her at least once a week for coffee, which made her feel better. I promised the same to Tethys, who I think just liked having me within teasing distance.

I arrived back at school by Shadow-Walking, and in good time for once. Windward Academy was surprisingly easy for me to find, even in the Shadow Realm, but then I had spent my most formative years there, so it made sense that I'd have a pretty serious connection to the place.

I found my room assignment quickly and unpacked before settling in to wait for my friends to arrive. Bill was first. He'd grown again and was now a good two inches taller than me and broader with it; he was still soft around the edges, though, with the same dark hair and easy smile. He was a frightful gossip but utterly and completely loyal to the end. We chatted and messed around while we waited.

Cathy's text came in around four. Bill smiled at me knowingly.

"Go ahead, I'll catch up when the saliva stops flowing," he said with a grin.

"You had to ruin it, didn't you?" I said, but I still jumped out the window and flew right over.

Cathy's father was still unloading the car when I landed next to her and scooped her into a hug that made her squeak adorably for a moment before returning it with gusto. We had a strict 'minimal contact around her father' rule, so it was just a hug... for now.

Cathy was the most beautiful girl I'd ever known, with a heart-shaped face, soft, full lips warm brown eyes and golden blonde hair. She had a dazzling smile, a delicate nose and wore thick glasses with heavy black rims, her hair held in a bun pinned by pencils.

"Missed you," I said, my arms and my Will combining to lift her a few inches clear of the ground.

"Missed you, too," she said, her arms hard around me.

There was a distinct cough from the direction of Cathy's car and I put her down, blushing as I went to shake her Father's hand.

"Good to see you again, Mister Campbell," I said after he'd barely avoided crushing every bone in my fingers.

"Graves," he said, with a brief nod, "Now you're here, you may as well make yourself useful."

He gestured at Cathy's trunk and suitcases.

I smiled and called my Will, lifting them easily into the air as Cathy led the way with a grin on her face. We climbed two flights of stairs and found Cathy's room quickly. I smiled at a couple of the girls I recognised. I put her trunk down and she was on me in a second, planting a deep kiss on my lips that left me in need of air.

She smiled impishly at me, and we kissed again, my world making sense once more.

"So, I go away for a couple of weeks and you move in with another woman, get engaged to a second princess and visit a brothel. What do you have to say for yourself?" she said in a serious tone, ruined by the mischief in her eyes.

"Sorry Miss Cathy," I said, whispering into her ear. She shuddered and nibbled my chin a little bit.

"You smooth talker, you," she gasped as I kissed her neck and cheek, "Was it terrible? Are you alright?"

"All better now," I said, smiling at her.

"God, Matty, I wish you would be more careful," she said, squeezing me tightly.

"I was, not a scratch on me!"

"Good," she said, nuzzling in close, "For every scratch you get, I will put on three more to remind you not to get hurt, understand me?"

"Remembering how you usually put scratches on me makes me want to go get hurt right now," I whispered, which made her squeak, blush and swat my arm.

"Stop that! I'm serious!" she said, giving me a glare.

"Alright, I'll be good."

She hugged me again, "You'd better be."

She saw her father off and unpacked. I was more of a hindrance than a help, but we had fun anyway. Bill arrived and we caught up some more, just messing around and doing as little as possible. It was good to be back, away from problems that I couldn't solve in places I couldn't stand. I was with Cathy, and all was well...

...for that first night.

The first day of my last term at Windward Academy dawned bright and warm and I woke with a smile on my face. I'd allowed myself to forget everything outside the place, and it felt good.

I dressed in my uniform, blue striped shirt, blazer, trousers, house tie, black shoes and headed off to the dining hall.

Cathy and Bill were already there and I joined them with a yawn before accepting a good morning kiss from my girlfriend.

"Did you hear about the new guy?" Bill asked.

"New what?" I asked, still not all the way awake.

"New guy," Bill repeated slowly, as if to a simpleton (my morning lack of intelligence was well known), "Mister Crippen said that his school closed down and he's finishing his A-levels here. Magician, apparently."

I yawned again, shaking my head. Not my problem, too early...

"What kind?" Cathy asked.

"How would I know?" Bill replied.

Cathy shrugged.

Belle dropped onto the bench opposite me while I was dozing, startling me back into consciousness.

"New hottie, closing fast!" she said, bobbing up and down.

"And a good morning to you too," I said.

Belle was a pretty, tall brunette, a Wizard-level Water Mage with striking features and a wicked smile. She was also my brother's ex-girlfriend, not that I held it against her; in many ways Des was my ex-brother.

"I just saw him coming this way, the new guy. He's... wow!" Belle said, not overburdened with subtlety was our Belle, "Ooh, there he is!"

Cathy turned to have a surreptitious look. I couldn't be bothered, still sleepy and hungry. He did walk past, though, and I could see why Belle was so interested.

The guy could have modelled. He was tall, at least six inches taller than me, and I was over six feet, with healthy skin, broad shoulders and the kind of muscle tone that made Bill and I immediately look like slugs by comparison. His face was finely chiselled, with strong bones and not a blemish in sight. He had grey piercing eyes, which reminded me a little of Kron, actually, and elegantly styled blonde hair.

"Oh, I would love to find out what that tastes like," Belle muttered.

"Belle, we're eating here," I complained.

"Not sorry, I want him to wear me like a hat," she said

huskily.

"What does that even mean?" I replied with a snigger, "You want him to hollow you out and wear your corpse? Or did you want him to skin you and use that to make a fedora?"

"Don't ruin this for me, Matty, I will beat you," Belle said, following the Adonis with her very lustful eyes, along with most of the other girls in the room.

"He is pretty, isn't he?" Cathy said.

"Boyfriend not six inches from you," I replied.

Cathy blinked and turned to stick her tongue out at me, I replied by pinching her bottom, which made her retaliate on one of my nipples. She kissed my cheek when she was certain I'd learned my lesson and went back to her eggs. I think Belle was drooling.

Blondie was looking around for a place to sit and naturally Belle decided to be helpful.

"Hey, New Guy!" she said, he turned, "Come sit with us!"

Bollocks. I didn't need new people so early in the morning.

"Thanks!" he said brightly, sliding in next to Belle, "I'm Tyler Storm."

Well, it's not like he *chose* the ridiculous name, but Belle seemed to like it. She introduced herself and us. Storm turned his eyes on Cathy.

"I must say that the young ladies at this school are a far more lovely bunch than I'm used to," he said with what was supposed to be a charming glance but came out as more of a leer.

Belle blushed hard and became unintelligible; Cathy rolled her eyes and leant against me.

Storm looked at Cathy and cocked his head.

I felt him call power, focussed on my girlfriend.

"What do you think you're doing?" I asked very quietly, my voice low and nasty. I was all the way awake now, and suddenly *not* in a good mood.

The Magic didn't stop coming. I wrapped a shield

around Cathy's mind as his Empathic probe was about to hit. I cast Mage Sight as he recoiled from the barrier.

Low level Sorcerer. Life Mage. That spell was designed to alter the emotional state of the target, of my Cathy. His eyes darted to mine as things started to shake... as *everything* started to shake.

I was that angry that my Magic was starting to act on its own, affecting objects around me. Plates and cups rattled, tables shuddered, lights started to flicker.

"He just tried to get in your head, Cath," I said softly.

"What?!" Belle asked, sliding away and raising her own shields.

"That's a lie!" Storm shouted, standing up.

Cathy, Belle and Bill were all glaring at him.

"What was he going to do?" Cathy asked quietly, her hands around my arm.

"I'll let you know when I find out," I asked, casting a Telepathic Probe.

For a kid who knew how to play with another person's mind, his defences were woefully weak. I was inside his psyche in less than a second and he gasped as I took control, putting his conscious mind to sleep while I went rooting. Searching a mind was a lot like searching the internet. You input certain words or ideas and then the subject's brain will bring up what you need, if it's there.

The first thing I saw was that he'd done this before. Usually to girls. He made them like him. When I looked deeper I saw that he'd never taken it to an extreme, but he'd wrecked a lot of relationships. That was where his enjoyment lay, not in taking advantage of the feelings he engendered, which was good for him, I'd have torn his brain into pieces if he had.

No, this was a creature who enjoyed feeding on the *pain* he caused. Literally, in fact, he drew energy from grief and loss, which was a *very* rare skill (not to mention a nasty one). He'd seen Cathy and me and wanted to wreck it so he could feed off the misery. He'd never had a relationship of his own. The ideas of love and affection were alien to him. I would have pitied him if it weren't for the fact that he'd gone after my Cathy.

The second thing I discovered was that he was a junior member of the Peace Legion, sort of their version of the Scouts. I probed deeper there, but the memories were fuzzy and indistinct, like I was trying to squeeze sand; they'd been deliberately scrambled. I might have pushed, but I didn't have the time to waste unpicking his head. Besides, I had enough to go on, and there weren't two ways to look at it, Sutton had almost certainly sent him to Windward, but why? As a warning? She had to know that Storm wouldn't get any closer to me than this, and there was no recognition in him; he hadn't known me, or Cathy, it made no sense.

I wanted to talk to Hopkins about it, but that would require yet more tact after the last time we'd discussed Sutton...

One problem at a time. What to do about this fellow? Obviously some sort of pain, lots and lots and *lots* of it. But how best to go about it? I thought for a moment and then smiled evilly before going to work. It took about a quarter of an hour to cast the necessary spell. It was a thing of horrific beauty and it slid into Storm's mind like an evil amoeba, seeking all the little cracks and crevices where it needed to go.

I released his mind and emerged to see my friends looking at me.

"What?" I asked.

"You've got a little evil on your face," Belle said, "What did you do to him?"

"You'll see," I said, waking him up with a mental prod.

His eyes fluttered and he glared, "You!" he shouted, darting towards me. He'd stayed stood up while I was working on him and was a little shaky on his feet.

He called his Magic... and fell to his knees as his pain centre fired off what would have felt like a first degree burn, over all his body. The more Magic he tried to call, the worse it would hurt. Needless to say, he wouldn't be able to use his powers anymore, not unless he could find a telepath to remove what I'd done, and people who could do *that* were few and far between. Vanessa Knowles, a professional Telepathic Interrogator with the S.C.A. couldn't get my hexes out, so I could assume that he was going to be without Magic for a *long* time.

The beauty of my Hex wasn't just the pain, but the fact that his own Magic shut down the part of his mind that knew how to use it, so even if he found a way around the agony, he wouldn't be able to work around the loop.

"Problem, Tyler?" I asked nastily, sitting happily as he flailed.

He stood and raised his hand again... and fell over once more.

"Wha... what did you do to me?"

"I revoked a gift you've been misusing," I said coldly.

"What?" he said, his eyes wide and staring, "My Magic?! You took my Magic?!"

"Yep," I said happily while the rest of the diners watched our little drama unfold.

"Give it back!" he said, crawling on his hands and knees, "Please?! God, please give it back?!"

"Come back in say... twenty years. If you've been good, we'll talk," I replied, turning my attention back to my breakfast.

"I've got connections," he said, the grovelling tone gone, "Give my Magic back or you'll be sorry."

"Go on, then," I said, turning my now black eyes back on him, "Make me sorry."

He backed away at the look in my eyes, tears streaming down his face as he ran out of the dining hall.

Silence descended.

"Wow, you really can't go one term without making an enemy, can you?" Belle said, "And did you have to do that? We could have been something special."

"He's asexual, Belle, he doesn't even know what his bits are for," I replied.

Her eyes went wide, "You're kidding?"

I shook my head.

"I could have taught him," she offered.

We sniggered, Cathy's grip on my arm never loosened.

After that, I went to find Hopkins, figuring I'd just lay it all out for her and let the chips fall where they may.

Back when I'd thought I was just your run-of-the-mill Shadowborn, she'd come to work at Windward as a teacher to keep an eye on me and chivvy me in the right mental direction. Even after I'd found out who I was, she continued to do the job she signed up for. Her contract would be up at the end of the academic year; she said she was looking forward to it, but there were times when she seemed to be a little sad about the idea of leaving teaching behind.

I found her in her English classroom just before first period.

"Jen? You won't believe what just walked into the school," I said.

"I know that tone," she said, turning to grin at me, "What did you do now?"

I explained and her face fell at my description of the guy and our brief interaction. I left out the Peace Legion stuff; I'd let her discover that on her own.

"Matty, I'm begging you, begging mind, to tell me you didn't break the mind of Tyler Storm."

"I didn't break it, I just blocked bits of it. It was the least he deserved, you heard what I told you about what he did, right?"

"Matty, you don't get it-"

The ground started to shake, the building with it.

"Oh no," Hopkins said as the door to her classroom blew open and a familiar, enraged figure stood in the doorway.

Storm is one of Kron's descendants, Matty, Hopkins said into my mind as Kron walked in, her face like thunder, *You hurt a member of her family.*

I saw Storm behind her, his face split by a sneering grin as Kron walked towards me.

Well... that sure did explain a lot. What happened next filled in the rest of the holes in my musings on motivation, cause and effect.

"You animal!" Kron bellowed, bunching a fist and slamming it into my gut. The air blasted out of me and I dropped to the ground, gasping.

"Vanessa!" Hopkins said, moving to my side as Kron dragged me up and socked me in the face.

My lip split, blood flowed and teeth loosened as I fell again.

You know, if she hadn't just played me like a harpsichord, I would be *very* impressed with Namia Sutton's Machiavellian talents. As it was I was too busy getting the snot beaten out of me to be anything other than quite pissed off.

"Stop it!" Hopkins shouted.

Jen, stay back, I'm sorting it, alright? Trust me, I sent.

Hopkins bit her lip and stepped back as Kron picked me up again, her face a mask of fury as she smashed me into the wall hard enough to crack something in my shoulder. I could already feel my face swelling up as she slammed her fist into the opposite cheek. I'd cast a numbing spell, so the actual wounds barely hurt, but every fresh injury produced a spike of agony before the spell could adjust and take it away.

It took her a while to punch herself out of her rage. I didn't know how badly I was hurt, but some important things were fractured and at least one limb wasn't moving properly.

"God, Van," Hopkins said as Kron finally let me slide to the ground, "What did you do?"

I saw through one working eye as Kron looked at her knuckles, covered in my blood. I coughed up a mouthful of the stuff and it stained my shirt red.

"You done?" I managed to lisp through split lips and broken teeth, "You ready to hear my side now?"

Kron looked horrified at my reasonable tone and backed

away, bumping into a table. I felt Flesh Magic as Hopkins went to work fixing things, which I appreciated; fixing your own wounds is trickier than fixing someone else's, and I'd taken a few good shots to the head, enough to make my concentration a bit iffy.

"What did he tell you?" I asked Kron.

"That you attacked him and took his Magic," she said, steel coming back into her eyes.

"Did he suggest a reason why? Did you ask?"

Doubt crossed her features.

"He's a Leech. He feeds on pain. When he can't find it, he makes it. He tried to do it to me and Cathy. I stopped him and made sure he couldn't do it again, that's all."

"That is a lie, Grandmother!" Storm said, "I didn't do anything to him!"

"Look in his head. Hell, look in *mine* if you want," I replied.

I coughed up another mouthful of blood. I felt Kron ready a probe and I deliberately lowered my defences. I felt her slide into my active memory while Hopkins glared daggers at her fellow Archon. She'd fixed my skull, teeth and jaw, bless her, and was moving on to my bruised and battered torso. I was already feeling miles better.

My head started aching again after a second; Kron wasn't being gentle in there. Before long, she yanked herself out, making me wince a little. Her face went white with fury again as she turned on her descendent.

"You can't believe anything he says!" Storm protested.

"Get out of my sight," she rasped, "What you have done is unforgiveable. Even worse is what you've had me do on your word. Step one toenail out of line and I'll make what Graves did to you seem like a gentle walk along the riverside! Now get out!"

Storm ran, tears in his eyes again, while I propped myself up into a more comfortable position against the wall where Kron had dropped me.

Lady Time turned to look at me.

"I don't know what to say," she said, letting her eyes drop.

Neither did I, really. She'd turned on me again. That hurt more than nearly being beaten to death (though not by much, that woman was freakishly strong). Thank goodness she hadn't wanted to use Magic. It was almost as if she'd just wanted an excuse to hurt me.

"Whatever your issues are with me, work them out," I said, "I am not your punching bag. I let you do that this time because you needed to realise that actions have consequences. It shocks me that Lady Time has to be taught a lesson that even I know, but there it is."

Kron glared, her eyes going dark.

"If you come for me again, I'll defend myself. I'll lose, but I'll try. So, next time, maybe act like Lady Time should and exercise some bloody foresight!" I shouted at the end, which made her jump.

"I mean, how did you not see that *this* was how it was going to end? Did you even check? I was never going to fight you; it was never even a *question*. Did you know you were just going to beat on me until you'd had enough?" I asked, my tone bitter.

Hopkins was squeezing my shoulder, still glaring at Kron.

"Is this about the last one?" I asked her, "He went bad on you and now I'm tarred with the brush?"

Kron looked away from me, her arms crossed under her breasts, defensively.

"I apologise for my mistake," she said at last, her voice empty.

"You apologised for the last one, too," I said, "and yet here we are again, only this time I'm bleeding. What happens next time?"

Kron winced. She kept looking down. She opened her mouth to say something, but seemed to think the better of it and stormed out the room, leaving Hopkins and I alone.

"Don't tell her I said this, but that woman has a mean right hook," I said.

Hopkins smiled sadly, fixing up the last of my injuries.

"I can't believe she did that," she said as she sat against the wall with me.

"Nash..." I asked, referencing my predecessor, "Did he hurt her? I mean, we've never discussed it, and I don't want to push..."

"No, maybe you should know. Nash... Nash was never a particularly good man. But he was our brother and we accepted him. He was the middle one, third oldest, about a hundred years older than me. When he went bad, nobody really noticed, as he was always a little dark. It started small, a little too harsh here, a little less patient there..."

She paused and I took her hand, squeezing the fingers, trying to offer my support. She took a breath.

"Anyway, he didn't want to share power anymore. And he destroyed centuries of work when he made his move. It was only through sheer dumb luck that he didn't kill at least a couple of us when he went bad. When he couldn't get to us, he went after our families, trying to draw us out. Kron didn't get to hers in time, a few died. Nobody really close, thankfully, but it still cut her deeply.

"We lost a lot of good people putting him down, friends and associates, whole alliances were torn to pieces. Nash wasn't a particularly smart man, or even a great Battle Mage, but he planned carefully and he exploited our weaknesses. The mess made was immense. We still haven't fully recovered."

"Oh," I said lamely, after an awkward silence, "No wonder she's wary of me."

"That's not the only reason," she said, sighing, "You... you're potentially far more dangerous than Nash ever was."

I turned and gave her a raised eyebrow. She smiled back.

"I'm serious. You make alliances and friends where you shouldn't. Bloody hell, Cassandra kills Shadowborn with only the teeniest provocation, and now she's your Warden. Tethys... well even I have to acknowledge that she adores you, and the way those Pixies drape themselves on you is only just this side of disturbing. Let's not even touch the other creatures that live in your garden or the princesses. But the big problem is that you're also *clever*, and that's more frightening than anything else."

"I'd never hurt anybody who wasn't trying to hurt me, I swear."

"I know that, Matty, but even I went into this relationship expecting the worst of you. It took me a while to get over that. It's going to take Kron a while too."

I nodded.

"How about the others?" I asked.

"Palmyra thinks you're great and Killian thinks you're a future partner in hilarious crime. They aren't the problem. Their bodyguards are something else, though, the Sisters of the Skull in particular. They lost nine-tenths of their ranks to Nash; they *really* don't like Shadowborn."

"Sisters of the Skull?" I asked with a snort, "Oh, Demise and the leather girls."

"They are a dramatic lot, aren't they?"

"Nearly took my bloody head off," I muttered.

She smiled, "Just give Kron time. She'll come around."

I chuckled.

"What?" she asked.

"Give her *Time*," I pointed out.

"I see why people keep beating on you," she said, planting a small peck on my cheek.

"Um, Miss Hopkins?" there were suddenly faces at the door, "Can we come in now? We didn't mean to disturb... you two."

Ho boy, I sent to her as her face went bright red, *how much do you think they saw?*

Shut up and go do something useful!

You're still holding my hand.

Sorry, she said, letting me go. I stood and helped her up.

Thanks for fixing me up, Jen.

Sorry I needed to, Matty. See you in class later.

I nodded and headed out to some giggles.

Rats, can't imagine that's going to end well. I mean, I know she's my sister, for me a peck on the cheek is just a peck on the cheek. But the rest of the student body don't know that. To them, she's a teacher and I'm a student. That could be... problematic.

CHAPTER 9

When lunch came around, Bill, Cathy and I had a double Physics class under our belts and I was looking forward to the two free periods we had that afternoon.

Bill and Cathy were waiting for me at our usual table, looking suspiciously amused...

I sat down with my plate of stew and yawned before shovelling it down at an indecent pace. Magical healing taxed my physical reserves something vicious and my stomach had been growling like a wolverine for the last two hours.

"You'll never guess what I heard today," Bill said a little too innocently, his eyes darting to Cathy, who was sitting next to me, trying to look nonchalant.

"Do tell," she said, forking up some macaroni and cheese.

"Micky Pratt, in fourth year, was in one of the outer buildings today, and he tells me that he walked in on a student and a teacher," Bill said.

I winced and turned a thirty-megawatt glare on him as his face lost its innocent smile and broke into a full-on evil smirk.

"Yep, full on heavy snogging. And groping. And grunting," he said.

"Really?" Cathy said, her tone so obviously faux-curious, I wanted to laugh (and beat Bill over the head with my tray, but mostly laugh).

"Oh yes, caught in the act, hot and heavy," Bill continued.

"I hate you so much," I said.

"Why, Matty? Whatever do you know about this situation?" Cathy asked brightly, her smile turning just as evil as Bill's.

"How far has this horror spread?" I asked.

"Everywhere," Bill replied, "your rep has shot through the roof, B.T.W.."

I groaned and rubbed my forehead, which was still aching after Kron's intrusion.

"Ah, the pitfalls of having a close secret sister," Bill said, "You didn't really use tongue, did you? They say you used tongue."

"I *really* hate you," I said. Cathy started laughing.

Well... that was awkward. Hopkins remained blissfully unaware of the mess for a while, but after she found out, she could barely look at me, blushing horrifically every time I was in the general vicinity.

Magic Class, which started in week two, was normally a fun time when I got to argue with my sister about all sorts of Magical nonsense. But it was a lot *less* fun when she was too mortified to talk to me and ran out of the building when I tried to see if she was alright. In the end, I had to resort to sitting in the classroom next to hers and connecting Telepathically.

Jen, what's wrong? I sent once she'd let me in.

You know very well. My reputation is in ruins!

Hardly. Nobody who knows you thinks you acted inappropriately, I replied.

Tell that to Kenilworth! He threatened an investigation. I almost cursed the little weasel!

Would it help if we went public? You can tell them I'm your brother, it's okay, I sent, slightly worried about that outcome, but not wanting her to be in a bad way because of me.

You forget, Matty, that we don't actually share any DNA. Just saying you're my brother doesn't make it so. We've only known each other a year; you are technically in my care, and while we're family outside these grounds, in here, I'm your teacher and what I did was inappropriate. It's even against the rules for blood-related teachers and students.

Alright, that I can understand, I just don't know why you've gone to such lengths to avoid me. We missed debate night. I love debate night.

I love it too, Matty, but I've been showing favouritism, and I shouldn't. I'm not just your teacher, I'm everyone else's too.

But don't you think that acting out of the norm makes you look more guilty, not less?

Don't try to confuse me with your well-though-through logic, I'm trying to spiral, here! she sent back.

Look, whatever else you are to me, you're also the best teacher I ever had. You taught me things about Magic I'd never even considered before. You made me think about things that really needed thinking about. A lot of how I choose to use my Magic is down to you and the example you set me. Don't let the mispercep-tions of idiots colour that, I replied.

She gave the equivalent of a mental sigh.

Fine, no need to be such a girl about it.

I smiled.

See you tomorrow. Try not to act inappropriately before then, I'll get jealous.

I will throttle you in your sleep, Graves, see how funny you are then!

Okay, that was one problem solved. But the problem of Storm was just starting to develop. He became something of a wreck as the days went on. He flinched at the sight of me, but that didn't stop him muttering behind my back, stirring up trouble.

And he wasn't the only one starting to mutter.

He'd taken up with Charlie Oxley, once my nemesis, and now a school outcast after being overly aggressive with a friend of mine. I didn't think anyone had even bothered to speak a kind word to him in over six months.

Serves him right, the little bugger.

The only problem was that now he had a knowledgeable ally in Storm, and people were starting to listen to what the Mage had to say.

Bill was also acting a little out of character, disappearing at odd times. He'd stopped going to the school shop for his morning sherbet and his afternoon ice lolly. I didn't pry, he'd talk when he was ready, but that didn't stop me worrying for him.

Even with whatever was bothering him, Bill was still keeping an ear to the ground on Stone for me through his web of gossip. Essentially, people were starting to whisper that having a Telepath wondering amongst them may not be the best thing in the world. It started with just Stone and Oxley muttering at meals, but then that mostly empty table started attracting more diners and then more still.

And then they stopped eating when I was around altogether, which was more concerning, not less. Bill managed to find out that this new 'club' (or whatever it was) had more than three dozen members by the end of the second week and they *really* didn't like me. They weren't giving the other Mages any trouble, thank goodness.

They *were* doing a pretty fair job of causing me problems, though...

"Thanks, Matty, I'll pay you back when I can," Bill said as I handed over a twenty.

"No rush," I said. Bill and I leant each other cash from time to time. He had been borrowing quite the chunk this last week, though.

We were sitting in the Big Square with Cathy. It was the third week of term and starting to warm up nicely. The leaves of the Old Oak and the grass under us were vibrant green, the breeze smelled of roses and fresh turned earth; we were happily chatting about absolutely nothing.

"Mister Graves?" Mister Kenilworth said, he had a pair of people with him, both tall and professional-looking, with short-cut hair and wearing neatly pressed suits.

"Yes, Sir?" I said, standing up.

"These gentlemen are with Stonebridge Police's Magical Liaison program. They'd like a word with you."

"Regarding?" I asked, thoroughly confused.

Law enforcement and Magicians were a complicated mix. Generally speaking, most of the work was done by the regular police, these very people, in fact; regular men and women with Spelleater amulets and other equipment, trained to deal with Magicians. They even had a few Adepts and Acolytes on staff.

If there was a problem they couldn't solve, they called in the S.C.A., which was staffed by actual Magicians, including Battle Mages, who were *not* to be messed with.

If *they* couldn't deal with the problem, then the Conclave sent in a Hunter Team, who were *very* dangerous. I'd dealt with them before; they cast attack spells first and... that's it. If you sent a Hunter Team, you weren't expecting a prisoner.

"There have been some troubling accusations made by a member of the student body. He says that you've been using Telepathy on your fellow students," Kenilworth said.

"Can he prove it?" I asked levelly.

I'd actually been doing that for years, for both fun and necessity, but nobody would ever be able to track it back to me... well, except maybe Kron, and she wouldn't tell on me.

"That's what these gentlemen are for," Kenilworth said, "D.C. Beck and D.S. Pike."

They both carried active Spelleaters.

"So you called the police on the word of another student without even talking to me first?" I asked. That was annoying, I'd always thought that Kenilworth was a good sort, a little weak and easily influenced, but essentially solid when it mattered.

"Well, if you're using Telepathy, then you might... that is to say..." he mumbled.

Beck was the taller of the two, broader at the shoulder

than his partner, with dark green, squinting eyes that never left me, he stepped forward, "We'll be asking you some questions, Mister Graves, and are you two," he consulted a pad, "William Hedrin and Catherine Campbell?"

"Yes," my friends answered.

"We'd like you to come with us and answer some questions, too."

"What for?" I asked, stepping in front of them, alarm bells ringing in my head.

"We'll be checking them for Telepathic influence."

"Not without their permission, you won't," I said.

"Which we don't give, just F.Y.I.," Cathy said.

"Miss, until we can be sure otherwise, we must assume that you are under a compulsion, so we must insist," he said, stepping forward.

"Do you intend to force my friends to go with you, then?" I asked, politely, but I felt Bill and Cathy tense, they knew my 'angry' voice, and what that generally meant for local property values.

This was getting out of control quickly, and was quite complicated besides. These men may well be legitimate officers, just doing their jobs as they saw them, even if they were acting on the word of an embittered sociopath. I needed to calm things down.

"They're both over eighteen," Pike said, his eyes narrowing as his hand migrated to the collapsible baton at his belt, "We can if we have to. Do we have to?"

"Yes," I said, "and you'll have to go through me to do it, best of luck."

So much for calming things down. It's not my fault, I'm protective.

I crossed my arms and stood my ground, already preparing the whopping amounts of energy it would take to break through two Spelleaters at such close range. I'd foolishly let them get too close.

"Mister Graves! These are police officers!" Kenilworth

squeaked.

"Who are acting like the Gestapo," I countered, "They have no evidence of a crime, no victim, no warrants. Do you have a warrant for any of this?"

"No," Pike said, now snarling, "But in the case of potential Telepathic abuse, we have the right to investigate."

"First you must have probable cause. Have you questioned the complainant? Have you checked his story? Examined his mental landscape?"

Neither of them were Mages, so that was unlikely.

"That's a police matter, Graves," Pike said, "and this conversation is over."

"That's a no," I replied, "Cathy, go get Hopkins please."

She would know what to do to fix this.

"Mister Graves, Miss Hopkins doesn't run this school!" Kenilworth wailed.

"No. If she did then these storm troopers wouldn't have gotten in the gates," I replied (perhaps a little unfairly).

"Hey, Miss, you come back here!" Beck said, stepping towards her.

"Touch her and the hand that does it comes off," I rasped, now getting really angry.

Beck stepped back at the tone of my voice.

"Enough of this crap. Beck, get the girl, Mister Graves, you are under arrest," Pike said, stepping towards me.

I called Will and yanked Pike's Spelleater off his neck in a shower of steel links before simply picking him up and tossing him at Beck, who'd started moving after Cathy. The Policemen went down in a pile of thrashing limbs and I yanked the other Spelleater away before tossing a pair of Sleep-Hexes that knocked them both out cold.

Three seconds from start to finish. I was getting better.

"Mister Graves!" Kenilworth said, "You assaulted two police offi-"

"Oh, shut up," I said sadly, hexing him too.

Bill looked on in shock as our headmaster fell to the

ground.

"Damn, Matty, this isn't good!" he said as I dragged the three bodies out of sight with my Will and threw an Illusion around them while we waited.

"True," I said, "but I've rather had my fill of heavy-handed authority figures lately."

Which was true enough; my experiences with Gardenia's police had likely informed what I'd just done, which was... regrettable, but better safe than sorry.

It wasn't long before Hopkins popped through a portal and came striding towards me. I felt her cast Mage Sight as she approached. She quickly saw through my Illusion to the three snoozing people inside.

"Oh, what did you do this time?" she asked.

I told her. She wasn't happy.

"I'm going to kill that kid," she whispered menacingly when I was done.

"What do I do about the police?" I asked.

"You're a pretty good Telepath, fix them," she suggested.

"Just like that?" I asked. "I would have thought that you'd object to that sort of thing."

"Matty, you have to do what you have to do. You're an Archon, trust your judgement."

I sighed, looking over at the heap. It had been my first inclination. Sort of an ironic solution to the problem, bearing in mind the very reason they were at Windward. I shrugged and headed over to them while Hopkins spoke to Bill.

Altering memory was a tricky and delicate business if you didn't want to create insanity, such as what had happened to Clayton. I slid gently into Pike's mind and started working. The best way to go about it was to build your fake memory on the framework of a real one, rather than shoving in something brand new. My way was more time consuming and focus-intensive, but was far more difficult to detect if done correctly.

I cast a delicate spell on the memory of our meeting, making the engram pliable and then I whispered into his mind:

I lead the way towards the kid. He's sitting under the tree with his friends. He looks harmless, but I'm taking no chances.

The memory shifted slightly as it adjusted to my words, which I was speaking as his own inner voice into the pliable architecture of the memory.

I ask him to stand and am about to take his friends to the station, but at the last second, I decide that it isn't necessary, and I am worried about my lack of warrant. So I question the kid carefully, forgetting to note things down in my book, like a fool.

I projected the kinds of questions he should have asked and my answers, instilling a sense of satisfaction and trust. By the end, he'd remember over an hour of conversation and be under the firm impression that I was completely harmless.

By the time I'm done, I'm convinced that he's innocent, and that the tipster has wasted police time. I decide that it's time to leave.

I stood him up and left him asleep while I put that same story into the memories of Kenilworth and Beck from their points of view, standing them up next to Pike when I was done with the alterations. I made sure that they were standing as they had been in the fake memories. I hid Hopkins, Cathy and Bill behind an Illusion of my friends sitting next to the tree (Cathy had come back while I was working). With a final effort, I reversed the Sleep Hexes, and the trio awoke.

"Sorry, spaced out there for a second," Pike said with an ingratiating smile, which I returned, "Well, thanks for your time, Mister Graves."

He offered his hand, which I shook.

"Sorry for wasting your time," he said sheepishly.

"No problem, Officer, you're just doing your job," I replied, "I'm just sorry I couldn't be more helpful."

He smiled and so did Beck before waving briefly at the Bill and Cathy Illusions, who waved back. Mister Kenilworth heaved out a sigh of relief as they left before following them.

"Tee hee!" I said happily as they vanished into the admin building and I dropped my Illusions.

I have to say, ethical considerations aside, I do love a successful manipulation. It makes me tingle in my evil little mind.

"So, before I set that 'better example' for you, you were kind of a little bastard, weren't you?" Hopkins asked with a proud smile on her face.

"Oh yes," I said with an evil grin, "Comeuppance was something of a specialty of mine."

"I have to say, that was some truly beautiful work, elegant. Just how much of your Uncle Thatcher's mind is in its original condition after all the practice you must have used him for?"

"Oh, most of... some of it," I said vaguely, turning away.

I heard on the grapevine that Storm was taken in for questioning the next day, which warmed my heart no end. I hoped they gave the little bastard a cavity search. Life started to calm down a little after that. And there were no more visits from the police, even if Storm's stink-eye had quadrupled in intensity after he'd returned from his probing.

Cathy and I spent as much time together as we could, but even we had to admit that this was an important term and started working harder for our upcoming A-Levels. We'd both applied to the same Universities, by design. Stonebridge was at the top of both our lists.

We were just getting settled into our weekend at the end of that third week. We were out under the Old Oak again, Cathy in my arms, her head on my chest under my chin. I was as happy as I could imagine being, and all that took was her.

There was a theatrical sigh from the other side of the tree that I ignored before the familiar voice accompanied it.

"Really, Beloved, I know you're fond of the concubine, but must you do that where I can see you?" Evelina said.

"Oh bollocks," Cathy said, sitting up so she could glare at the Sidhe as she came around the trunk in her interestingly (short) tailored Windward uniform... with Gwendolyn in tow.

Cathy looked to the blonde Sidhe, who was smiling sweetly, her eyes locked on me in what was a very intense way.

"Who's your friend?" Cathy asked Evelina.

"Princess Gwendolyn," Evelina said with a smile more at home on a shark looking at a minnow.

Gwendolyn looked at Cathy and extended her hand, "Hello," she said, coming closer. Cathy took the hand and they shook.

"Hello, Mathew," Gwendolyn said, moving towards me.

"Hi," I said, snapping out of my brain-shutdown and standing up to greet the princesses, "What brings you two by?"

Apart from ruining what was shaping up to be a carnally interesting evening...

"Our mothers hammered out an agreement at last, and if you and your... little friend are willing, I'd like to resume our talks," Evelina said.

Gwendolyn coughed pointedly.

"Oh, and she'll be coming too, I suppose," Evelina added with a dismissive wave.

"I like your outfit," Gwendolyn said to Cathy while Evelina was talking to me, "it's nicer than hers, I don't like that cut."

"Thank you," Cathy said with a blush, "I think yours is pretty, too."

She was wearing a white and yellow sun dress with flowers in her hair. It was rather lovely.

"Thank you," Gwendolyn said with a dazzling smile, "It's my favourite."

"Oh, good grief," Evelina sighed, rubbing her eyes, "damned Seelie, can't keep their minds on the job. Show them something shiny and off they go."

"Sorry, Evelina," Gwendolyn said, winking at Cathy.

"Anyway," Evelina continued, "our mothers have agreed, in principle, to you being a consort to both of us, with precise terms and living arrangements to be determined at a later date."

"Say what now?" I asked.

"Oh, can I tell your mother the happy news?" Cathy said impishly, earning her a glare.

"This isn't what any of us had in mind," Gwendolyn said, "and we're all willing to be patient with you, just know that we'll wait as long as it takes."

"Look, that's very flattering," I said, "but I have always been firmly of the opinion that love is one of those things that isn't shared. You can be in love with one person. That's it. And for me, also her, incidentally."

I gestured at Cathy, who waved.

"And that's what we are," Evelina said, smiling at me, "in love with one person."

Cathy sniggered.

"You are not helping," I said.

"Not trying to," Cathy replied, quick as a flash.

"Nobody's pressuring you, Mathew, just let us come by and see you from time to time? Now that we've met you, it really is painful to be parted from you for so long," Gwendolyn said in a voice that broke my heart.

"Of course you can see him," Cathy said, sticking her two penneth worth in and getting me deeper into the pit.

I nodded along, trying not to scream. This was *not* acceptable...

"Thank you," Gwendolyn said, smiling again.

Oh, don't thank me, thank the girlfriend who's apparently trying to drive my blood pressure through the roof...

"Good," Evelina said, with another of those shark-smiles.

"Well, I'll leave you three to it," Cathy said, smiling again.

What?! I sent to her mind, making her jump, *Why?!*

Because it takes time to put on a corset, and the blonde is so adorable, I'd feel like I was kicking a puppy if I didn't throw her a bone.

What's this about a corset? I asked.

Don't take too long coming to my room to find out.

She kissed my cheek and walked away leaving me with the Fairies.

"I like her," Gwendolyn said.

"She's name three on my revenge list," Evelina said with a pout.

"Oh, must you always be so crotchety?" Gwendolyn said.

"Yes," Evelina replied.

Gwendolyn rolled her eyes and looked at me, holding out her hand, which I took automatically, like an idiot. Evelina stepped to my side and linked her arm through mine. I felt comfortable, safe. That was a seductive damn feeling, I've got to say.

"So," I said, walling that feeling away behind some mental defences, "I know quite a bit about you, Evi, why don't you tell me about yourself, Gwendolyn?"

She smiled, "Well, I have eight sisters and three brothers, I'm the youngest. My sister Loni is the heir, like Evelina. My best friend is my dragon, Lenia. She's got turquoise scales and eats fish..."

And so on. It turns out that she was the family's best Magician, other than her mother. She loved flowers, trees and swimming. She talked about her homeland, which sounded as close to beautifully idyllic as anything I'd ever heard of. Evelina's home was beautiful in its own way, but the way a Bengal Tiger was beautiful, which is to say, untamed and lethal.

We'd sat down some time during this, Evelina playing with the fingers on one hand while Gwendolyn held the other.

Gwendolyn talked about her servants, one of whom had been her nanny, whom she loved so much that she'd persuaded her mother to make her Gwendolyn's companion. She told me about her siblings, their quirks, likes and dislikes, about her eldest brother who had pitched a fit at the idea that a human was to be his little sister's consort.

She spoke softly and emotionally, always smiling, her touch tender. It distracted me from Evelina's stroking and sniffing on my other side.

"Easy, you," I said as her nose got to my neck.

"Why?" she replied, "Am I making you nervous?"

"You tried to kidnap me once. You'll always make me nervous."

"I'd never do that, Mathew," Gwendolyn said, echoing Evelina's sentiment from back at the conference, and earning her a glare from the Unseelie. Gwendolyn smiled, a trace of mischief there.

"Well, I think that's enough for one day," Evelina said.

"Aww," Gwendolyn said, squeezing my hand.

"I have a tutorial in half an hour and you know the rules, we're both here or neither of us is," she said.

"Okay," Gwendolyn replied as I helped her up.

The Seelie pecked me on the cheek before blushing, "See you next time, Mathew," she said.

Not to be outdone, Evelina placed a much wetter kiss far closer to my lips, licking the cheek a little before pulling back.

"See you soon, Beloved," she said.

"Bye," I managed, blushing from those kisses. They vanished.

I stood there like a half-wit for a few long moments before I took a deep breath and went to find Cathy.

Bloody hell, I just didn't need that sort of additional complication in my life...

CHAPTER 10

And speaking of complications in my life...

My mobile rang at one o'clock in the morning the following Wednesday.

"Hello?" I said groggily.

"My lord? Vivian Price. There's been a development."

"What sort of development?" I asked, suddenly very awake.

"I found the factory."

"I can be with you in about..." I gave it some thought, taking into account inevitable detours, "...an hour, call it, maybe sooner."

"Aren't you in Stonebridge?"

"Magician," I explained simply.

"Ah, of course," she replied, a hint of amusement in her tone, "My place. See you in an hour."

She hung up and I dressed in my hoody and trousers. On a whim, I picked up the staff I'd taken from Des when he went insane the second time (or was it the third time? Hard to keep track of my brother's loose screws). It was useful thing, it weaved a dispel into whatever attack I channelled through it, which might make all the difference in a punch-up.

I picked up my phone to call Cassandra, but decided against it, she'd yell. I pulled my satchel around my shoulder and opened a Gate.

And I found that I wasn't alone on the other side.

It wasn't the Leviathan, the presences were smaller, and there were a *lot* of them. There had to be a couple of dozen, at least.

"Hello?" I said into the darkness.

Greetings. Friendship to the One. Joy of meeting.

Elementals, and very friendly ones. The way they communicated was quite refreshing, no obfuscation, nothing but pure emotion and intent.

"Nice to meet you," I said as the little Shadows flitted around me, some touching, most just observing. They, like all Elementals, were usually quite harmless, unless you *really* annoyed them; then you'd better watch out. Shadow Elementals, in particular, could be especially dangerous as they could come from any dark patch and do you a mischief you wouldn't soon forget.

Loyalty to the One. Protect the One. The ideas and emotions became more complex, seemingly projected by the whole as a collective, rather than any single Elemental. *The One calls and we come.*

I connected to the Shadows, *Gratitude, Joy, Pleasure, Honour,* I sent back. There was a happy tremor, and the little Elementals flitted away, except for a few which hovered around at the edge of my perceptions.

That was... a wonderful thing. Shadow Elementals were the most passive of them all. They never got involved with the Newtonian World. I wondered what the Leviathan had told them to change that.

Well, that was an issue for later, back to my journey. This time, I decided to try something a bit different, flying high into the Shadow Realm's 'sky' before jumping in relatively short thirty or forty mile hops, rather than trying to get all the way there in one go. This allowed me to keep track of where I was and where I was going.

I found myself over the channel in short order, which looked beautiful in the Shadow Realm, a whole sea of rolling, transparent fog, with the Isle of Wight's Shade ahead of me. I smiled. Ten minutes was all it took to get that far. I was over Gomorrah in another ten, and I opened a Gate on top of one of the taller skyscrapers, so I could check Google maps. Another three miles to the South-East.

Back in for a brief jump and I was floating high above the Red Carpet's spot in the Realm. Now that I could see it, jumping into it was nothing. I could hear the usual sounds through the mists as I drew myself towards the front door and opened another Gate in a darkened patch next to Bianca's desk. I stepped out and she squealed in surprise, which forced me to apologise profusely before she could call in someone to shoot me.

"Please don't do that, Sir!" she said after she'd stopped squeaking, "Things are quite tense enough around here!"

"Really sorry," I said sheepishly, blushing and feeling guilty.

"Oh, don't worry about it," she said, calming down, "I know you did us a good turn a few weeks back, you've earned a dramatic entrance or two."

I smiled and she led me through the place to the alternate office I'd visited the last time. The receptionist was there at the same desk that had been in front of the other one. Bianca smiled at me and retreated; Francois announced me.

Price was dressed in a sensible suit and stood as I entered, smiling as she looked me over.

"That's more what I had in mind," she said, "much more 'modern magician'."

"The staff's a rental," I said with a grin, she chuckled, waving me to the same chair I'd occupied before.

"I've found their lab, in a church, after not a small amount of work, I might add," she said, pulling out a city map and pointing out the particular building, I marked it in my phone's map.

"Thank you," I said, "I'll go have a look-see."

"Miss Vivian, do you think he'd prefer the red or the bla-oh! Hi, Mathew," said a cheery voice from behind me.

"Hi Crystal," I said turning to see the vampire in what couldn't really be described as underwear, there simply wasn't enough of it.

152

I looked away immediately, turning red.

"Aw, he's blushing again," Crystal said, bending over to plant a little kiss on my cheek, "That's so sweet!"

Without any further preamble, she sat all that perfect *everything* in my lap and wrapped her arms around my neck.

"Crystal, don't torture the First Shadow, you know he's attached," Price said with a wicked smile on her face.

"But he's so comfy," she replied, brushing my cheek with her nose, "and it's not like he's objecting."

"That's because he doesn't have the necessary social skills," I replied, really not knowing what to do, I was too flummoxed and Crystal was too endearing to just toss off my lap.

"I like your staff," she whispered in my ear, "Can I play with it?"

Oh for heaven's sake...

"Now, just keep it clean, would you?" I asked (begged, really).

"But I like it dirty," she replied instantly.

Well, I walked right into that one, I'll admit. Price looked on the verge of hysterics.

"I'm sorry to tell you, but the same accident that did this to my eyes also broke my man bits, nothing works down there, sorry," I said.

It was the first lie I could think of, don't look at me like that.

"Oh," she said, hugging me tighter, "I'm sorry."

"Not at all, you weren't to know," I said as she hopped up and moved over to the seat next to me.

Price's eyes narrowed as she looked at me. She didn't buy it for a second.

"Anything I should know?" I asked, trying to move the conversation along.

"A few things, Crystal will fill you in on the way," Price said.

"My method of travel isn't really passenger friendly," I replied, not wanting a bystander if I was going to be knocking a building down (which I was quite looking forward to, hadn't done that before, well, not on purpose, anyway).

"That's why we have a car," Crystal said, having darted to my side while I wasn't looking. She fastened her lips and teeth to my ear while emitting what had to have been the dirtiest sound I'd heard in my entire life, during which her left hand pinched some things she had no right or cause to be pinching.

I jumped, but there was no concealing the... physical reaction she'd stimulated.

"Mm, knew you were lying," she whispered, "You'll pay for that."

"Crystal, down," Price said, "You're his guide for this evening. Keep it civil."

Crystal sighed while I broke out into a sweat and started thinking about number sequences.

"Oh, please Miss Vivian, I only want to be his friend," Crystal said with a pout.

That blend of cute and sinful was just doing nothing good for my circulatory system.

"Isn't the sun about to rise, or something?" I asked, a little desperately.

"Not for a while, you and Crystal can spend all the time you'll need," Price said unhelpfully.

I rubbed my aching eyes, "Before my head just pops clear off, can we please head to the church?"

"Oh, so polite," Crystal said, "but I'll need a firmer hand in the future, Mathew."

"And that's all I can handle this far from dinner and breakfast," I said, standing up.

"Give me five minutes, I'm a little under-dressed," Crystal said, bouncing away.

Price smiled, "She really likes you," she said once the younger vampire was out of earshot.

"She's a nice girl. A little more forward than I'm used to, mind."

Price smiled, "You'd be amazed how far treating a girl

with respect goes with someone in Crystal's profession. We don't meet a great many gentlemen around here."

"Oh," I replied, not really knowing how to reply, "I'm sorry to hear that."

She shrugged, "Pigs are easier to part from their money, anyway. And one feels less guilty about fleecing them."

She had a point, I know that was one of the pillars Tethys built her businesses on, though she didn't take it to the Red Carpet's extreme (I hoped, I hadn't asked).

"Okay, I'm ready!" Crystal said, coming up behind me. She was wearing motorcycle leathers and high-heeled boots, all in black, tight and very well fitted.

"How can you run in those?" I asked.

"Vampire. We're graceful," she said, twisting the boots slightly so I could get a good view.

"Don't those things snap?"

"Steel reinforcement," she said, "You don't know much about shoes do you?"

"Y-chromosome. If it fits and isn't pink that's all I need in a shoe."

Crystal sniggered, it was an adorable sound.

"Come on," she said, taking my hand, "I'll show you the way."

"Be back by four!" Price said.

"Yes, Mummy," Crystal said ironically, dragging me along before I could say goodbye.

Nothing I could do about it, she could pick me up and carry me if she wanted to.

She set a pretty fast pace, and I had to ask her to slow down after I'd nearly tripped over the staff for the umpteenth time.

"Don't handle the staff very often?" she asked coquettishly, I replied with a look that made her smile as we exited the house. There was a BMW waiting for us with a burly driver, and heavily armed guards everywhere, it was almost like an armed camp, I assumed in response to the recent attack.

We hopped in and I wedged the staff in somehow. Crystal slid over so she was sitting hard up against me. The driver started the car and pulled away from the house.

"So, this girlfriend of yours... serious?" she asked.

"Very."

"First love?" she asked, holding my hand.

"First one that matters."

"That sounds like a story."

"Oh, not really. First girlfriend cheated on me with my brother because my sister told her to in an attempt to distract me from casting a Black Magic spell that would have turned me into a monster. You know, that old chestnut."

She laughed, stroking my fingers in a very distracting way.

"You ever cheat on someone?"

"No," I said, frowning.

"Would you like to?"

I snorted.

"Faithful type, huh?" she asked.

"I try to be," I said, "What about you? You have somebody?"

"My line of work isn't conducive to a healthy relationship. I have friends, work friends, mostly. Miss Vivian's people are like a family, we support each other."

"That's good. Everyone should have someone to turn to."

"Even us monsters?" she asked; this smile a little sad.

"I've met a great many things far more deserving of that descriptor than you. Monstrosity is a matter of the soul, not biology."

"You've got some strange ideas for a Magician," she said, rubbing her cheek on my hand.

I shrugged.

"What can you tell me about the church?" I asked.

"Catacombs, lots of same," she said, "Our people tracked more than a dozen men and women coming and going. Don't know who they were or what they were doing, but one of the suppliers gave up the location to our Mimi while in the throes of ecstasy."

"Alright," I said, "Any maps of the catacombs?"

"The plans were mysteriously absent from the county offices, which should be a clue all on its own, and nobody was going to risk trying to go in there with a notepad and a compass."

"Fair enough. That's a solvable problem," I said as I thought it through.

We arrived a few minutes later and I stepped out of the car, which the man then parked discreetly in an alley, drawing a gun.

"Which way?" I asked.

"This way, I'll show you," she said.

"I'd prefer it if you stayed here."

"Why?" she asked, crossing her arms, "I can take care of myself!"

"I know that, but there may be Magicians, and I don't want you getting caught in the crossfire."

"I'll be fine," she said stubbornly, "Miss Vivian told me not to let you out of my sight."

"Look, if you come with me, I'll worry. If I worry, I'll be distracted, and that might get me killed," I explained.

"You worry about me?" she asked with a smile.

"Don't change the subject."

"We can discuss it on the way," she said, gesturing for me to follow.

"But..." I said, but she was already striding ahead.

Seriously, did nobody feel it would be a good idea to do what the First Shadow said?

I muttered and followed after her.

She paused at an intersection and held up a hand. I stopped.

"It's around there," she said, "There are six guards, rotating shifts around the building, irregular patrols."

I cast Mage Sight and took a peek.

And yikes, there were a lot more than six people in that building. Closer to sixty, most of them below ground. Most of them were... different. I didn't know what the hell I was looking at, really, but the Auras were warped by something. And there were at least seven Mages, nothing more powerful than a mid-level Wizard, thankfully.

"Ho boy," I said, laying out what I saw.

"We can't deal with that!" she said.

"Very true," I said, patting her shoulder, "You go get help."

I stood and cast a set of shields, wrapping myself up in Shadows as I approached the Church. It was wide and crumbling, missing most of its roof and half of its East wall.

"Psst! Mathew, come back here!"

"Just a sec," I whispered back, expanding the cloud of Shadow to envelope the street.

The first guard saw the darkness coming, but I dropped him with a sleep spell. There were five more, and I made my way around the perimeter after each. Most were in teams of two, but it was simplicity itself to drop them with wider Sleep-Hexes and then solidify the enchantment. The final one fell into a heap and I dropped my Shadows, using tendrils to drag them into a covered vestibule with a heavy door in front of it.

"Wow," Crystal said, startling me, "That's cool."

I chuckled, searching them and finding little of value. I used Shadows to tie them up and to each other before using a solidifying spell to make the bonds permanent. I smashed their weapons and their electronics before shutting the door using a reversed lock-pick spell to lock it.

I went to the middle of the church and started to concentrate.

"What're you doing?" Crystal asked, looking around for more enemies.

"Mapping spell," I said, pulling my phone out, and handing it to her, "Take pictures when it's done?"

"Sure," she said taking the phone while I worked.

It took about fifteen minutes to cast the spell. Subsonic waves darted out and down before bouncing back to the receiving enchantment in my hand, forming a map of everything below us, every room, passage, person, door and bit of stone.

"That is so amazing!" Crystal gushed, snapping pictures from every angle with the camera.

"It's annoyingly complicated," I replied, "but it does the job."

There were about a dozen levels of catacombs beneath us, with a massive chamber in the bottom three floors. The entrance was through the nave ahead of us, a hatch in the floor.

"You really ought to stay here," I said.

"No, I worry, too, you know," she said, "besides, you need me."

I disagreed with that, but wasn't going to argue with her.

"Fine, but we're doing this stealthy, and nobody dies, alright?"

"What?"

"I don't kill people. It's a whole thing for me. And nobody else dies on my watch, either, understand?"

"Oh, alright," she said theatrically, "There's no need to be quite so restrictive."

I glared.

"Fine, fine," she said, following me. I went over to the hatch and opened it slowly, there wasn't anyone close, but I didn't want the sound to carry.

"Do you have a mask?" I asked, "I don't want cameras to see your face."

"No, no mask," she said, "besides, you're not wearing one."

"I don't live in this city," I said, shrugging off my hoodie and pulling a set of sunglasses out of my bag, "put these on."

"Is this cotton?" she said with a grimace.

"Either put them on, or you wait out here."

She rolled her eyes and made a disgusted sound, but she took them from me.

"Ooh, smells nice in here," she said as she pulled the hood over her head and put the sunglasses on.

"It smells like my most recent terror-sweat, if anything."

"That's what I meant," she whispered back.

I rolled my eyes and led the way down. I kept my Shadow Magic to a minimum so as not to alert the Magicians that we were coming, but I could still see just fine, and so could she, as we descended into the earth.

"Oh, if I say 'Exit', you need to get to me fast and close your eyes. We won't be leaving in a sanity-friendly way. Don't open them again until I say so."

"Usually when men ask me to close my eyes and come to them, it's in much more comfortable circumstances," she replied.

I shook my head and pulled my phone, looking at the improvised map for the next stairway. We found it and carried on, down and down (too deep for my claustrophobia's liking).

After about half an hour of careful movement, down stairs and ladders, slinking our way through passages and moving too slowly for my sense of well-being, we came upon the uppermost part of the big chamber, where we dropped to the floor and crawled towards the edge of the upper gallery.

The room was a huge cylinder, maybe a hundred metres across. There were two galleries above the ground floor, both packed with bone-filled alcoves. The room itself was brightly lit, almost painfully so. I looked down into it and nearly ran screaming for the Shadow Realm.

It was full of Demons, which explained those twisted, alien auras I'd seen.

Each was bound to a summoning circle, thank God, but they were very definitely demons. No two looked alike, but about a dozen were humanoid, with red skin and bony protrusions of various length and location. Most had black eyes, some had red, some had tails or wings. The others vaguely resembled animals, some were quadrupeds, some looked like snakes or slugs or masses of spiny tentacles.

A word on Demons. I may not know a great deal, but I had the basics down. There were two kinds of them, very broad categories, really, sentient and bestial, in which there were various grades, based loosely on those for Elementals, lesser, common, greater, arch and titanic.

Everything in that room was a lesser Demon. That's right, every horrific, lethally dangerous thing in that room was the *least* nasty thing that comes from down *there*. Just to compare for you, Gabrielle, being a purebred Succubus, fell under the general heading of 'greater'. If I didn't have Magic, and she'd been summoned instead of assigned, she could kill me with a look, she was *that* powerful. But, even with all that power, she could still be held in a circle like one of these.

Each circle had a device attached to it, silver, spindly and about nine feet tall, almost like a hospital frame used to hold drips and IV bags. Each device was packed with an intricate array of enchantments and spells that was drawing power of some sort from the Demons. As time went by, I saw little chunks of red fall into receptacles on the front of the machines.

I blinked hard as I realised what I was seeing.

Source.

My God. They were making the drug out of Demonic Essence! Were they insane? What the hell would it do to a person over time? Certainly nothing good, that stuff was literally pure, distilled *evil*.

I looked around with Mage Sight. Six technicians, all armed with guns. Four Adepts, Flesh, Air and two Earths. Three Wizards, two Water and a Pryo. I could take them, not even a problem, really. But doing that might bring the whole place down on us.

Do you see that man at the bottom? I sent to Crystal.

EEK! Are you in my head?

Yes, you see the man? White beard, dark jacket? Can you knock him out without alerting anyone? I asked.

Sure.

Okay. The two across from him to the right are Earth Mages. I'm going for them. If you can get your guy, that means that the chances of anything dropping on our heads are greatly reduced, at which point I'll act as a magnet while you start beating people over the head. Stay away from anyone if they are shimmering, it means they have a Shield cast, you won't be able to get through it, alright?

Okay!

I'll go when you knock out your guy.

I disconnected and she was gone, darting silently down the stairs.

This was the great weakness of the Magician. We had human reflexes and (generally) human bodies. Surprise by a more physically imposing enemy was the greatest danger. That's why Archons had Wardens, not to fight our battles, but to see one coming in time to allow us to react. A vampire attacking from surprise was a terrible danger, even to me.

And just like that, the Pyro was down, silently, perfectly, and hidden behind some gear where I only saw him because I was looking. A tiny blur and another man was down, and then another while I was still casting shields and calling my Shadows. I used my Will and destroyed the massive set of lights in the ceiling, plunging the whole place into darkness that my Shadows and Crystal exploited.

There were shouts of panic as my Shadows enclosed me and I directed a bolt of force through my staff at each of the two Earth Mages. The poor buggers were still too shocked by the sudden destruction of the lights to do anything useful and they both went down hard. I got one of the Water Wizards the same way before the last one got his shields up, and so did the last two Adepts.

Crystal switched her aim to the men without magic, and they started dropping like flies as she choked or knocked them out. My staff flared with more force and the last Wizard went down with six broken bones. The Air Mage started casting, screaming for help, obviously panicked and terrified (neither a good state of mind for Magic use, by the way; I knew *that* from painful experience). Crystal darted behind cover as the moving air created static that he hurled at my Shadows in the form of forked lightning. The attack missed the vampire by a hair's breadth.

I had my constructs converge on him, tearing his weak shields to shreds before battering him into the wall, where he slid to the ground, unconscious. Just the Flesh Adept left. His body expanded, his muscles bulging, and he sprinted for the stairs. I aimed Force and missed, blowing up a chunk of wall and creating a cloud of dust. I recharged, aimed and fired again and hit him hard in the shoulder. He smacked off the wall with a scream and I tossed a Sleep-Hex that dropped him, ending the pain of his shattered shoulder.

The demons were roaring or screaming, smacking off their summoning circles as they saw the battle in their midst, and tried to get at their downed tormentors. I lowered myself to their part of the room, checking carefully for any more threats.

"I think we're clear," Crystal said, appearing in front of me.

"Apart from the Demons, you mean?" I asked with a smile.

"Yes, Mathew, apart from the Demons," she said, rolling her eyes.

I used my Shadows to drag all our prisoners into an alcove at the side of the room, where I dropped Coma-Hexes into their heads one by one until they were all sleeping soundly. Crystal watched me all the while, holding my staff while I worked.

"What do we do about them?" she asked when I was done, gesturing at the Demons, who'd all grown quiet, watching us.

Demons weren't my speciality. I knew how to blast them, but I didn't know anything about summoning circles or even what kinds of demon were currently in those ones.

"That is a problem," I said, reclaiming my phone, "Could you go up top and make a call for me?"

"To who?"

It took her about forty minutes to get up top and make the call before bringing Palmyra back down with her, a globe of light above her head.

"Mathew Samuel Graves, what the hell are you doing in Gomorrah?!" she said, her normally friendly voice filled with worry and anger, "And why are you in a room full of bloody Demons?!"

"I can explain most of that," I said as Crystal came back over to stand with me again.

"It had better be good. Do you have any idea what Jen will do when she finds out about this? You think you've heard her yell before, just you bloody wait!"

"What is she, your mother, or something?" Crystal asked while Palmyra came over and glared.

"Sister, actually."

"From the top, leave nothing out or I will silent treatment you into the ground!" Palmyra said.

I cleared my throat and filled her in on my efforts to find out where Source was coming from, leaving out why I'd started. Palmyra likely knew about the whole Liaison thing, but Crystal didn't, and she didn't need to, either.

"And that's when I asked Crystal here to go call you. I'd have done it myself, but I didn't think it was the best idea to leave a few dozen Demons alone."

One of Palmyra's battle-nuns came down the stairs as I was finishing.

"All clear, Milady," she reported, "the guards have secured the area and we're holding."

"Good," Palmyra replied, "Give me a few minutes with my brother, would you?"

"Of course, Ma'am," she said with a bow before retreating.

She waited until the nun was out of earshot before speaking again.

"Oh, Matty, can't you just stay out of trouble for five minutes?" she asked, squeezing my shoulder as she turned. She raised her hand and called Life Magic before releasing a wave that made every sigil flare and then wink out.

Leaving the Demons still in place.

And suddenly free.

CHAPTER 11

"That's not possible!" Palmyra said, barely getting a Will Shield in the way before the first Demon could bite her head off.

"Crystal, get up top and warn her bodyguards!" I shouted, but she was already gone, clever girl.

I started bringing up my own Shields, which snapped into place a second after Palmyra's, just in time to catch a black lion-looking thing. A Shadow darted after it, spearing into its torso before expanding, ripping outwards and leaving it in pieces that turned into black mist and vanished. Palmyra gestured and a trio darting towards her simply immolated, screaming as their flesh turned to ash and their bones crumbled to dust.

I sent my Shadows to our flanks and started attacking, leaving the centre to Palmyra, who was an expert at dealing with those things. I speared finger thin, razor sharp tendrils through skulls and chests, which seemed to be effective enough. I banished two of the smaller quadrupeds before they could leap at us, as well as some sort of snake-frog-deer thing with black scales, yellow eyes and horns that tried to climb the wall and drop on us.

I moved up to stand next to Palmyra, and we fought back to back as the Demons closed on us. Their wordless roars of hunger and fury mixed with screams of pain as we threw them back into the Pit. But for every one we dropped there was another to take its place; every one that died allowed the rest to get closer.

Some of the bigger ones started using their Infernal

version of Magic. I threw a dispel just in time to intercept a spinning ball of crimson fire, which exploded messily, coating several smaller Demons in sticky red flames.

Just as they were getting close enough to attack our shields up close and personal, I felt Palmyra reach out with her mind. There was a flare of power, Magic flowed throughout the room, and white shapes seemed to materialise out of nowhere, pure Life Magic radiating from them.

I couldn't believe my eyes...

Life Elementals!

My God, they were beautiful! Bright and soft, with difficult to define shapes, casting a soothing light over everything, undulating gently, as if they had all the time in the world. Their very presence calmed and invigorated me.

The Elementals' light touched the Demons, and the monsters screamed. It wasn't long before even the big ones were backing away. I redoubled my efforts, gathering Force and Light to sear into their retreating ranks, cleaving off arms and heads. Palmyra pointed a finger and several of her Elementals pooled their power into a beam of golden light that washed over half a dozen Demons.

Two of the humanoid ones and four of the animals fell, screaming, their skin burnt and flaking away to reveal charred muscle and bone. This was the stuff of life itself, pure Creation given form; demons didn't do well when exposed to it. The energy tore the Demons' forms apart and flung what little was left back into the Pit, searing their very essences into practically nothing. One of the monsters spread its wings and darted up and over the light, apparently unhampered by its missing arm (which might be expected, it had seven others). It leapt at Palmyra.

It never even got *close*. In an act so graceful it almost seemed planned, one of the Elementals intercepted the creature far short of her shields, wrapping the Demon up in its form and power. The red-skinned brute vanished in a flare of light, and my sister's protector returned to its slow patrol.

Between the two of us (mostly her), the demons were down to a handful, maybe ten, all being pushed back by her Elementals' Light and my attacks. I kept channelling huge amounts of Force, Light and Fire through my staff, blowing Demons apart with Chaos Bolts and Balls (called Chaos Magic because the combination of different energy types into the same attack spell could be powerful, but also unpredictable).

It was just about done, and then there was a roar from above, and half a dozen women descended on what was left of the creatures like the hammer of God. They wore close fitting armour, their robes discarded. Each piece was enchanted to a spectacular degree, and their power blazed as energies collected in their hands.

They hit like thunderbolts, energy flaring with every strike of fist and foot. One woman bodily charged an ox-like thing four times her size and bore it to the ground where she broke its neck with her bare hands, spinning in time to block an attack on her vambrace and rip off the hand that did it! Another's whole body was wreathed in white fire, and she put her hands through the torso of one of the humanoid ones, coming out again with organs that burned into ash (I nearly threw up after that one, but held it together).

The tallest one wielded a broadsword like it was a toothpick, slicing straight through three demons with a single strike and leaving them in rapidly disintegrating pieces. Two others were surrounded by razors made of air, and simply stepping towards Demons made them come apart.

And then it was over. The last of them fell into dust.

I was breathing hard, half mad with terror over what had happened, barely keeping my dinner down through sheer stubbornness. Palmyra looked over at me, relief in her eyes that it was all over.

"When you tell this story to Jen," I said, "be sure to mention that everything here was perfectly under control- Ow!"

She pulled back the fist that she'd used to hit me and

yanked me into a hug, patting my back.

"Dumb Shadowborn. You know very well that when I tell this story it's all going to be your fault," she said. I sniggered.

"Figures. Story of my life, when something goes wrong, 'blame Mathew, he's probably guilty of something anyway'..."

"Shut up," she said, tweaking my nose.

"Mathew, you take me to the funnest places," Crystal said, coming up behind me and wrapping her arms around my torso.

"This is fun for you?" I asked, "How do you relax? Dental surgery?"

Palmyra laughed and moved towards her people, who had already sheathed their weapons.

"Now that's done, my place or yours?" Crystal asked in a sultry whisper.

"I am going home," I said, "where I intend to sleep until I can forget all about Demons."

"How can someone so young act so old?" Crystal asked, her hands moving gently up and down.

"I'm sorry, but us cowards like to deal with Magical combat with denial, sleeping and eating until we puke the terror out."

"Yes, that sounds healthy," Crystal said, letting me go, "The next time you're in town, come see me. We'll have dinner, on you of course."

Yes, you stand in front of a *Vampire* that says that and see how well *you* deal with it.

She grinned, deliberately showing fang.

"See you, Mathew, don't let it be too long," she said.

She stroked my cheek and walked away, up the stairs and out of sight. I let out a breath and called a Shadow to sit on while Palmyra finished chatting to her people. She came over to me and I called another Shadow for her, which she dropped into.

"Oh, that's surprisingly comfy," she said.

"I know my seats," I replied with a smile.

She snorted, "You were great tonight, Matty, I'm proud of you, little brother."

I flushed a little, it was nice of her to say.

"Needs must and all that," I said, looking away.

"Now that we have a minute, you want to tell me how you got started on this nonsense?" she asked.

"I don't know if I'm allowed to. Would the term 'Liaisons' mean anything to you?"

She went pale, "Oh Matty, already?" she said, squeezing my hand, "They don't... they usually give you a while before they start on this stuff. But say no more about it. We know, but we're not supposed to know. So we pretend we don't."

"Well, hopefully that's done now," I said, leaning back in my chair, yawning widely.

"God I hope so, I don't need this sort of stress."

"Yes, what happened? I'm assuming you intended a different outcome."

"You think?! I cast a simple circle inversion, it was supposed to send them back downstairs, but someone put some sort of enchantment on the bloody things, and the circles vanished instead! I am not happy. What if some idiot had tried it instead of two Archons? It would have been a massacre!"

"Well, with any luck, the prisoners we took can shed some light."

"What prisoners?" she asked, looking around.

"Those pr-" I said looking into the alcove where we'd stacked the lab's workers, "They're gone!"

I darted over and found the whole alcove soaked in blood, claw marks dug deep into the flagstones. There wasn't a scrap of flesh or clothing to be seen.

"You don't think..." I said, swallowing hard, my heart pounding in my chest.

"The demons ate them? No, I'm sure they just... left. Or something," she said, rubbing the back of her neck guiltily.

"I had them under Coma-Hexes," I said, very quietly.

"Oh. Well... it's their own fault. They summoned and tortured Demons; that was never going to end well."

"But... I... I left them defenceless," I whispered, "They died because I put them to sleep."

The guilt was like a knot in my guts, churning and biting, burning into my chest. I wanted to throw up, to scream, to crawl into a hole and just die. Thirteen people... dead because of me. They'd still be alive if I hadn't been there.

"Matty, no!" she said, spinning me around to look at her. I couldn't meet her eyes, "They died because they chose to break the laws of nature. They died because they sacrificed their souls to the pursuit of money. You tried to put a stop to something that would have killed tens of thousands, maybe even more. You did nothing wrong!"

I nodded, not really hearing her, and unable to believe her.

"Could I ask a favour? Could you portal me back to Windward? I'm not sure I'm up to Shadow-Walking just now," I said in a small voice.

"Tell me you're okay, first. Tell me you know you aren't to blame," she said, squeezing my arm.

"Sure," I said, "I'm fine."

I doubted I was convincing, but she opened the portal for me anyway.

"Thank you," I said, "and thanks for coming. I wouldn't have known what to do."

"Any time, Matty, you know that," she said, tears in her eyes.

I gave her a tight smile and walked through the portal into my room. It snapped shut behind me.

It was maybe four in the morning. I was exhausted and miserable. I could see the faces of the people who'd died, like a horrific parade inside my mind.

God, what had I done?

It wasn't the ones who'd died that was *really* tearing

me up, though that was bad enough to leave me gasping for air that wouldn't come; no, it was all the others, the ones who would now have to grieve for those who'd died. Mothers, fathers, siblings, cousins... wives, husbands, children, friends. How many lives had I just ruined? How many of them didn't have the slightest idea what their loved ones were doing for a living and would now find out in the worst possible way?

That was assuming that someone in the Source organisation was keeping records and would inform the families, because goodness knows there weren't any remains to be identified...

I threw up and didn't stop until I was completely empty, at which point I just dropped to the floor, sore and miserable.

Eighteen years, and I'd never even killed a *fly*.

And now thirteen people were just... gone because of a mistake that I'd made.

It wasn't like I was an innocent, or anything, I'd done some pretty terrible things, but I liked to think that what I'd done had always been in proportion, and always to people who'd had it coming. Those people may have been drug-dealing, torturing bastards, but they didn't deserve to be... eaten alive.

The thought brought about more nausea, but there was nothing left to throw up. In the end, I just sat there, knowing that I would have to live with what I'd done, but without the faintest idea how to go about doing that.

I knew that if I said the word, everyone who cared about me would be there like a shot, ready to help and make me feel better, but I couldn't bear the thought of their understanding, if that makes any sense. I knew that not a one of them would blame me; I doubted any of them would shed a tear over a few dead drug-makers, but the thought of being comforted after what I'd done was unbearable.

So I allowed myself one good, long scream into my pillow, after which I showered, dressed, deployed my stiff upperlip, and went off to breakfast, determined not to let anyone know that anything was even remotely wrong (yes, I realise *now* that wasn't the healthiest way to deal with the problem; it's been established that I have issues).

As I might have expected, Cathy immediately noticed that something was off, so I told her what had happened, sugar coating the details only where it would have been distressing for her to know them. She asked me if I was alright about a dozen times before the end of the meal, and I replied in the affirmative every time. My emotionless delivery, constant cold sweat and shaking hands may have been a bit of a giveaway that I wasn't quite in the right frame of mind.

Bill did what all best friends did, ignored the whole thing and offered food, which I accepted, though didn't eat, which was almost certainly another giveaway, but I wasn't really in a state to notice.

I essentially white-knuckled my way through that first day, saying as little as possible and doing my level best not to draw attention or cause anyone distress, which was inherently self-defeating, as the people who knew me could tell that I wasn't myself, but they had the decency to leave me to it.

I didn't have English that day, for which I was grateful, I didn't want to have to face Hopkins. I thought I'd gotten away with it, too... until she came to my room that night. No doubt at least one of my friends had told on me.

"How's it going?" she asked lightly, perching on the edge of my desk, her eyes sliding over the small heaps of screwed up paper that marked the nine attempts I'd made to get my prep done. I'd found that even writing properly was a bit of a chore as my hands still shook from time to time.

"Fine thanks, Jen," I said, my voice as cheerful as I could make it.

She lifted an eyebrow.

"Uh-huh," she said, "Anything you'd like to tell me?"

"I presume that Lucille had a word?"

Hopkins nodded.

"That about covers it."

"Matty..." she said, her voice very soft.

"Please, Jen, not now, okay?" I begged, my voice cracking a little.

She nodded quickly and stood, "You know where I am if you need me, okay?" she said, her tone firm again; she knew what I needed and did me the immense favour of not making me cry in front of her.

"Thank you, Miss Hopkins," I said.

She nodded and left. I went back to work, but my damned shaking made it three times as tricky... and the parade of dead men's faces in front of my mind's eye didn't help either.

When I slept, I found some peace, apart from some half-remembered nightmares, but I awoke back into a world where my mistake still existed, and it came crashing down on me like a wave, dragging me down into an ocean of guilt.

Maybe I was a fool for feeling like that about what had happened, but being responsible for the end of a life... that's not something that should ever be taken lightly or dismissed. A human life is all about potential, the endless possibility of choice, from birth to grave, to chart our own course and affect change in the world around us. My actions had taken all that away from *thirteen* people.

I did know that they were doing bad things; I was smart enough to realise that how their lives had ended was not entirely my doing, but enough of it *was* that it felt like a great anchor around my very soul, crushing the heart of me.

I won't apologise for feeling like that, because the part of me that *let* me feel that way was likely the best bit, and the day that the loss of a human life, because of something I'd done, becomes trivial is the day that the world will be in a very great deal of trouble, because I will truly become the monster everyone is afraid of.

I was like that for two more days, and they weren't very good ones for me, as you might expect. I like to think I put up enough of a front that Cathy and Bill didn't worry so much, but they both kept trying to feed me, so I couldn't have been that successful (those two normally hang onto food like a starving bear holds onto a fresh salmon, and with the same basic ferocity).

It was on the evening of the second day that Hopkins discovered that my Magic had stopped working.

She'd come to host the chess club for the night, and had brushed past me on her way to play a game with Cathy, the only one of us, aside from me, who gave her a consistent challenge. She gasped as we made contact and spun me around to look me in the eye.

"Ow," I protested weakly.

She took my hands, which still shook, then used her fingers to open one eye after another.

"Come with me," she said.

I followed her out of the room, under the gaze of the other members, trying to look nonchalant.

"How long?" she asked once we were out in the corridor.

"How long what?"

"How long have you been blocking your magic?" she asked, eyes narrowed.

"Blocking?" I asked, "I'm not."

"Yes you are; try calling your Shadows."

I did as I was told... and nothing happened.

"What?" I said, "How's that?"

She sighed, "Damn it, Matty."

"What's happened to me?" I asked, a little worried, though a not insignificant part of me felt that I probably deserved it.

She shook her head, "You've tied yourself up so tight in knots that you've closed off the top of your Well. You can't draw Magic from it."

"How do I fix it?"

"You have to release whatever's got you like this."

My hands started shaking again.

"Yes, that's healthy," Hopkins said, gesturing at my

hands.

I stuffed them under my armpits.

"Talk to me, Matty," she said, squeezing my shoulder.

I did what she told me, to make her feel better if nothing else. I told her what had happened and she listened. It didn't bring my powers back and the evening ended with Hopkins looking *very* worried.

The door slammed open late on Saturday. It must have been about half past six, something like that. I was trying to get some work done, and was making progress. I was learning how to ignore how I felt, to concentrate on better things, but it hadn't stopped the shaking, and it hadn't brought my Magic back.

Cassandra barrelled into my room, an angry look on her face.

She took one look at me and winced.

"Sorry," I said. Cassandra was a Life Mage like Palmyra, a little less powerful, but almost as sensitive and not as able to shield against powerful emotions, I could hide nothing from her in my state, as I couldn't really shield.

She shook her head and sat down next to me, looking me over very intently.

"Well, you idiot," she said.

"I'd protest, but..."

"But I'm right, you *are* an idiot."

"There's that," I replied, smiling a little.

"It's not like we didn't warn you about bloody Gardenia!"

"I know."

"And?" she pressed.

"And what?"

"You know what," she said, her eyes narrowing.

"Really?" I whined.

"Really."

I sighed, "And you were right."

"And...?"

"Come on, Cassie..."

"*And*?"

"And I was wrong."

"There, was that so hard?"

"Nobody likes a know-it-all."

"That explains your situation, then," she replied quickly, smiling nastily.

"Walked right into that one, I'll admit," I said.

She nodded, leaning back, "Lady Hopkins said you've walled yourself off like an idiot, care to explain?"

"You say that like I know what the hell I'm doing," I replied.

"Yes, that was assuming a bit much."

"Hey!"

"You got thirteen people eaten by demons, Matty."

I shuddered, feeling sick again.

"Well, you did," Cassandra said, though there was no judgement in her tone, which confused me enough to keep the nausea at bay.

She pulled a satchel from her shoulder and extracted a cardboard folder before I had a chance to spiral.

"Take a look at these, will you?" she said, handing me a series of eight by ten photos.

"God, what the hell, Cassie?!"

There were about twenty of them, all of women between the ages of eighteen and twenty-five or so. Each picture was of a face, their eyes held open to reveal gaping sockets full of red and black mush, their mouths and noses hooked up to machines. It was a disturbing set of images.

"This is what you stopped," she said quietly.

I looked away.

"I know you, Mathew Samuel Graves, I know that you're desperate to punish yourself for what you've done, but *this...* this is what your actions stopped. We've had reports from the Healers dealing with these cases. Believe it or not, these were the *lucky* ones. Habitual users who don't overdose suffer what is defined as a complete moral inversion. Do you know what that means?"

I shook my head.

"It means that this stuff *corrupts* them, Matty, brings out the worst in them, and it doesn't go away when they've had a fix. It just keeps getting worse and worse until the person is simply a grotesque, evil caricature of who they once were."

She picked up the first picture and looked at the back, "And then there are these poor souls. Anastasia McLaren, twenty-two, was studying to be a nurse, overdosed on Source three days ago, killed her father and two brothers with uncontrolled electricity before the drug and the magic burned out her brain."

She picked up the next, "Shana Twill, twenty-six; she was a primary school teacher. Someone slipped her a dose of Source on a night out. A week later, she was addicted and crippled three people with chemical burns trying to get enough money to pay for the overdose which made her like this and contaminated two underground wells in the resultant Magical explosion, severely poisoning seventy-three people before it was discovered."

She picked up the third, but I put my hand over hers and she stopped.

"I know, Cassie, really, I do. I know that in the grand scheme of things, the good more than outweighs the bad... but it's still my fault that they're gone. It's still my fault that their families have lost their loved ones... and wasn't it you that told me 'two wrongs don't make a right'?"

She glared at me again, "Don't use my own words on me, that's my thing!"

I chuckled, "I'll be alright eventually, you know that. It's just taking me a while to get past this one."

"I'll say, you're being a real little bitch about this whole thing."

I laughed and she pressed her forehead against mine.

"You know how I feel about Shadowborn, Mathew; and

you know how I feel about Shadowborn taking lives. What happened has *not* changed the way I feel about you, do you understand?"

I nodded.

"Good. When you've stopped being a little girl, come see me and we'll catch up. Until then, your emoting is making you a complete downer."

I laughed again and she smiled back before kissing my cheek.

"Hopkins is thinking about this, okay? You listen to her when she comes."

"Yes, Ma'am."

"Manslaughter has made you very polite, I'm already seeing the bright side."

"Do you want me to throw up on you? Because I will!"

CHAPTER 12

She left me then, extracting a promise to call her, and I went back to my homework. To my surprise, I felt... better, just a little, but enough to get me going again. The fact that Cassandra didn't hate me made a big difference; I'd anticipated her being disappointed at the very least.

I should have had more faith in my friend. She'd understood, both the situation and my reaction to it. That allowed me to start moving forward; to start moving on.

Sunday was a whirl of near chaos as Bill and Cathy did their level best to completely distract me. I appreciated it, and let myself be diverted with Bill's Doom tournament and Cathy's Keanu Reeves movie marathon.

The funny thing was that even though I was feeling better in myself, my hands were shaking worse than ever. I was an idiot not to realise why.

Monday came and I felt happy enough to sink back into routine, the memories not so sharp, and easier to bear after what Cassandra had showed me and told me. One might argue that there should be no difference between being responsible for the death of a drug-maker or an innocent person, but knowing that their choices in life led to so much suffering *did* make it easier to bear (which made me feel even more guilty, but in a different way; I'm complicated).

Monday night was a bit of a sticky point for me, though, as it was the Magic class. I stood outside the gym door for a solid twenty minutes. My powers should have come back now that I was starting to resolve my baggage, but they hadn't, and that sent me into a spiral of fear and doubt; what if I'd broken them forever? What if they weren't coming back?

In the end, I couldn't face finding that out, and I ran like a chicken (though with considerably less speed).

Naturally Hopkins wasn't going to take that without comment.

I was reading at my desk when the door opened.

"You weren't at class tonight," Hopkins said, letting the door shut behind her.

I turned from my book to talk to her.

"I couldn't go," I replied.

"Why?"

"I..." I started but couldn't finish. I was ashamed of myself in a variety of ways and still feeling so guilty.

"What is it, Matty?" she said, her voice soft as she knelt next to me.

This was a hard one, and I didn't want to talk about it; it wasn't even something that I'd even been able to properly articulate to *myself*.

"I'm afraid," I admitted, "what if someone else..."

Again I couldn't finish.

She wrapped her arms around me and squeezed me tightly.

"Oh, you poor, sweet idiot," she said, and then stopped for a moment, looking like she was thinking, "Would you come with me for a bit? I need to show you something important."

I nodded and she stood, offering her hand as she opened a portal and led me through.

We walked into a graveyard, one of the big ones in Stonebridge. I swallowed hard.

"It's okay," she said, leading me by the hand. It was dark out, after ten. There were a couple of lights around the perimeter of the yard, not much, but enough to let us see grave markers of every type imaginable, from simple sandstone crosses to small marble mausoleums. It was large enough to need a series of paths, and we were on one of the big ones, making our way to the far end, where there was an overgrown plot with a simple brown headstone, so old that the writing had completely faded.

She squeezed my fingers as we stood next to it.

"This is where a woman called Lillian Van Otre is buried," she said before taking a breath, "I killed her."

I squeezed her fingers, trying to offer comfort.

"There was a Vampire terrorising Stonebridge in the seventeen-hundreds. Long story short, I destroyed it. Lillian was the woman who lured his victims away from their friends so her master could feed. In exchange, she'd get to keep anything the victims had on them. She was his partner, for all intents and purposes; the Vampire's human servant, like Renfield from Dracula. When the Vampire died, she went insane, threw herself off a roof, broke her neck."

"That wasn't your fault," I said, "How did you kill her, for heaven's sake?"

"If I hadn't destroyed the vampire, she'd be alive. Simple as that."

"But you weren't to know," I argued, "You were only trying to save lives- oh..."

"There you are," she said quietly, "Now, if you can argue so strongly for me, why can't you accept that the same might apply to you?"

"I don't know. I can't explain why. I just... I want to take it back and I can't!"

"I know, I know," she said, holding my hand again, "Look, this is important, you need to really listen to this, alright?"

I nodded.

"The life of an Archon is long and complicated. Lives change based on the choices we make. You made a choice and lives ended. If you'd made a different choice, many more may have been. Those men died, and that is a tragedy, but you can't forget that it was their choice to use their lives in a way that led to that end. I'm sorry that what happened hurts you so much, but you are the First Shadow, Mathew. You made a choice to save lives and end a horrific thing."

She turned me around to look at her.

"And let's not forget the Demons. They may not be the cuddliest victims in the world, but they *were* victims. Those Magicians and technicians were leeching sentient beings of their life force. When they were used up, they'd have disintegrated and been sent down below, where their weakened states would have left them easy prey for the other things that live there. I'm not entirely certain about how things work down there, but I can't imagine that's fun.

"There may have been Demons in that room, but those drug-dealers were the biggest monsters, Matty. At least they got to die painlessly in their sleep, which is far more than the victims of their business can say."

She stood with me while I processed what she said. I thought about it for a long time, and then I asked myself an important question, one I'd been avoiding: if I'd known how things were going to turn out, would I have stayed away? Would I have let things carry on just to save my own conscience?

The answer scared me.

No. No, I would not have stayed away. Because instead of thirteen drug-makers, I'd have hundreds or *thousands* of innocents on my conscience, not to mention whatever horror Rose and Gabrielle had in mind when they set me on the path that eventually led to that lab.

I think that's what was really getting to me, that even with all my regrets, I was willing to do it again if I had to; that made me question who I was, and who I might one day become.

Finally I nodded, taking a deep breath.

"Good. Now, I'd like you to do me a little favour, can you do that?" she asked.

"Okay," I said warily.

"Cast me a Magelight. Just a little one."

"But-"

"Don't worry. You can. I know it. You've fallen off the horse and you ran before getting back on it. Cast that spell, because the longer you leave it, the harder it's going to get. For me, alright?"

I nodded and concentrated. It was the easiest spell in the first spell book, a tiny little construct that converted pure Magic into light. Even the weakest Acolytes could cast it, it was that easy. I could cast it in my sleep, with barely an effort. With my Shadow Magic, I didn't need it, but I still knew how.

"Take your time, do it right and, above all, *relax*."

I nodded and pictured the spell, a construct that looked like a tiny inverted umbrella that held a little shard of pure Magic which was then steadily released as light.

My hands shook hard as I stretched them out put my Magic into the Spell. It guttered for a second and then flared into bright light above my right palm.

Hopkins had told me what the problem was, but I hadn't realised just how clenched I'd been, how hard I'd been fighting my Magic. I staggered and nearly fell as what almost felt like a boulder lifted off my soul. Hopkins caught me and held me as I sagged.

She grinned broadly and yanked me into a hug, patting my back.

"Never do that again, Matty. Magic is part of who you are. It's one thing not to use it, but walling it off will damage you, it's like wrapping a computer in loft insulation, it fries. That's why your hands were shaking; the feedback."

"I don't even know what I did," I pointed out, making her roll her eyes. My hands were steady again, though. Thank God, I'd thought I was developing a twitch! Red eyes, facial scars and a twitch; Cathy was a very understanding girlfriend, but that was taking it a bit far...

The light floated away, a little piece of me, shining in the night. The world seemed to pop back into shape, like I'd been looking at it with one eye closed. I felt a little more balanced now, more like me again.

"How do I live with it, Jen?" I asked after a gentle silence.

"One day at a time, little brother," she said, kissing my forehead, "You take comfort from the fact that you've made a real difference in the world, and that it's been a good one. You've done your best, and even if it hasn't turned out exactly how you've wanted, you keep trying. That's how you carry on."

I nodded, taking a calming breath.

"Okay," I said, closing my eyes.

My Shadows came from everywhere, almost desperately. They flowed around me, surrounding me and wrapping me up to the neck, whispering soothing things. They'd missed me.

"Oh, that's just peculiar," Hopkins said, "Even I can hear them, now."

She squeaked as a few brushed against her before subsiding back into their cracks and crevices.

Sorry I was gone so long, I sent.

I felt my connection buzz slightly with... harmony, I think. I knew that Elementals lived in there, but the Shadows themselves were alive too, in a way, or were alive through me, I'm still not entirely sure on that one. But I'd missed the connection, and I'd stuffed it down so far.

"Oh, that's better," I said.

Hopkins smiled, "Stupid Shadowborn."

"Hey!"

"Don't 'hey' me, you got people eaten."

"Really?"

"Too soon?"

"Just a smidge!"

"Well, we're going to be holding this over you for a while. Don't feel too bad, we all still remind Kron of the time she took a trip to Sarajevo and accidentally facilitated a little assassination."

My eyes narrowed, "This wouldn't have been around

1914, would it?"

"She doesn't like to talk about it," Hopkins warned.

"How do you *accidentally* facilitate an assassination?!"

"She healed the wrong guy, it happens; moving on."

"Have you ever done anything like that?"

"Caused the outbreak of a world war? No; I'm clever."

"I wonder what Killian would say if I asked him that question about you."

"You wouldn't discover anything, but I suspect that a lot of your course work would suddenly and inexplicably vanish two days before it's due in to the examining board."

"You wouldn't!"

She turned to give me an evil look.

"Withdrawn," I said quickly, "I always knew you were perfect, never made a mistake, I'm sure."

"Good boy, I'm glad you can learn. It makes me worry less about future demon-related eatings."

"Seriously, this is already getting old."

"Unlike the people those demons ate. They're dead."

"Alright, this is now approaching poor taste," I protested.

"*Taste*, you say?"

Alright, I knew this was comeuppance for all the bad jokes I'd made at *her* expense, but this was getting ridiculous!

I put my hands over my ears and she laughed, pulling them away to smile at me.

"Everything will be fine," she said seriously, "And I'm glad that you're taking it like this. A human life should never be a cheap thing, Mathew; it's an immense comfort that you know that."

"Thanks."

Hopkins portalled me back, and we emerged outside Kimmel House. She gave me a hug that was spotted by a clutch of students, who giggled, causing Hopkins to swear creatively once they were gone and hit me when I sniggered.

"See you tomorrow, Matty," she said, "You going to be

alright?"

I nodded, "Thanks for giving me the kick I needed."

"Always happy to lay hands on you," she said before real-ising what she'd said and hitting me again.

"Ow! I didn't even laugh!" I complained.

"You were laughing in your head, I could feel it," she said before spinning and walking away.

I smiled, feeling a bit better and Shadow-Walked back into my room.

Just because I could.

In the days that followed, I found it easier to put the mess behind me. Cathy made me feel a little better every time she held my hand, or... did other things with me. It was all helpful. Bill's combination of outrageous gossip and evil hu-mour drew me back into the real world, and the weight hang-ing from my heart started to ease.

I knew that it wasn't going away for a while, if ever, but that was important. I was determined never to make a mistake like that again.

So, things started to return to an even keel. Bill asked for more money. Apparently he had a girlfriend in Stonebridge, and I fervently hoped that didn't mean anything tawdry, he was spending a *lot* of money.

Friday rolled around.

I swear, when people have bad news, they always deliver it at night.

It didn't start off *so* bad...

Now, when I was asleep, I was out like a light. I slept deep, and I didn't wake quickly, which is why Tethys could get away with so much; I honestly had no earthly idea what she was doing.

It started with a slow movement over my hips.

A very pleasant one, actually. The pressure built ever so slowly, at such a rate that I only slightly woke up, and it wasn't enough to register a problem. The movement turned into a gentle grind, and I reached out, still mostly unconscious, towards the source of this rather pleasant phenomenon.

I found shapely hips and tight leather, and my hands moved around to a bottom I suddenly became aware I was unfamiliar with. Still trying to come out of sleep, I smelled the barest whiff of rotten eggs as I squeezed something soft and warm.

Rotten eggs? That was familiar. Where did I know that smell from?

Well, the obvious answer would be sulphur, but why would that be in my roo-

Brimstone.

Demon!

I slammed a set of mental shields into place just as a pair of moist and warm lips fastened onto mine. My eyes snapped open, revealing Gabrielle straddling my hips. Her hands found my shirt, grabbing on as she let out a little moan. I felt her power squeeze my shields and thoroughly fail to penetrate. I grabbed her shoulders and tried to push her away, a stupid idea if ever there was one. Physically, she was about twice as strong as Tethys, and Tethys made me look like a baby jellyfish going up against a Great White shark.

Gabrielle took both my hands in one of hers and pushed them to the bed above my head before sticking her tongue deeply into my mouth. I attempted to protest, but she just held my head in place with her free hand.

I bit her tongue, she just laughed, it may have had the same texture as a human tongue, but it was far tougher. And I nearly chipped a tooth on what I was certain was some sort of stud.

Potential danger to my soul and freedom, it was sexy as hell. But enough was enough. I called my Shadows and they wrapped around her torso, yanking her off me and pinning her to the ceiling. I shook my head to wake myself all the way up before glaring at the Demon, who was smiling down at me, her arms and legs pinned by coils of Shadow. I cast a muffling spell around the room.

"Can't you just call like a normal person?" I asked.

"I can't imagine that being anywhere near this fun," she replied.

"And you didn't think it might be an idea to stop any of that?" I asked Rose, who was standing in the corner.

"You were doing just fine," she replied, "my action was unnecessary.

"That, and the winged freak likes to watch," Gabrielle said.

"That is a blatant lie!" the Angel replied, glaring at the woman on my ceiling.

"Pfft, please, you think you're the only one who watches him? I've seen you," the Demon replied, "and I've seen what you do while you're watching."

"One more word and I'll banish you," Rose said, blushing.

"No you won't," the Demon said with a giggle, "Without me you'd be back to the goody-two-shoes beat, and you don't want that, do you?"

"Do I need to be here for this?" I asked, "And by the way, you two are just ruining Christianity for me."

"In that case, do you have some time to hear about the gifts the Dark Prince offers?" Gabrielle said in a tone of voice that reminded me of a Jehovah's witness Burglar had intimidated once (don't ask me how. Burglar had been known to run away from *ducks*, goodness knows how he frightened off a grown man).

"Dracula?" I asked.

Rose sniggered, Gabrielle glared at her.

"I'm a Demon, who do you think I'm talking about?"

"I don't assume, you could be moonlighting," I replied lightly.

Rose burst out laughing, it was a thoroughly wonderful sound and warmed the corners of my soul.

"Oh shut up!" Gabrielle said, "And let me down, this is

undignified, and all sorts of interesting."

I shrugged and let her go. She fell straight down and landed perfectly. Rats, I was hoping for a face-first impact.

"Nice try," she said with a glare.

"I might say the same to you," I replied.

She licked her lips, looking me over. I met her eyes, my Shadows close and ready.

"Next time, Shadowborn," she said huskily.

"Doubt it."

"You wouldn't be the first to say that."

"He would be the first to hold you off not just once, but twice," Rose said helpfully, "And after you had a free shot, too, are you slipping in your old age?"

Gabrielle's glamour slipped and she appeared in her full red-skinned, black horned glory. Still sexy, by the way; even more so, if that's possible (I really need to deal with those issues). Her every curve and feature was just that little more sensuous, more inviting, even the black and spiky tail at the base of a bony crest over her backbone. What I had taken for gloves, way back when, was actually black, toughened skin over her forearms and hands with razor-sharp nails on the ends of her delicate fingers. Her four curling horns stretched above her hairline, and her eyes became an even deeper crimson.

Just looking at her, I knew that if she's wanted to, she could have filleted me without any effort whatsoever. I mean, she wasn't *allowed* to, but she could.

"I can take him right now, and there's nothing you could do to stop me," she said in a growl.

"I disagree with your assessment, but even if it *were* true, even if I couldn't stop you, he could," Rose said, gesturing at me, "already rather demonstrated his willingness. So why don't we just leave this one alone for the moment and get back to the task at hand?"

Gabrielle turned to look at me again while I scratched my head, trying not to yawn. Her glamour fell back into place and she stepped away.

"This isn't over," Gabrielle said, as much to me as Rose.

"Can't I just stipulate that you're the superior seductress and just skate over the eternal battle of wills?" I asked tiredly.

"No."

I sighed, "So, what brings you by?"

"We're curious as to when you're getting back to work on the problem we brought to your attention," Rose asked.

I suddenly had a sinking feeling.

"I already solved that problem," I said, "Didn't I?"

Gabrielle snorted, "Even if you'd disposed of the distribution channels, the warehouses, the dealers, the pushers, the masterminds, the designers, the enchanters and the drivers, you've still only managed to destroy *one* of the labs. *Labs*, plural."

"Oh no," I said, "There's more of them?"

"It's a nation-wide enterprise; did you really think it was being supplied from that one tiny base? Get your head out of your arse, Shadowborn," Gabrielle said.

"Bollocks," I said, using my Will to pull my mobile to me from the chest of drawers, scrolling through to Price's number. The Angel and the Demon were gone before I'd finished dialling.

Price was not happy when I told her about the other labs, and she promised to get back to information gathering. I left a message for Tethys telling her the same thing. I didn't want to wake her. She'd be cranky.

Bugger, bollocks and crap!

I thought this was done! Damn it! Damn it to hell!

The last lab had left me little better than a drooling wreck, and now there were more?

Just... bloody hell!

And also there was the small issue of getting groped by a pureblood demon! How the hell am I going to explain *that* at the Pearly Gates?

Or to Cathy?

CHAPTER 13

I decided to keep the intrusion to myself. I was supposed to keep the whole 'Liaison' thing under wraps anyway, and so I figured that nobody really needed to know about Gabrielle's antics. Hell, I wish *I* didn't know. That whole mess was just... confusing.

So I pushed it to the back of my mind, which didn't really work, because an impending catastrophe was a difficult thing to ignore. As a result, I was thoroughly distracted when I walked right into the lynch mob.

It was the following Monday and I was on my way back to Kimmel House after Magic Class. It was about ten, the class having run long as Hopkins and I had our usual debate, which rumour was now saying was down to sexual tension. A rumour Bill was helping along for his own amusement, the bastard.

It was dark, not that this was a problem for me, and I actually had a little spring in my step as I anticipated a warm shower and my comfortable bed. I was walking across the fields, flipping through a couple of notes I'd taken in the class, which had included a lecture about the Fairy Realms; information I knew would come in handy one day.

I'd just crossed through the arch leading to the Big square.

"Mathew?" said a small voice from ahead of me. I looked up to see one of the second years, a girl called... Kelly Ashton, I remembered after a bit of thinking.

She was a pretty little thing, her eyes and nose running with tears and snot.

"Yes? Are you alright?" I said, walking towards her. I stuffed the papers back into my satchel, completely unsuspicious, but worried about the poor kid.

"I don't know," she said, letting out a sob. She started crying, great wails of sound that concealed the footsteps behind me until it was far too late.

There was a whistle, a crack and my world exploded with stars before fading to black.

I woke surrounded by torches and tied to a post in the middle of a copse of trees.

I couldn't *believe* that I'd fallen for that... *again*. That was almost exactly the same way I'd gotten the bloody scars on my face. Crying girl, trap, club to the back of the head. It was embarrassing; fool me once shame on you, fool me twice and nobody would ever let me forget about it, and I already had 'accidentally getting people eaten' to live down.

I groaned in pain as I started moving; my head was bleeding freely and I could feel the blood oozing down the inside of my collar. I felt the effects of Spelleater amulets on my Well and tried not to throw up as the world spun around me. That meant a concussion; terrific. Using Magic in such a state was unwise to say the least. Almost as dangerous to me as it would be to them.

Of which there had to be about thirty, arranged in a semicircle around my stake. They wore Windward Academy rain coats, hoods over their heads. About a third were girls, I could tell by the cut, which surprised me. I knew that there were a great many boys around school who disliked me, but I got on quite well with the girls. I started to pick out features in the crowd, a nose here, hooded eyes there. I knew some of those people, considered some of them friends, acquaintances at the very least.

I tried to move, but found that I was tied up tight by my arms, legs and ankles; there were twigs at my feet.

Kindling?

Then I smelt petrol. It was soaked into my trousers and the wood.

No... they wouldn't!

"Mathew Graves! You are accused of witchcraft and altering the minds of your fellow students!" said a voice I recognised, Storm, the son of a bitch, "How do you plead?"

"Traditionally speaking, an accused Witch has the right to representation," I replied, getting some saliva into my dry mouth as I started focussing hard, trying to get my aching head to work properly.

"How do you plead?!" he repeated, he had a road flare in his hand and was wearing one of the amulets. I had no doubt that he intended to immolate me no matter what I said.

The crowd started shouting, some threw things at me, they hurt when they hit.

"The fact that I'm tied to a method of execution would tend to indicate that pleading with you is an exercise in futility," I replied calmly, playing for time, hoping I could talk my way out of this before things got *really* ugly.

"Smart mouth," Oxley said from under his hood, "We'll see how smart he is when he's burning."

"You could talk to my ashes and still find something smarter than you, Oxley," I replied.

He stepped forward and socked me in the gut. I gagged and dry heaved, which made the crowd laugh.

"Something else to say, funny man?" Oxley said.

"Oh yes," I gasped, "But I'll be saving that for your trial."

"Oh you won't be saying anything ever again, Graves."

I snorted, "Whether you win or not, you're going to prison for a very long time, Oxley. Kidnapping, assault and conspiracy to commit murder. That's approximately... fifty years in prison, for each of you, about double if you let Storm throw that flare, because then you become *accessories* to murder. I doubt Storm himself ever gets out for *premeditated* murder, assuming of course that his grandmother doesn't simply eviscerate him."

There was uncomfortable muttering from the crowd. Had they really not thought this one through?

"Oh, didn't you realise that murderers go to prison?" I said icily, "That's what you're doing here, by the wa-"

Storm punched me in the face and stuffed a rag into my mouth.

"Don't listen to him! We know he lies; we know he gets in your head! We're on the side of the angels; don't let this Shadowborn freak get to you!"

He snapped the top off the road flare and ignited it.

"Does anyone have anything to say on behalf of the accused?"

"I thought I might offer an opinion," said a familiar voice, a very *angry* familiar voice.

Storm turned, a look of horror on his face as all three Spelleaters were yanked away from the group and into Vanessa Kron's outstretched hand, where she crushed them with brute strength and dropped the mangled pieces to the ground. That was funny because Spelleaters cost somewhere in the neighbourhood of two hundred *grand*, if they were well made. Whoever those kids had borrowed them from would be hopping mad.

Storm shook in fear as my sister came over to the stake, waving her hand to throw the kindling out of the way. She gestured and force parted the ropes, the gag slipping out of my mouth. She caught me before I could fall and drew the petrol out of my clothes before igniting the resultant ball and burning it away. She lowered me gently to the ground.

She looked horribly ashamed as she attended to my wounds, working quickly and efficiently. My head tingled as the wound closed and my mind cleared. Thank God she'd turned up. If I'd had to fight my way out, then I wouldn't have had the control to take the amulets, my Shadows would probably have torn someone to pieces in my state.

When she was finished, Kron stood and turned towards the crowd, her eyes boring into her great (times twelve) grandson before shifting over the whole assembly.

"You are a disgrace," she said acidly. The kids flinched back, "This young man stood between you and an army of monsters. He risked his life to keep your school and your persons safe. And you... *animals* repay him with murder?"

Kron glared at each and every one. I heard Kelly Ashton start crying again.

"Mathew Graves is a Sorcerer, do you understand what that means?" she asked, "It means that the second he woke up, he made a conscious choice to try and talk to you rather than just killing each and every one of you, as I would have done," this last directed at Storm, "You just tried to lynch the most decent Magician you could ever hope to meet. So, congratulations, you've just proven that in the half a millennium since the witch trials began, humanity has not advanced at all."

She helped me to my feet. I was still a little dizzy.

"As for you, Tyler Magnus Storm, you are no longer a member of my family," she said, glaring at the boy, "As of this moment, you are unwelcome in my home or any city where I hold sway. If I should see you again, I'll make you suffer like you wouldn't believe."

He nodded, crying again.

"The rest of you will go to your headmaster tomorrow. You will admit what you did, and you will accept punishment. If you don't, then I'll come back," I felt her throw a pulse of terror into her words. It was actually an elegant bit of Magic, transmitting the emotion directly into their minds by means of sound; it made me even more impressed with Lady Time, "You don't want that, do you?"

They shook their heads, a few of the girls burst into tears.

Kron opened a portal and held my arm as we walked through. We emerged onto Blackhold's front drive. She walked me slowly up to the front door. I staggered a few times.

"Easy, Graves, you had a fractured skull, it'll take a while to get you up and running again," she said.

"Thanks for coming when you did," I said, "That was about to get ugly."

"I know. Saw something very nasty coming, just in time to stop it. You don't want to know how badly that could have ended," she said with a sad smile as a couple of my Wardens came forward.

"Lord Shadow?!" one said, taking my other arm, "Are you alright? Jillian, get the Captain!"

"That's unnecessary," I started, but Jillian was already through the doors.

"I'm going to go and speak with Jen," Kron said to me, letting go of my other side, "I'll be back tomorrow morning; don't return to the school until one of us tells you it's alright."

And just like that, she was gone, stepping right back through a portal.

My head ached, and I kept staggering as I walked through my front doors.

I was grateful for Kron's foresight, but wished it would have kicked in *before* I got smacked about the head...

"Shall I summon a healer, my lord?" the guard propping me up asked.

"No thanks Lacy, but I'd appreciate a sturdy arm up to bed, if you wouldn't mind?"

"Of course, Sir."

The house's lights started coming on as the commotion spread. Tethys met us as we were coming up the stairs, dressed in a very interesting set of night things.

"Matty?" she said, darting towards me, "What happened?"

"Oh, the usual, lynch mob, tied to a stake, nearly got immolated, you know, Mondays," I said as she took over from Lacy.

"Thanks, Lacy," I said.

"Of course, Milord," she said before darting back down the stairs.

"Will I have to order them to call me by name?" I asked

Tethys.

"You could try, but it might short-circuit something," she replied, helping me into my room and lowering me to the bed, which looked distinctly slept in. Tethys saw me notice and grinned.

"What? It's comfy," she said.

"Could you make sure Cassie knows where I am, when you've got a sec?"

"Oh, it's fairly safe to say she'll be along right abou-"

The door banged open.

"Shoot, so close!" Tethys said, smacking her thigh.

"What happened?" Cassandra asked, rushing over to me.

"It wasn't my fault!"

"That means it was."

"Before we get into that, could you send two of your most discreet guards to Windward, one each for Cathy and Bill, just until I get back there? I'm a bit worried, so if you could have them on site within the next thirty minutes, it would be a load off my mind."

"I'll arrange it now," she said, "but you'd better believe that there's going to be a conversation."

She turned around and jogged back the way she came.

"Wow, you're in trouble!" Tethys said with a snigger.

"Why? I was the victim!"

Tethys just kept giggling.

I pulled my mobile out of my pocket and texted Bill and Cathy. If two strangers showed up and started shadowing them, they might fret. I kept it simple. I didn't want them to worry about me, either.

While I did that, Tethys took off my shoes and gently shoved me into bed before pulling the duvet over my legs. She curled up under it with me, her arms around my chest and her head on my shoulder.

"You want to talk about it?" she asked once I'd finally put the phone down.

"I do," I said, closing my eyes.

I was out like a light before I could start.

When I woke up, my head felt like it had been split in two. Tethys was sleeping on my chest, looking peaceful. I cast a numbing spell that took care of the pain and closed my eyes again.

"You know, it's hardly fair," said a far too chipper voice not too long afterwards.

Kandi dropped onto the bed next to me, jostling me awake, "I'm here all the time, working my perfect arse off, but the second you come in the door, herself drops everything, including whatever part of me she was handling at the time, and drops right into bed with you."

"Sorry?" I offered, still half-asleep.

Kandi snorted and slid under the covers with us, "Oh, it's not so bad. I can see the appeal," she said, resting her head on my other shoulder, "What's this I hear about you cavorting with Vampire working girls?"

"You have my attention," Tethys said, suddenly awake and staring me in the eyes, "Kandi, Honey, where did you hear this delightful piece of gossip?"

"The Captain was muttering something last night after you got in, 'Bloodsucking hookers, demons labs and now a bloody lynch mob, is he trying to give me an ulcer?!'," Kandi said in an impressively accurate impression of Cassandra, "and then she said some un-ladylike things about having you neutered so girls couldn't lead you around by the nose so easily."

How did she know what had happened with the mob?! I hadn't had the chance to tell her yet!

Oh, Kron.

"Oh, Matty, what have you been up to?" Tethys said with a chuckle.

"I told you everything on Wednesday," I said.

"Nowhere in that conversation was there a mention of an escort, Vampiric or otherwise," she countered.

"I told you about Crystal."

"You said she was your borrowed muscle, that conjures up a certain image, you sneaky boy," she said, nosing my ear.

"What the young lady does when she's not knocking drug-dealers on the head is none of my business," I replied with as much dignity as I could muster.

"She started sniffing you, yet?" Tethys asked.

"Not that I'd notice."

"What sort of Vampire is she? Quad, Lupin, Strigoi?"

"There's more than one type?!"

"There's twelve that I know of," Tethys said, "Any powers?"

"Strength, speed, telepathy, as far as I know; doesn't do well in sunlight, I think."

"Add beautiful to that and we get a Saphyron," Tethys said, "I presume beautiful, going by her profession?"

I nodded.

"Don't... don't let her bite you. She'd likely get very... clingy," Tethys said with a wide grin.

"You don't say?" I asked in a heavily ironic tone, "Don't let the creature that feeds on human tissue bite me, never would have figured that one ou- Ow!"

Tethys bit me on the cheek.

"Sarcasm, Matty? And in our bedroom, have you no shame?" she said mischievously.

"Why is nobody afraid of me? I'm a dangerous man, you know," I complained.

"Saw you run away from a rubber spider," Tethys said with a smile.

"Watched you cry during Bambi," Kandi offered.

"Damn it," I said, pulling a pillow over my head, rolling over on my side.

"Come out from under there, we're not done with you," Tethys said.

"I'm going back to sleep!"

"Can't you tell us about your new gal-pal first? We want more material to tease you with later, and I just know you've bungled this one somehow," Kandi added, trying to pry my pillow away.

"No," I said.

"It's not worth it, Kandi, knowing our Matty, he was a nauseatingly perfect gentleman," Tethys said, patting my arm and settling back down, "I'll bet you didn't even ogle the girl a little, did you?"

"Sleeping now, can't hear you," I replied.

"Yeah, that's what I thought," Tethys said, curling up again.

That was at about seven o'clock.

Hopkins came in about nine, Cassandra right behind her, looking poised for that promised scolding.

"A lynch mob?!" Hopkins shouted, startling me out of sleep. The numbing spell had lapsed and the headache was back, though somewhat diminished, Kron did good work.

"God, why are you yelling at *me*? I didn't form the mob," I said, sitting up as carefully as I could.

"How did you even get caught by a lynch mob?!" Hopkins continued, shuffling Kandi out of the way so she could sit on the bed.

"Morning, Jenny," Tethys said, stretching as she hopped out of bed.

"Morning, Tethys. Spill!" Hopkins said.

"You mean that you're yelling before we've even gotten to the stupid part?" I asked, "I don't think I want to tell you."

"Matty!" Hopkins almost shrieked, making me jump. Tethys and Kandi sniggered.

"Fine, fine," I said. I told her.

It didn't take long. The look on Hopkins' face wasn't one of amusement.

"A girl. Again? Did you learn nothing from that Puritus thing?" Hopkins asked, clearly exasperated with me (not that I could blame her).

"I knew this one!" I pointed out.

"Yes, that makes it better," Tethys offered.

"Please stop," I asked her.

"Pwease big stwong man, save me fwom de mwonstwers," Kandi said in a tiny lisping voice. I called my Shadows and she shrieked as they tickled her mercilessly before pulling her off the floor by her foot.

I dangled her in front of me upside down and she giggled, blushing hard.

"Oh, you touched me in places no man ever has before," she said, limp and bedraggled.

"Must you make everything tawdry?" I asked.

"Hey, you're the one who enveloped me in tentacles, which one of us is more guilty here?" Kandi asked.

I dropped her on the bed and she stretched out like a cat before rolling onto my legs with a happy little sigh.

Hopkins rolled her eyes and rubbed her forehead. Cassandra looked like she was about ready to beat me over the head with my bedside lamp.

"If I ever see that little wart again, I'm going to gut him, I swear," Hopkins said.

"Assuming Kron doesn't beat you to it," I said, trying to get out from under Kandi, who wouldn't let me. In the end I just rested my hands on her back and tried to make the best of it.

"I really can't leave you alone, can I? I turn my back and it's a Demon drug lab, or an angry mob, or a sentient suit of armour, a Fairy princess or some other such nonsense. Bloody hell, Matty, you have a Warden for precisely this reason!"

"Not at school, I don't," I offered, looking hopefully at Cassandra, who didn't look any happier, or inclined to help me out of my scolding.

"She could go in disguise," Kandi offered.

I put my hand over her mouth, and she giggled, "You are not helping," I told her.

Hopkins and Cassandra smiled at her antics. Kandi tried to say something else, but I kept my hand in place, not wanting her to put any more ideas like *that* in anyone's head. Naturally, this didn't discourage the redhead; it just made her make happy grunting sounds (the little weirdo liked it for some reason, so did Tethys).

"Anyway," Hopkins said, moving on, "your little friend may have a point. You need a Warden around."

I grunted something and let Kandi go, who was now flushed again.

"Love it when you do that," she whispered in a shaky voice.

"She's right, Matty," Cassandra said ignoring Kandi, "People keep trying to kill you."

"Look, I know that the day is coming when I'm going to need full time security, but let me have my illusions a little longer, okay? This isn't likely to happen again, after all."

"You said that after the Puritus thing, and yet here we are," Cassandra pointed out.

"I know, I know, just let me have this last term, alright?" I gave her my best puppy-dog eyes, which don't really work when your eyes look like something a demon would be proud of, but they were successful enough that Cassandra growled and stomped off.

Hopkins shook her head, "Just be more careful, will you?" she asked.

I nodded and she left me to it.

"Kandi, I need to pee," I said.

"Should have thought of that before you did things to me," she said, wrapping her arms more tightly around my legs.

"Tethys, control your staff," I begged.

"Tell you what, Matty, rub my back, we'll call it even," Kandi said.

"One inappropriate sound, and I'm stopping."

She nodded and I ran my hands up and down her back gently, kneading it carefully. Naturally, she fell asleep after a few minutes of this and Tethys grinned evilly as I looked desperately towards the bathroom.

"Help!" I mouthed.

Tethys shook her head and Kandi started snoring.

Cassandra came back about an hour later, barging in before dropping on the bed next to me, where she proceeded to turn the most ugly stare I'd ever seen on me. It made me uncomfortable.

"Tethys, would you give us a moment?" Cassandra asked.

"Sure," Tethys replied, picking Kandi up and slinging the girl over her shoulder. Kandi squeaked as she was handled, but that quickly subsided into yet more happy sounds.

"You could have done that any time?!" I asked.

Tethys stuck out her tongue and disappeared with her nearly-purring burden.

"I'll be right back," I said, running for the bathroom. It was a close-run thing!

"Okay, shoot," I said, returning to my spot.

"Bad choice of words, Shadowborn," Cassandra said with a smirk, patting her hidden holster.

I sighed.

"I'm worried about you, Matty. This isn't sustainable."

"It's not like I enjoy it, you know," I pointed out, earning me an elbow to the ribs.

"Be serious. You aren't trained for this sort of thing. You nearly died *at school*. Who manages that?!"

I leant against the headboard and looked over at her.

"I know," I said quietly, "and I'm sorry for worrying you; I will be more careful in future. I wasn't expecting something like that to happen at Windward."

"Didn't they tie you to a set of Rugby posts that one time?"

"Well..."

"And to my recollection, no less than four groups have tried to kill you on those grounds."

"That doesn't count."

"Why?" she asked sweetly.

"Um..."

"That's what I thought. Now can I send a Warden with you?"

I gave her a look.

She snorted and yanked me into a hug.

"Fine, but if you die, I'll kill you," she said, squeezing hard enough to bruise.

"That makes no sense!" I gasped through the constriction.

"Shut up, Shadowborn."

She held me for a while; it was a nice moment, which Kandi ruined.

"Yeah, that's right, now go for the bra..." whispered a sultry voice from the door.

We both turned to glare at Kandi, who was peering through a crack.

"Um," she said, "It wasn't me."

The door shut as she ran for it.

"You just had to move the Succubus in, didn't you?" Cassandra asked.

"You told me to get the paperwork under control, this is your fault."

She leant her head against mine.

"You hungry yet?" she asked.

"I could eat."

I checked in with Cathy, who hadn't noticed the bodyguard. She was worried about me, but was reassured by my explanation (as she should have been; it was all complete waffle that concealed everything important).

Miss Jenkins laid on a fantastic breakfast, as always. Hopkins joined Tethys, Kandi, Cassandra and I, and we all ate like it was going out of fashion. Cassandra stole half my food, just like normal. It felt good. Just like it should. I smiled, more than I had since the church. I actually relaxed, really relaxed.

CHAPTER 14

Cathy dug the real story out of me over the phone as I was being driven back to school. She tried to hide it, but I knew that she wasn't taking the latest attempt to do me a mischief very well. She smiled when I arrived back at Windward (just in time for lunch), but broke down in tears the second I looked in her eyes. I held her as she cried it out, whispering soothing things to her as she squeezed me.

People started to stare, but my red-eyed glare soon had them minding their own damn business.

"Oh, Matty, I'm not sure I can bear too much more of this," she whispered in a tiny voice as she sat on my lap.

"I'm sorry, Cath, really I am," I said, "I'll be more careful, I promise."

"I don't want you to change, Matty. I just hate that you live in a world where who you are puts you in danger."

I kissed her forehead and held her hand.

"Me too," I said, "God, me too. I wouldn't tell anyone else this, but I'm getting tired, Cath. It seems that every time I turn around there's another enemy, or another creature trying to get its hooks in. I just want to pick you up and carry you to the Grotto and stay there until it all goes away."

"I'd like that," she said with a smile. She kissed me gently, that simple gesture a balm for all my worries.

"How do you do that?" I asked with a smile.

"What?" she asked.

"Make it all better," I replied, cupping her cheeks.

"I'm Cathy," she said with that lovely smile of hers back in place, "I'm amazing."

"That you are."

She seemed to calm down a little and we went back to our day. But we kept close to each other. I think we just needed the other to be there when we turned around. I was so glad she was there, even as I felt horrible that I was making her worry.

Mister Kenilworth called me into his office to discuss the various confessions he'd received that morning, and I told him what had happened, laying the lion's share of the blame on Oxley and Storm's shoulders, largely letting the rest off the hook.

As much as I would have liked to bring the hammer down on all of them, I knew that even powerless, Storm was an expert manipulator; I'd seen that in his memories when I went poking through them. Half the time, he didn't even bother using Magic to break people up, he just talked to them. It should have come as no surprise to me that he'd managed something like this.

Storm and Oxley were expelled by the end of the day and I never saw either of them again. Half the student population either thought I was a snitch or a monster, but at least that meant that they weren't inclined to make trouble.

After that, the week passed quietly. Thank God, I needed the break. I had lunch with Tethys as usual; she'd already managed to grow my not-inconsiderable holdings, and was raking it in. Cassandra was there, too, as she was from time to time. She said it was to make sure Tethys didn't try anything, but I knew those two were starting to get along quite well, it was actually beginning to worry me. It was hard enough getting my nonsense past *one* of them; both would be impossible.

We parted ways and I started walking towards the bus stop that would take me back to school. It was a pleasant day, and there wasn't much of a crowd, so I took a detour across Giles' Park, hoping to get myself some home-made ice cream from my favourite parlour before an afternoon of Chemistry.

I didn't make it very far.

"Mister Graves?" said a bowel-loosening voice from behind me that had me breaking out in a cold sweat right on the spot.

I turned.

Yep, Namia Sutton.

"I think it's past time we talked," she said, her voice musical, her smile perfect.

I looked around. The sun was shining down on us, and there wasn't a cloud in the sky. A perfect battleground for her, being a Light Magician, especially as there weren't too many witnesses around.

Then I remembered the warning. *No Magic on Namia Sutton.*

I calmed myself down slowly, putting my hands in my pockets to conceal the shaking.

"What about?" I asked.

"Shall we make this a frank conversation?" she asked sweetly.

I nodded.

"I know who you are, I know everything. Vanessa told me, all I had to do was ask. I have nothing against you personally. There is nothing in my agenda that includes you or anyone you know. But if you keep sticking your nose in my business, that's going to change, and I'm going to come for you," she said.

Her tone was respectful, almost sorrowful, actually.

"Allow me to be equally frank," I replied, "I saw the look in your eyes the day we met. I saw your hatred, your bile. This cutesy exterior doesn't fool me in the slightest, I know what you are. You're a drug-pusher, a torturer and a thug. Do yourself a favour and shut Source down now, because either you do it, or *we* will."

"You don't speak for the others, we both know that," she said, her mask dropping away as her face twisted into a sneer and her voice became hard and cruel.

"When one speaks, it is with all our voices. You may be a

friend of Kron's but you shouldn't believe that she'll take your word over mine forever."

"I'm her daughter. You are a replaceable part. One that's going to be made obsolete very soon. You are nothing but a weak, ineffectual *man*. I'm going to enjoy tearing you down."

"I've been threatened by the best of them, Sweetie," I replied, "You're barely a blip on my radar."

I sneered right back at her and her face coloured. *That's it, get angry...*

"You know what I did to the last man who spoke to me like that? I took him from his home while he was eating with his family. I hurt them while I took him, his last sights of his wife and son were them screaming. And then I started working on him. It took me a week to break him. I tore his mind apart and made him my slave. I still keep him around, crawling around one of my houses. He licks my boots clean. You won't have a tongue by the time I'm done, but I'm sure I can find something for your husk to do."

I sniggered.

"Oh, you really are a little drama queen, aren't you?"

"You think this is funny? You think someone who could build the Source trade under the noses of the Conclave is to be taunted, trifled with? I'll eat you *alive!*"

"Go on then," I said calmly, "Give it your best shot. I'll wait, take your time."

"Oh, you'd like that wouldn't you? Give you the provocation you need to have me up on charges," she said, eyes narrowed suspiciously.

I sighed theatrically, "Do you know what Sovereign Immunity is?" I asked, "If you were important enough for me to kill, I'd kill you. You're not. You're just a broken kid with man-hating tendencies and a penchant for power. Not worth an Archon's time."

"I'll take your family," she said icily, "Would that make me worth your time?"

"Indeed it would," I said neutrally, "but be very careful of wandering down that road. Because as creative as you may be, I have a Grimoire *packed* full of horrific ways to keep a soul in unending agony and far away from whatever peace waits beyond this life. Keep this fight civil, because the second you take someone I love from me, I'll open that book. And you'll find out what *real* pain is. Do we understand each other?"

She actually had the good grace to swallow in fear, her teeth chattering. You'd be amazed what being the bound owner of the ancient repository of evil magic does for your reputation.

She nodded.

"Good. Then let the games begin," I said, "I'll see you when I see you."

Her face went white with fury, but she turned on her heel and walked away. I waited until she was out of sight and pulled my mobile out of my pocket, hitting the 'stop' button on the recorder.

Yes, that'll do *very* nicely...

It took her two days to make her move. Less than I thought.

Friday afternoon. I knew something was up when Hopkins wouldn't look at me during English, I didn't know exactly what was happening until she showed up in the Big Square just before dinner.

"Mathew, come with me, please," she said.

"Something wrong?" I asked.

"Yes," she said, opening a portal. She stepped through and I followed her.

Killian, Kron and Palmyra were waiting for us in a big cylindrical room, almost like the inside of a stone silo. Sutton was with them. The walls were black marble, inscribed with runes and sigils. They hurt to look at, but I didn't have attention to spare for them. I did notice that I couldn't access my Shadows, which gave me a little insight into the room's purpose. There was no door that I could see.

"What's up?" I asked, deliberately not mentioning the nature of the room (which was quite clearly some sort of Shadowborn's trap).

"Namia is a member of my family," Kron said, her eyes narrowed and furious, "You were told to leave her alone."

"And I did," I said.

"She says different," Killian said, "She says you attacked her. Threatened her with violence and accused her of drug trafficking. This is unacceptable behaviour. Even from you."

"*Even from me?*" I asked, "What's that supposed to mean?"

"Nothing," Killian said, his expression inscrutable.

"Wow, we are really getting down to what you people think of me, aren't we?" I said.

"Are you saying it's not true?" Palmyra asked hopefully.

"Did she offer evidence?" I asked.

"She gave her word, and Palmyra monitored her as she offered testimony. She wasn't lying," Kron said.

I snorted in amusement.

"So you deny it, then? You didn't accost her? You didn't threaten her?" Palmyra said.

"I didn't accost her. I *did* threaten her," I said.

Kron's form flickered with power, so did Killian's.

"You two stop that right now!" Palmyra shouted, "For heaven's sake, Van, you've already screwed up with him once, are you so desperate to do it again?"

Kron growled, but settled, Killian just looked glacially calm.

"Why did you threaten her?" Hopkins asked.

"She threatened me first," I replied.

"That's a lie!" Sutton said, striding forwards.

"Palmyra?" Kron said.

"They... they're both telling the truth. But that's impossible. One of them is fooling me!" Palmyra said.

"We all know that Graves is a practiced liar," Killian offered.

I rolled my eyes.

"Purely for the sake of interest, what were you planning to do to me? I assume that my guilt was more or less determined before I arrived."

"You'd be facing punishment. Under our judgement," Killian said.

"Meaning?"

"Meaning that you'd lose your privileges and status as an Archon," Killian said.

"All on her word against mine? Well, I lived seventeen years without those things, I could probably survive," I said.

Kron turned away, disgusted.

"What do we do?" Killian said, "They can't both be telling the truth."

"I guess it comes down to who you trust," I said, "Her or me."

"There's not enough evidence to damn him," Hopkins said, looking at me, "and even if there was... I wouldn't vote for it."

"I will," Killian said.

"And so will I," Kron added, wrapping her arm around Sutton's shoulders.

"Lucille?" Hopkins said, "There has to be a majority."

"There's no evidence, none at all!" Palmyra said.

"Namia's word is evidence!" Kron said, "And that's all you should need!"

"Lucille," Sutton said, "you know I wouldn't lie to you. Think back, how many years have we been friends, taken care of each other?"

Palmyra dithered. Then she deliberately turned away from me, "She's never lied to me before," she said, "That must mean... that Matty is."

I smiled sadly.

Palmyra noticed and stared at me. I felt her empathic sense fire up with a vengeance.

"Oh, God," she said, taken aback.

"What?" Killian asked, looking at me with hatred in his eyes.

"He has something," Palmyra said, "He was just... he was waiting to see which ones of us would believe in him. Oh, no..."

I pulled my phone and played my and Sutton's conversation for the other Archons.

Their faces fell as they listened, and then they turned towards Sutton.

"You..." Kron said, "Namia, how could you?"

"It's not true! It's a fake!" Sutton screamed.

"Jen, take me home, will you?" I asked before I could see any more. It was done.

"Sure, Matty," she said, her hand on my shoulder as I turned my back on the others and followed her back to Windward.

The portal closed behind us and I turned to look at her.

"Thank you for believing me."

I couldn't describe how much that had meant, but I think she got it.

She smiled, patting my shoulder, "I'm sorry it happened that way."

"Meh, I'm used to it at this point."

"You shouldn't have to be," she said, anger entering her voice, "and Palmyra... I wouldn't have believed it if I hadn't seen it."

"Peer pressure. Why do you think we have an assembly on it every year?"

She smiled again, sadly.

"She and Namia have always been close. Please don't hold it against her?"

"Of course I won't," I said, "She's saved my life a bunch of times, she's more than earned the benefit of the doubt. Would you tell her that for me?"

She nodded.

"And Kron?" she asked, elbowing me.

"Oh, she's dead to me," I said, earning me a swat to the head.

"That was quite an elegant little setup, Matty. Give everyone enough rope to hang themselves with," she said, "And you made three Archons look like idiots. They won't like that."

"Yes, *I'm* the bad guy."

She snorted and nudged me hard enough to make me stagger.

"Do you have any idea what a mess you've made?" she asked, "How long it's going to take everyone to cool down?"

"That's assuming that Sutton doesn't manage to lie her way out of this and turn them right back on me," I suggested.

She sighed and leant her head against my shoulder.

"You're just a ray of sunshine today, aren't you?" she said.

"Guys! They're doing it again!" said a tiny voice from behind the bushes.

I sniggered as Hopkins flew away from me and started glaring.

"Don't you have anything better to do?" she snapped. The three second years ran away, giggling.

"Aw, you scared them," I said with a grin.

"Shut up. And go away. Apparently I shouldn't be seen with you."

I laughed and pulled her into a hug before walking away. She blushed hard and hit me as I left, smiling all the while.

CHAPTER 15

I didn't hear from any of the others for a while, though Hopkins kept me updated. Apparently, Killian and Kron didn't really believe either of us anymore, and Palmyra was simply miserable about everything that had happened. So there was now a series of rifts, and nobody was talking to each other except Hopkins and I.

Thankfully, I was presented with a distraction that Thursday night.

Well, sort of.

The phone rang and I groaned. I rolled over and reached out with my Will for the phone, but ended up accidentally dragging the chest of drawers into my outstretched foot instead, which hurt.

Magic + Lack of Sleep = Oops.

"Hello?" I said groggily, wincing as I rubbed my stubbed toe.

"Mathew? It's Crystal. I... I need your help."

Oh, I just knew that wasn't going to be good.

"Where?" I asked.

It took a bit longer to get to Gardenia this time. I accidentally detoured into Brittany. To this day, I'm still not sure how.

She stood, waiting for me, in an alley outside a nightclub a couple of miles away from the Red Carpet. She was dressed in *my* hoodie, over her motorcycle leathers (so that's where it went, I'd completely forgotten I'd leant it to her and been looking for it, like an idiot).

"Thanks for coming," she said, not looking at me as I dropped out of the sky in a Shadow cocoon. I was dressed in dark clothes and a raincoat, the hood down and a glamour in place to make me look normal.

"No problem," I said, "What's going on?"

"It's..." she started, and then she stopped before taking a deep breath; she pointed to what I'd thought was a nightclub, "That's a 'Seven-House'. My sister's in there."

This was one of those places where you went to indulge the seven deadly sins, hence the name. I wasn't entirely clear on what that meant, but then I'd gone to some effort *not* to find out about the less wholesome aspects of life in Gardenia.

"Alright," I said, "what do you know?"

"I haven't seen her in a while, five years. The last I heard, she was working down in Orleans as a hostess. But tonight, I get a note from her begging me to come get her. It's her writing, and it had her blood on it and it said this address. Oh, Matty, I don't know what to do! What if she's one of the victims?!"

"Victims?" I asked.

"Seven-Houses cater to those people who want to act out their darkest desires. Sometimes that's harmless enough; be praised and adored, have a little rough sex, sleep in a tub of caviar, beat up a shape shifter who looks like their boss, that kind of thing. But sometimes it's worse, much worse. Sometimes the client wants to kill, or cut or eat someone. Michelangelo's is where the people who want to do *that* go. What if they're killing her?!"

I took her hand, "Easy, we don't know anything yet, and I need you to be as calm as possible, alright?"

She nodded, but she was clearly still distressed.

"Look, you went into Hell with me, so you call, I'm here. But why me? Isn't Price far more able to get in and out of a place like this? Make a deal or something?"

At this, she looked shifty, "I'm not supposed to be here; ordered not to come, in fact. If Price found out that I'd prodded one of the territories... Well, suffice to say, I'm on my own, and you were the only one I could think to call who'd even turn up, much less be able to help me."

That made me sad and the look in her eyes was just so... lonely.

I nodded.

"One step at a time, okay? First, think of... what's your sister's name?"

"Amber."

"Amber. Think of her so I can see who we're looking for."

I slid a probe into her mind and saw a bright, beautiful looking blonde girl, about Crystal's height, but with a slimmer build and less generous curves. Her eyes were a lovely dark blue and her fangs were small and dainty; she was the spitting image of her sister.

"Good," I said, sliding out again, "Now, I'd prefer to go in quietly and not give them any warning that we're coming. You'd better put that hoody up. Do you still have the sunglasses?"

"Yes," she said, sliding them on.

I was proceeding under the assumption that Amber was being held against her will. She may not have been, but it was better to assume the worst and plan for it, rather than hope for the best and be caught flat-footed (I wasn't making *that* mistake again). With that in mind, Crystal looked so much like her sister that bringing her in as she was could only cause complications. Hence, the disguise.

"Good, then this next bit is up to you. You know how these places work; get us in and to a private area where I can cast a mapping spell and look for Vampire Auras. Once we do that, we'll slip away and start going through the matching signatures one by one until we find Amber or someone who can tell us where she is. Sound good?"

"Absolutely," she said firmly.

I offered my arm and she took it. We walked around the

corner at an easy pace, taking our time, pretending to be relaxed (Crystal was better at it than me). There was a guard on either side of a heavy metal door, above which the place's name shone in red neon. Both guards were tall, bulging with muscles and dressed in suits with lumps under their arms that told of weapons.

"Good evening," I said brightly, "I'm told this is the place to come to relieve certain tensions?"

The one on the right snorted but he opened the door. Crystal and I walked through.

"All yours," I whispered to Crystal.

She nodded, and we sidled through a wide lobby to a receptionist's desk.

"Good evening, Sir, Ma'am," she said, "How may we be of service tonight."

"We're starting slow tonight; can we have one of the L-rooms? Top tier to begin with, ease him in," Crystal said conspiratorially.

"Oh," the woman said knowingly, "Of course. You're a lucky man, Sir, if you'll pardon me saying."

"I'm well aware, Ma'am," I said with an ingratiating smile.

"Oh, he's so polite," the woman replied, "how... new is he to the scene?"

"All the way," Crystal said, giving the receptionist a naughty smile.

"How nice. Three hundred for the hour, four fifty since there are two of you. Did you have a preference for companion?"

"No companion," Crystal said, showing fang, "I want to enjoy *myself* tonight."

"Of course, Ma'am," the woman said with a knowing smirk.

"Pay the woman, Honey," Crystal said.

I pulled out the gold MasterCard attached to one of the Stone identity's slush funds. The lady smiled and took it with a flourish.

"There's a ten percent charge for credit cards, Sir," she said.

I nodded my assent.

I tapped my pin into the machine; the woman smiled and handed Crystal a key, "Behind me, on this floor are the tier one rooms. If you're ready for a lower one, come back and we'll make arrangements."

"Thank you," Crystal said, "Come on, Darling."

Crystal led me by the hand through the door behind the woman and into a black-painted room. There were seven doors, each with a letter on it - P, W, L, E, G, S and A (Pride, Wrath, Lust, Envy, Gluttony, Sloth and Avarice respectively). Crystal pulled me through 'L' and into a short corridor with three doors down each side. We went to room three, at the end on the left. She opened the door and led me through.

And, oh dear.

The room was almost all bed. It looked comfortable enough, with pink pillows and a thick mattress. Less comforting were the fur covered manacles all over the shop. There was a door leading to a bathroom and a set of drawers labelled 'enhancements and safety gear', whatever that meant, I wasn't eager to find out.

Not that this wasn't quite enough to be going on with, but my problem was the immediate, mind searing wave of desire that flooded through my system the second I stepped through the door. A problem Crystal was rather evidently suffering from too, because she turned very slowly to look at me, her pupils dilating, turning black as she stared at me with almost laser-like focus.

She closed the distance between us in a heartbeat, kicking the door shut and fastening her lips to mine, wrapping her arms and a leg around my body. For an instant, a very long instant, the enchantment of that place got under my skin and I responded to her, kissing her back with all I had, my arms around her, running all the way up and down her body, until my brain finally turned over and got back into gear.

I called my mental shields and almost immediately felt normal again (and also rather ashamed of myself). It took a couple of extra moments to craft a set for Crystal, and all the while she was trying (quite successfully) to get my clothes off and kiss every exposed part of me. I cast the shield just as she'd gotten my shirt off; hers had long since fallen by the wayside, along with her jacket, hoodie and bra. She'd even pushed me onto the bed.

And she didn't stop.

"Crystal!" I said, "Did you forget why we were here?"

She was breathing hard, her lips on my belly, her hands on my chest. At the sound of my voice, she halted, pulling back a little. Eventually, she slowed her breathing down and laid her head on my chest.

"Oh..." she said, nuzzling away happily; all sorts of interesting parts of her were all over me, "I didn't want to stop."

"Well, that's Magic for you," I said, controlling my own breathing, "Speaking of which..."

"Yes, right!" she said, sitting up and blushing at her state of dress, "These rooms really work well, don't they?"

"Too well," I said with a cough, "I wish you'd have mentioned this little effect *before* we came in. I could have been prepared."

And bloody hell; that had been a close run thing. A little less conscious thought on my part and I would have done something unforgivable. And enjoyed every second of it. I was going to find whoever set this place up and do them one hell of a mischief. I could only imagine what horrors would arise if you put two people in the 'Wrath' room.

"Sorry, I haven't been in one of these for a while," she said, "I wasn't expecting it to be so... strong, and normally there's a button or something to turn me- *it*, I meant *it*, on."

She blushed and I patted her newly clothed shoulder.

"Don't worry, could have happened to anyone," I said.

"I don't see you complaining," she said, her eyes drifting

over me as I pulled my shirt and jacket back on.

"That's because there was nothing to complain about," I admitted. It was hardly her fault (or mine, just to clarify).

Even with the... 'randy field' turned off, I was still very aware of her, I felt an almost primal need to touch her, which worried me enough that I double and triple checked my shields, but everything was fine, it must have been some residual thing.

"Really?" she said, up against me again, "Am I getting to you, Mathew?"

She kissed my neck, just a little one, but it made me shiver and she giggled.

"Oh yes, very definitely getting to you," she said.

"Do you mind?" I asked, turning to look in her eyes, "I'm working here."

"Yeah you are," she purred, nuzzling my cheek and neck.

"If I miscast this mapping spell because you distracted me, then I could break every pane of glass and shatter every ear drum in this place, including yours and mine."

She sighed, "Fine. Work your Magic. We'll discuss returning to this room later."

I knew how that discussion was going to go. I started casting the mapping spell, but didn't get half way done before the door slammed open and there were suddenly four goons in the room with us.

Not just regular goons, they were *Ghouls*. I *hated* Ghouls; carrion eaters, yuk. As a species, they tended to look just like regular people, perhaps a little more attractive. These four, not so much, they looked like bruisers and they stood like they knew how to do violence.

"Miss Sabeta," said a voice from outside, a slick sounding one, "sorry to intrude on your evening."

That was not good. They'd recognised her after all, and that was just annoying. A hoody had worked just fine for years as a disguise for me. But then it was a lot easier to conceal an average looking male than an astonishingly attractive Vampire...

The slick-sounding one was taller than the other ghouls, but thinner. His skin was pale and unhealthy, his head bald, his eyes dark and staring. I immediately brought up a number of discreet shields, just in case; that guy looked *dangerous*. He took in our clothed state with some confusion, but he didn't let it phase him.

"Would you be willing to have a word with management?" he asked, "I believe we have a guest who's eager to see you."

Crystal nodded, a little too eagerly and I stood with her.

"Is your pet trained?" he asked, "I don't want him slobbering on anything."

"He'll be good, won't you, boy?" Crystal said, her eyes urging me to play along.

I nodded, and was almost immediately forgotten as we walked out.

Two thugs led the way, and I trailed behind Crystal and Baldy; the last two heavies bringing up the rear.

This was starting to stink like a trap. A convenient note, a club built like a fortress. Guards and vice and torture rooms...

This may have been a mistake.

"Where'd you find the meat?" Baldy asked.

"Needed some money for tonight," she said with a shrug.

"Hey, I don't judge," he said, "Ate me an heiress yesterday, she left me quite a few diamonds to pick out from between my teeth."

He and the other ghouls started laughing nastily. My eyes narrowed, my Shadow straining to show my displeasure.

"Did it get darker in here?" one of the guys at the back said.

"Don't think so," said another.

I controlled my temper and sent my Shadows away, but after we found Amber I was burning this place down to the bedrock.

Baldy led us through some back corridors and into a wide lift. I kept my expression neutral while we descended to the floor labelled 'B-3' and they chatted.

"So, that mean you're done with the guy? He looks pretty spaced," Baldy asked.

"I haven't fed yet, and the night's still young," Crystal replied.

"Still, he doesn't need all his fingers, does he?" Baldy asked, eyeing me up in a very unpleasant manner.

Thankfully the lift doors opened and we were walking again before we had to meander any further along *that* conversational tangent. We made our way through some drab rooms filled with what looked like junk strewn onto worn carpets, to a pair of wide, wooden doors. Another Ghoul opened them and we walked through.

The office was wide and comfortable, with an aquarium built into the far wall over a fitted sofa. There was a massive desk next to one wall, covered in papers and a computer monitor. The whole thing reeked of money.

On the sofa was a young-looking man, a Ghoul, tall, good looking with blue eyes and dark hair, but with terribly mismatched teeth and a rather nasty under-bite. Amber was sitting next to him. She didn't look like she was in need of rescue. She wore a tight black dress and had her hair in a severe bun, which made the most of her high cheek bones. There was a half-dead girl gasping on the sofa next to her, blood trickling from her neck. A man sat in the far corner, oozing Magic, a Wizard-level Magician, Flesh Affinity.

Crystal went towards her sister, but was pulled back by the bouncers. I kept quiet. It wasn't time yet.

"Amber? What's going on?" Crystal asked.

Amber grinned evilly, showing fang, "What do you think?"

Oh dear...

"What?" Crystal said, sounding genuinely confused.

"You're Price's favourite," the Ghoul next to Amber said,

let's call him... Tusk, "Do you have any idea what she'll pay to get you back?"

"And if she doesn't... well, there's always a room for you here," Amber said nastily, "And what's this? Who's the morsel?"

"He was with her. We figured you'd want him," Baldy said.

"Ugh, he's not very attractive, how rich is he?"

"Very," Baldy said, "Sandra said he had a gold card."

"That explains it, still latching onto anything with a wallet, eh, sister mine?" Amber said, walking around me.

"Still latching onto the lowest piece of pond scum, Amber? You always did enjoy the smell of rot," Crystal said coldly.

Amber laughed nastily, "Osrik, Darling, may I?" she said, gesturing at Crystal.

"I can't refuse you, Love," Tusk (Osrik) said.

"Tie her up. Put her in a Wrath Room, level *three*," she said, her eyes flashing with pure evil triumph, "Let them do whatever."

Crystal was a Vampire, it was unlikely that a human could kill her with their bare hands, but they could still hurt her... a lot. I was now starting to get angry.

"What happened to you, Amber?" Crystal said, her voice trembling.

"I found a place where I wasn't just your sister, any-more," she said, "Where I am valued and loved. Something you'll never have. Do you have even *one* friend? One person who's not with you just to get in your panties or make money off your arse?"

Crystal's eyes shed tears, she was completely devas-tated.

Baldy grinned and reached for Crystal.

He never made it.

Because that had really been the last straw.

Crystal may not necessarily have the most... friendship-conducive lifestyle.

But she had me.

And, if I'm honest, Cassandra was right about me. I was a bit of a Neanderthal. I didn't like it when people hurt women. I didn't even like it when they talked about it. You can imagine how I'd feel about it happening right in front of me. And the whole sibling betrayal thing cut a little close to my open wounds, too. That likely made me just a smidge more brutal than I'd otherwise have been...

I took Baldy's arm off at the shoulder with a Shadow tendril. Black blood spurted out and he screamed. The Wizard was surprisingly quick off the mark, and was on his feet calling energy in the time it took me to put two more Shadow tendrils apiece through two bouncers. They flew apart, arms legs and organs flying everywhere, coating the room in blood and viscera while Crystal went for Amber and they blurred around the place, tearing into each other.

I wasn't holding back. These were monsters in every sense of the word, and needed to be knocked out of the fight as quickly as possible (don't worry, ghouls and vampires could take a lot of damage; nobody died). The Magician was conjuring light and his form swirled with Chemical Energy as he started casting at me. This was no place for a duel. It was too easy for a stray shot to take someone's head off.

He gestured, and a great gout of energy smashed into my shields, peeling away the outer layers before splattering all over the place, including Osrik, whose arm melted down to the bone, leaving him streaked with grey slime that used to be his flesh. He screamed, clawing at the wounds, not that it did him any good.

I sent my Shadows, swatting Osrik like a sack of potatoes on their way past to tear into the Magician's shields. The Light weakened my attack, but not enough, and the sheer power and violence behind my Shadows ripped his defences to pieces. His were made of Chemical energy, not particularly strong to begin with, but worse against a Shadow attack, because there's nothing for them to eat at. The chemical light drained more energy from me, but combat was obviously not this man's speciality, and it showed. His shields were feebly made, poorly executed and his attacks were unfocussed (if potent).

I tore his shields down and threw a curse that set his nerve endings on fire from the impact point on his abdomen. A nasty little spell, but it didn't do any actual damage, and it distracted him enough to allow me to drop a Coma Hex into his head and drop him like a stone.

Meanwhile, Osrik had reached his desk and slapped his hand down on a control of some sort. I heard an alarm blare, and felt minds converging on us, well, something like minds, anyway. Focussing on them allowed me to recognise some of them, and I grimaced before turning back to the irate ghoul.

He moved fast, heading for the door. By this point I was surrounded by a cloud of Shadow, impossible to see, much less attack, for someone without Magic. Just getting close to me would be nigh impossible.

He must have realised that, and was trying to escape, but my Shadows were there, and a tendril caught him around the middle. I thought about trying something fancy, but in the end I opted for cutting him in half with a mental flick. Being chopped in half wouldn't kill him. As long as the heart and head were intact and connected, he'd live.

Reinforcements arrived, two ghouls at the back, along with four Vampires, behind a small pack of Hyde monstrosities. These ones were of the smaller variety, men combined with goats or sheep, all the stitching crude, but effective. Some of the magic leaking off them was recognisable as belonging to the Flesh Mage behind me, though I didn't think he'd made them, not enough magic. Perhaps he was their controller? Their focus?

That was a telling arrival. There seemed to be a connection between those who'd attacked the Red Carpet, and these people. If the Hyde were mercenaries, then was it the same employer? Had these Ghouls been behind everything?

Well, that was hardly my problem, and I had better things to do than play detective at that moment.

There was no reasoning with the Hyde, so I sent my Shadows and started pulling them apart, which was *disgusting*, if quick. George Romero, the great zombie master, had one thing bang on, take the head or the brain and the Reanimate snuffs it for good. It wasn't long before I was left with a corridor full of twitching man and animal bits and a *repulsive* smell, which didn't blend well with the stench of Ghoul guts and Vampire viscera.

The Ghouls and Vamps behind them looked shocked, wavering between attack and flight, so I threw the still screaming half-Osrik at them. They chose to run, which was clever of them.

They didn't make it far. I got them too, and revelled in tearing those people to pieces. Something very ugly in me enjoyed visiting on these things the pain they'd inflicted on others.

"Hey! Freak! Stop what you're doing or I'll pull this bitch's head off!"

I turned.

Crystal was on her knees, bleeding from her neck, face and chest. Amber had her nails dug into her sister's neck, her knee braced on her back, ready to pull.

"Don't listen to her, you surrender and she'll kill us both!" Crystal croaked.

I didn't bother to speak to her; I just tossed a Sleeping spell. Amber never knew what hit her and simply collapsed onto Crystal. The damage was done, though; most of the monsters got away.

I ran out of my Shadows and over to Crystal, who was curled up in an agonised ball, blood seemingly leaking from everywhere.

I adjusted my Mage Sight and cast a numbing spell while I went to work, calling Flesh Magic.

Right, wounds. Long gash in her belly, stab wound to

her chest, puncturing her left lung; severed veins in her left arm and right thigh. I started to weave Flesh Lattices, but when I tried to apply them, her body rejected them. I took a look, and saw that the energy of her body was all wrong. It wasn't anything like it should be, nothing worked the same way. She was regenerating, but was losing more blood than she could afford to while it was happening. I nearly panicked, looking in her eyes, knowing that I couldn't help.

"Mathew," she whispered, her eyes glazing, "hungry."

I slapped my forehead.

Oh, right, Vampire. I didn't know how I'd forgotten that...

I used a painless extraction spell to remove about a litre of my blood, which formed into a ball above her mouth. Her eyes went wide at the sight and she stuck her face into it, sucking greedily. Her wounds closed before my eyes as she moaned and shuddered. I saw her Aura brighten as she drank.

It was only at that point that it occurred to me that feeding a Vampire the blood of an Archon might not have been the *very* best idea...

Creatures like Vampires had a Well, very much like a Magician, which allowed them to do things like lift cars or move faster than the eye could see. Different creatures refilled that well in different ways. Ghouls ate rotting flesh, Ogres had to sleep in their element (Earth or water, usually), Vampires drank blood. Drinking mine deepened and widened Crystal's well. She wasn't exactly a kitten to begin with, but now her powers had as much as doubled. Permanently.

I wondered if that sort of thing was cumulative... though I doubted it. A piece of my power integrated with her Well, almost a foreign entity. It shouldn't have the same effect a second time.

The last of my blood flowed down her gullet and she fell back with an ecstatic sound before smiling broadly, squirming interestingly.

"Oh, that was amazing," she said, her eyes lidded as she

stared at me. I was feeling a little woozy and cast a spell to re-place my blood volume.

"How are you feeling?" I asked.

"Better now," she said, curling up around my legs with her head on my thigh, "Is she...?"

"Sleeping," I said.

"The others?"

"Alive, but very unhappy."

"Good," she said, her eyes closing.

"Crystal, I have to take a look at that girl, I don't think she's well," I said.

"Oh, fine," she said, sighing, "but I reserve the right to resume my previous position."

I snorted and she let me get up. I went to the girl who'd obviously been fed on, still lying on the sofa. She hadn't moved at all.

I looked in her eyes, opening my senses.

Brain damage. Severe. She was a vegetable. Severe muscle wastage, she'd been that way for a while...

No soul.

Bastards!

Crystal stood over her sister; knife in hand, a snarl on her face. She grabbed Amber's head and moved the blade to-wards her sister's throat.

"Crystal..." I said gently, "Don't do something you can't take back."

"She needs to die," Crystal whispered.

"Maybe. But don't be the one that does it," I said, mov-ing over to stand next to her. I put my hand on her shoulder, squeezing gently, "Whether or not she dies, if you're the one that does it, that'll be a scar on your soul. Don't let her hurt you again, not like that. She's not worth it."

"How would you know?" she asked, her voice shaky, aggressive.

"My brother... my *twin*, he... went bad. He keeps trying to kill me. But I know that killing him won't make anything better. All it will do is drag me down to his level."

She turned her head to look at me. She knelt like that for a while, the knife poised. And then she dropped it.

"Manipulative Magician," she muttered as she hopped to her feet and wiped her eyes, "That bitch wrecked my clothes!"

"Whose clothes?" I asked with a grin, gesturing at the hoodie.

"Mine," she said, turning a very intense gaze on me, implying perhaps that she didn't just mean the top...

"Alright, alright, not coming between a lady and her things," I said, walking over to the twitching heap that was Osrik.

She growled and followed me.

"Ozzy, old boy," I said, flipping over his torso with a little shove of Will. His mouth was full of black blood and his eyes were staring and insane, "Let's have a chat."

He let out a stream of invective that would have made a sailor blush; I waited for him to finish.

"Creative, isn't he?" I said to Crystal, who had linked her arm through mine and was leaning on my shoulder, sniffing me from time to time, I tried not to notice.

"I don't know, I accidentally stepped on a man's testicle during an inventively athletic evening, and he was far more expansive with his cursing," she replied.

"That is just far more than I needed to know."

She chuckled.

"Ozzy!" I shouted, smacking him upside the head with a Shadow, he shut up, "I have questions, answer them and maybe I'll let you go with what you have left. Don't, and I'll take the rest before dropping a curse that removes your powers of regeneration. Your choice."

He growled, but nodded.

"Good man. Who told you to try this little scam? This reeks of someone far more clever than you or my friend's idiot sister."

"You're wrong. All my idea," he gurgled.

"Oh," I said, "Funny, your mind just lit up with all the telltales of someone fibbing. Did I mention that I'm a Telepath? Maybe I should have."

He swallowed.

"Look, you're stressed, you're humiliated, you're hurt, so I'm going to let you have that first lie for free. Tell me another and it's going to cost you, understand?"

I think it was my quiet, neutral tone that convinced him as much as anything else. I've noticed that a jovial nonchalance in the face of horror scares people far more than shouting would.

He nodded.

"Good. So, same question."

"He was one of Greg's friends, our Magician is Greg. He told us to use the sister to get your girl and then call him. He said she'd be valuable to the right people."

"Did he say who?"

"No," he replied.

"Call him now. Tell him you have her."

"What? No! He'll kill me!" Osrik said.

"Do we really need to go through this again?" I said, letting a coil of Shadow congeal in my palm, becoming barbed and spiky. He swallowed again.

"Alright! Alright, damn you! My phone's on my desk."

I saw it and Willed it into my hand before dropping it on his chest.

"Get me a name, a location, something I can use to get him in close. And don't give the game away, alright?"

He nodded again and scrolled through to the right number.

"On speaker, please," I said.

It rang twice before someone picked up.

"What?" the voice was male and gravelly, unpleasant.

"I have the girl," Osrik said.

"She give you any trouble?"

"Killed one of my guys," Osrik replied.

"Keep her close, I'll be in touch," he said.

"Wait!" Osrik said, looking at me, "I want to meet. Right now. She told me about a Magician. He's been sniffing around. She told me some stuff, dark stuff. I don't want to talk about it over the phone."

I heard a grunt.

"Fine. Twenty minutes, your place, but this had better be good."

They hung up, "Well done. Now, you wait here while I go have a chat with my new friend."

I took his phone and left him there, heading towards the lift and up to the front door, Crystal with me.

"Can I interrogate the next one?" she asked brightly.

"Sure, why not?" I said as I pushed the button for the ground floor.

"Well, you've been having all the fun, chopping things up and eviscerating people."

"Don't remind me, I have a delicate system."

She snorted and cuddled up close to me.

"Still have a girlfriend?" she whispered.

"Yes. And anywhere up to three fiancées, depending on who you ask."

"Now that sounds like a story," she said, working her nose into my collar.

"Maybe we could leave that for a time when a Magical duel isn't in the offing?" I suggested.

The residual effects of that damned room were still bouncing around my lymphatic system and I wanted very much to take Crystal in my arms. Thankfully, time with Tethys had taken what had been already relatively strong willpower and turned it into something iron-clad.

Still, having her pressed up against me like that just wasn't helping my blood pressure at all...

CHAPTER 16

The place seemed to have emptied of staff, which was good; I didn't want bystanders getting in the way (even the sort of people who worked at places like Michelangelo's). I sensed a few minds on the lower levels (aside from the ones I'd fought), but they wouldn't be in the way down there. I'd go have a 'chat' with them later.

We waited by the front door, I was sitting on one of the sofas with Crystal next to me, holding my hand.

"Why are you doing all this?" she asked after a while.

"What do you mean?"

"I mean all *this*. You... you went to war for me. Why? When men do things for me, it's because they want... something. But you... you don't. So why?"

"Why wouldn't I? You needed a hand, and goodness knows you were there for me. And this is hardly a war. I could tell you stories. But as for motivations, I look out for my friends, and I look out for my allies. You're both, how could I do anything else?"

"But this could get you into real trouble," she said, her tone worried.

"Hardly," I said with a chuckle, "this is the least stupid thing I've done in a while."

She sat there for a moment, chewing her lip, looking thoughtful.

"Thank you. In case I forget to say it later," she said finally.

"Any time," I said, squeezing her fingers.

"Magicians don't tend to go out of their way for non-humans. You're different from the others. I like that."

"Some of my best friends in the world are supernatural beings. I live with a Succubus, my land has Fairies on it and I can't get my Pixies to let me bath in peace. The one thing I've discovered is that humanity has very little to do with biology. It's who we choose to be that matters."

"You really believe that?" she asked, smiling at me.

"I have to."

"That sounded ominous," she said, nudging me.

The door opened before I could answer.

Showtime.

He was tall and thin, with dark hair and a neatly trimmed beard speckled with grey. My Mage Sight told me that he was a Sorcerer, a strong one, with an Air affinity. He wore a dark pinstripe suit and carried a cane, which was enchanted heavily, probably a weapon.

"Hello," I said as he walked past. He jumped. His energy surged and I recognised his signature instantly.

This was the man who'd scrambled that poor bugger Clayton's brain for Namia Sutton. Things started to fall into place at long last.

He raised his Shields and an impressive set of Mental Blocks that would have taken me half an hour to smash through. My defences were already in place and I had been steadily collecting force and heat over the last twenty minutes. I was in a good state for a fight, while he was caught on the back foot and he knew it.

"Let me guess," he said, looking us over, "Mathew Graves."

I nodded, not taking my eyes off him. He struck me as dangerous.

"I told that bitch we shouldn't try this. I told her,' you don't screw with the Archons'. Would she listen? Of course not."

"Namia does have some strange ideas, doesn't she?" I

replied.

He nodded. I felt him gathering static, readying lightning bolts, no doubt. I let him.

"So, how hard are you taking the whole 'kidnap the girl' thing?" he asked.

"They were going to put her in one of these rooms," I said coldly.

He winced.

"I told them they should treat her right. I gave *specific* instructions," he said, his tone almost pleading now.

"Why?" I asked, "Why do any of this?"

"I'm not telling you that! She'll kill me!"

"Only if she finds out, and who's going to tell her?" I pointed out.

He swallowed, "The idea was to turn her, or if she proved unwilling, adjust her; then use her as a Trojan Horse and have her either kill or enthral you after trading her back to you for some concession or another, that bit wasn't my department."

"Who are you, by the way?" I asked, digesting the information.

"Dirk Wallace," he answered slowly.

"And you support places like this, Dirk?"

"It's a free country," he said, rubbing the back of his head, looking uncomfortable.

"You know what they do here. You're a Magician, for heaven's sake! How can you allow it?"

His face went red.

"Not all of us are cut out to be heroes, Graves," he said, "I don't want to die. I barely want to live like I have been. But it's better than the alternative."

His voice was tortured, agonised.

"Then why stay with her?" I asked, "Why not just leave?"

"You think I'd be the first to try and leave her?" he asked, "People have tried! She finds them, she takes them to pieces and she makes the rest of us watch."

I looked him over, up and down. I looked in his grey eyes,

full of fear and desperation.

"Can't you go to the Conclave?" I asked, "Tell them what you know?"

"I wouldn't last a week, and that's assuming they believed me."

I nodded, understanding that idea better than anyone.

"What's her connection to Source? There have to be easier ways of making money."

"I don't know, I swear! All I know is that she's using her Legion to do the technical stuff. Nobody except Sutton really knows what Source even does. What I do know is that every time the subject takes a dose, he loses a little something, energy of some sort. I don't know where it goes or what Sutton's doing with it, but by now there has to be buckets of it stored somewhere."

"Do you know where the other factories are?"

He shook his head, "Since you hit the first one, all that information's been clamped down on."

I sighed, "Can you tell me anything that might be useful?"

"She hates you. Sutton. I've never seen her hate someone this much. And she's also scared. She gave explicit orders that your family and associates are to be avoided at all costs. They are untouchable."

"Then why go after Crystal?" I asked.

She squeezed my hand a bit tighter.

"The idea was to *turn* her. She'd have made the choice," Dirk said.

"Like hell, I would!" Crystal chimed in.

"Ten million. That's what I was going to offer you. And we'd have let you keep him if you could enthral him."

"Enthral? An Archon?"

"Saphyron Venom," Wallace said with a shrug, "It's potent stuff."

I shook my head, "What about the business side of things; distribution, sales; is there anything I can exploit?"

He shook his head, "Not that I can think of, but that's not where I work."

"Okay," I nodded, "You can go. Tell her whatever you want."

"Just like that?" he asked suspiciously.

I nodded again, taking a card out of my pocket and writing a number on it, "That's one of my people's numbers. If you think of anything or learn something I can use, leave a message there."

"Yes my lord," he said, "and... and thank you. I'll not forget this."

He started backing towards the door.

"It goes without saying that anything concerning my friends or family should be passed on with great speed?" I said.

He nodded quickly and left. I relaxed back into the sofa.

"You're just letting him go?" Crystal said, aghast.

I nodded again, "I know that look. Hopeless desperation. If we'd fought, we would have levelled this place, and he would probably have killed himself trying to escape. Besides, he was the hand, not the brain."

"You realise what he wanted for you? What he wanted me to do to you?" she asked.

"Not really. Vampires aren't a speciality of mine."

"Every Vampire race's venom is different," she explained, "Most are some variant of a painkiller and sedative; with the Strigoi it's a simple paralytic. Mine is... an enhancer of sorts, kind of a social lubricant, if you could put it like that. It's like a chemical aphrodisiac. If we give enough of it to our thralls, they become little more than mindless slaves to our desires. Hell, even a single bite is enough to make a victim very pliable to the Vampire that did it."

"Oh," I said.

Damn, Vampires were dangerous, who knew?

"I... I want to do that to you," she said, looking away, "Not the slave thing, I mean. But I want you to be my servant. That's the term, not the sentiment. I'd never want you subservient to anyone, especially me. I want to bond with you."

Well, that was a little terrifying.

"You've already fed me," she continued, "If you didn't want more, then you shouldn't have done that. If we feed and the victim remains alive, we start to bond with them; we can always find them, as long as they're within a dozen miles or so."

Ho boy...

I swear, no good deed ever goes unpunished.

We sat like that for a while.

"Say something," she said quietly, and then in barely a whisper, "And please don't hate me."

"Oh, I don't hate you. I mean, I'm a little more wary of letting you near my neck, but I don't hate you. It's your nature after all. But like I told you, I'm not a cheater. I'd not hurt my Cathy for anything in this world. It doesn't matter that she'd never know. I couldn't live with it, do you understand?"

She smiled, "Figures, I find a man worth spending time with, and he's too honourable to do it. This girl, she human?"

I nodded.

She grinned evilly, showing fang again, "So, what do you think, eighty, ninety years left to go?"

You know, that was the first time I'd ever thought about that?

I swallowed hard. Cathy...

When I thought I was just a Sorcerer, I knew I had centuries in terms of life span, more even. As an Archon, I didn't really have an expiry date. I was functionally immortal, not that this meant I couldn't die. I could die, alright, just not of old age.

Cathy wasn't a Magician. She was human, she was *mortal*.

She'd... eventually she'd...

I couldn't say for certain, but I think I went white as a sheet; certainly my hands started shaking.

"Sorry! Sorry, oh, God, sorry!" Crystal said, taking my shaking hands, "I meant it as a joke!"

"I know," I gasped, "Not your fault. Just never... never thought about it before, that's all."

There were tears in my eyes and she threw her arms around me.

"Hey, look," she said, "It's not all that bad. There are any number of ways a human can live longer. I know for a fact that living around Magicians makes people live longer and healthier. I can only imagine that she'd live a lot longer around an Archon."

I nodded, shaking with fear. How had I never thought of that before? It felt like there was a spectre hovering behind the girl I loved, one that was getting closer and closer with every passing second. One that I couldn't shield against. I'd fix it somehow. I'd find a way, damn it.

Crystal kissed my cheek and held me tight (which was very reasonable of her, bearing in mind the circumstances).

"It's okay, I'm good," I said. She pulled back and planted a little peck on my lips.

"Okay," she said, "You know, for someone as dangerous as you, you're surprisingly touchy-feely and girly."

"You're not the first to notice that," I said as I walked back towards the lift.

I spent the next half an hour turfing everyone out of that place. The rooms that were still full... those were some things I couldn't unsee. Crystal seemed to enjoy watching some of what was happening in the L-Rooms though.

I dragged the pile of mangled Ghouls out with Magic and left them in a twitching heap in an adjacent alley.

Then I had an awful time removing the fish from the aquarium.

"What are you doing?" Crystal asked after coming back from scaring off the last patron.

"Rescuing the fish?" I offered. I'd found a cooler and it was now full of the things and their water.

"Why?" she asked as I hefted the vegetable-girl in a

Shadow and led the way out.

"Because they'll die otherwise."

"Am I missing something? And why are we moving everyone out into the street?"

"You'll see," I said with a smile. She shook her head.

"You know, I'd have expected police by now," I said.

"They don't really respond to calls for help from this neighbourhood," she said sadly.

"I am really starting to hate this town."

"You and me both! I loved it before, you know? Before you came and messed it up with your ideas and your girl-feelings."

"Well, if you ever feel like moving, Stonebridge is nice."

"And what the hell would I do in Magician central? You know they actually enforce laws there? It's annoying."

I chuckled, "Just a thought."

We walked out into the night and I felt relief as we finally left that place behind. I took one more look with my Mage Sight to confirm that the building was empty of living things, and then I set to work. Gravitational Energy was not my thing, I had no aptitude for it, so this one was a strain, but it was also the cleanest way to do what needed to be done.

I was crafting the spell for half an hour. Crystal was getting impatient by the time I finally cast it.

The Earth shook and I felt nine tenths of my weight drop away for a long minute before there was a great, almost subsonic, 'whoomph' of energy, and the spell went into effect.

It was actually quite simple, if fiddly, and a bit of a power hog. The spell was a circle enclosing the warehouse under which Michelangelo's was built. The idea was to redirect gravity, absorb it into the fabric of the circle, and when enough was gathered, release it into the building.

In the two minutes the spell was charging, it reduced the gravity over three square miles to about a tenth, and absorbed all of that into an area approximately... one-hundredth of one percent of that.

The spell discharged it all in a little under two seconds.

The result was loud, and though I say so myself, impressive as hell. One second there was a warehouse on top of four sublevels. Then there was a massive, screeching clank, and approximately ten thousand gravities went to work. Suddenly there was just the one sub-level at the bottom of a pit, with everything compacted down to almost nothing. Heat wafted from the bottom of the hole, the pressure releasing it. I could smell molten metal and rock dust.

I turned to see Crystal staring, her mouth wide open.

"What?" I asked.

"Remind me never to make you mad," she said, awe in her voice.

"Still think I'm girly?" I asked.

"Darling, you're still holding a cool box full of rescue fish," she said with a smile.

Damn it...

"What do you want to do about Amber?" I asked (also dumped in the nearby alley).

"Nothing," Crystal said after a minute's thought, "She's made her bed."

I called an ambulance and ensured that they took the girl away first, for all the good it would do, and then I led Crystal around the corner with the fish-bucket in hand.

"Would it help if I came back with you? Smooth things over with Price?" I asked.

"You've done enough already."

"That's a yes. Where's the 'Carpet from here?"

"About two miles that way," she said, pointing to my right.

"You mind flying? It'll be faster."

She blushed, "Okay."

I wrapped us up in Shadow and she 'whooped' in glee as we darted up and over the buildings, a Will Shield in front of her face so she could see out as we flew.

"This is amazing!" she squealed. It made me smile.

It didn't take long to find the place, and I brought us in for a gentle landing on the driveway. Guards pointed guns until Crystal made herself known and they calmed down. I added a little extra warmth to my casket of fish (it was a cool night) and followed her in, up the stairs and to Price's office.

Francois didn't say a word except to announce us. We had to wait a few minutes before we were invited in.

"Good evening, my lord," Price said, "Crystal, where have you been?"

Crystal swallowed under the scrutiny as she sat down.

"I must apologise, Miss Price," I said, trying to lend my friend a hand, "I decided on a little entertainment this evening, and, needing a guide, I called Crystal. She agreed to lend me some of her time, and we adjourned to a lovely little spot called... ooh, what was it? Michael something. Anyway, a great time was had by all."

Price was tapping her long fingers on the table, glaring at me.

"You were with her the whole time?" she asked.

"I was."

"You made sure that there were no... complications with management?"

"Nothing that will ever come up again. I think that place was a little flat, nothing to recommend it. I should think they'd be shutting soon."

Crystal seemed to choke for a moment over my terrible pun. Price smiled slightly. We understood each other, and yet we still had our parts to play.

"You'll have to pay for her time," Price said, "This isn't some candy jar for you to stick your fingers in whenever you want. That's what, four hours? Premium time. Five thousand, and I must insist that all bookings go through my people in the future, understand?"

"Of course, Ma'am," I said, reaching into my satchel, "I trust that Crystal won't be penalised for my poor behaviour?"

I put five grand on the table, and Price took it, counting it quickly and professionally.

"Of course, not. You were to blame, I'm sure."

I nodded, "Any luck with our other enterprise?"

"Some, I'll let you know when I have something concrete. Can Crystal be of any further use to you tonight?"

"Oh no, I'm quite exhausted as it is, thank you," I said, standing.

Price smiled, "Alright then. Feel free to come back whenever you like, my lord."

I bowed slightly and withdrew with Crystal.

"Best of luck," I whispered.

"Thank you, Mathew. For everything. For helping me through that."

"You're welc-"

She planted another kiss on me, and I have to say that it was one of the sweetest, most gentle ones I'd ever received, full of meaning, but not in any way tawdry; it was a kiss for a dear friend, and a truly wonderful thing.

"Don't wait too long before visiting me again," she said, stroking my cheek before biting her lip with those cute fangs of hers.

And then she was gone, darting through a convenient doorway.

Bloody hell, I needed a shower. First a hot one to get the stink of that town off me, and then a cold one to wash the memory of the Vampire away.

Can't say that I was expecting the second one to be entirely successful.

CHAPTER 17

Even after all of that, my night wasn't quite over. I had to go to the Grotto and persuade the nymphs to look after my rescue fish. Well, that didn't take too much work, they thought they were pretty and the water was more than warm enough to accommodate them. The trouble was getting away from the Pixies once they'd found me. Not just because they wouldn't let me go, but because I couldn't bear to leave them. In a world where Gomorrah existed, and pain was just a corner away, those three girls were a soothing balm that let me remember that Creation was a beautiful thing.

In the end, I settled down against the roots of my Willow tree and slept with the Pixies wrapped around my chest. It felt good.

Naturally, as so often happens these days, I didn't wake up with the same number of women I'd gone to sleep with...

This time it was Gwendolyn.

She was propped up on an elbow, lying next to me, her lovely eyes watching me as she stroked my hair. I smiled, and she did the same.

"Gwen?" I said groggily, no idea why I said that, and she blushed, waking me up a little, "Sorry, Gwendolyn. What are you doing here?"

"No, that's okay, I like Gwen," she said, "I felt you. Your connection to this place, it buzzed through our bond."

The Pixies perked up enough to yawn and glare at us for waking them. I stroked their heads one by one and they relaxed back onto me. Gwen smiled and laid down next to us.

"I love it here," she whispered, "it's beautiful, and so

peaceful."

I nodded my agreement, relaxing again.

"Oh, you little snake!" Evelina said, startling everyone. The Pixies legged it immediately and ended up in the branches above us, glaring down at the interloping Unseelie.

Gwendolyn started giggling, "I sent a note," she protested, "You were invited."

"You sent it by pigeon. By a very *fat*, very *slow*, pigeon," Evi said with a glare, dropping down on my other side.

I groaned and sat up, rubbing my face. I was running on maybe three hours sleep, and I had the headache to prove it. I looked at my watch and found that it was just before seven. Classes started at nine, and I needed to be at breakfast in an hour or Cathy would be crotchety all day.

"Atticus is a lovely pigeon. Very reliable, always gets where he needs to go," Gwendolyn replied.

"If it weren't for the fact that you'd use the resultant tears to lure him into another cuddle, I'd have *eaten* that pigeon," Evi muttered.

Gwen smiled at Evi and the Unseelie glared back.

I rubbed my eyes again and reached into the lake to splash some water on my face.

"You're usually more alert than this, Beloved, long night?" Evelina asked.

I nodded and yawned, "Destroyed a torture house in Gardenia; stayed up past my bed time."

I felt soft hands on my neck and shoulder as Gwen touched me, soothing and relaxing. It felt terrific, something utterly sincere in the gesture that made me want to go right back to sleep and stay there with them.

Naturally, Evelina's touch was a little different, but no less interesting. I sighed happily, but forced myself to wake up.

"I wish I could stay longer," I said sadly, looking around at them.

"Really?" Evelina said, "How interesting."

She grinned evilly and I shook my head. It took me the

better part of my hour to rouse the Pixies and say goodbye to them and the princesses. I felt an awful wrench leaving the Grotto, but I did it, and Shadow-Walked back to Windward in record time.

I showed up to breakfast half asleep, but perked right up after Cathy kissed me good morning. She had that effect.

I was feeling a bit more recovered when English rolled around. 'Romeo and Juliette' this term. Allow me to summarise: Love, cock-up, bad communication, sad ending; waste of time that could have been spent reading 'The Hobbit'. Hopkins was still making us plough through it, depressing though it was.

"Mister Graves, a word?" she said as we started filing out. Some students started tittering, which made her glare and them run.

"Yeah?" I said.

"Lucille needs you. She... she's not in a good way, Matty. She feels so guilty."

"Of course I'll see her," I said immediately, "When?"

"You have a study period now, right? Then now," she said, waving her hand to open a portal.

I followed her through and into a foyer. It was white and beautiful, with a small fountain in the centre, the basin filled with bright fish. Some of Palmyra's battle nuns were in evidence, looking tense and upset.

"Come on," Hopkins said, leading the way around a corner and deeper into the house.

The whole place seemed homey and comfortable; the floors were polished wood or covered in thick, bright carpet. There was some beautiful art on the walls and the windows were wide and let in bright light. The house was warded like mine, and was surrounded by trees and lakes from what I could see. It was a beautiful place.

Hopkins opened a set of double doors leading to a bedroom. It was dark in there, but I saw my sister on the bed, curled up into a ball.

"Lucille?" Hopkins said, "I brought him. You have to talk."

"No, no," she whispered, "I can't bear it, go away!"

She radiated misery and pain, it nearly made me weep.

I lowered my shields as I approached and she gasped as she felt me. I sat on the bed next to her and she looked up after a moment. I smiled down at her tear-streaked face and took her hand.

She could feel my emotions, each and every one. By looking at her, I made sure she understood the context. There was nothing but affection in me for her. She was my sister; I knew there wasn't a mean bone in her body. I knew that Sutton's word and her two siblings' opinion were against me, and I was sorry that she'd been upset by my gambit.

"Really?" she asked in a small voice.

"Of course. I could never stay mad at you. You mean too well. I put you in a horrible position, and I'm sorry. If I'd know for a second it would do this to you, I'd have brought out the evidence I had at the beginning and had it done with."

She burst into tears again. I rubbed her shoulder, and she sat up to hug me tight.

"I'm sorry I doubted you," she said, "I've known Namia so long. I never thought she'd say things like that. I never knew she was like that."

"I understand," I said, stroking her hair, "Jen told me about Nash, I know that you and the others have every right to be wary of a Shadowborn."

"But we have no right to feel that way about *you*. Not a one! You have proved, time and again, that you're a good man, that you're doing your best for us and those around you. I mean, even the idea of being responsible for people dying broke your heart. How could I have forgotten that?"

"Namia's your friend, you've known her for centuries. You've known me for months. I understand, really I do. I swear, you can check, I don't blame you at all."

"I can't believe she fooled me," Palmyra said, "The sheer Will she must have to control her emotions like that... And that should have been a clue! They were always clear and perfect, no variation at all, like they were programmed responses. Yours are raw and alive, I wasn't thinking."

"Alright," I said firmly, pulling back to look in her eyes, "I'm going to say this once and then we're going to forget all about it, okay?"

She sniffed but met my eyes.

"I forgive you. I never blamed you to begin with, but I forgive you. You're my big sister, and you were trying to be someone else's too. I couldn't hold that against you. You know I'm telling the truth?"

She nodded, smiling a little.

"Good, now why don't you get up and, for God's sake, shower? Because I lived in a forest for a three week camping trip that involved getting covered in Basilisk faeces and didn't smell this bad."

She squawked a little at that and swatted me hard enough to knock me off the bed.

"You arse," she said, stepping on my stomach as she went towards the shower, hugging Hopkins on the way. It was as if the room had lightened, the oppressive atmosphere gone in an instant. She radiated contentment and relief.

I smiled as I stood and saw Hopkins cuffing away a tear.

"You tell anyone, and I'll brain you," she said with a glare as she saw me noticing.

I nodded.

"So, how do we convince the others that I'm not a bastard? I take it they still believe Sutton?"

Hopkins nodded, "That may take some more doing. You may not like it."

"It's worth it," I said, actually meaning it.

Hopkins smiled proudly at me.

"Stupid Shadowborn," she said fondly.

That was how we ended up back in that black room a few days later. All five of us again, plus Kron and Killian's body-guards, none of whom were looking at me fondly. Palmyra and Hopkins stood behind me. Palmyra had arranged the meeting, told them I wanted to make nice.

"You called this meeting, Lord Shadow," Killian said, using the title ironically, "Speak."

"You think I'm a villain," I said simply, "How do I fix that?"

Kron's expression changed, confusion crossing her features.

"What do you mean?" she asked.

"I've lost your trust, how do I get it back?" I asked, "I'm willing to do anything you reasonably ask."

"You put qualifiers on it?" Killian asked, glaring.

"Trust is a two-way street, Lord Death," I replied, "Would you fully trust two people so willing to cast you in the role of the antagonist? One of whom very nearly beat you to death?"

At this, Kron looked chagrined, but she held her position and her glare.

"I ask again, what's it going to take? You want another look in my head? Do you want me to hold a Truth Stone? What?"

Killian stepped forward, his dark eyes boring into mine.

"You're serious about this?" he asked.

"The alternative is making enemies of you two for life, and I don't have the energy for that," I said, "Just tell me how to make this right."

His eyes softened, just a very little, but enough that I had hope of a rapprochement. The others conferred Telepath-ically for a few moments, I could feel it but didn't intrude, even if I felt a little snubbed. Finally Killian nodded and turned back to me.

"Trust must be rebuilt. As far as we're concerned, you attacked a member of our extended families. You are a declared

Danger. So, the first thing you must do is agree not to go near her again."

"Without conceding the point or the issue, I agree to the term," I said.

He nodded, "And you will have a Watcher until we can be sure that we can trust you again."

"What kind of Watcher?" I asked.

"Demise," Killian said, the bodyguard walked forward, "Where you go, she goes, what you do, she does. For as long as it takes. You shower, she does, you sleep, she sleeps. You need to take a piss in the night, you wake her and she goes with you. There is not a time when she is not with you. The second you leave her sight is the one in which you fail, understand?"

Hopkins was quite right, I didn't like that at all (which wasn't good; she was the *worst* 'I-told-you-so-er' I knew). I wanted to point out the million or so problems and complications that this would cause for my daily life, not to mention all the ethical issues inherent to having a *woman* shadow a *man* in such intimate conditions, and indeed I opened my mouth to do exactly that... but then I thought about it, and I looked at Killian and Kron. I saw the look in their eyes and I realised that the very conditions of the test were themselves, a test (very crafty of them, actually), and that protesting not only wouldn't do me any good, it would damage my standing further.

I was trapped, locked into *months* (or maybe more!) of a stranger watching my every move, seeing everything I did. It represented a complete removal of privacy and the idea repulsed me more than I can reasonably describe. But in the end, I accepted it, because I'd been telling the truth when I said I didn't have the energy to make enemies of them. I had quite enough problems in my life without adding them to the list.

"There are certain things relating to my Liaisons that may require some leeway," I finally said, suddenly feeling a little sick.

"No," Killian replied, "It's all or nothing. She will not interfere with anything you do. She will only report back, and keep you safe should the need arise."

"Alright," I said, still unhappy, "She won't be sharing my bed or anything, will she? Because my girlfriend's nearing the limit of her tolerance in that department."

Demise looked disgusted. Palmyra laughed.

"Oh these two are going to get on just fine," Hopkins said, trying to conceal a smirk (and failing *dismally*).

"And how do we explain this to the school?" I asked her.

"I'll have to do a little mental Magic," Hopkins replied, "But it's not an issue. This isn't the first time Demise has been a Watcher. She knows how to blend in. We'll tell anyone that asks that she's an exchange student, not that I expect too many questions."

"Well, if you're sure," I said, with a resigned sigh. I didn't see how this was going to work. Demise may not have been very approachable, but she was beautiful enough that at least some of the four hundred or so hormonal boys were *bound* to notice her, but that wasn't my business.

"Demise, how are you with Shadow-Walking?" I said.

"What's that?" she asked, her eyes narrowed.

"Nothing much," I said lightly, "You don't mind staring into infinite darkness, do you?"

"Matty, don't be a prick," Hopkins said, swatting my arm.

"Fine," I said, "How long is this to last?"

"Until you've persuaded us you can be trusted again," Killian said, not answering the question. Like I suspected, months or worse.

I sighed; this was going to be *interminable*.

Hopkins portalled the three of us to a dark room some-where, where Demise collected a few things into a duffel bag. From there, it was back to school; Hopkins hadn't stopped grinning the entire time.

"Would you stop that?" I asked.

"This is pretty funny. If there was one person on the face

of the Earth who'd *hate* a Watcher of this invasive nature, it's you."

"She'll break before I do, she has to watch me shower and pee."

"And how much alone time did you think you were going to get with Cathy in this situation?" Hopkins asked, her smile turning positively *evil*.

My mouth dropped open in horror.

"No..." I said.

"Yes," Hopkins replied gleefully.

"No!" I said, turning to Demise, "Tell me you're not planning to watch *that*?!"

"You do it, I have to watch it," Demise said, hefting her duffel into a more comfortable position, "Including any and all intimate activities."

"Oh... just bollocks," I said, now feeling thoroughly down.

"I can't wait to hear how you're planning to tell Cathy about this," Hopkins said.

I muttered something and led Demise out of Hopkins' classroom, her laughter following me.

I led her towards Kimmel, "So, how did you get this job?" I asked her.

"I'm the best," she said simply, glaring at me as we walked, she didn't elaborate.

"You don't like me much, do you?"

"Do I have to?"

"No, but it might help if you didn't hate me quite so much. I'm not Nash, you know," I replied.

She snorted, "Nash was much stronger than you."

"Can't argue with that."

I showed her my room and she dropped her duffel on one of my chairs.

"This is it?" she asked, "This is where you live?"

"No, this is just school. You can take the bed, if you like, I have a sleeping bag."

"As do I. I don't need your creature comforts, Shadow-born."

"Mathew. If you're going to be here, my name is Mathew."

She snorted again; it was beginning to annoying me.

I went to lunch, where I found Bill and Cathy. Bill wasn't looking well; he was pale and a little shivery. He perked up immediately after seeing Demise, though.

"Well hello," he said, standing to offer his hand, "William Hedrin, at your service."

She ignored him and put her tray down at the far end of the table from us. She'd drawn a few looks (surprisingly few, actually) and cheerlessly ignored them all. Thankfully she looked young enough that she could just about blend in, even if her outfit wasn't exactly school-friendly (black on black).

"So, who's the icicle?" Cathy asked.

"My new minder," I said with a grimace, I explained the situation and Cathy looked over at me.

She, very deliberately, so that Demise could see, turned my head and planted a kiss on my lips that made me tingle from forehead to toes.

"She wants to watch? I can live with that."

I went bright red and Bill started choking on his fruit salad, "God, don't say that kind of thing where I can hear you! Damn!" he complained.

Fun though the thought was, neither Cathy nor I were into that sort of thing. We were firmly of the opinion that while public displays of affection were just fine, public displays of genitals were *not*. She wouldn't even take off her jumper without three locks and a shield spell between her and potential witnesses, goodness only knew how she changed her clothes every day.

Essentially that meant that I was rather thoroughly screwed (just not in the fun way), and had a great many cold showers to look forward to (if I wasn't already harbouring a pretty healthy dislike for Namia Sutton, this would have clinched it, let me tell you...).

"You alright, by the way?" I asked Bill after he'd coughed up an unfeasibly large strawberry that had somehow gone down the wrong pipe, "You're looking a little sick, want me to take a look?"

"Naw, that's alright," he answered, "My new girl kept me up late is all."

"Bill, calling your left hand a girl doesn't fool anyone," Cathy said.

"Damn, Cath, I'm eating here!" I said.

"She's real!" Bill complained.

"Sure, sure," Cathy said, pinching a spoonful of my pudding.

After that, Demise followed me everywhere, and Cathy seemed to take her presence quite well, even if she did have to tone down our time together a little.

True to her instructions, Demise did everything with me. Showering was a nightmare, but in the end, I just covered the important bits with Shadows and carried on. She showered at the same time, in the same stall, and I put my back to her while she did (a courtesy she never did me, by the way). She slept in my room, watched me work, went to the bathroom with me (same arrangement). It wasn't fun.

There were times when I thought that students or faculty were going to comment, but they seemed to barely even notice Demise, a glazed look coming over their eyes when they looked at her. It didn't take me long to discover a discreet spell that clung to her aura, which made her hard to remember, see or hear with any clarity. I asked her about it, but she refused to teach it to me.

After that kind of start, I was fairly certain that I would go insane before we were done, but I eventually found out that Demise wasn't *all* bad.

It was late on the third day, about nine at night and I rubbed my eyes to clear them as I finished up a bit of Physics prep before heading out, walking towards the Maths department.

"Chess club tonight," I told Demise.

"You play?" she asked, it was the first personal question she'd asked me.

"I do. You?"

"Some," she replied.

And wow, was she good. She beat Bill twice and Cathy once in the first half hour. She and I then set to and had a marathon match that lasted well past the end of the hour and ended in a stalemate.

She grunted, "Not bad, Graves. You were careless in your opening."

"And you were sloppy with your Steinitz Gambit," I replied.

"I thought I had the advantage," she said with a shrug.

"That's what I wanted you to think."

She actually gave me the littlest smile at that.

"I'll get you next time," she replied.

"Promises, promises."

"You talk big for someone who barely managed a draw," she said.

"I'm eighteen, what's your excuse?"

She snorted again, but this time it was a little more friendly.

As promised, she slept on the floor in a sleeping bag. She did accept my spare pillow with ill grace (and used it every night).

She came on dates with Cathy and I. She watched what we did with what can only be described as disinterest, but wow, did she watch everything. I think she paid more attention when we were kissing than when we weren't, though, the pervert.

When we went out to eat, I bought food for Demise. When I asked her what she liked, she just said 'anything'. It took a good seven meals before she was willing to express a preference. She liked beef a lot, though she also tried to hide it. When I bought her ice cream, she almost cried; I don't think she'd had it before.

"You don't eat out much, do you?" I asked once we were alone again, which was often.

We were in my room, and I was reading a book just before bed.

"Not really," she said from her sleeping bag, "It's a waste."

"Of what?"

"Time, money, capacity. Food is fuel, nothing more."

"Even triple chocolate fudge?"

"Especially that."

"What do you do for fun?" I asked, "Life can't be all about duty."

"I play chess with my sisters. I practice my Magic, I spar. I learn; I make myself a better Magician."

"So, chess and fighting? That's all?"

"I need nothing else. It is an honour to serve my Lord," she said with finality.

"I know you don't *need* anything else, but don't you want things?" I asked, "Everyone wants something."

"Not me. I have everything I want."

She went quiet for a while before speaking again, "What do you want, Shadowborn?"

"I have Cathy," I said with a smile, "That's all I've ever *really* wanted. If I could trade all my Magic for one more day with her than I'm supposed to have, I'd do it in a heartbeat."

I felt her attention on me and turned to see her eyes boring into me, "That kind of attitude has led to more destruction than you can possibly imagine."

"Meaning?" I asked.

"That Love put more spells into that Grimoire of yours than hate ever did," she said, closing her eyes again.

"I don't get it."

She sighed and looked at me again, "Goddess forbid, but if your Cathy died tomorrow, is there any length you wouldn't go to if you thought you could get her back? To see her, hold her again?"

"I... I can't answer that."

"That means no, and that's what I'm talking about. The power of the Archon is the stuff that dreams are made of... or nightmares, depending on the man. You could be an awful nightmare, Mathew Graves. One that I will have to dispose of, or die trying. And you're too smart for my comfort, too smart by far, and too patient. The last one was ruthless and strong, but he wasn't smart."

"I'm not him!" I protested.

"I know. Whether that's a good thing or a bad one remains to be seen."

She went to sleep and I muttered as I followed suit.

I swear, it would be easier to list the people who *don't* think I'm a monster in waiting than the ones that do...

CHAPTER 18

Days passed, and pleasantly enough. Demise wasn't as oppressive a presence as she'd been, and playing chess with her before bed was actually quite fun. We won, lost and drew about equally as we got used to each others' strategies and adapted.

She swore blind that she hated movies, but she started shushing me mercilessly whenever I had one on and asked her a question. She loved listening to the radio; she was actually quite sweet to watch as she tapped her foot along to something and then immediately stopped when I noticed.

She appeared quite determined not to enjoy anything she was exposed to, but couldn't seem to help herself. Cathy seemed equally determined to corrupt her, too, and even offered to take her to the hairdresser, which led to me being dragged there and spending two hours on a sodding sofa while I waited, Demise's eyes constantly darting at me to make sure I was still there.

Bill... he was getting strange. He now owed me something in the area of five hundred pounds, and Cathy another two, and he was spending every free afternoon in Stonebridge. His grades had dropped to dead last in our classes, and he always seemed to have a cold. I kept offering to have a look, and he kept refusing.

Events came to a head that Saturday.

I never saw it coming.

My phone rang in the afternoon, just after lunch, as Cathy and I were settling in for a few hours under the Old Oak and, if things proceeded the way they usually do, a few interludes in a large bush behind the bike sheds.

What with Cathy lying on my shoulder, her nose and lips happily moving on my neck, there was no way in hell I was answering the damned thing. It rang and rang, and I just kept ignoring it until Cathy eventually grunted and pulled the thing out of my pocket and pressed accept.

"Bill, so help me, you'd better be dying," Cathy said.

She went white and passed it over with a shaking hand. I took it from her.

"Hello?" I said.

"Matty, you've got to help me," Bill's terrified voice said, "I'm hurt and I'm somewhere I shouldn't be."

"Where are you?" I asked.

He gave me a meaningless (to me) address in Stonebridge and I stood, "Alright, I'm coming. Hang in there; I'll be there in ten minutes."

I hung up.

"I've got to go get him," I said.

Cathy nodded, her lip trembling.

"He'll be alright, Cath."

She nodded again and I ran for the indoors, where I'd find a patch of Shadow deep enough to open a Gate.

"Don't forget your agreement, Shadowborn," Demise said, right on my heels.

"What? Oh, sure," I said, finding a dark enough alcove under the stairs in a nearby corridor, "put your arms around my torso and close your eyes. Don't open them until I tell you. The Shadow Realm isn't something you can unsee."

I wasn't entirely sure anyone but me *could* see in the there, but it felt like the right thing to say, and any sensible Magician would trust those instincts.

She nodded and followed instructions. I wrapped my Shadows around her and opened the Gate, stepping through.

I still wasn't used to seeing the Shadow-version of everything, but I was getting better at navigation. I found the right street in only a couple of tries (I'd consulted Google-maps before going). The address was a large house in one of the newer districts of Stonebridge, to the north of the City Centre.

I stepped out of the Shadow Realm under a tree in front of the house. It was a tall, red brick building with a tiled roof and small windows, three stories high.

"We're clear," I said. Demise let go and stepped back.

I cast Mage Sight and saw a single aura in the house, towards the rear. I started moving cautiously. Demise was hot on my heels.

"Something's off," I said.

I'd felt something strange... something I didn't recognise. I didn't even know if it was Magic, but it was very definitely there...

"Like what?" Demise asked.

"I don't know," I replied, "Shields up, just in case."

She nodded and I felt her defences snap on, much faster than mine, I might add. I strode up to the front door and set a lock-pick spell into it. It clicked open and I pushed it away from me.

We walked into the house. Nobody and nothing presented itself.

The whole place was tastefully furnished and elegant. The owners were apparently comfortably well off. Was the owner's daughter Bill's new girlfriend?

Bill was lying on his side in a large conservatory, right in the middle of a rug. Demise stepped towards him. I clamped my hand around her arm (well, her shielded arm), and she glared back.

"What?" she asked impatiently.

"He's not bleeding. None of his bones are broken. He's just sleeping."

"He's not hurt?" Demise asked, now suspicious herself.

"And I don't detect any Magic, either."

"Then it's safe," she said, trying to move forwards.

"Not what I said."

I called my Will and tried to move Bill. My Magic hit the

edge of the rug and just drained away.

"Sneaky bastards," I said, seeing it at last, "Spelleater trap built into the floor under the rug. Very clever work, you couldn't see it before it was activated."

I called extra power and probed the edges of the mat with my Will. I yanked on two corners and pulled both it and Bill away, revealing a sigil carved into the tile that hurt to look at.

"Bloody hell, who made that?" I asked, rubbing my eyes.

"Someone very powerful and stupidly talented," Demise said, looking around her.

I called force and aimed at the Sigil, putting extra strength into the Spell before releasing it. It smashed into the stone and a crack broke the enchantment.

"Idiots, it wouldn't have held me," I said, "The best it would have done was slow me down a little, and why would they bother?"

I should learn not to say things like that. The Universe likes answering questions of that sort in hilarious ways. That hurt.

There was a Magical crump, and a weight descended on the whole place. My nose started bleeding and I felt light-headed. Worse, I couldn't feel my Shadows. They were just... gone, like that part of me had been cut off. It wasn't pleasant.

"Wha?" I managed as more Magic poured into the perimeter, and I saw black flames surround the house as the sky turned black. Before my eyes, the fire burned hotter and dissolved into a massive, surrounding portal.

I saw fire, darkness and molten rock through that hole in the universe. And Hell poured through. Demons by the dozen. They looked confused at first, but then they looked right at us, even though we were concealed by walls; it was like they could feel us. Some didn't even have eyes, but still they turned to face us.

"Graves, what's going on?" Demise asked.

"Unless I'm very much mistaken, we've walked into a

Dimension-Trap, I've just lost my Shadows, and in a very short time, we're going to be overrun by Demons."

"Upstairs, now!" she said, yanking Bill up and onto her shoulder before leading the way up the big stairs as the Demons came for us, horrific creatures, every one of them, things drawn from the darkest human nightmares. I saw leech-like horrors with piercing limbs, massive spider-creatures with human faces, quadrupedal horrors with hooves and scales, a hundred different things, and no two exactly alike.

I was reminded of a verse from a hymn. It used to be one of my favourites. Not so much now:

...I danced on a Friday when the sky turned black,
It's hard to dance with the Devil on your back...

I was calling Light, Fire and Force as we ran, I felt Demise leeching Entropy from the environment.

She pulled us into one of the front bedrooms.

"Are we in Hell, or has Hell come to us?" she asked.

"The latter," I said, "I think that they surrounded us with a Dimensional wall. It's not my area, only barely touched on them in my reading, but we just have to hold out long enough for whoever's casting it to run out of juice."

"Are you sure?"

"No, but it's our best bet."

A demon ripped through the floor next to Bill. I used my Will to yank it away from him and a lance of Force to rip its head off. It fell to the ground in pieces as another one came through the door, a snake-looking thing with insect legs and a mouth full of acid. Demise got that one, a beam of deep purple searing through it and killing it instantly, leaving it to crumble into ash.

"Definitely still on Earth," I said, "The Demons are being banished. They aren't dying!"

I used my Mage Sight to track the Demons and send Chaos beams at them. The attacks were effective, but draining. I missed my Shadows.

That house was getting torn up pretty badly; my attacks

had already ripped enough holes in the floor that a good third of the rooms across from me simply collapsed, crushing several Demons on their way down. A bit of the ceiling fell in on us, and I barely got a dome of Will in place to deflect both it, and the Demon that tried to land on Bill.

Demise banished it, tearing another hole through one of the supporting walls; the house creaked ominously.

"We need to get out of here!" I said over the groans, picking Bill up with Will and aiming Force at the Wall behind us. I blasted it away, raining brick and cement onto the lawn. Demise jumped out first, Death Magic lashing out as she fell, disintegrating half a dozen of the monsters. I came after, throwing out Chaos Spheres that detonated on impact and threw bodies and limbs all about the place.

My Will deposited me gently on the ground, and I laid Bill down under my Shields. Really speaking, these Demons weren't much of a threat to me. They were mindless animals, not a one was sentient and none of them had that Hell-Magic that might have posed a problem. Any that got to my shields simply bounced off, not even denting them.

I was actually feeling pretty confident... but then these little black, scaly goblin-looking things came out of nowhere. They screeched loudly, but otherwise appeared harmless. When you had seventeen feet long, six legged, horned and spiked black lions with six inch fangs charging at you, things that looked like mutated toddlers weren't something you sweated.

We started paying a lot *more* attention when they exploded against out shields. I lost half of my layers to that first hit, and barely deflected the next two out of the way before they detonated.

Demise wasn't so lucky. Her shields didn't have as many built-in redundancies as mine, and she lost the lot on the first hit. If it weren't for the temporary clearance made by the explosion, she would have been torn to pieces. She staggered back to her feet, weaving a little, and I covered her as she began to restore her defences.

And that's when the *real* attack materialised.

I felt it coming. My heart soared at its presence, my soul cried out in joy and my mind nearly collapsed in dread.

Black Magic. My temptation, my darkest desire.

I got a Will shield in the way, the only defence I could manage without my Shadows. But it wasn't aimed at me.

Demise saw it coming as well, but too late. She still managed to twist mostly out of the way. The beam grazed her side instead of piercing her heart, but she still fell to the muddy earth with a horrible scream. I threw out a wave of energy that tossed and burned every Demon nearby so I could reach for her and drag her under my shields.

"You alright?!" I shouted over the cacophony that surrounded us.

"I'll live, but I can't fight them and this," she said, gesturing at the already black wound. Her voice trembled and tears ran down her face.

The Demons gathered for another leap, and then a voice dragged from the deepest pit of Hell spoke out in a language that made my ears feel dirty just hearing it. The Demons halted, some even retreated. Two men appeared through a hole in the Demon ranks, tall and strong-looking, perfectly attractive, in dark suits and tasteful jewellery.

At least that's how they *wanted* to appear.

The reality was something quite different.

My Mage Sight let me see them how they really were. They were twisted, hunched little things, their wings, once massive, white and beautiful, were black and bent, feathers missing in clumps. Their skin was green-tinged and blotchy, their eyes black and staring, like sharks'. They wore rags and the tattered remains of armour, once burnished gold and now encrusted with what looked like eons of muck and filth.

Angels. Of the Fallen variety. They all but *pulsed* with the Black. That dreadful power called to me, begged to be used, to be a part of me. I clenched my fists and walled that temptation up behind a barrier of sheer stubbornness.

"Greetings, Lord Shadow," said the one on the left with a deep bow, "I am Illiel. I have an offer for you."

"Oh? Do tell," I said ironically, replenishing my energy stores while I talked.

"Don't bargain with it!" Demise hissed, still focussing on her injury, which seemed to be spreading, but one lethal problem at a time.

"She would say that," Illiel said, "Give us the woman, and you and your friend may leave unmolested, my word."

"You know, Dee, I have to say it's nice that I'm not the one they're after for a change," I said. She glared at me.

"You're waiting for the barrier to drop; stalling," Illiel said, "It's not going to. I am its power source. And I think we can both agree that you are no match for me."

"Is that so? Then why are you trying to bargain?"

Illiel laughed heartily, it made me feel sick.

"Clever, clever boy, I can see why *he* likes you so much, but this isn't the time to go to war with Us. Give us the Death Mage. Now, please."

The other one stepped forward, and a black sword appeared in its hand, radiating Death.

"What's his name?" I asked, pointing at the swordsman.

"Rashur, why?" Illiel asked.

"For my biographer, mostly."

I let Rashur have it, a Chaos beam that would have taken a lesser creature's head off. But he was so *fast*! He dodged and took the tiniest hit to his shoulder, which was barely enough to scorch something and send him tumbling back, grunting in pain.

"Is she really worth your soul, Magician?" Illiel said, darting away as I sent a similar beam after him and missed entirely, "Think of what we could give you. I'm willing to bargain. But if we take you here, that's it, you come Home with us."

That horrified me no end, I can tell you. But even if I could trust him, which I couldn't, I wasn't leaving Demise to them. She was only here because of me. I'd be damned before I just left her to face Hell alone.

Even if it cost me everything.

Rashur threw a lance of Shadows right at me, and I had to redirect Light to break them.

That steamed me a little. Using Shadows against *me*? That was annoying. I let the Light continue its path, and Rashur howled as the beam grazed him, tumbling and running out of the way. The Demons resumed their advance.

Light! It was as if the word popped into my mind.

Light of the Soul.

What?

The easiest thing in the world...

Oh!

No, that wouldn't work, surely?

Then again, the Fallen Angel had howled when the light had hit it. And it was still smoking...

Worth a try, if it didn't do the trick, I could just go back to what I was doing.

I called a big chunk of my Magic and let it gather in my hand. I took a moment to deflect a ball of Black Magic with Will before it was ready. Then I lifted my hand, and cast Mage Light.

But not just any Mage Light; this one burned like the sun, I had to close my eyes to keep from being blinded. It made me grunt in discomfort, but I heard the Fallen Angels and Demons *scream*.

Light of the Soul. In a very real way, that's exactly what it was, a burning piece of the very heart of me. It wouldn't have worked this well in any other situation. In a way, Illiel had made it possible.

He'd brought Hell to Earth, soaking this little patch of the Newtonian World with the full power of the Pit, making the demons stronger and faster, giving the Fallen the power to manifest fully. But that came with a cost, because along with all the strength of Hell came its weaknesses.

Under normal circumstances, this sort of light wouldn't

be that much of a threat to a Demon; sure, it would make them uncomfortable, maybe give them the equivalent of a sunburn, scare them a little, but *here*, where Hell soaked into the Earth, it was something different, something... more.

Light of the Soul, light made by a human soul, itself a tiny piece of Creation, the part that brought forth the stars, a teeny piece of what gives life to our little blue marble. Hell couldn't tolerate that.

Hell burned at the sight of it and Hell *screamed* at its touch.

It was a little strange for me. As a Shadowborn, I hadn't really made use of Light before, not in any subtle way, but now it was saving my life, and using it felt as natural as breathing, like it was *precisely* the right thing to do.

Demons started to smoke, sizzle and burn. Many burst into flames right there. A couple of those Goblin-things exploded, causing more carnage. The rest started running.

The Angels screamed as their feathers caught fire and their skin turned black. Rashur leapt for me, sword held high. His eyes were burnt out; his lips were charred, pulling back over his teeth as they burned away.

He brought his sword down and I caught it with my Will, wrenching him forward along with it and right into my ball of Light. He let go of his weapon and screamed one more time as the light touched his skin and turned him to ash. There was a boom as he was banished, flattening what remained of the grass for twenty metres in every direction and taking a chunk out of my shields. There was no killing him in the Newtonian world, but that *had* to hurt.

Illiel was running. He had to, his wings had been burned down to stumps. If he got away, he could continue sending waves and waves of Demons into my Light until I was all out of energy, or he was, and I didn't like the idea of having to out-last him, not if he was standing in Hell.

He had his back to me and was running for the barrier between Hell and Earth. I picked up Rashur's sword with my

Will and I aimed, putting every scrap of Force I had into it.

I let it go. I don't know how I managed that shot, but it hit him square between the shoulder blades just as he crossed over back into Hell.

At which point it occurred to me that I might have made a bit of an oopsie.

Because that was an Angel's sword, used on another Angel, in his home realm.

I'm pretty sure it killed him.

I'm just going by the explosion.

Illiel screamed as he tried to drag the blade out of his chest. I saw lines of black spread from the wound site. What few Demons remained in the general area ran like hell (so to speak). I put up a whole mess of shields, and a good thing too, because there was a flash, a whining thump, and then noise that I barely prevented from shattering my ear drums. The blast wave tore the portal apart in an instant. And just like that, we were standing back in the world.

The transition was jarring. One second I was fighting for our lives and the next... we were safe! We'd survived!

My Shadows surged back to me and I whooped with joy as the connection re-established itself. I turned to look at Demise and she smiled sadly, a tear rolling down her face as she clutched at her side, now a mass of black muck as the Fallen Angel's spell continued killing her.

"No...," I whispered, dropping to her side, all thoughts of triumph vanishing in an instant.

"It's okay, Mathew," she whispered, "I'm ready."

I switched the mode on my Mage Sight and nearly cried.

The Black had spread its tendrils from the impact site and well into the surrounding tissues. Skin, muscle, and organ were already little more than sludge. She was down to a fraction of her power, and without it, she wouldn't be able to stay alive very long.

"Thank you for letting me live a little," she said to me, "I never knew what I was missing."

She closed her eyes.

CHAPTER 19

"Oh no you don't," I said, slapping her face.

Her eyes darted open, and she glared.

"You die when I say you die, understand me?"

I had exactly one trick that would fix this. Only a Death Mage would be able to survive it, and it might well kill me to do it.

She glared as I reached out and put my hand over her heart.

"What are you...?" she said, "No! Mathew, don't you dare!"

Lifelink.

I *hated* that spell. It hurt like hell.

I felt her injury like it was my own and nearly screamed. I bit back on it and went to work. I knew that I could share my Well with another Archon, but I'd never initiated the sharing before, much less with a Sorcerer. I was muddling my way through, searching through the heart of her through my Lifelink, which was slowly but steadily killing me. I had minutes in that state. I was already shaking as my Vitality was drained to keep her alive.

"Mathew, stop, d'you hear?" she shouted.

I looked her square in the eyes and she recoiled from the stare.

"Just this once, do what I say!" I barked.

I found it, her Well.

"Let me in," I said, "That is a command from an Archon. Do it!"

She swallowed, and I felt her relax her defences. The

power in our Wells merged, which is to say, my power flowed into hers refilling it right to the top in an instant.

She gasped and her energy surged, driving right back into battle with the Black, Entropy versus Evil. She could hold it a while.

"Keep at it, we're almost there," I said weakly.

It's a good thing I'd become good at carving off pieces of myself, or I'd never have managed while in so much pain. I yanked away a chunk of my living energy. Normally it just went straight into my Well, but this time I held onto it with every fibre of my being, in spite of the unspeakable agony it had caused to remove it. I shielded her from my pain as I moved that ball of life force into the breach in her side, and let it flow.

Life Magic. The quick and ugly kind; the desperate kind. The kind I'd unknowingly used a long time ago to save my brother. It very nearly didn't work.

But Demise was on the ball, and as I attacked the Black from the outside, she rallied and fought it from within, eradicating the tiny tendrils I couldn't reach while my Life Force neutralised the main site of infection.

The black flesh turned grey and then a healthy pink as I trickled my energy into it, and Demise's own power met mine at the surface of her skin, stripping away all the death from within as I restored life from without.

It took seconds that felt like hours.

And then the Black was gone.

Demise caught me as I fell, the last of my enchantments and spells petering out. I was down to practically nothing, Magically. My life force had been reduced by a half, what with the Lifelink and the chunk I'd removed. I felt sick, I could barely breathe, and I certainly couldn't move.

"Why?" Demise asked, tears in her eyes as she looked down at me, "Why would you do that?"

"Why wouldn't I?" I managed to gasp out.

Portals opened. I barely felt them, I was so sleepy. I

recognised the new arrivals. Hopkins generally noticed when I left the planet and also tended to show up to yell when I got back.

"Demise?" said a familiar voice, "What's happening?"

"Lady Hopkins..." Demise said, "I can't explain it, there was a trap, and a portal. Demons and Fallen Angels. He... he saved my life. I can't get him to tell me why."

"It's alright now," Hopkins said, kneeling next to me, "Mathew Graves, what stupid thing did you do this time?"

I smiled and she took my hand, "Crap, we told you not to do any more Life Siphons!"

"S'fine," I managed, "Just a little chilly is all."

"Bloody hell, now what?" Palmyra said, landing next to me and looking between me and Demise, "Oh my, just how dead were you?"

"Dead?" Demise said.

"You're full of his Life Force," Palmyra said running her hand over me, "and he's almost down to a level that would put him in a coma."

"I didn't mean... I begged him not to... he ordered me to let him," Demise protested.

"Look at that, Matty, someone actually did what you said," Hopkins said, patting my shoulder.

"When I can sit up, I'm going to get you for that," I mumbled, feeling awful.

"Bugger, he's already got three infections making progress," Palmyra said, finishing her diagnosis, "and I'm worried about his heart rate and B.P."

"Can you do something?" Demise asked.

"Of course," Palmyra said, "But most of this, I can't fix. He needs to replenish it on his own, over time."

She did something, and suddenly everything sharpened up. My breathing improved, my heart stopped pounding, and I felt a little more energetic.

"Oh, that's so much better," I said.

"Report, Guardian!" barked a voice from behind us, making me jump.

Demise shot to attention and dropped me on the ground as she turned towards her master. She started telling him what had happened while Kron glared.

"Ow," I said. Palmyra smiled.

Hopkins helped me sit up again and I took a look around.

Bill was where we'd left him, Magically asleep. The house... well, it wasn't so much a building as a pile.

"When you break something, it really stays broke, doesn't it, Matty?" Palmyra said.

"That wasn't entirely my fault," I said.

"Which bit, exactly?" Hopkins asked with a grin.

"The first floor. Demise did that," I said sheepishly, "And the house died honourably. Saving lives and squishing Demons."

"We should all be so lucky," Hopkins said gravely.

"Ha!" I said, "If I die, it's going to be from too much indulgence and debauchery at a tender old age after my important bits stop working, thank you very much."

"I do enjoy your outlook, Matty," Palmyra said with a snigger, "Reminds us what priorities we should have."

"Thank you, I do my best to keep my eye on the ball," I said seriously.

Killian approached us after a while, sitting carefully on the ground next to me, "Demise told me what happened. I'm... I'm impressed, Kid."

I went red and muttered something deflecting.

Killian smiled, "Demise hasn't many good things to say about anyone. If she says you did well, it's nothing to sneeze at."

I smiled a little, "Any idea why those Fallen Angels were after her?"

He sighed, "They weren't. They were after you."

"That's not what they said," I pointed out.

"Think about it, Demise was hit by the Black. They knew

it. She was dead; it was damn near a certainty. Why offer you the trade at all?"

I shrugged, "No earthly idea, now you put it that way. But maybe they knew I'd be able to help?"

"Palmyra maybe, but you?" Killian said, "Nobody would have thought you could do that."

"I didn't do all of it, Demise did as much to save her own life as I did," I said.

I think Demise coloured a little at that, strange girl. I say girl, she was about two hundred and ten years older than me, give or take. Still looked like she could be my older sister, though. Sorcery sure was fun...

"The idea was to make you pick your own life over another's. To make you be selfish, to take that first step down the wrong path. The way Demise tells it, you didn't even hesitate."

"It was literally Hell. You don't leave someone there," I said.

"Many would. Many have," Hopkins said, "Some do it on purpose, for advantage."

"Hey, you know what my record for atomic cock-ups is, I'm just putting some karma in the bank for when the day comes that I try driving to Tesco's and end up in Hell myself, that's all," I said.

"That sounds more like it," Hopkins said, squeezing my arm in a way that said she didn't believe me.

"Yep, nothing selfless going on here," Palmyra said, nudging my ribs.

I grumbled and they sniggered.

Kron was still glaring at me like I'd exploded her puppy, but Killian seemed to be warming back up to me. I yawned widely. My Well was refilling, so I had enough to drag Bill over to me. I reached into his mind and removed the Sleeping Hex he was under. It wasn't a particularly powerful one and came out quickly and easily.

He woke up with a snap and seemed immediately twitchy as he saw me.

"Matty?" he said. He was already shivering, "You're okay! Oh, thank God."

"Why wouldn't I be?" I asked neutrally.

He started sweating almost on the spot as he looked around at the rather spectacular collection of Magical firepower gathered around him.

"Um, no reason," he said lamely, distracted and staring as his hand occasionally patted his pocket in unconscious gesture.

"What's in your pocket, Mister Hedrin?" Hopkins asked.

"Nothing, Miss Hopkins," Bill said, moving his hand away.

"Show us, Bill," I said softly.

"There's nothing there, Matty, I swear on my life," he said, scuttling back.

"Do you understand what it means to speak an oath like that among Magicians, Boy?" Demise said. She'd drawn a blade from somewhere, that long black one she'd nearly taken my head off with back in the Grotto.

"Where were you hiding that?" I asked her.

She winked at me. It made me grin until I remembered our current situation.

"I... I... I...," Bill stuttered, covering his pocket protectively, "You can't have it!"

And then the damndest thing happened.

He called Magic.

I was so surprised, I did absolutely nothing, not that I was in much of a state to do anything.

It was Flesh Magic of all things, a spray of Chemical Energy that would have acted much like acid and burnt our exposed skin down to the bone.

Five overlapping, and stupidly powerful, Will shields erupted into being between Bill and us, the work of my brother, sisters and Demise. Bill threw more into his attack, but it was barely a spark of Magic, and any one of us was a firestorm compared to it.

Bill ran out of Magic after maybe two seconds and fell to the ground, scrabbling for his pocket. Out flew the packet, filled with shards of red crystal.

Oh, Bill, you utter idiot...

Source, lots of it.

He tore the packet open, but three different spells hit it before he could stuff any down his throat, spraying the crystals into the mud. Hopkins lifted him up and away with her Will. My friend screamed as he tried to gather up his drugs, thrashing against Hopkins' mental grip to get at it.

"Did you know?" Hopkins asked me.

"Not a bloody clue," I said, thoroughly shocked.

Well, that wasn't strictly true. There were a whole *bunch* of clues, now that I thought about it.

I told Hopkins about his absences, his requests for money, his shivers and paleness and his refusal to let me take a look.

"I should have seen it," I said as Bill stopped thrashing and started crying his eyes out, the poor bastard.

"I never suspected a thing, either, Matty, don't beat yourself up," Hopkins said.

"He's more of a brother to me than the one I was born with; I should have noticed," I said, tossing a Sleep Hex that put him out again. Hopkins lowered him to the ground next to me.

"Is this fixable?" I asked.

"The physical effects, I can deal with," Palmyra said, waving her hand over Bill, "The mental effects? I don't know. Yikes, that stuff really isn't good for you!"

I felt her Magic pulsing through Bill's body.

"Liver cirrhosis, kidney damage, perforated lung tissue, pre-cancerous cells in his stomach... it's a mess in there."

I rubbed my eyes and focussed on his mind, calling up my Telepathy.

"Oh, get out of the way, Graves," Kron said, kneeling next to Bill, "I was playing in people's heads fifteen hundred years before you were born. You'll leave him a vegetable with your ham hands."

I did as I was told and watched as she went to work. It was a thing of beauty, what she did. There was a subtle elegance to her manipulations that I couldn't hope to match. She altered his memory and thoughts like a master, moulding here and pressing there, adjusting ever so carefully. It was spectacularly well done, I could have worked on him for ten times as long and not have managed something even a fraction as effectively neat.

It took her half an hour, and Palmyra about half that, to put my friend back together.

"They used him to get to you, Graves," Kron said after she was done, "They gave him a sample when he was out shopping, and then another. They got him hooked and then they upped the price, then they asked him a favour and he was too strung out and desperate to say no. He would have given them his own mother in the state he was in."

I'd met his mother; I'd have traded her for a Mars Bar and still think I'd been overpaid, but that wasn't the point.

"Who?" I asked, hoping that maybe there might have been a glimpse of a certain troublesome pain in my arse...

"They were well disguised. Male, average height, always wore a hood. Your friend didn't have a name."

Damn it.

"Is he alright now?" I asked.

"I excised all the memories associated with the drug, and Palmyra cleared the effects out of his system. There will be some holes in his memory, but he won't notice them. He's a sedentary fellow, I replaced them with naps."

"Thank you," I said to them both.

"You're very welcome," Palmyra said with a beaming smile.

"I didn't do it for you," Kron hissed icily.

Hopkins rolled her eyes.

I really hoped that Bill would be alright, I knew that Source changed people, and not for the better. If Bill had been permanently altered, then it was *my* fault; these bastards (almost certainly Namia Sutton's bastards) had only gone after him because he knew me. I watched him carefully as he woke up again, looking slightly bleary-eyed but otherwise fine, that manic light gone from his eyes, much to my relief.

"Matty?" he said, sounding just like my friend, "Where the hell am I?"

"Stonebridge," I said, "You got yourself in a little trouble, Pal."

He looked around at the devastation, "Did I win?" he asked.

I sniggered, "Yes, you did," I said, patting his shoulder.

"What happened?"

"And that's our cue," Palmyra said, standing along with the others.

"Need a portal?" Hopkins asked.

"Yes please," I said, standing and then staggering, only for Demise to catch me and prop me up, "Thank you."

She nodded and Hopkins shook her head before opening a portal. We walked through and back into the Big Square, where Cathy was waiting under a tree and ran for me. She threw herself into my arms, and in my depleted state, I buckled and went down with her on top of me.

"Now *that's* a hello," I said with a smile as she squeezed me into a huge hug.

"I'll see you later, Matty. Go eat something, alright? Lots of somethings," Hopkins said.

I nodded and she patted my shoulder before walking away.

I held my Cathy while Bill stood nearby, almost dancing from foot to foot with curiosity. Cathy nuzzled into my neck and I kissed her cheek.

"I wish you'd stop doing that," she whispered.

"I'm sorry."

"I know, I just wish I could handle this better."

"I love you," I said, not knowing what else to say.

She snuggled in tighter.

Explaining things to Bill was complicated.

Eventually I settled on telling him he'd been kidnapped. I didn't mention the drugs or the betrayal. That Bill was gone. My friend, Bill, was back where he was supposed to be.

When Bill went off to the school shop for his afternoon treat, I smiled, and told Cathy the real story.

"Oh, the poor bastard," she said, echoing my earlier thoughts.

"He'll never know," I said, "And I'd prefer it if it stayed that way."

She nodded, "Okay," she said, kissing me gently, "though I don't know if I can look at him the same way again after this. He could have gotten you killed, Matty."

"But he didn't, and that's the important thing," I said.

Cathy spent the rest of the day anchored to me, and I didn't complain at all. I hated having to leave her at bed time, but I went to my room with Demise after a long kiss that made the world right again.

"You didn't tell her what you did," Demise said once we were ready for bed, "You didn't tell any of them."

I'd called Tethys and Cassandra to let them know what had happened, leaving out the Life Siphon and any other really dark stuff, they'd just have yelled at me. They *still* yelled, which was par for the course, but they yelled less than they would have.

"Sure I did," I said.

"You didn't tell them the important parts," she insisted, "What you were willing to do to save me. What you *did* do."

"They don't need to know that sort of thing, it would terrify them. And I don't need an audience."

"You saved my life," she said, "If our positions had been reversed, I might have made a different choice."

I shrugged, "I wouldn't have blamed you."

"Your people should know what kind of man you are," Demise said quietly.

"They do. Knowing what I did today... I don't care about credit. I'm just happy knowing that things turned out alright. That's more than enough for me."

"I won't forget it," she said.

I smiled and closed my eyes.

I was thinking hard over what had happened. I shouldn't have won, or not as efficiently. That Light idea had done it, and it hadn't come from me. It had come from someone who knew their Demons but couldn't act to help me.

Thank you, Rose, I thought as loudly as I could.

"You're welcome," a tiny whisper said from somewhere close to my ear.

I smiled and fell asleep, relaxed like I hadn't been in a long time.

CHAPTER 20

The next Friday was the start of Half Term. Cathy and I had rarely been apart since Bill's 'fixing', and leaving her was a wrench and a half.

Naturally, Demise hadn't gone anywhere. My parents had been miffed at the idea that I needed a minder, but my mother was polite when she arrived to collect me and I introduced them. Conversation on the drive back was somewhat stilted, Demise wasn't exactly a font of verbiage at the best of times, and she was even worse with strangers.

I got home and was mobbed by the dog and the Pixies, who attached themselves firmly to my head and shoulders with every intention of staying there. Demise looked at this quizzically, but seemed to take it in stride like she did everything else.

My mother still had a lot of work to do, and spent most of her days in her study with her nose in reports and insurance claims, so I spent mine in the Grotto with the Fairies. I swam with Nymphs and slept under my tree while Demise watched. I chatted with Lunson, debating the differences between Fairy and Human Magic while his daughter and her mate taught his granddaughter, Kay, about the woods and how to use the bow; which nearly ended in calamity and an arrow in my bottom but for the protective enchantments of the woods.

The poor thing was so mortified that she darted into the Centaur's caves and refused to come out until I promised that I wasn't angry, and told her that I appreciated her not aiming for my head. She was an adorable little thing, a seven year old girl's torso attached to a pale, brown and white horse's body, shy as any kid that age, but lively as any ten of me. She was always running and laughing with the Wood Sprites and playing with Bayano (the talking otter).

It was idyllic. Even Demise relaxed, sleeping next to me under the tree.

"She smells funny," Meadow declared one afternoon while I was sitting with my feet in the pond. Demise looked up from her book and raised an eyebrow, "But you don't anymore."

"Really?" I replied.

"Nope," Jewel said, stretching across my stomach, "I can't tell the difference between you and us anymore."

"It's your link to this place," Demise said, "The blending of Magics, there's a little of them in your Well, and a little of your Well in them."

"Yuk, human magic," Melody squeaked, "How do I wash that off?"

I tickled the little Pixie and she squealed, almost rolling onto the ground in her attempt to escape. I caught her before she could get too far.

"No fair!" Melody complained, "You're using your size to pick on little Pixies!"

I have her a little hug and she subsided back onto her spot in the crook of my arm with a happy sigh.

"That's not fair, either," she muttered, "You know I have a weak spot for a good hug."

I stroked her hair and she soon started snoring, along with the other two, who'd quickly drifted off. Any excuse for a nap, those three, they were almost as lazy as I was.

"This isn't normal," Demise said, "this blending of Fairy and Human Magic is unprecedented."

"It's fine. My Magic hasn't been affected. And if it makes my friends more comfortable, it can only be a good thing."

"It's like mixing oil and water, it shouldn't work," Demise said.

I shrugged, "It's not like I can use Fairy Magic, and I

haven't seen them use mine."

She grunted and went back to her book, but I could tell she was confused.

I knew that sort of ease couldn't last, though. I felt it in my bones, something *had* to ruin it.

At least this time, Price had the decency to call while I was awake.

"Hello?" I said as I sat up from my half-nap, dislodging Melody, who I had to catch before she rolled off onto the carpet.

"Ah, Mathew," Price said huskily, "I have news. There are two more laboratories; that's confirmed. We've found one of them, want to come and play?"

I shuddered in fear, remembering what had happened at the last one. It took me a moment to get it together, but the job needed to be done, and it was my responsibility.

"Address?" I said.

She told me and I wrote it down.

"I'll let you know how it goes."

"You'd better," she said, "In person. And I'd like to hear all about that little trip you took to Michelangelo's. Crystal's told me all sorts of details, but she does exaggerate. Rather taken with you, though."

Crystal had called from time to time since we'd gone after her sister; talking to her was a refreshing change of pace. She had a certain outlook on life I found interesting.

"I can't promise to improve on her story," I said.

"Oh, I'll bet you can."

"I'll come by when I'm done."

"Excellent," she said, "I'll make sure Crystal is ready for you."

We hung up and I stretched.

"Dee, we're going to Gomorrah," I said.

She sat up with a start, one of my books falling off her face.

"What?" she said, confused and half-asleep.

Demise did not like Shadow-Walking any more the second time, and was less than amused when I got lost on the way. She held her eyes tightly shut as before until we emerged in Gomorrah, high up on a roof.

"Ugh, I hate that," she muttered, "I feel sick."

I rubbed her back and she sighed as she bent over, recovering her equilibrium.

"How can you stand it in there?" she asked, "It feels so wrong."

"We'll make shorter jumps on the way back, alright?"

She nodded and stood, "I'm fine."

I consulted my phone. We were about a mile away from the warehouse.

"We can walk it from here?" I suggested.

"It's a mile, you'll be dead before we get there in your state."

Palmyra's enhancement spell could only do so much to keep the edge off my lack of Living Energy. Even a mile would likely exhaust me.

"I'm doing my own flying, though," she said, calling her Will.

I pulled up my map for her to see, "We'll land in this alley. I want a good look around, this time, I'm not taking any chances."

"O-" she started and then just... stopped. Frozen there.

"Dee?" I said, scared out of my wits, starting to cast Mage Sight.

"It's alright, Mathew, she's alright," Rose said from behind me.

I turned towards her. She wore white leather armour over her body, her red hair was pulled back into a bun. She looked... martial, like a warrior. And she looked miserable.

"You scared the crap out of me," I said.

She smiled back sadly.

"I'm sorry to do it this way, but... but I need your help."

"Are you alright?" I said, stepping towards her.

She nodded.

"It's Gabrielle. *They* have her."

"They? As in *Source* 'They'?!" I asked, my eyes going wide.

She nodded.

"How?"

"She was looking around their operations, making sure that she knew who was doing what, maybe doing a little gloating over Demons she didn't like too much. There was a trap-circle. She got caught. Apparently she wasn't the only curious Demon to come looking. They've been draining her like the others. She's strong, Mathew, but I don't think she has much time left."

"I'm heading in now. I'll get her out."

"You don't understand, she's at the other one," Rose said.

"Oh. Rose, I don't know where that is," I said.

"I know. And I can't tell you. I have to take you. And you have to promise me, on your word of honour, that you will do nothing except free her and come back to me. You can't use anything you see or learn to come back later. You must come by the knowledge in your own time. Will you do that?"

"Yes," I said without hesitation, "My word."

"I don't want to ask you this, Mathew. But it's forbidden for me to act, especially in this situation. I'm bending a whole mess of rules far too far. But she's... she's my friend. I work well with her, and I trust her more than I'd trust another Demon in her place. Please help her."

"If it can be done, I'll do it," I said, and then gestured at Demise, "I take it she can't come with me?"

"No, just you. Are you still willing?"

"Yes," again, no hesitation.

People are people. Even the ones with horns. And Gabrielle's never done me harm. And even if that weren't the case, Rose's word was good enough for me. Even if it cost me Demise's respect and made me an enemy of my brother and sister. Hopkins and Palmyra would understand. Killian and Kron wouldn't.

Screw 'em.

Rose's wings unfurled and she pulled me into an embrace. The wings wrapped around me.

"Close your eyes and you must absolutely keep them that way, understand?" she said.

I nodded.

We moved.

There was a wrench and we were somewhere... else. For a long moment, I felt warmth and acceptance that made me feel safe like I never had in my entire life. Just before we left, I heard a wonderful sound, what can only be described as a note of pure joy and love that made me cry on the spot, and then we were back in the world. I don't know where we went, but it hurt not to be there anymore. That instant of peace and elation... I shivered as I bent over and breathed hard, trying to get my equilibrium back.

"I'm sorry to have done that to you, Mathew," she said, "Just be glad you didn't see."

"I agree," I said, standing again. What the hell was that?

"This is the back door," she said, pointing at a blue door, snapping me back to the present, "Come back here when you've finished and I'll extract you both. Be quick, Mathew, she doesn't have much time."

I nodded and went to the door, which was locked. Rose was already gone by the time I'd cast the lock-pick spell. I surrounded myself with an Illusion and cast Mage Sight.

And... oh dear.

I thought the *Church* was bad.

The building was a factory that had made televisions once upon a time. The top floor was entirely empty, but for a few boxes with pictures of the wares on them. There was a walled off area where there would once have been offices, another set of rooms for lockers, which were bent, mangled and rusty. At the far end, there was a set of wide concrete stairs leading into the ground; a recently refurbished freight lift was set into the wall next to them.

There were two floors below, the same size as the one I was on, both carved from the living rock, by an impressively powerful Earth Mage, if I was any judge. My Mage Sight let me see all this, and more, it let me see the fifteen Magicians, the fifty or so technicians (many of whom were armed) and upwards of two *hundred* Demons.

That was *bad.*

If those circles failed like last time, there would be *such* a mess.

And that was something I just didn't understand. These were drug dealers, they knew they were doing bad things, they *knew* they were hurting people *and* torturing demons... so, how could they be so dumb? They had to know that their afterlife was far more likely to involve pitchforks than harps, so why did they think that tormenting their future neighbours was going to end well for them? It was just insane.

I shoved that thought aside, it was a distraction I didn't need. I walked quickly to the stairs and disarmed the rather crude alarm spell I found over the threshold. My Illusion let me pass a security camera without a problem. I still moved carefully, though, keeping the amount of Magic I used to a bare minimum so as not to alert the Magicians. I also kept well clear of them, just in case they were paying attention.

It took me the better part of half an hour to search the upper level for Gabrielle. The Demons' Auras all looked very similar to me, so I had to inspect each one up close. Thankfully most of the workers and guards were either fast asleep or dozing. The few technicians who collected Source from the machines looked bored and careless (not a great condition in which to be handling Demons, but that wasn't my business).

I found the steps leading down and made my way to them, growing steadily more worried as time stretched on and I hadn't found Gabrielle. It was colder down there, and I was tired, but I started searching again.

I found her at the far end of that second floor in a silver circle. She was crouched, bent over and in obvious pain. Her frame was wasted and thin, her clothes ill fitting, like she was wasting away, but her eyes were still very much Gabrielle. The Technicians and Magicians were as far away as they were going to get, and I knelt next to her, casting a muffling spell around us.

"Gabrielle?" I said, feeling around the circle for a weak point, "Can you hear me?"

She raised her head slowly, "Come to gloat, Shadow-born?" she rasped.

"Hardly," I said, extending my Illusion around her.

"Then why are you here?" she asked, her eyes intent on me as I focussed my Will.

"I think that would be quite obvious."

I kept it simple and just yanked the energy out of the circle. Without Magic, a silver circle was just a silver circle, and easy to break with a little effort of Will. It was designed around enchantments built right into the metal; nasty, ugly little things which allowed demons to be bound within it, as well as making the silver alloy more durable and harder to break, attributes that weren't much of an obstacle to yours truly.

There was a faint crack as the spell was broken. Gabrielle collapsed and I caught her before she could hit the concrete.

"Ugh," she managed, "Too late."

"You'll be fine," I said.

She snorted, barely moving against me. Her energy was low and getting lower. She was close to being banished, and in her state... who knew what she'd find on the other side waiting for her.

"They took it all," she whispered, "Bastards. Want to kill them..."

Her eyes were fluttering, her skin was ashen. She had seconds left.

"Bugger it. Never tell *anyone* I did this," I said crossly.

I pulled her chin up, lowered all my shields... and kissed

her.

Maybe not the brightest idea in the world, but needs must.

Her arms went around my neck and her mouth opened against mine. What with the... lack of 'intimacy' I'd endured over the last few weeks on account of Demise, there was quite a bit of pent-up desire for her to feed on and she moaned hard as she took it in. Her grip strengthened and the kiss deepened, her tongue sliding against mine.

I lost myself a little bit to that kiss. She was all, her scent, her touch, her taste. I told myself I was simply feeding her, but damn if I wasn't enjoying it. I felt her form swell, filling her clothes out again. She was suddenly warm and vital and she flipped me over and pressed me to the concrete, her hips straddling mine. In the throes of that kiss, I forgot everything for a long minute, and it felt amazing, seductively so. I would happily have done it until it killed me...

And *that*, ladies and gentlemen was the real danger of the Succubus. One might think that they're harmless, just a bit of fun, right?

Wrong. They were, if anything, one of the very most dangerous predators in the universe. They were a living, breathing *trap*, perfectly evolved to draw men and women to their death. All it took was a touch, a kiss, and you could quite easily lose yourself to them, and that would be it. If Gabrielle had wanted, she could have killed me right there, right then, and even with all my power, all my skill, there would have been exactly *nothing* I could do about it.

Essentially, I'd put my entire future in the hands of a demon, and trusted her to do the right thing... damn, but that was *dumb*!

But then, just like that, it was over, she pulled her lips away from mine and I sagged, panting and exhausted.

"Oh, no, Magician, not like this," she said, leaning over me, her voice a happy purr again, "I'll win you fair and square. I'm not taking you by default."

She planted another little kiss on my lips as I rebuilt my shields. I was shaky and horribly randy. It took a lot to put that away.

She looked... perfect again. And she was still sitting on me, her hips grinding a little bit against mine.

"How may I show my gratitude, Shadowborn?" she crooned, leaning to whisper into my ear.

"Helping me up would be a start."

She sighed, but hopped up, "You're just no fun when you're not making a donation," she said, offering her hand, which I took. Skin to skin contact... not a great idea, either. It was as if letting her in to feed from me had put a tiny chink in my armour she could worm her way into.

"Stop it," I said, looking her in the eye.

"You started it," she said in a whisper, gently rubbing at my fingers.

"It may have escaped your attention, but I am rather *not* supposed to be here, and we need to go before we're discovered."

"I can smell our mutual friend all over you," she said, sniffing hard at my neck, "How ever did she persuade you to come for me? Did she have to do anything drastic? Or did you just come running at the thought of little old me in trouble?"

"No doubt you can spend the next couple of centuries torturing me over this, but for the moment, can we please just go?"

I cast an in-place Illusion of Gabrielle as I found her and led the way towards a darkened part of the room.

"Ugh, I looked like that? Someone's losing some intestines for this!" she snarled.

"On your own time. We're on Rose's schedule right now."

"You're just no fun at all, are you?"

"Nope," I said, "Really not worth the trouble at all."

"Oh, my dear Shadowborn," she said, letting her fingers drift over my neck, "You're worth *all* the trouble."

"Focus."

"Oh, I am," she replied.

"I was talking to myself," I said as I reached out for a patch of Shadow to open a Gate.

Before I could, the room was suddenly filled with blinding light. Gabrielle ducked behind me with a hiss.

"Well, well, well," said a familiar and ghastly voice, "What will your brother and sisters make of this?"

Namia Sutton, Light Magic charged and ready, seven mages alongside her, marched towards me.

Well. That just wasn't good...

"No Magic on her," Gabrielle hissed, "Remember!"

Aw, bollocks...

"Miss Sutton," I said confidently, "Gentlemen. Why did you steal my pet?"

Gabrielle tensed, but she went with it, remaining cowed behind me.

"What?" she asked, stopping.

"This one. It's mine. You captured it," I let my voice descend into ice, "I'm seriously considering releasing the others just so you can learn your lesson."

She swallowed for a moment, but continued towards me, more cautiously now, though.

"You summoned it? A Demon, all by yourself?"

"Do I need to remind you who I am, Sutton?" I asked, stepping towards her. She stopped approaching, "This one was the first. My first. My first of a great many more than you can imagine."

All utter crap, of course, but people like her tended to assume that everyone else was just as rotten as they were, so hopefully she'd buy it long enough for me to think my way out of this mess.

"And you came for it? It must be very... valuable to you," she said with a knowing smile.

"Oh yes," I said casually, "enough that I'm willing to put aside your blatant provocation so I can leave in peace. This *one* time."

291

"I don't think so," Sutton said, "I promised you certa-"

I blasted the nearest circle. It broke and a massive Demon roared as it leapt free, bounding straight for the pack of Magicians. It was eight feet of blue flesh and black eyes, with three foot, razor-sharp horns and wings twice its height, not to be messed with, and definitely not to be ignored. Sutton turned and fired off a burst of Light that cleaved off the Demon's wing, not that it slowed down any.

I called my Shadows and wrapped Gabrielle up in them, pouring buckets of power into them to overcome Sutton's Light Magic. We darted towards the stairs and straight to the upper level. I wasted no time, and yanked us across. My cocoon was pursued by Magic and bullets, and it drained me awfully to keep it going, but there was no time for anything else.

Sutton screamed in frustration as we flew away and tore a ragged hole through the Demon's face as it bore down on her. She'd turned back towards us, but by then we were up to the top level and darting towards the back door. I didn't bother with subtlety and simply ploughed through it as the first Magician came up through a hole he'd blasted in the floor, readying a fireball.

He threw it, and it simply... stopped, along with him and everything else.

Rose appeared out of nowhere and I relaxed, lowering Gabrielle to the ground and then myself.

"Oh, that's useful," I said, gesturing at the approaching fireball, "Any way you could teach me that?"

Rose smiled, "You'll learn yourself one day," she said, stroking my cheek, "Hello Gabrielle."

"You sent the Shadowborn," Gabrielle said, "Idiot. He must not be risked, you know this."

"Not be risked? Did you see the last place I ended up in on account of this nonsense?" I asked.

"Quiet, Magician, Higher Beings are talking," Gabrielle replied.

"Should have left her in the basement," I muttered.

Rose snorted, Gabrielle glared.

"Go back to your place. Heal and rest, stay away from this poisonous city. I have to return him before he's missed," Rose said.

"I will, but not because you told me to," Gabrielle said, and then she simply vanished.

Rose rolled her eyes and approached me.

"Thank yo-," she started and then she gasped, her nose lifting, "oh my..."

She pressed herself up against me, her nose nuzzling my chest and neck. Her hands were suddenly on my back and travelling lower.

"Um... Rose? Whatcha doin'?" I asked, a little nervously.

My voice seemed to give her pause, and she jumped back.

"Oh!" she said, blushing hard, "Oh, I'm so sorry!"

She shook her head and rubbed her eyes before looking at me again.

"I saw what you did, and I forget sometimes that Gabrielle is what she is. You let her in of your own free will. That... marks you in a way, so that you can better feed her in the future. It draws... female attention," she said, fanning her face, "Even mine apparently. I'm so embarrassed."

"This isn't permanent, is it?" I asked, horrified.

"Oh no, not from a single feeding, two days, three at the most. Here, I can mask it a little. But try to stay clear of women you don't want to bed. Enough time in their company might cause... problems."

She waved her hand and my skin tingled for a moment.

"I live with a minder," I said.

"Right... Demise. I recommend cold showers. For both of you."

She smiled evilly, her eyes wondering over me.

I ignored it, "I've been taking those for weeks, it doesn't help, even if that woman is a walking mood-killer."

"Well, she's not here now, need some help with tha-

Sorry!" she said, turning away and fanning her face again.

"How bad is it?" I asked, now really concerned.

"Pretty bad," she said, breathing hard, "It won't be so bad with normal people. But I can smell past the enchantment I put on you. It'll also be worse with those who liked you to begin with."

"Rats," I said.

She sniggered, "You have to be the first man to *ever* say that in regard to this issue," she said, "Most would be dancing with glee."

"I don't want to be with someone who doesn't really want to be with me. It's not right."

She smiled, a great, beaming thing that lit up that dark alley.

"Don't feel too bad, the mark doesn't create lust, it only enhances what's there. A girl that doesn't like you to begin with won't like you under its influence."

I raised an eyebrow at her, and her eyes went wide as she realised what she'd admitted. She spluttered incoherently for a solid few minutes.

"I didn't mean it like that," she said, "Here, I'll take you back. You'll arrive at the same instant you left."

"Time travel? That's useful."

"Not as such," she said, as she approached with a trembling lip, "You might say that I... stretched your timeline a little and now I'm letting you... snap back."

She wrapped me in another hug, wings and all, and had me close my eyes again. That same tone, that same sense of serenity, and I was back on the rooftop with a frozen Demise.

Rose took a little longer stepping away, shivering as she did, "Thank you, Mathew," she said, "For saving my friend."

"You helped me save mine. It's the least I could do," I said, remembering that crucial piece of advice that had helped me get Bill and Demise out of that trap.

"You earned that, Mathew Graves. You were given a choice and made the hard one, the good one. That's enough wiggle room for someone like me to act," she said, brushing a little muck off my shoulder. Then she wasn't brushing so much as stroking...

Then it wasn't just one shoulder.

"Rose, Demonic musk," I pointed out as her slim fingers brushed my neck.

"Right, right. Sorry," she said, stepping back and taking a breath, "We'll be in touch."

She vanished.

"-kay," Demise finished.

Right. The other lab.

Still have *that* to deal with...

CHAPTER 21

We darted into the air and flew towards the lab. My heart was still pounding in my chest after the rescue, and it was jarring to just have to carry on with the next thing. I shoved all that down and concentrated, I wasn't going to screw up this time, I swore to God...

This location wasn't buried under an abandoned building, but was part of a fully functioning warehouse, which was how Price had found it; they'd been indiscreet with their purchasing orders.

Not that I knew about the other one. That *didn't* exist. And I *hadn't* been there and had my tonsils inspected by a pure-bred Succubus... again.

Oh boy... I'm never telling anyone about that. I'd never hear the end of it.

We landed in the alley I'd selected (I seemed to spend a lot of my time in Gomorrah lurking in alleys).

I cast Mage Sight and took a long look at the building. There were lots of regular workers there, in addition to the Source-makers. The operation seemed to be on the upper floors this time, which was a nice change. I'd had enough of the underground.

There weren't as many Demons there as there had been at the Factory, but there were still more than a hundred and fifty. There were about forty men and women working the actual warehouse, including some people loading a big truck out front. I had no idea how much they knew about what was going on above them, but I needed to get them out of the way before I tackled the lab. In the upper floors, there were four Magicians, none stronger than a Wizard, hardly worth bothering about, really, and a dozen technicians.

"This isn't good," Demise said as she stood next to me. Was it my imagination, or was she standing closer than usual?

"I have to agree," I said.

"How would you normally deal with something like this?"

"Hide in a corner and call my big sister to come beat up the bad guys for me."

Demise smiled and then shook her head like there was a fly.

"You alright?" I asked.

"Fine, just... something smelled funny is all," she said, looking at me.

"Yeah, sorry about that," I said, thinking up something on the spot, "I was playing with my body chemistry earlier, trying to increase my available energy. I may have accidentally over-triggered some pheromone production. I'll be keeping clear of anyone female for a while after this. I should be back to normal in a couple of days."

"You shouldn't play with your endocrine system. You can cause all sorts of problems."

She was looking at me very intently, biting her lip.

"I know that *now*, won't do it again," I said, "Just left me more tired, anyway."

"I could have told you that."

"You were napping."

She glared and I stretched, walking towards the building.

"What are you doing?" she asked, following behind me.

"I thought I'd go make a mess."

I walked up to the loading dock, calling a set of shields around myself as I went.

I approached a portly fellow with a broad moustache loading sacks of something into the truck.

"Excuse me?" I said politely.

"What?" he said, not as politely, I frowned.

"Where's your manager?" I asked.

"Who wants to know?" he replied, glaring.

"Someone with little time and less patience," I said coldly, staring him down.

He swallowed at my tone before he remembered that he was just dealing with a kid and got in my face.

"Run home, Kid," he growled, "and take your mother with you."

"Sir, do you imagine that someone like me walks through Gardenia late at night without knowing precisely how to prevent a messy end? I'll ask one more time. Manager?"

He spat on the ground.

"Now what?" he asked, grinning nastily.

Before I had a chance to do a damn thing, Demise had him six inches off the ground by his overalls, one delicate hand clenched in the cloth, her form crackling with power.

"You speak to him with respect, understand?" she whispered, her eyes boring into his.

"Y-y-yes, Ma'am, sorry, Sir!" he said, "She's through there! Office to the left."

Demise dropped him and stepped back behind me, resting her hand on my shoulder protectively, which was new.

"Thank you," I said, "You may wish to take the rest of the night off."

I walked past him, Demise close behind. The man scuttled off at speed, I smelt pee and wrinkled my nose.

"You're a little scary when you want to be, aren't you?" I asked Demise, who flushed like it was a compliment.

"I get by."

We drew a few looks as we crossed along the side of the factory floor. Demise drew some whistles, which stopped when she looked in their direction. I smelt pee again...

I knocked on a door which said 'Manager' on the front in black. A female voice told us to come in and I obeyed.

"Who are you?" she said. She was middle aged, with a matronly look, wearing overalls and a comfortable shirt. Her brown hair was greying at the top and she wore something of a scowl.

"Hi," I said cheerfully, "I'm here to destroy the drug lab upstairs. You and your people have about five minutes to clear the area."

She blinked hard.

"There isn't a-"

I raised my hand and it burst into flames. An Illusion, but a good one. She shoved her chair backwards until it smacked into the wall.

"Five minutes starting now. Warn them, don't, makes no difference to me, just be gone within the time limit. This place might not be entirely... here when I'm done."

She nodded and pulled the fire alarm on the wall next to her with shaking hands before sprinting out past me and onto the floor.

"You're a little scary yourself, Milord," Demise whispered in my ear.

The place cleared out pretty quickly. As the last of the workers left, two Magicians came down a set of concrete stairs, dressed casually; jeans, work boots and shirts, one carried a heavy rod. One was a Fire Wizard, the other a Flesh Adept.

They saw us and readied shields. I yanked the electricity out of the Fire Alarm system and it shorted out, plunging us back into silence.

"Gentlemen," I said, "I'd advise you to leave now."

The Wizard snorted and raised his hand.

He didn't even get to finish his first spell, as an image of Bill, strung out and desperate, filled my mind. I saw him screaming for Source, desperate to get more of it as he willingly lured me to my death.

My Shadows went for them. The Adept's shields were abysmal; they fell in a less than a second. The Wizard may have put up a fight, but I think the wall of darkness shocked him so horribly that he didn't do a thing. In fact, he lost control of his shields and my Shadows hit home a little harder than I meant them to. They were both flung into the wall with sickening force, bones breaking in their backs and shoulders; nothing fatal, but still painful and debilitating enough to drop them to the ground unconscious.

I walked over them and up into the first floor, where the last two Magicians were waiting. They didn't even bother fighting, they ran out the back the second they saw Shadows. The technicians were hot on their heels. That just left us with Demons.

"Well," Demise said, "That was no fun at all. Now what?"

"I call Palmyra again," I said, pulling out my phone, "Demons aren't my thing."

"Sure," Demise said dryly, giving me the raised eyebrow.

"Oh, not again, Matty!" Palmyra said when she turned up, her usual clutch of nuns in tow.

"I was just out for an evening stroll, when I happened to hear the roars of Demons..." I said.

"Shut up," she said without heat, giving me a hug before approaching one of the circles, "Right. Once more, but without the screw-up."

"Only if that wouldn't be too much throub- Ow!" I said as she hit me, "Am I just the designated Archon punching bag?!"

"Well, certainly mine. You make delightful sounds, sort of like a mouse with its tail caught in a blender," she said.

"Couldn't you try to make that sound a little more butch?" I begged.

"Would you prefer rat?" she asked sweetly.

I grumbled while she sniggered. This time, she took things slowly. First she banished one, and when she was sure that it was gone (and not lurking in a corner, or something), she did another and another; then in pairs, by threes until she got the rest in a big final spell.

She stretched a little and I yawned, desperate for my bed after what had been a *long*, stressful night.

"That was fun, not as fun as last time," she said.

"Oh ha, ha!"

She sniggered and came over.

"You smell funny, is that..." she stopped, and her eyes went wide.

Shush! I sent, *I told Demise I messed up playing with my pheromones. She doesn't know I got... groped.*

When did this happen?! How did she not see that? Palmyra asked.

My Liaisons had a... problem.

Ohhh, she sent back, *Time Sling, huh?*

Yep.

Alright, say no more. And stay away from the women-folk for a while, you'll be a liability.

I know that!

Okay, no need to be so touchy.

I glared and she grinned.

We chatted a bit as we walked out, followed by our retinues. We emerged into the sightlines of an army.

There had to be two hundred policemen out there, every one armed with a rifle or a pistol, all pointed at us. Many had Spelleaters. Palmyra smiled.

"You want to take this one?" she asked.

"Sure, ears and eyes?" I suggested.

She smiled.

"This is the Gardenia Police!" said a voice over a loud-speaker, "Surrender n-"

I cast Sensory Overload.

And *wow* was that a lot of vomit! I may have... *accidentally* loosened the visual section.

"Oh, Matty, that's just mean," Palmyra said with a grin.

"Wait for it... and there we go, they all land in their own sick," I said as they passed out at last.

"You know, Mathew, it's Magicians like you that give the

rest of us a bad name," Palmyra said.

"So, I shouldn't mention the additional stimulant I added to the visual component that you should be able to smell in few minutes?" I said.

"What are you-? Oh, damn, Matty, that's just plain wrong!" Palmyra said, holding her nose against the smell of two hundred voided bowels and bladders.

I chuckled evilly.

"What? They're at the beck and call of drug dealers. That makes them- oh I wish I had sunglasses so I could do this properly- *crap* cops."

Naturally Palmyra hit me again.

"Why?" I whined.

"Bad pun, you deserve it."

"I disagree!" I said, rubbing my shoulder.

Palmyra snorted and raised her hand; three dozen Spelleaters darted into her palm. She squished them and they fell to the ground in a single ball of metal.

"I'm beginning to get the impression that you and the others know far more about Spelleaters than I do," I said.

Palmyra smiled.

"Give us a sec, would you?" she said to Demise and her people.

Demise stepped back with the nuns, getting out of earshot.

"How much have you figured out?" Palmyra asked.

"I'm pretty sure that your signets, not mine incidentally, make you immune to them. And, unless I'm very much mistaken, just about everything else?"

"The Signets aren't actually... rings. They are symbols of what we are, that happen to *look* like rings. In a way, they're alive, siblings like we are. They keep us safe. Yours agreed to... limit herself to a symbol and certain general protections."

"Why?" I asked, "I think I know, but let's hear it."

"Well... First Shadows can go bad. The Spelleaters were made with... that in mind."

"That's what I figured," I said with a sigh.

"And, of course, our ancient, mystical, semi-living items of power trump Sorcerer made piffle. So does an Archon, but enough can slow you down."

"Ain't that the truth?" I said.

"You're not mad?"

"I'm actually relieved," I said, "I always had this worry at the back of my mind that someone would ambush one of you with enough Spelleaters to actually hurt you. Or kill one of you."

"Nope," she said, patting my shoulder, "Pretty much the only thing that can hurt an Archon is another Archon. Generally speaking, when one of us dies, it's because we don't want to live anymore."

"Or they're a First Shadow who played around with the Black," I said.

"Yeah, or that," she said, smirking, it shouldn't have been endearing, but it was, "you're not supposed to know a lot of this, you realise? We don't tell the First Shadow about the signet, or the Spelleaters."

"Then why tell me?"

"You know, that's a good question- Ah! That bloody Succubus-thing!" she said, stepping back.

"Oh. Still not my fault, just want that on the record!"

"Shut up, Mathew, I am so mad at you!"

"Me?! What did I do?"

"Well, you're standing there with those puppy-dog eyes and that little sort of smirky smile I like, and you're talking... and stuff," she said, biting her lip.

"What sort of puppies have eyes like this?" I asked, slightly off topic, but I wanted to know.

"Hellhounds," she said, waving it off, "Ah, you see? You see?! You're doing it again, distracting me, drawing information out of me with your clever double-talk."

"My clever what-what?" I asked, a little baffled.

"Well, it's not going to work, you'll get no more information out of me, not even if you tied me to an interrogation chair, maybe with those little furry cuffs..." she said, her eyes glazing a little.

"Alright, this conversation is scarring me for life, and I have an urgent appointment with a Vampire that I'd like to get out the way so I can sleep," I said.

"In the Companion House?" she said, her voice a little squeaky, "Can I come?"

"What?! No! Go when I'm a county and a body of water away, good grief!" I said while Palmyra sniggered.

"No goodnight kiss?" she said as I walked towards Demise.

"When you get home, you're going to remember this conversation with a clear head, and I think you're going to throw up."

"We'll see!" she said as she called a portal and her people piled through.

I went over to Demise, who was still staring.

"This pheromone crap is a menace!" I said.

"I hadn't really noticed," she said, deliberately looking away, blushing a little.

"Thank goodness for that, at least," I said, patting her shoulder, "let's get this conversation with my Information Broker over with. I don't want to be there more than ten minutes."

She hopped on my back again and I Shadow-Walked us to the edge of the 'Carpet's grounds. The guards were even more obvious than before.

"Mathew?" Demise asked.

"Yeah?" I said as we walked up the drive.

"Is this a brothel?"

"It's the location of my Information Broker's office, and that's all that concerns me."

"Then you've never...?"

"Why does everyone keep asking me questions like

that?" I asked, turning to glare.

"Well, you are a man, and eighteen. You live with a Succubus, and now I see that you get your information from a place oozing sexual temptation."

"Alright, for what I hope will be the last time, I have a girlfriend!" I said impatiently.

The door was pushed open by a security guy and we spoke to Bianca, who greeted me fondly.

"Crystal's been going on about you, Mister Graves, or is it Stone? Anyway, I think you helped give her a little peace over her sister," Bianca said as she led us towards the original office, which had apparently been rebuilt.

"I'm glad," I said, "nothing can get to us quite like family."

She nodded and handed us over to Francois.

Demise and I waited for about fifteen minutes, chatting idly. I yawned and leant my head on the wall. I closed my eyes for a second...

"You don't have much in the way of stamina, do you?" said Crystal before there was suddenly a new weight in my lap.

She wore tight jeans and a crop top with half-sleeves. Her hair framed her face and her eyes were dazzling.

"Keep that in mind," I said as I rubbed my eyes, "and adjust your desires accordingly."

She snorted and kissed my cheek, rubbing her nose against it.

"My, my, you smell amazing tonight," she said before nuzzling my neck.

"Oh!" I said, remembering, "You have to keep away from me tonight. I messed up some Magic, and now I'm throwing out enough chemical attractant to draw in a Succubus."

Literally, in fact...

"I like it," she purred, "makes me want to do naughty things."

"Crystal, it's not real. I'm a walking aphrodisiac."

"Doesn't feel any different to me," she said, sniffing a bit harder, "Oh, that's so nice."

"I can drop you in cold water."

"Go on then," she said, nibbling on my ear and making me shiver.

"Mistress Price will see you now," Francois said, a little impatiently (or was that jealously?).

"Crystal?" I said.

"Busy," she said, kissing her way down my neck.

"Crystal!" Price barked. The younger Vampire darted to her feet and backed away, which allowed me to get up.

"Thank you," I said to Price while Crystal giggled from her spot against the wall. Price led us into her office, and I stayed standing, not giving Crystal another chance to sit in my lap.

"You were quick tonight," Price said.

I explained what happened, the setup, the layout and the numbers. She noted some things down on a pad, but she was starting to eye me up as time went on, and it was becoming very intense.

"Good, good," she said, leaning back in her chair. She undid the top button on her jacket. I heard snoring behind me and saw that Demise was curled up on the sofa, Crystal sitting next to her, stroking her hair.

"Is she alright?" I asked.

"Of course," Price said, drawing my attention back to her, "she's just sleeping."

I never even had a chance to see it coming.

Price distracted me and Crystal was at my back before I had even the slightest idea what was happening. I heard my jumper tear, and there was a sudden sharp pain in my neck. I didn't even have the chance to call my Will, I didn't even think I was under attack. This was a safe place, these were my friends...

Warmth spread from the wound, and I felt lightheaded. The pain left almost immediately, and a sense of intense peace and relaxation came over me. The last thing I remember of that night was Price standing up, her fangs prominent in a wide and hungry smile as she moved towards me.

CHAPTER 22

Okay.

Not good.

Still woke up, though, so I took that as a good sign.

I found myself lying on a wide, comfortable bed and even though my head was trying to kill me, everything else was where it was supposed to be (I checked). The sheets were soft and clean, smelling faintly of Crystal's perfume, which I hoped wasn't a sign that I'd done something I shouldn't have. I wasn't quite naked, still in my shirt and underwear, which reassured me a little, though I was even paler than usual (and it didn't take a genius to figure out why). The room was elegantly decorated, the bed a four-poster with transparent silk curtains. There was a very dim light coming through a gap in the heavy blinds, so it was probably what passed for daytime in Gardenia.

God, my mother was going to flip her lid; I'd just disappeared on her!

Demise was sitting in an armchair next to the door, looking at me, she didn't look happy. She was fully dressed and otherwise looked none the worse for wear.

"Are you alright?" I asked.

She looked away.

"Did they do anything to you?" I asked, my voice instantly cold and a little nasty, Shadows flickered from all the dark places as I prepared to knock the building down.

"No!" she said, standing up, "No, Mathew, I swear. They didn't feed on me at all, they couldn't... Death Mage."

"Ah. Then what happened? You look like someone kicked your puppy." I asked, looking around for the rest of my clothes and finding them in a neatly folded heap, freshly laundered. I hopped out of bed and dressed quickly. I wasn't as clean as my clothes, but I didn't feel grimy, or even dirty, really. I did notice that there wasn't a scratch on me, so there was that.

"How much do you remember?" she asked, swallowing hard.

"I remember getting bitten, and that's it."

She sighed, releasing a breath, "Good."

"Good?" I asked.

"I made an arse of myself. I'm just glad you don't remember it."

I frowned, that didn't sound right, "Are you sure you're okay?" I asked her, "They didn't... do anything to you?"

She smiled, just a little, "Nothing I didn't ask for in the heat of a stupid moment, and, like I say, I'm just glad you didn't see it."

I might have pressed, but Demise seemed pretty adamant.

"If you ever do want to talk about it, I'll listen," I said, "And you know I don't judge."

She smiled again, and I'd have sworn that her eyes went a little moist, but that might have been my imagination.

"Thanks," she said, patting my shoulder a bit awkwardly.

"Any idea where Price is? I'd like to get home for breakfast, and I'd better check in before we go."

The door opened right on cue, but it wasn't Price.

Crystal wore a grey silk dressing gown, and that was it as far as I could tell. It was a good look on her.

"You bit me!" I said, making her jump before she broke into a smirk.

"That's hardly my fault, you smelled like sexy food and you turned your back on me, what was I supposed to do?!"

"Well, that's fair enough, but still very bad form," I muttered.

Just like with Kandi, it was more or less impossible to be angry with Crystal for more than a minute, she was too... bouncy, too sweet.

And it wasn't like it was her fault, she'd made her intentions towards me very clear (repeatedly), and since I was the idiot who came into her parlour sporting Succubus musk (which was essentially throwing myself into a shark tank while wearing a swimsuit made out of fresh meat), I had only myself to blame that she sunk her fangs in. I was just grateful that I woke up with my ability to enjoy sunbathing intact (as well as all my appendages).

Crystal slid up to me and drew me into a very nice hug, which was surprisingly affectionate, rather than carnal.

"You still smell *terrific*, by the way," she whispered, dragging the tips of her fangs along my neck.

"No, bad Crystal," I said, pushing her back to arm's length, "and I did tell you that I'd made a Magical mistake with my hormones."

"And? You say that like it matters," she said, still smiling.

I shook my head, having trouble not smiling myself.

"How far did you take the biting?" I asked, exasperated.

At this, she looked a little shifty.

"Oh, you didn't, did you?"

"Sorry," she said, blushing, "I couldn't help myself, you were so tasty! And then I took a little too much, so I had to give you some of mine so you wouldn't snuff it, and then it was easy to make the bond, so I did..."

"Damn it, Crystal!"

"Well don't blame me! You were Vampire Catnip, how was I ever *not* going to scratch?"

"Self control?" I offered.

"You realise what I do for a living? Does that really scream 'self control' to you?"

Again, fair enough.

"Still, bad form," I repeated, it just made her laugh, which banished my grump.

"It's not a problem for you?" I asked, "The blood bond thing? It doesn't produce a dependency or anything?"

"Hardly, just makes feeding more fun and nutritious and you'll have some wild sex-dreams about me, so it's not like that'll be anything different," she said, her smile turning a bit naughty and sending my heart-rate up.

"Ha, ha," I said dryly, tweaking her nose, which only made her shiver. I needed to get out of there, she was still under the influence of the musk.

Naturally Price came in just as I was contemplating a swift exit.

"Ah, you're awake," she said with a smile. She was dressed in her usual business-casual, "And upright, I was worried for a moment there."

I glared at Crystal, who whistled innocently, staring at the ceiling.

I shook my head, "My apologies for any... problems caused last night," I said.

"Oh, you were no trouble at all," Price said in a predatory way, turning her eyes on Demise, "*absolutely* no trouble."

Price's eyes swivelled back to me, taking me in from head to toe, "You know, my lord, if you have some time today, I'd love for us to have a nice, long... chat about how our business interests could further... combine."

I swallowed hard.

"I'd like that, but today is rather packed for me. If you still want to talk, it would have to be in three days or so."

At which time, she'd have forgotten, and the musk would have worn off... hopefully.

She licked her lips and took a step towards me.

"Easy," Demise growled at Price, the Death Mage's hand in her jacket.

"Come, come, we've been through a lot together, sweet Demise," Price said pointedly, surely you don't mean to get in my way, who knows what might slip out in the heat of the moment?"

"Ms. Price," I said in a hard voice, which startled her enough to make her turn around, her eyes clearing, "You're not yourself. I'm still putting out that pheromone, remember? Would you really break a confidence like that under any other circumstances?"

I respected Demise enough to let her keep her secrets, and even help her do so if it were that important to her.

Price's eyes cleared, and her cheeks coloured. She bowed to Demise, "My apologies," she said, sincerely.

"Not your fault," Demise replied, quite graciously. She even took her hand off whatever weapon she'd been reaching for.

"Look, we've all had a bit of a night, some of us did some things we shouldn't have," I said, "Let's agree to move on and *never* mention it again, alright?"

"Nope," Crystal said, beaming happily as she continued to stare at me.

"Agreed," Price said, pinching Crystal's wonderful rear end, which made the younger vampire squeak and glare. I couldn't help but chuckle, and feel a rush of affection for those two. Even under chemical influence, when they could have easily done me all manner of harm, I'd been able to trust them (more or less).

I nodded, "I'll be in touch."

"I should hope so," Price said, her eyes narrowed and interested.

"See you soon, Mathew?" Crystal said, a glint in her eye that reminded me of Cassandra eyeing up my last packet of chocolate digestives.

I nodded and opened a Gate, smiling at them both as I took Demise back home.

Half an hour later, we emerged out of the Shadow under a tree on my front lawn. It was just after eleven, and we walked up to the back door. I found Mother in her study, hard at work. She hadn't noticed I'd gone, which was good, in a way, but also a little sad.

I walked and fed Burglar, who was near-manic to get out of the house. Then I went to the shower and took care of my morning ablutions while Demise watched as usual. I still wasn't used to that, but there seemed to be less of a barrier between us since last night, like we knew each other a bit better, perhaps. There certainly seemed to be less reserve on her part, and I found that I was just that little more comfortable in her presence as well, which was nice.

"Are you hungry?" I asked her once I was in a new set of clothes.

"A little," she said.

I nodded and led the way to the kitchen so she could eat. I wasn't that hungry, and I was just a bit worried about Crystal and what had happened. I knew that nobody had been in their right mind, but it seemed to be a very hard thing on her, like I was leading her on.

That sounded idiotic, even to me, but I was nothing if not a sucker for a pretty face. So I tried not to think about it, which led to me thinking about it; it was an irritating cycle. I needed a book, a movie, something to distract me.

"The Starborn Lady told me that you spiral," Demise said, sitting down at the kitchen table, Burglar hard on her heels looking for titbits (he'd discovered her to be a soft touch), "Don't spiral. That girl is not some ingénue flower that will wilt at the first sign of strangeness. She's older than you by a solid margin and has more experience of men and relationships that I hope you'll ever need. She understands, trust me."

"I still feel like a..."

"Cad?" Demise offered.

"As good a word as any."

"You're not."

I smiled at her and she returned the expression.

I felt a bit better and made some breakfast, which the dog stole while I wasn't looking.

Afterwards, I pulled out one of the Level Ten Magic textbooks and headed outside. I'd been neglecting my Magical education for too long, what with one thing or another.

At Level One, the book was the width of my thumb with big writing, comforting pictures and detailed descriptions. The Level Ten 'book' consisted of *five* volumes, each two inches thick, and you needed to know every spell in every volume to pass the tests, and these were spells that required sub-spells to cast and a variety of energy types to work properly.

I loved every frustrating page of it.

I'd made my way through the first volume and part of the second. Though complex, it wasn't really hard to understand. Magic came to me like breathing did, as naturally as life itself. It just took time to learn that much material, though retaining it was much easier than Shakespeare, it just sort of... went in and got stuck, particularly if I cast the spell in question.

The book was arranged by loose 'Schools' of Magic that had so much overlap at that level that categories were more or less pointless. I was studying an 'Enhancement' spell, the principle of which was to grow a field of something from a single seed of same. So, take a wheat seed, and make a whole field of it.

It was about fifteen different spells in one construct, and awfully complex. It had to be, so as not to rip all the nutrients out of the soil and leave it barren, while also avoiding horrific mutations in the plant, in this case, apple trees.

My mother always said she wanted an orchard.

Demise sat down on the grass next to me in an open stretch of our back garden. I'd taken an apple from the fruit basket in the kitchen for my experiment. She peered down at the book as I studied the spell frameworks.

"Complicated," she commented.

I nodded.

"You're Level Nine?" she asked.

"Certified," I said, a little proudly, "You?"

"Seven. Highest among my sisters. We mostly focus on Battle Magic, but I always liked studying the general spells."

"You getting ready for Eight?"

"I... I have trouble with some of the transjunctions and sensory input spells," she said self-consciously.

"I still have all the Level Eight books," I offered, "I had some trouble with sensory input, too; I can show you how I solved the problem, if you like?"

"You're busy," she said, turning away.

"This'll keep," I said, standing up, "and reviewing the theory is always useful before trying something new."

It certainly helped pass the time and to focus my mind on better things. Demise was an exceptional Sorceress, powerful and versatile, but holding multiple spell effects in her head at the same time was a bit of a problem for her. That, and she wanted to do everything quickly, like ripping off a bandage, which was a battlemage thing. It took me a while to persuade her that advanced sensory alteration spells *shouldn't* be rushed (that's how I ended up with purple vision for a week).

I helped tighten up her spell groupings and her constructs. She only took four hours to progress. That was far quicker than I'd managed, just so you know, it took me days to get those spells right.

She smiled as she succeeded, casting one of the more complex variations on Mage Sight.

"You're a natural teacher," she said.

"You did the work, I just helped you scrape off the rough edges," I said, going back to my Level Ten book while she started leafing through some of the other spells in the Level Eight.

"A natural teacher, but a terrible fighter."

I snorted, "I hate fighting," I confessed.

She looked surprised.

I nodded in reply, "It's true, I absolutely loathe it."

"They way you fight, I'm not surprised."

I grinned and went back to reading.

"But why?" she asked.

"Why what?"

"Why do you hate fighting so much? An Archon would be exceptional at it."

I closed my book and looked at her.

"You know what my first piece of serious Magic was? I don't mean practice or little stuff around a house. I mean Magic in earnest, when it *really* mattered?"

She shook her head.

"My brother fell down a gorge. It was a bad fall, maybe thirty feet down a rocky slope and right onto a broken fence post, hit him right here," I said, pointing at my chest, mid way up where my right lung was.

"He nearly bled out before I got to him. I knew a few bits of Medical Magic, barely anything. I cast a Lifelink without even knowing what I was doing; all I knew was that I wanted Des to live so badly that I was able to reach out and give him what he needed. If Magic can do *that,* let a clumsy young Magician save his brother when he shouldn't be able to... then using it for... hurting people, killing them... how could I do that? When Magic can bring my brother back from the brink of death, how could I use it for *that*?"

She sighed, looking at me for a long time, "We do it, Mathew so that the next person's brother doesn't die. We do it because people need someone willing to stand between them and the things that would eat them. And often, we do it because the next person wouldn't survive trying."

"I still hate it," I said.

"Learn to love it, that's what I did. And learn quickly, spending time with you is making my sword hand itchy."

I laughed.

I did some spellwork, and made some progress.

Then I called Tethys.

"Oh, good, I was just about to call you," she said.

"Regarding?"

"I need some paperwork signed, what was your thing?"

I told her about the previous night, leaving out a couple

of details, but she was able to infer. She wasn't an idiot and knew that my skills at Medical Magic were too far advanced for a hormonal mistake like that.

"Can she hear my side of the conversation?" Tethys asked, referring to Demise.

"No."

"Was it really a malfunction?"

"No."

"Was it Gabrielle?"

"Yes."

"Get over here. I want to see how bad the damage is. Vampire and Demon."

"I can't. I dare not risk being around women right now," I said.

"I can control myself, Matty, and your Captain doesn't think of you that way. I'll keep Kandi out of the room, I promise."

I let out a breath.

"Okay, be there in ten," I said.

"Now what?" Demise asked once I'd put the phone down.

"Tethys wants to take a look at me after the whole... Vampire thing. Just to be on the safe side."

I told my mother I was going out, and then Demise and I Shadow-Walked to Blackhold. We emerged into a downstairs loo and opened the door to the sudden surprise of Jillian, who shrieked and nearly shot me, before calming down and telling us that Tethys was in her office. I led the way and knocked on the door.

Cassandra and Tethys were waiting for us.

They said hello, and I hugged each of them. Cassandra was just the same as always, but Tethys... well she didn't want to let me go.

"This may have been a mistake," the Succubus said as she pushed me to the nearest sofa; she bit my ear and kissed my neck, "Matty, you're going to have to stop me. God, I'm sorry."

She didn't sound too sorry. She moved and straddled my

hips, her hands going for my shirt. I called my Shadows and wrapped her up in them as gently as I could. I deposited her on the sofa next to me.

She groaned, her eyes on me.

"Matty, it's fine, you can let me go again, really I'm okay," she said, but I could feel her straining at the wrap.

"I'm just going to pop next door," I said, "You should be fine in a minute."

"No, Matty, don't go, please," she whispered huskily, biting her lip.

"I'm not going. I'm right next door. Where you can't smell me."

She growled in frustration, but I managed to get out and move into the adjacent room with Cassandra and Demise in tow.

I opened my mind and reached for Tethys'.

How are you feeling? I sent.

Better now I can't see you. My God, Matty, what did she do to you?

I told her everything in more detail, including the entire story of Gabrielle and Rose.

Oh, you idiot! No wonder the Vampires went for you! I'm actually quite amazed that you came out of that in one piece!

Yeah, me too, actually.

The fact that Crystal was actually fond of you would have helped. I know it sounds hokey, but friendship and other positive emotions do provide a certain defence when dealing with Hell-related problems like this. Not enough to stop her, but enough to keep her human part in something resembling control.

That surprised me... a lot. I would not have thought the world worked like that. It left me feeling a little hopeful, actually.

Is she going to be okay?

I don't know her, but Demise is probably right. And you've demonstrated a willingness to be there for her when it matters, so I don't think this will negatively affect your relationship. Just be careful not to turn your back on her for a while, you are at least ten times more delicious to her now, that's what the bond does; she'll nip at you every chance she gets.

Terrific. And how am I going to explain this to Cathy?

Tell her you swapped bodily fluids with a sexy escort, that should do it.

Not funny, Tethys.

Then why am I laughing?

I could hear her guffawing through the walls.

That is not a ladylike sound, you know!

Don't care.

She carried on for a while before coming back to the conversation. I loved Tethys, but she could be a bit of a monster at times. Laughing at other people's discomfort was one of her favourite things (not that I'm one to talk).

Anything else I should know about the bond?

Not really. It just makes all those fun things girls and boys like to do to each other even more fun, it'll let her find you if you're in the general area; she'll be better equipped to get past your mental defences, that sort of thing.

Mental defences? that worried me.

I wouldn't worry, you're still an Archon, Matty.

An Archon who let himself get bit and knocked out by a tiny little vampire, I reminded her.

She started laughing again.

What was Demise doing during this, by the way? I would think she'd have been quite able to stop any of this happening.

She told me they knocked her out with some sort of Telepathic attack.

Then how was she conscious for this 'embarrassing event' she mentioned?

My forehead furrowed at that.

No idea.

I'll ask. I smell dirt! She obviously doesn't want you to know, so we'll have to make arrangements if we've any hope of discovering anything juicy...

Tethys... are you drooling?
What? No!
I chuckled.

That part was complicated.

Demise always had to keep me in sight, as you know. So I sat at one end of the house at the far end of a long corridor, while Tethys and Demise sat across from one another at the other end, with Demise able to see me.

Cassandra sat with me.

"I want this drug crap over with," Cassandra said, "I'm not sure how much more of this stress I can take."

I snorted.

"How do you think I feel? I'm not cut out for derring-do," I replied.

She chuckled and leant her head against my shoulder.

"Is it odd that I'm not affected by this Succubus thing?" she asked.

"For me it's infinitely reassuring," I said, taking her hand, "Don't take this the wrong way, but you're exactly the sort of big sister I always wished I'd had. Someone I could look up to. That's how I think of you."

She smiled, "You really are such a girl," she said, squeezing my fingers, "much like my little sister was."

I grinned widely and she nudged my ribs with her elbow.

"You know I was the only Magician in my family?" she said.

I nodded.

"Well, you remind me a lot of my sister Karen. After we got away from Benjamin, she became an apothecary, wanted to help people. Even after everything she'd been through, the training and the loss, she was still so sweet. She lived a long, happy life and died fat and happy surrounded by her children and grandchildren, as sweet as the day I first took her in my arms as a baby. You have a lot of her inherent decency, Mathew.

I like the way you remind me of her."

We smiled at each other and watched as Tethys and Demise talked. The look on Tethys' face wasn't pleasant. She looked immeasurably pissed off.

"That doesn't look good," I said.

"No, it doesn't," Cassandra said.

"Maybe you should go make sure nobody's about to lose a body part?" I suggested.

"That might be best," she said, hopping up and moving towards the reception room.

I waited where I was. Three women, all of them dangerous, two of whom I loved like family, not a great idea to get in the middle of that.

"WHAT?!" Cassandra bellowed.

Oh dear. I stood up.

"STAY WHERE YOU ARE!" Cassandra shouted in my direction.

I sat back down. What brought that on?

It took a while, but Cassandra and Demise came back with Tethys. The Succubus looked calmer, but still miffed. Cassie looked like she was about to blast something.

"Is everything alright?" I asked.

"Fine," Cassandra said through gritted teeth, glaring at Demise, "we had a nice little... chat. Demise has explained herself. You will not ask her what happened. You will not make any further enquiries, do you understand?"

"You're making me very nervous," I said.

"Don't. Ask. Questions," Cassandra said very firmly.

"But..."

"Mathew, have I ever lied to you?" Cassandra asked.

"No," that was a certainty, Cassandra didn't lie, as a rule.

"Then you'll believe me when I tell you that you mustn't prod at this, understand me? It's important. Maybe we'll be able to discuss it one day, but not now, understand?"

I nodded.

"Then no more questions," Cassandra said, "or I will beat

you like a throw rug."

"Okay."

"Come on, let's eat something, then we'll get you out of the bloody way before some other critter takes a fancy to you," Cassandra said, dragging me to my feet and in the direction of the breakfast room, "Honestly, as if the Succubus wasn't bad enough, and that werewolf girl you took a fancy to, now there's a bloody vampire!"

We ate, Cassandra, Demise and I, and then Demise and I went back to my home.

I spent time with the Pixies and the Nymphs, none of whom were affected by the musk, thank God. Demise kept staring and she started sleeping next to my bed, and by the time the third day rolled around, she'd moved her sleeping bag *onto* the damned thing. A slight invasion of personal space, but at that point, I barely noticed.

I told Cathy everything I remembered; I was completely honest. She wasn't mad at me, she trusted me. But she was upset at the idea that things may have fed off me. The fact that they were female things barely registered. The whole blood-bond thing made her... furious is too mild a word. I heard things hitting walls over the phone.

CHAPTER 23

I went back to Windward in a mood. Thankfully, that blasted musk had worn off, at least. I met Cathy in her room and she threw herself at me and refused to let me go, not that I complained. Demise sat unobtrusively in the corner, watching as always.

"I missed you," I said as we sat on her bed, her head on my shoulder and her legs over my lap.

"I missed you too, Matty," she said softly, her hands tangled in my shirt.

"Are you alright?" I asked.

"I'm worried, so worried. It seems that every time I see you something else has happened to you. I can't bear it, Matty, I can't," she said with a sob that was like a knife in my heart.

"I'm sorry, Cath. I love you. I'd never do anything to hurt you, not if I can avoid it, I swear."

"I know that," she said, squeezing me again, "But, Mathew, I'm not strong enough for this."

"Yes you are. And you won't have to worry any more, alright? You will not hear about any more of this. I'll stay safe."

She looked me in the eye and those lovely soulful eyes of hers seemed to bore into me. She nodded once, slowly, and leant back against me. I held her and closed my eyes. Having her close made everything better, like she was my tether and letting go would mean I would float away into this world of Vampires and Demons and looking over my shoulder for the next knife coming at my back.

Could I disappear with her one day? Could I just leave? I choked back a sob when I realised that it didn't really matter how far I ran, or what dimension I decided to hide in, those 'Liaisons' would always be able to find me. And then I'd have to deal with whatever they wanted or there'd be some sort of apocalypse...

I wanted to scream, to thrash and burn something to the ground. But then Cathy held my hand, and it wasn't so bad anymore.

Crystal called after a couple of days (once the musk had completely worn off), thoroughly apologetic for biting me without permission. I told her it was alright. Though as soon as I dealt with that last bloody factory, I wasn't ever going near Gardenia ever, ever again. Or even Stonebridge at this rate, cities just caused me trouble.

Days passed slowly, routine re-established itself. It allowed my mind to shift into more comfortable areas, and forget about... everything. The fact that Demise was still there like a spectre at the feast didn't help. She was sleeping in my bed with me these days. I didn't really like it, but I was too tired of fighting to make an issue of it.

As days turned into weeks, Demise... started getting peculiar. She started being... nice. She had always been courteous enough, if a little distant, but now she was friendly. Or as close as she knew how to be, I suppose. She talked to me, told me about her life, which was mostly learning to fight and then beating the snot out of people.

She was a soldier, and I couldn't really relate to her on that level, but she was also a student with a love of Magic, and that was something I could very much relate to. So I talked to her about that, which may have been a mistake, because it turned out that she had a lot to say, and once she started, she wouldn't stop.

I didn't think that her sisters encouraged intellectual pursuits. Cathy and Bill tried to follow the talk, but it was rather technical, and it was *all the time*. Questions and comments, not always about Magic, either...

Just as an example, a few days into this, Cathy and I were happily occupied in our favourite bush, and things were progressing in a very interesting direction. She was all teeth that day, her breathing loud and arousing as she nibbled my ear and I kissed her neck.

And suddenly, there was Demise, looming through the hole in the bush above us.

"You do this a lot," she said, startling both of us, which made Cathy bite down hard enough to draw blood.

"Dee, for heaven's sake!" I said, clutching at my neck.

Cathy looked aghast, but she was also trying to conceal a laugh while looking at the damage she'd caused.

"I've been with men. They don't do this with as much enthusiasm as you do," she said.

"I don't know how to answer that."

Cathy sniggered and pulled out a hanky to press to the tooth marks that were oozing.

"What makes what you do better than what they do?" she asked.

Cathy actually laughed that time.

"I... I... I...," I stuttered, Cathy continued laughing at me, "What makes you think I'm doing it better?"

Why the hell I asked is beyond me.

Cathy was on the verge of hysterics at this point, still in my lap, by the way.

"The sounds she makes," Demise replied, "I don't normally make sounds like that."

Cathy was shaking with laughter, and the effect was rather... stimulating, bearing in mind how she was sitting.

"Well..." I said, trying to come up with some response, just to get her out of my sight line as much as anything else, I was in the middle of something, damn it, "It's... it's all about being comfortable with your p-partner, I guess... help me Cathy."

"Nope," my girlfriend said, nosing into the uninjured side of my neck.

"But why do this?" Demise continued, "You won't have sex while I'm your Watcher, so why bother?"

"This has to be the most uncomfortable conversation I've ever had in my life," I muttered.

"Why?" Demise asked.

"I do not discuss the intimate details of my life," I said.

"But you're willing to conduct them in front of me?"

Cathy was crying with laughter now.

"Would you let us conduct them in private?" I asked.

"Of course not," she said.

"Well, then this is sort of a..."

"Middle ground?" Cathy offered with a chuckle.

"Close enough," I said.

"And you enjoy it? Without completion?" Demise asked.

"Very much," Cathy said, kissing my cheek, "You must have... you know? Kissed a boy, cuddled?"

"I've been with a few men, but like you two? Only once," Demise said, a strange look coming over her face, "and then it was part of a larger... experience. The only time it was... good. So, I want to know what makes things like that different."

"It's about who you're with," Cathy said, looking at me, "About trusting who you're with. What did you feel with the one you liked?"

Why the hell were we going into this? This was girl talk, damn it. I didn't know what I was doing, there! And I didn't need to hear it, particularly when there's an agitated Cathy on my lap! For heaven's sake, this woman was older than the two of us put together times six!

"Like... like I was where I was supposed to be," Demise eventually answered, "I felt like he wanted to be there, and that he loved what he saw."

"What happened?" Cathy asked quietly.

"He woke up," Demise answered softly, and then she disappeared, though I knew she'd still be where she could see me.

"Oh, that's so sad!" Cathy said, leaning against my shoulder.

Mood completely killed, thank you, Dee.

And that wasn't the last time she did that, oh no.

It seemed like every time Cathy and I adjourned to a bush, or a bedroom, behind a shed or just to steal a kiss, Demise was there with a question, or a comment, or simply standing *way* too close and killing the mood again and again and *again...*

I begged her, begged her, mind you, to give us some space. She replied by periodically checking if she was far away enough. As if it wasn't bad enough that she was preventing greater intimacy, now she was trying to break the smaller stuff too.

I knew she didn't mean to. It was just her way. But damn it, I was getting frustrated, and Cathy just seemed to find the whole thing utterly hilarious.

It was the third Monday after half term ended and I was in a state and a half when Magic Class came around. Direct spiritual draining by Succubus aside, it had been a *very* long time, and I was just about ready to start chewing the concrete.

Hopkins had started teaching basic self defence, which gave me time to nap, seeing as how my life was more or less one long advanced-class in same. Cathy was sitting to my left, Bill my right and Demise was sitting behind me. Belle was in front of me with the other Magicians in the school, occupying the first three rows.

I knew them all to one degree or another, a nice enough group. Lilly, Wilbur and Shelly were the new people. Wilbur was a friend, I helped him with his spell problems from time to time.

"Alright, which poor fool wants to volunteer for a practical demonstration?" Hopkins said.

I cast a glamour and became invisible.

Demise rapped me on the head and my glamour dissolved.

"Ow!" I said, rubbing my crown and turning around,

"What the hell?"

"Mister Graves, excellent," Hopkins said.

"Oh, please no," I said.

Hopkins tapped the duelling ring with her foot. I slumped but stood. She liked to use me as a practice dummy from time to time. She had everybody line up and blast my shields. I received a round of applause and some catcalls on my way. Hopkins tossed me a gauntlet. They worked with the Duelling ring to produce protective shields around the participants.

Naturally, I dropped it and there was jeering as I picked it up and strapped it on before stepping into the circle.

"Nothing flashy," Hopkins said to me.

"I'm not a well man, you know," I protested.

"And whose fault is that?" she replied.

"I need a nap just from walking down the stairs," I complained.

"Just put up a shield, you weed."

"You know, in other parts of the world, them'd be considered fightin' words."

"Oh really? After the spanking you got last time?" she said with an evil grin.

"As I recall, it was a draw," I replied snarkily.

"Did she say spanking?" Lilly asked Belle, which caused a giggling fit among the girls.

Hopkins growled and turned away, "McFadden, get up here and do something useful!"

Lilly squeaked and darted to her feet, nearly falling over in her haste to get into the circle.

"Hi Matty," she said as she slid her own gauntlet on and stood opposite me.

"Remember, quick is key; fast and nasty," Hopkins said.

"Okay," Lilly said. She called Magic and drew in energy. It took her a couple of seconds.

"Relax," I said, "don't drag it in, let it in."

She nodded, sweating. She thrust her hands towards

me, shutting her eyes. A trio of weak lightning bolts flew out. One hit my shields, the other two smacked into the ground.

"Good, Lilly," I said, "but I've seen you do better. Remember, it's relaxation and concentration. It's a balance between the two."

She nodded, "I don't like shooting lightning at people," she said, pulling in more static electricity from the air.

"Good," I said with a smile, "But you don't learn because you *like* it, you learn for the day that you might *need* it."

She closed her eyes and nodded.

Two out of three hit me the next time. I helped her tighten up her spell work, and on her fourth try, she hit me with all three. Then she got it right three times in a row. I smiled at her and she grinned back.

"Alright, very good," Hopkins said, "You may sit, Miss McFadden. Next?"

And so on and so forth until everyone had taken some pretty decent shots at me. It took well over an hour for Hopkins and I to get everyone blasting in the right direction and on target (me). It was good practice for me too. I worked on my adaptive shields while they had at me. Generally, I used general Force-Shields layered with Dispels for my defences, but I could also tailor specific, far more efficient, shields for each type of incoming energy. The drawback being that they were useless against everything else.

Still good practice, though.

Finally, Belle sat down after exhausting herself trying to get through my shields. She liked to come up with surprises for me, trying to get past me. I didn't mind; she was getting better, and it kept me on my toes. Belle had been advancing in leaps and bounds since she stopped trying to be a duellist and focussed on Magic as a subject rather than as a means to an end. She was about to take her Level Three tests, and I was helping her study for the theory part in between everything else on my plate.

"Alright, if everyone's quite finished trying to kill Mister

Graves-" Hopkins began.

Demise stood and Hopkins looked up as she walked down the steps and took the gauntlet from Belle before stepping into the ring.

"Oh," Hopkins said, a little surprised, "well, why not?"

"I can think of a reason. Or five, mostly involving my imminent injury," I said.

"Do I have to call you names again?" Hopkins asked.

"If it gets me from here to the nap I had pencilled in to start ten minutes ago, then sure."

There were some laughs from the crowd, but more in the way of anticipation. Demise was a largely unknown quantity, and barely even noticed on account of her concealing Magic (which she was *still* refusing to teach me). What few people even remembered her thought that she was some sort of exchange student, which was the story we'd told them.

Demise stood in front of me. She looked utterly calm and focussed.

"What's up, Dee?" I asked.

"Spar now," she said, tightening up the gauntlet.

"Any particular reason?" I asked.

"May need to kill you one day. Good to know what I'm dealing with."

She said it so coldly, so clinically, that I took a step back.

"I don't think I want to do this," I said, stepping back out of the ring.

"Why?" she asked, "Are you a coward?"

"As a matter of fact, I am," I said, pulling my gauntlet off.

"Is that what you said to Puritus?" she asked as I stepped out of the ring; I froze "When they held you down and carved that thing into your face? Is that what you said? 'I don't think I want to do this'? Did you cry? Did you beg?"

Hopkins was white with fury as she stepped towards Demise. I put up a hand and she stopped, but I could feel Space starting to warp a little in her rage.

"What did you say to me?" I asked Demise, turning

around. My voice was very low, very cold. People recoiled from it. Lilly broke into tears on the spot.

"You heard me," Demise said.

I yanked the gauntlet back on and stepped into the ring.

"Miss Hopkins, would you mind refereeing?" I asked as gently as I could, now pretty angry myself.

"Of course," she replied, her eyes boring into Demise.

"Best of three touches," Hopkins said, "No High Magic."

I nodded.

"I will not be restricted," Demise said.

"Yes you wi-" Hopkins began.

"It's fine with me," I rasped.

The scars were something of a sore point for me, as you may have guessed. If she'd also mentioned my brother, all that would be left of her would right now be a greasy stain on the floor.

Hopkins nodded, "Both ready?"

Tear her a new one, Matty, she sent.

Oh, you betcha.

"Begin!"

The first round lasted exactly one second.

I lost.

In that first second, while I was still calling my Shadows, she'd drawn her sword out of nowhere, closed the ten metres between us, and cut a trough in my cheek.

It bled heavily, and my face burned with sudden pain. I yelped and turned, my power ready to blast Demise right off her feet, but the chime sounded. I stopped automatically, thank goodness. That remembered response was quite possibly the only thing that kept me from... I don't know. I was *that* angry.

"What the hell is wrong with you?" Hopkins said to Demise as she darted into the ring to look at my face. The cut had been straight through the pentagram, and blood was pouring down in a sheet, dripping onto my jacket.

"Duels are to the first blood," Demise said.

"I'm fine," I whispered, retaking my stance.

"At least let me fix that," Hopkins said.

"Later, please, I just want this done," I said, still whispering.

Hopkins looked almost as angry as I was, "Will first, Matty. She's a War Mage, trained to murder, not just battle. Get something between you and her."

That, I'd already figured out.

"Thanks," I said neutrally.

She backed out again and Demise retook her place. I tried to calm down and think it through. She was physically faster than me, but I was smarter, mentally quicker, Magically stronger and far more versatile. The mismatch was actually laughable, and yet she'd cut my face open.

In front of Cathy; who was now crying as well.

She'd made my Cathy cry...

"Both ready?" Hopkins said.

We both nodded.

"Begin!"

She bounced off my Will shield almost the instant I'd called it. I strengthened it and she came from another angle, that bloody sword of hers slashing and pounding at my shields. I felt her calling Death and cast my standard shields. They sprung into being between us, and she cast her Entropic beam at them. I shifted my Will shield to deflect it. Force-based shields weren't too useful against Death Magic, Will worked just fine, though. The only problem was that Will was draining.

That wasn't as much of a problem for me, though.

I called my Shadows. They came from everywhere all at once and converged instantly on her before flinging her bodily from the ring. It was the most gentle I could be, and she still broke the doors clear out of the wall as she smashed through them.

The chime went off.

Demise didn't care. She came right back at me, silently,

her sword held high. She threw great gouts of Death Magic through the one-way barrier that kept my Magic contained in the ring. My Shadows were shredded, but there were always more of them, solid and reassuring. I slammed them into the shield, running them through with pure Dispel, I drained huge amounts of power to make a hole and walk out with my spells and defences intact. I'd have had to leave them behind otherwise.

Slight problem, the gauntlets didn't work outside the circle, and also the crowd wasn't protected from splash damage.

So I decided to take it outside. I sent a whole mess of Shadows. They wrapped her up in a cocoon and I simply tossed her out the door, the Shadows dragging her out and away before dropping her into the playing fields half a kilometre away.

I followed, wrapping my Shadows around me and darting into the air. I landed nearby as she was dragging herself groggily to her feet. I felt her calling more Death Magic. So I hit her again. It took all I had not to let those Shadows grow barbed and ugly. I wanted to take her head off (I'd done that before, to a reanimated Sorcerer-corpse, so it was doable).

"So, you *can* get angry..." she said as she brought herself to her knees, dizzy and tired.

I didn't respond.

"I was beginning to wonder. Always so reasonable, so kind. It'll kill you one day," she said.

"I want you gone," I said, my voice vibrating from the Shadows, I sounded ugly and awful.

"That's not your choice."

"Right here, right now, it's very much my choice."

"Only if you're willing to murder me," she said.

"You pull a weapon on me again, that's what happens."

"As you will, Lord Shadow," she said, lowering her eyes.

I dropped my Shields and released my Shadows.

"You stay away from me," I rasped.

I turned and walked back towards the gym, where there

was quite the crowd gathering. My collar was soaked in blood. Ever since I'd torn out half my living energy, *for that woman*, I'd been healing and clotting slowly. The cut had been deep, and my face was burning.

Hopkins was close and she moved in next to me, her hands gentle on the wound. She grunted, and I felt Flesh Magic at work while Cathy came to my other side and tucked herself in under my arm. Hopkins had to be careful. Flesh Magic used the injured person's resources to heal them. With my living energy so low, Flesh Magic could do me as much harm as good if handled improperly.

Thankfully, Hopkins knew what she's doing.

"I want her gone," I said.

"I'll call Killian."

"I won't have her sleeping next to me. I can't look at her."

"She'll be gone within the hour."

"Doubt it," Demise said from behind me, "Watchers aren't disposed of because the Danger is uncomfortable with us. I was assigned. I will stay."

"You would be well advised to remember who you're talking to," Hopkins said, "And don't all of you have rooms to get to?!"

The crowd dispersed very quickly, leaving Bill and Cathy with me.

"I know who I'm talking to, Lady Hopkins. And it doesn't matter, with respect. This was one of his tests. How he responds to anger. It had to be known."

Hopkins scowled.

"And how will you report to Killian?" she asked.

"Any other man would have murdered me. I used secrets told to me in trust to hurt him and he didn't hurt me back. He passed, thoroughly. Even when he's angry, he's a good man."

Hopkins finished patching me up, which took a while. Demise watched passively, her eyes very intently on the wound she'd caused. I didn't look at her, focussing my attention on Cathy, who was recovering and now incredibly angry with Demise.

"Warden, a word," Hopkins said, nodding away from us.

They walked out of earshot. Well, most people's earshot. It was dark, I heard what they were saying through the Shadows like a spider feeling a fly in his web. I didn't want to listen, but I was too frazzled to block it out, exhausted and weakened.

"Are you insane?" Hopkins whispered, "That was supposed to be the *final* test! What were you thinking?"

"I won't have that be the last thing he sees of me," Demise said, "This way he has time."

"You don't know Mathew Graves. He holds epic grudges, he won't forgive what you just did. If he even speaks to you again, it'll be a minor miracle."

"He'll forgive me," Demise said firmly.

"You listened, you drew his pain from him, and then you used it to goad him into anger. Would you forgive him if he did that to you?!"

"He's better than me," Demise said softly, "He understands. Even the monsters. He even loves the monsters."

"That's because even the monsters don't do *that* to him!"

"I must see to my charge, my Lady," Demise said.

"He is not your charge! He's *my* charge. He's your Danger. And you just gave him every reason in the world to drop you, which puts his relationship with Killian and Kron in jeopardy, which puts him in danger!" Hopkins said, her voice rising just a little, "Why? Why would you do that?"

"I told you, and it's like you said, this test should have been his last. I won't have him remember me like that, like I'm just his tormentor. I wanted to give him time. I knew he'd hate me. I also knew that he'd forgive me if I made him, if I gave him that time. He gave me a part of himself so I could live. I know his soul. I know his character. He'll forgive me."

I really wished I hadn't heard all that. It makes it very difficult to hate people when you empathise with them. Demise... she was just following orders. But I was still so mad at her! She... I thought she was my friend. I should have known better. And yet she obviously thought well enough of me to want to make things right. How much longer was this whole 'Watcher' thing going to take?

Demise came over and stood to one side. I ignored her, still too angry. Cathy was glaring hard and squeezing me tightly enough to bruise.

"Okay, Matty, you can go back to your room now. She'll have to stay. She... she's in charge of your case."

I nodded.

I walked away with Cathy and we chatted idly as we walked, trying to ignore the spectre.

"She wouldn't have really hurt you, would she?" Cathy asked quietly.

"Couldn't if she wanted to, Cath," I replied, "She's no match for me."

An utter lie. If she'd wanted me dead with that first strike, I'd be dead. But Cathy didn't need to know that. And she'd suffered enough for one night. I said 'good night' to her and hugged her tightly to me. I told her I loved her and she went off to bed.

Bill ran like the wind (more or less) once Cathy was gone. I rounded on Demise.

"I don't even know what to say to you," I said, "I am so angry with you right now, I want to spit!"

"What was done needed to be done."

"I heard what you said, I understand *that*. That's not the problem. You did it in front of *her*. You hurt me, you humiliated me. You *cut* me in front of Cathy. You scared her, you upset her. She's already terrified for me, and you made it worse."

"The life of an Archon isn't going to get any easier, Mathew. She can either accept that, or she's going to suffer horribly just being near you, much less with you."

"That is not for you to say!" I shouted back, "You don't know her!"

"But I do know *you*," she said, pointing at her chest, "In here. You can't stop yourself. You see pain and you slam your head straight at it trying to make it go away. That will hurt you from time to time. One day, in spite of what your Wardens will be able to do, that is going to get you killed. You should have tried to kill me today. At the least, you should have broken me for what I did. You lack that instinct, that warrior's heart that will be all that keeps you alive. Even Palmyra has it."

I shook my head and continued walking.

"Never do that in front of Cathy again."

"As my lord commands," she said.

"There's no need to be facetious," I said with a snarl.

"I wasn't," she said, perfectly seriously, which took me by surprise and made me feel ashamed of myself.

"Sorry," I said, "generally when people say something like that to me, they're being sarcastic."

"You are the Lord Shadow. You've earned my respect many times over. When I use your title, I mean it. When you give me a command, I obey it, to the limit of my orders as your Watcher, and that only because the will of all the others is the only authority greater than yours alone."

"What about Killian?" I asked, expecting his name to be in there somewhere, and curious why it wasn't.

"He is my master. I obey his commands."

"Unless there's more than one other Archon around with contradictory instructions?" I asked.

She sighed.

I was probably just being unnecessarily nit-picky, but I was still pretty pissed off, and that was how it manifested. I could and would passive-aggressive a recalcitrant donkey into the ground if it had annoyed me as much as Demise had.

"I am sworn to the service of Lord Killian. I am a servant of Lord Death. I also serve the Archons, as all Magicians do; you are our liege lords."

"Sounds complex," I said.

"It would to a man who never does as he's told. Or asked.

Or begged."

"Oh yes I do," I said sadly, "All too often."

CHAPTER 24

Weeks passed. May began, and A-Level Exams started to loom horrifically.

Demise was always there, and our relationship seemed to recover somewhat. It took me a while to stop being so mad at her, but I got there. She even helped me with my revision for exams. By that point, she'd been in every class with me for months, after all; she knew the material almost as well as I did.

Cathy grew a little distant, not that I could blame her; her life depended far more on the A-Level results than mine did. Between the simple fact that I was an Archon, and the existence of the trusts, I was financially and vocationally secure, but I still wanted to go to University, to learn; to experience a bit of a normal life, and I really wanted that to be with Cathy.

That's what I worked for.

Bill, Cathy and I helped each other out as best we could. Mostly we studied together, under a tree, in a library, wherever it was quiet. As we started getting deeper and deeper into the month, lessons and extra tutorials crammed ever greater amounts of revision into each day. Our first exams would be in the third week of May. Windward did the AS and A-Levels at the same time, rather than splitting them up over two years as most other schools did. It would be painful.

Start to finish, the whole thing took a month. A long, frustrating, ugly, intensive month. Demise was, to my immense surprise, kind of a rock about the whole thing. Steady and constant. She tested me; she re-read the material with me; she made sure that I ate and rested and slept enough.

Cathy was a mess. I tried to do for her what Demise did for me, but more often than not, she wouldn't let me. I hoped that it was just the stress of exams, but she was getting very snappy towards the end. She wasn't as affectionate, she barely even looked at me; it worried me, but I didn't push, hoping that she'd be alright given time and space.

Bill just seemed to drift through the whole thing, largely unaffected by all appearances, but he still put in the work. He kept our spirits up, but I think he detected the underlying and growing tension.

The exams were straightforward enough, if long-running and complex. I think I did alright. I would have used a little Magic, but Hopkins had told me categorically that I wasn't to do that and Demise glared her disapproval when I brought up the topic.

Finally it was done, on a sweltering Thursday in June, and all three of us were too tired to do much more than sleep, and so that's what we did, but we were planning a celebration of some sort for the weekend.

That night I staggered into my room and fell on the bed. I didn't bother to undress, I just closed my eyes and relaxed. It was done, one way or the other, my future was decided. The die was cast and all that.

At some point Demise slid in next to me, but I was completely conked out, just glad that I could sleep without facts and figures flashing before my closed eyes.

Naturally, while I was at my lowest ebb of energy, while the summer cold I'd been desperately fighting off with my diminished Life Energy was starting to gain ground and a good night's sleep would have made all the difference... Price called.

"No, just no. Whoever this is, no," I said without even waiting to see who it was. I had been blissfully asleep, and had no inclination to be in any other state. Demise was still asleep on the bed next to me, wearing almost nothing, far too many bits of her draped over me or entangled with me. It might once have been distracting, but I'd largely become immune to it (which was just *sad*).

"So forceful, but save that for when we meet in person," Price said.

"Price?" I asked groggily.

"Lord Shadow," she said softly, sensually, "But aren't we really on a first name basis by now?"

"What can I do for you, Vivian?" I asked, settling back down. Demise sighed sleepily and latched back on, her arm around my chest, thoroughly dead to the world.

"Found the last factory. Well, you did. I received an interesting communication. Anonymous source. I believe you met the gentleman in question in a building that is now a hole in the ground? He provided a little sliver of information that led us right to it."

"Oh. And Crystal wanted to kill him."

"She's always been impulsive," Price replied, "You may know something about that?"

"Let's not go there."

Price chuckled, "Oh but we must, and soon and repeatedly."

"Before I try thinking of ways to curse someone over the phone, address, please?"

She laughed out a throaty chuckle that was rather pleasant to listen to. She gave me the information and I thanked her before flopping back down.

Oh... bugger.

"Dee?" I said, pressing her shoulder.

She muttered and held on tighter.

"Dee!" I said and she woke up with a glare.

"What?" she said, as bleary-eyed as I was.

"Drug lab," I said.

She grunted and sat up, allowing me to dress.

I called Hopkins.

"Matty, you'd better be dead or close. It's one in the morning!" she said.

"I know," I said with a stifled sneeze; terrific, that was

starting... "but my people found the last Source lab. I need help. This one... this one's big and I don't know if Namia Sutton's there."

"Sutton?!" Hopkins said.

Demise was suddenly very awake and intent. Sutton must be one of those words she was told to listen out for.

"Liaison information," I said pointedly.

"Crap, crap, crap!" Hopkins said. I heard clattering and swearing, "Location?"

I sent it over. She tapped at what sounded like a keyboard.

"There's a park two blocks South-east, meet there in... an hour?"

"Sounds good," I said.

We said goodbye and Demise frowned as I put the phone down.

"Don't start," I said.

"That city will eat you up and spit out the pieces."

"With any luck, this is the last time I'll have to go there."

"As Milord says," Demise replied, which I have discovered is her code for 'Bullshit'.

I grumbled and dressed, hoodie, trousers, heavy shoes. I remembered my staff this time.

We emerged into the park that Hopkins chose after I only got lost a couple of times. Demise wore her usual jeans and shirt. She was already under shields and I felt Death Magic flowing. Hopkins was late, but she brought heavies.

The portal opened and about a dozen of her Wardens came through, all dressed in tactical gear, carrying weapons, including some very impressive enchanted rifles that almost screamed 'don't stand in front of this thing'. Hopkins herself came through, wearing a set of dark blue robes and a variety of items that oozed power. She had a short stave in her left hand, about three feet long and ivory-white.

"I suddenly feel underdressed," I said.

"That's because you are," said Palmyra, who opened up a portal behind me and came through with seven of her nuns, dressed in white and carrying a dark red staff taller than she was, "I mean, you called this gathering, at least put in the effort. I mean, you're not even wearing the signet."

Palmyra gave me a hug and grinned at me. Hopkins too.

"Tethys is fond of it," I said sheepishly, which made both my sisters roll their eyes.

They introduced me around their people, though I knew quite a few of them already. The nuns were just as inscrutable as ever, just as crotchety. Hopkins' people were much more cheerful. Her bodyguards were obviously devoted and utterly loyal. Eight men and four women, most of whom were confident and smiling. They radiated competence and decency. Good people.

"Shall I go take a surreptitious look?" I asked.

"You have all the subtlety of a boulder among pebbles," Hopkins said before turning to her people, "Minnie? Would you?"

"Sure, Boss," said a short, but solid looking girl with a broadsword over her shoulder and a long rifle in her hands. She vanished without a trace and I didn't even hear footsteps.

"I can do invisible, you know," I said, slightly put out.

"Sure you can, Sweetie," Palmyra said, patting my head like I was an errant labradoodle.

I glared and she stuck out her tongue.

Minnie came back a minute later.

"It's empty," she said.

"What?" I asked.

"Three floors, vacated summoning circles, silver apparatus at each one. No people, no other equipment," she said, giving me a glare.

"I am going to stake that vampire," I said.

"Yeah you are..." Palmyra said lasciviously.

I glared again and started stomping towards the factory.

"Where are you going?" Hopkins asked.

"I can break the extraction devices, and knocking down the building will make me feel better," I said.

"Ooh, sounds like fun," Palmyra said, walking up onto Hopkins other side.

"I know, I so rarely get to do mayhem anymore, it's a pain to be respectful in the information age," Hopkins replied.

"That's why I wear a disguise," I said.

"Yes, and who would ever penetrate such a well thought through outfit?" Palmyra asked.

"You're not very nice to me," I said.

"I was fast asleep, you bugger. I had a pretty, pretty man underneath me, and now I'm in Gomorrah; you deserve it," Palmyra said.

"I called Hopkins, *she* woke you," I pointed out.

"You are such a weasel," Hopkins said.

"I'm not having the best night, either, you know," I said.

"He was also sleeping with someone pretty," Hopkins pointed out.

"I'd electrocute you if you weren't so much stronger than me," I said.

"Get used to that, it's well known that the First Shadow's the littlest Archon," Palmyra said nastily.

"How pretty *was* that guy that you're this snarky right now?" I asked.

"Think you, only with muscle tone, and a nice arse," Palmyra said, "and big, manly arms."

"You're scarring me for life again."

She blew a raspberry at me and we strolled into the factory. It was just as it had been the last time I was there.

It was a testament to just how stupid I can be, and how tired I was, that it took until *then* to occur to me that this wasn't quite right.

Now that I thought about it, wouldn't Sutton have moved the whole thing after she'd caught me making my way out with a Demon?

So why would the extraction equipment still be there?

Except to provide a juicy target that was easy to smash, and almost entirely without risk...

"Stop," I said.

They did, the Wardens too.

"What?" Palmyra said.

"I think it's a trap," I said.

That was enough for the Wardens.

They had their hands under Palmyra and Hopkins' arms faster than you could say knife, and had bodily dragged them back out the door while I was still turning to run.

Demise was carried away by the crowd. I ran after them as fast as I could. Naturally, I was too late.

Far, too late...

A circle flared into existence, and I smacked into it, to rebound and fall to the ground. Palmyra and Hopkins were already working Magic to get me out, but that was a Fortress Shield, it wasn't coming down quickly.

And then I felt the binding circles firing up below me. All of them.

"Ladies, please get me out of here!" I said, backing against the field.

I started casting, my shields snapped into place and I started conjuring globes of Light, Force and Heat. I moved away from the barrier, to get a little manoeuvring room.

I felt them coming for me, hundreds of them, and even more arriving every second. I needed to keep them contained. I might just manage, too, there was just the one hole leading to the lower levels.

And indeed quite a few came out of there.

But just as many simply tore themselves a path up through the concrete.

And these weren't the little ones either. Not just Lesser Demons. They were at least Common. Bigger, stronger, more vicious, all bestials, thank God. The earth shook, and I heard a scream of joyous freedom as something even nastier made itself known.

The Demons were all of a similar type, looking like carnivorous black squids crossed with sea anemones, all reaching tentacles, snapping mouths and beaks. Their skin was black streaked with other evil-looking colours without a human name, slick and oily.

I channelled my power through my staff, and Demons started flying apart, any innate defences no match for the dispels my staff wove around my attacks. The air reeked from gasses discharged from their mangled bodies as I cut them down. Only hits to the central mass did any real harm, anything else was shrugged off, as any severed tentacle was only one of dozens or even hundreds.

There were so many of them! They rolled out of the holes in the floor, grotesque spinning masses of inhuman horror. I used my Shadows, but these ones seemed... resistant somehow, the darkness sliding off, unable to get traction, so I stopped using them, they'd just be a drain on the energy needed to keep me alive.

I took in a breath of that reeking gas and coughed, my throat searing with heat. I spat and red came out to land on the concrete floor. I barely noticed.

I kept fighting, but every one I banished threw out more of that gas as it was torn apart. I started coughing more and more. I redirected some of the Force into the surrounding air. Air Magic wasn't my thing, I'd never had much use for it, other than calling a little Electricity, but I focussed hard, and the gas swirled, dispersing and spinning away. It didn't help much as there was always more gas. I was coughing with every other breath, which were becoming harder to draw, each accompanied by burning pain.

The Demons were getting closer; they were coming from all directions. One leapt and bounced off my shields, taking a few layers away with it before I could fire on it and banish it. If enough of them got close to me, they'd take all my defences apart.

My strategy wasn't working, there were too many, and

most of the offensive Magic I knew for crowd control was either non-lethal (which would be useless) or Shadow Magic (same problem).

My breath was becoming ragged and I could taste blood in my mouth. The situation was becoming desperate.

I gestured, and a bright ring of Chaos Energy assembled above my staff. I released it, and a blast of lightning-blue power washed over the incoming ranks of horrors. About twenty of them evaporated, burned and blasted away. I did it again and again, burning through my gathered energy far too quickly.

I actually thought I was making progress... until the floor fell out from under me, and a mass of black tentacles wrapped themselves around my shields. I put Will into a sphere around me that shoved back those reaching limbs, and it bowed under the strain of a ten foot beak as it closed on my construct.

I gritted my teeth, choking back another wracking cough as I flexed the sphere and shoved the crushing beak apart. This was the thing that had screamed. Huge and awful and insanely powerful. A Greater Demon, thank God it didn't know any Magic.

My Will met infernal muscle and tendon.

Will won, and the beak came apart in a fountain of gore. The Demon recoiled and I pointed my staff right at the heart of it, releasing a lance of pure, focussed light. It screamed even louder as my attack speared straight through it and carved it up into chunks.

More gas billowed out as it came apart. I took a great lungful of it this time and fell towards the ground as it vanished. I was at the bottom of the building, having fallen through two holes in ceilings, but I was still far enough above the ground that when I fell, and landed badly, my ankle snapped with a wet crack. That thing has been broken so many times at this point, you'd think I'd be used to it...

I screamed, but couldn't spare the time to take care of the injury, as the rest of the Demons were already coming after me, and some were too close for comfort. I quickly cast a numbing spell that released me from the pain and called my Shadows to prop me up as I continued blasting and reinforcing my shields. There was too much to do at once, I was reduced to channelling simple energy through the staff, which wasn't as effective as a Chaos strike, so more Demons were getting closer before they were banished.

I flew to the far end of the room to buy myself some time, and just managed to cast Shade Armour before a whole wave of them converged on me. Shadows erupted from crevices, surrounding and covering me before condensing into hundreds of micron-thick layers of hardened darkness, moulded and shaped into a suit of heavy-looking armour. It actually weighed nothing, but made me vastly stronger and more resilient. Most importantly, it would keep me alive just that bit longer; hopefully long enough for Hopkins and Palmyra to get through that barrier.

I surrounded my Staff with Will and laid about me. I had no talent for close combat, but it didn't matter. They were everywhere, and not even I could miss. The hits were hard enough to send them flying, but their forms were too flexible to take more than superficial damage. They didn't even have bones I could break.

But I cleared myself a space and recast my shields. I channelled pure Force straight through the staff, condensed down to a needle thickness, and Demon pieces went flying. I backed away, fetching up against the wall so that they couldn't get behind me, though that left me without a line of retreat. Again, that didn't matter, as I was feeling dizzy, breathing very hard, and yet still felt like I wasn't getting enough air. I wanted to throw up, but to pause was to die. Even Shade Armour wasn't invulnerable.

My heart was pounding, both with terror and injury. I was hurt, and the gas was everywhere. I couldn't smell it inside the armour, which hopefully meant that there was a built-in protection (or it could well have been that my nose had been burned as well, as I couldn't smell anything else, either). I tried to open a Gate, but the whole place was a maelstrom of light and flickering shadow, nothing stable enough for me to use. I gathered more energy, as much as I could from every source within reach, and released a blast that lit the room up like the sun.

Dozens of them were banished, but there were always more, so many more. Always coming, always hungry.

Too many of them.

My shields started taking hits. And then more hits. Every Demon I threw off or banished was replaced by two more. My shields fell and they had at my armour. Layers fell away, damage built up faster than the regenerative spells could keep up.

I lost my staff, wrenched away and smashed to pieces by one of the horrors. I laid about me with Force and Will, trying to cut my way free, but they piled on, wrapping around all of me, dragging me down. I called more Light, and seared them off me, but more came.

The armour around my head was down to its last few layers. I could see my death coming.

Then, just before I was about to die, I felt a great 'pop' at long last, and the world around me exploded with light as my sisters simply tore the concrete separating us away, sucked into a massive portal above me. I focussed and locked my armoured feet to the ground as the Demons flew up, screaming into the rift. Palmyra shone with terrible, vengeful light, her elementals diving by the dozen into the fray, tearing the demons apart with their energy as she disabled the summoning circles with a single wave of her hand.

That power washed over me, and the Demons recoiled, darting away. I borrowed some of her Light and let their retreating forms have it, banishing a few more of the monsters. The Wardens dropped into the pit Hopkins had made and went to work with Fire, Lightning, Air and Death. It was an astonishing display of Magical might, and I was deeply impressed.

The monsters were driven back, foot by foot. Demise was suddenly at my side, just as my legs turned to jelly and I fell to one knee. I released the armour and collapsed to all fours, vomiting up a stomach-full of blood. I started shivering as I fell against the wall, barely able to breathe.

"Don't you leave me, Mathew Graves," Demise said, touching my chest. I felt Death Magic go to work as she pulled entropy from my dying cells. You'd be amazed just how versatile Death Magic could be. But it wasn't enough. I was poisoned; badly if I was any judge.

"Lady Palmyra!" Demise all but screamed.

My sister looked down and her eyes went wide. She flew to my side, held up by her Will. She landed next to us and I felt Life Magic begin to flow into my aching chest.

"Oh God..." she whispered as she went to work.

"That's reassuring," I tried to say. All that came out was a bloody gurgle.

"Hold on, Little Brother," Palmyra said, her hands glowing brightly, "You're going to be alright. Just hold on, please..."

I tried to do as she asked, but darkness surrounded me, and I couldn't fight it for very long.

CHAPTER 25

It took me a while to come out of it again.

When I finally did... I wished I hadn't.

My chest was on fire, and I opened my eyes to see a hospital room. It was clean and quiet. I was hooked up to monitors and drips. There were a couple of tubes in places where only Cathy had any right touching me, and another in my nose.

I coughed, which turned into a fit.

Warm hands appeared on my shoulders, supporting me as I coughed. A glass of water was pressed to my lips and I took a sip.

"I'm never letting you out of my sight again. You can't be trusted," Cassandra said, stroking my hair as she helped me back to a flat position.

I tried to say 'Hello', but my voice came out as a rasp.

"I know. Blessed silence for a while," Cassandra said, "I think I prefer you like this."

I glared. She smiled sadly.

She gave me a tiny whiteboard and a marker.

Everyone alright? I wrote.

"Of course. You're the only idiot who got caught in the trap," she said, perching on the bed next to me.

Magic feels fuzzy.

"It would. Don't touch it yet, it's helping to keep you alive. Palmyra did something that turned it inward."

Voice?

"A couple of days, Palmyra fixed the deep damage, but there's a lot of inflammation that needs to go down. Same with your lungs. Don't get up for a while."

With this many tubes?

She snorted.

How bad was it?

She looked away, "You... you died a couple of times. Your heart stopped. That Demon toxin shredded your lungs. Palmyra barely got you going again. It took her three days to fix you up, what with that Life Siphon damage."

Three days?!

"Yeah. Your parents aren't happy. I finally got them to go home this morning. They were exhausted. Tethys and Kandi are around here somewhere, too, probably violating the chapel."

Feel like an idiot.

"As well you bloody should!" she snapped, "Sticking your face in a bloody trap!"

Not my fault? I offered.

"How? How is it not your fault?"

Fair point.

"It's good you were out for the first couple of days. I wanted to kick your arse."

I smiled.

Phone?

She rummaged in my bedside table and came out with my mobile. Texts from Bill and Cathy. None in the last three days after an initial flurry when I disappeared. I texted them telling them that I was awake and laid back while Cassandra watched me like a hawk. There were missed calls from Price. I would have called her, but... well, couldn't speak.

What?

The gaze had been getting a little intense.

"Nothing."

Sure?

"Yep."

Where's Demise?

"She's alright, she's elsewhere. Hopkins will explain the details when she turns up, but, essentially, you're off the hook.

No longer a Danger; Palmyra and Hopkins read the other two the riot act, and they agreed to give you the benefit of the doubt at long bloody last. Demise went home."

Well, that was a nice surprise! Though, funnily enough, now that Demise was gone, I found that I actually quite missed her. I was a bit conflicted, so I shrugged and relaxed a little. I coughed from time to time. We chatted a bit, but to be honest, I felt like total crap. Even the effort of operating the pen was tiring me out. A doctor came in, for all the use he was going to be. He talked to me, made sure I stayed in bed. No unnecessary movement. I didn't argue.

Tethys and Kandi came in while I was dozing.

"He woke up," Cassandra said and I opened my eyes to see two of my most favourite people, who wrapped me up in a huge hug that immediately made me feel miles better.

"Well, you idiot," Tethys said as Kandi crawled onto the bed and sat up next to me.

Does rather look that way.

Kandi snorted and started playing with my phone. She has her own, but apparently mine's nicer. I know, crazy, but still lovable.

"I contacted Price on your behalf. I'm confident that she was just as fooled as you were."

Reassuring.

"She expressed an interest in visiting you," Tethys said with an evil grin, "Her little friend, too."

Not until I can cast fireballs again!

Tethys smiled and held my hand while Kandi yawned and leant on my shoulder.

"So are you just like... the worst Archon?" Kandi asked.

I turned to tickle her and was quickly overpowered, Kandi was probably stronger than me at the best of times, but right then it was just laughable. She straddled my waist and pushed my hands down above my head.

"Kandi, he's sick, and that is just all sorts of arousing," Tethys said, picking the little redhead up by her sides and plopping her down in a chair.

"You're no fun!" Kandi said.

"You know that's not true, but if you kill him now, we can't play with him later," Tethys said, tweaking her assistant's nose.

Kandi pouted adorably and I looked at my phone. No replies to my texts. Odd.

Tethys took Kandi's spot on the bed and looked at the phone.

"Worried?" she asked.

I shook my head.

Tethys shrugged and my friends chatted. I fell asleep again.

When I woke up, it was much later. My parents were sitting in with me, and I smiled at the sight of them.

"Hi Matty," Mother said. Normally, my mother is the most reasonable, gentlest person you could hope to meet. But she was an unholy terror when one of her sons got so much as a boo-boo.

My father was solid and utterly dependable, dark haired with a wicked sense of humour. He was the most moral man I knew; the person I became is mostly down to trying to live up to the example he set for me.

He looked worried, his eyes tired. He squeezed my arm while my mother buried me in a hug.

"How are you feeling?" Father asked.

I gave him a thumbs-up.

"Liar," Mother said, plumping my pillow.

I smiled. It was so good to see them.

Sorry I scared you, I wrote on my board.

"Jen told us you were getting better," Mother said, "but that you'd need a few days here. What happened, Matty? Why were you even there?!"

She was upset, and her eyes were moist.

My job. Don't like it much.

"Mathew, you're eighteen years old! You haven't even finished school yet!" Mother said, "How is this your job?!"

Okay, this part isn't my job. This was a cock-up.

Ran out of space.

My job is more along the lines of poking around and directing-

And again.

-more qualified people in the direction of the problem. This was really-

This was getting ridiculous.

-more of an aberration.

Cassandra and Tethys had ducked out and left me to try and explain this mess on my own, the bastards. Kandi was actually waiting at the door, waving, with an evil grin on her face, making the occasional crude gesture that made me smile.

They quizzed me on what had happened, and I provided them with a *very* watered down version, one which didn't make me look like a complete idiot. After that, I was tired again, and didn't even notice that I was falling asleep until I woke up the next day.

Hospital food was horrific as always, which made me very grateful for Cassandra who brought in sandwiches and treats every day. One of my parents was always with me. Cassandra or Tethys was always in the building, often with Kandi. Cassandra watched over me while I slept, often holding my hand. It made me feel safe.

My voice came back on the second day after I woke up. Bill had texted back.

Cathy hadn't. She didn't pick up when I called, either. Bill didn't know why, or claimed that he didn't.

Palmyra came by that day, I mean she came by when I was awake, she'd been in and out a lot since my snafu.

"Wow, you look terrible," she said with a smile.

I glared and she hugged me before pecking my cheek.

"Thanks for putting me back together again," I said, my

voice a little dry, but it was working.

"It's rather becoming my hobby," she said, putting her hand on my chest. She grimaced.

"That good, huh?" I asked.

"The poison you breathed in dissolved big chunks of your lungs," she said, patting my chest lightly, "I neutralised it and stabilised you as best I could; but because you're so low on Living Energy, I couldn't use a lot of the usual shortcuts. Currently, you're working on about sixty percent lung capacity, and expending the resources needed to do the repair left you badly vulnerable to infections, one of which is starting to take root in your left lung.

Cassandra looked worried and stood next to me so she could hold my hand.

"I've cast a series of spells to enhance your stamina and speed up the replenishment of your Living Energy, but I can't risk just get rid of the infection in your state, you're going to have to ride it out, and that's going to be very unpleasant for you."

"But I'll live?" I said.

"Of course," she said with a smile.

I nodded, "Maybe they'll give me the good drugs?"

"They will provide you with everything they can to help," she said, "but you have to stay here, where they can monitor, and I can come quickly if I have to. This is going to be really rough, Matty."

"Hey, alive is alive," I said, "I can't complain."

"That's a first," Cassandra muttered.

I glared again, she smiled.

Palmyra filled me in on a few details. She talked about the meeting the other four had attended to discuss me. Kron wasn't willing to let go of the fact that Sutton and I were at odds, but she was willing to admit that I had acted with enough integrity to get me off the Danger List, even if she still wasn't very fond of me. Killian had apparently sat with Demise for hours, going through every detail of our time together until he was satisfied that I was safe. It had been he who had finally convinced Kron.

Hopkins was apparently very miffed with me for nearly getting killed again and would be along to express that displeasure shortly, God save me.

Palmyra got on well with my parents, who couldn't say enough nice things about her after she'd left. Everyone liked Palmyra, but my parents were bordering on worship for the woman who kept patching their son back together.

Cathy came on the third day. Cassandra left to give us some privacy. I smiled at her, and saw that she wasn't in a good way. Her eyes were wet and downcast, her hair was mess, her nose was red, her complexion blotchy.

I reached for her, but she wouldn't come any closer. I let my hand drop to the bed as she stood there. She took a breath and looked me in the eye. She looked like she'd been gathering herself for a plunge.

"How are you?" she asked, her voice neutral, almost cold.

"Better," I lied, "What's the matter, Cath? Are you alright?"

I wanted so much to go to her, but there were too many things stuck in me.

She swallowed and sucked in a shuddering breath.

"No, I'm not," she said, her eyes darting away again, "I'm here... I'm here because I can't, anymore, Matty. I can't do it. I can't wake up every morning and wonder if you're going to be alive at breakfast. I can't deal with that fear anymore... I'm sorry, I just can't."

I swallowed; the monitor beeped alarmingly as her words sank like a pick into my soul and my body started going haywire in response.

"What... what are you saying?" I asked, my voice trembling.

"Mathew, I love you," she said, her voice cracking, "but I can't be with you. I can't give my heart to you and wait around for the day that you die. Because I'll die with you."

I could see the way this was going, and I simply didn't know what to do.

"Cath, please," I whispered, almost desperately, "You're... you're my reason. You're why I can get up and do what I need to do, because you're there, because you are the person I love, the one that makes me believe that humanity isn't just a collection of monsters in waiting. Please, Cathy, please don't do this."

"You're the reason I have to *force* myself to get up," she countered, "You make me terrified to pick up my phone in case it's someone telling me you're dead or hurt. I can't bear it, Matty. You're the best man I know, but I'm not like you. I'm not strong enough."

"Yes, you are!" I said, trying to get up. She backed away, "Please, Cathy..."

She put up a hand.

"This isn't a sudden thing. I've thought about this," she said.

Tears ran down my cheeks, she wouldn't look at me.

"I'm breaking up with you Matty," she said finally, sobbing, "I want to be clear. I haven't been coerced. I made this choice, the right choice for me. You need someone who's able to cope with who you are. That's not me. I want a quiet life, husband, kids, career, a *life*. Not this Magical horror show."

"I want those things, too!" I said, my heart pounding, my soul aching. Tears were flowing freely as I pulled the sheets off and pulled at tubes and patches.

"But you can't have them," she said, "Your life is Magic and monsters and duty. I don't want to be cruel, Matty, don't force me to be. Do that one last thing for me?"

"Cathy..." I sobbed.

"Do you understand what I'm telling you?" she said, her voice cracking.

"Can't we just talk?" I asked, "Just for a while? Please, just let me talk to you."

"No. You won't talk me out of it. And I don't want you

to," she said, her back straightening, "Don't call. Don't text. I won't pick up, I won't reply. I'm assuming that you're going to Stonebridge University if you get the grades, which you will. I'll be going elsewhere. This is goodbye, Matty."

No...

She finally broke down. She turned and ran from the room, leaving me half disconnected from wailing monitors as I pulled things off me. Blood flowed from IV holes, heart monitors left red patches of skin. I pulled out the nasal cannula and took a good grip on the things in my private parts.

I had to get to her. I had to change her mind.

She can't have meant it, she couldn't...

Cassandra came in as I was psyching myself up to yank out the tube in my man-bits.

"What happened? Cathy looked like she'd committed a murd- What are you doing?!" she said running for me.

"Help me catch up to her, please," I said desperately. I couldn't see for tears. It hurt so much, but there was still a chance, there had to be...

There *had* to be...

"Matty," she said as I started pulling.

She put her hands on mine, "Matty, listen to me," she said.

I looked at her, "She was moving fast. In your state, you'd never catch her now. If you tried, there's a good chance you get another infection or injury that finishes you."

"Then give me back my Magic!" I said, "Please, Cassie, please?"

"What happened?" she said softly, "Tell me."

I did, haltingly, my voice breaking and trembling.

By the time I was half way done, Cassandra had pulled me into a hug and was holding me so tightly, like she could squeeze the pain out of me.

"What can I do? Ask me anything, Matty, tell me what I can do."

Tears were running down her face. She was likely getting a colossal taste of my emotions as well.

"You'd better arrange for some relief," I said softly, "I can't shield, Cassie."

Which meant I couldn't stop her from getting a continuous blast of everything I was feeling.

"I'm not leaving you," she said, "No way in hell."

She wiped furiously at her tears, but they were just replaced by more and more.

"Just for a while," I said, "until I get my head together, I'll be alright."

I coughed heavily, turning my head away.

Concentrate, focus, breathe.

Was actually having trouble breathing...

Alarms were sounding and nurses came in to see the mess. Sorting it out wasn't pleasant. They had to stab in a new IV, replace the stickers on my chest, and the cannula in my nose... and they had to adjust the catheter I'd half pulled out.

Learned my lesson right there. No leaving until they let me.

But the pain distracted me a little. Cassandra was sitting in the corner, crying openly as she shared my pain. Finally, the nurses were done, they warned me not to do it again, told me off and left me to it.

"Please go home, Cassie," I said, "I can't bear to watch you like that and know it's my fault."

"It's not your fault!" she said, standing up, her voice as shaky as mine, taking my hand, "It's hers! Who dumps someone while they're in the hospital?"

A new spike of agony to add to the growing pile.

"Oh God, sorry, I didn't mean... I'm just going to wait outside for a bit, okay?"

"Out of range, okay?" I said, "I'll make it an order."

"You're not the boss of me," she said, leaning in and kissing my forehead, "I'll see you in a while, okay?"

I nodded.

She left.

I cried.

It was the worst night of my life. All the lives I'd imagined for myself had Cathy in them. She was my anchor, my rock, the foundation on which happiness was going to be built. And she was gone. I tried to work through explanations, excuses, some reason why she'd have done this. But all I had were her words, which roared through my mind like a forest fire.

My parents came back and I put on a good face for them, but that was about all I could manage, and I simply went quiet, and then silent.

I wanted to sleep, but I was coughing too much. So I simply sat, staring at the wall.

Tethys came in with Kandi and they sat on the seat next to my bed. They knew. Cassandra must have told them. Tethys looked like she wanted to kill something. Kandi looked like she was going to cry, too.

I simply closed my eyes and begged for it to be over with.

The next day I took a fever. A bad one. I coughed hard enough to hurt my back; I felt dizzy, my chest started to burn with every breath and my head ached. My temperature hit one hundred and two and stayed there. They put me on fluids and antibiotics. The day stretched on in a fugue of pain, coughing and tears. I stopped talking completely.

My temperature climbed, hitting one hundred and ten on my sixth day in that hole. They started pumping more drugs into me, but I didn't really notice, I was pretty out of it by that point. I think I'd largely given up, truth be told. I don't remember eating much, and I think they started feeding me intravenously.

I was delirious by the fifth day, and spent the next three in a waking nightmare where I saw Cathy over and over, telling me that she hated me. I saw her as the person who'd cut my face, as Namia Sutton, Lord Faust; all the enemies and evils I'd seen defeated had come back for me with her face, it was horrifying.

I remember waking up on the seventh night, sitting up and coughing hard before spitting blood into a kidney dish Tethys held for me. I could barely breathe.

"It was a dream, right?" I asked her, groggy and weak, "It was all just a bad dream? None of it happened, did it?"

"Of course it was, Sweetheart," Tethys said softly. She held my hand and settled me back down, "Everything's alright."

I remember being relieved and falling back to the pillow. Every breath was pain, every movement a horror in my chest.

My fever broke on the ninth day. As it turned out, delirium had been a blessed relief compared to reality. I wanted to cry, but I didn't want to upset anyone. My parents were with me when Palmyra came by to check me over. She could shield better than Cassandra, so she was able to be in the room with me without feeling the need to jump out the window.

"Much better, Matty," she said, patting my shoulder, "your lungs are almost three quarters fixed, and the infection's gone. A couple more days and I'll be able to put your Magic back."

"What if you didn't?" Mother said.

"Beg pardon?" Palmyra replied.

"What if you just left the Magic gone?" Mother said, "What if you just left him normal?"

Palmyra visibly bristled, "He is normal," she said icily, "but to answer your question, I can't leave it pointed inwards when there isn't something to heal. It would be damaging, and when something dangerous turned up, he would die when he couldn't fight it."

"There must be a way," Mother said, "some way to keep him safe from this... hell he's been dragged into. Can't you just take the Magic away? Can't you just leave him in peace?"

"You can't take someone's Magic. You might suppress it-" Palmyra said.

"Do that!" Mother said, slightly desperately.

"Matty? You've been quiet," Father said, looking intently

at me, "What do you think?"

"No," I said simply.

"Good enough for me," Palmyra said, patting my shoulder, "I'll be back tomorrow, okay?"

I gave her a fake smile and she vanished.

"Wait!" Mother said, but Palmyra was gone. She rounded on me, "Happy? She was going to do it; she was going to help you!"

"Help me what?"

"Careful, Sweetheart," Father warned my mother, recognising the dead tone of my voice. He knew I was barely holding it together.

"Help you be normal!" Mother said.

"Damn it," Father said, leaning back in his seat, rolling his eyes.

"Like Lady Palmyra said, I am normal," I said quietly.

"What sort of life is this, Mathew? Pain and hatred; prejudice?"

"Those things won't go away if I lost my Magic. They'd just be a lot more difficult to defend against," I pointed out.

"I want it gone, Mathew! I want that filthy Magic gone from our lives. It took your brother, and now it's taking you! One piece at a time!"

I sighed and closed my eyes. I'd had enough. I needed to sleep again.

"Did you hear me?" she said, "I said I want it gone!"

"Then kill me," I said, she gasped, "That's how you get rid of it. But just wait a while; no doubt someone will be along presently to grant your wish."

She slapped me. I deserved it. It was a terrible thing for me to say, and she didn't understand what she was asking for.

I heard feet clattering out the door.

"That wasn't fair, Mathew," Father said.

"In a very real way, I am Magic, Father," I said tiredly, "It's in me down to the bones. To say that she wants the 'filthy magic' out of her life is to say she wants rid of *me*. Something which seems to be going around."

"I'm sure she didn't mean it like that. I'm certain," he said, "and you are too. You know she loves you and is just so scared for you."

"Yes," I said.

I rolled onto my side and tried to sleep.

My parents stayed. Mother was always angry, she wouldn't speak to me. Oh well, the lid's on the coffin, what's another nail? Father tried to get us speaking from time to time, but I wasn't inclined to speak at all, much less to someone who felt like that about me.

I just laid there in the awkward silence, almost yearning for the day when I'd get my Magic back and... what? Do what?

Go where?

Palmyra came back again a couple of days later.

"Okay!" she said after her examination, "Looks good! Lungs back up to capacity. No more infections. She touched my forehead and it felt like a heavy lid had come off my Well. Palmyra darted back with a squeak as my Shadows darted out from under my bed, wrapping me up, moving gently, little tones of worry and messages of relief coming from the link.

I smiled slightly, relaxing as they slid back under the bed, satisfied that I was alive and well. Mother was looking at me. There was a new note of horror in her eyes, one that hadn't been there before.

"Just because it looks odd doesn't make it evil," I said, making one last attempt to repair the growing rift.

"Can't you..." she began, "I don't want you to be a Magician anymore, Mathew. It's killing you. And that's killing me."

"I am what I am, Mother. It's not something that can be switched off. And even if it was, it's too late now."

"What? Why?!" she asked.

"Too many enemies. And Cathy's already gone. No way out but forward now."

"No, I won't accept that," she said, "Just think, you get rid of it, and maybe she'll take you back?"

I couldn't believe she'd said that. It was such a cruel manipulation; I couldn't accept that it had come from Mother...

"Miriam!" Father said, his eyes flinty, his tone very like mine when I'm mad. Palmyra smiled slightly, recognising it.

Mother recognised it too and stood to look at him, regret in her eyes.

"Outside for a moment, Dear?" he suggested, waving at the door. He led her out.

There was yelling.

"He's just like you," Palmyra said, "I think I'd enjoy biting the apple that fell out of that tree..."

"That's me, you realise?"

"Shh, don't ruin it," she said, hopping on the bed next to me, "How are you really?"

"Bad," I said, gesturing at the door, "this rubbish isn't helping. Don't tell anyone?"

"Of course not," she said. She waved her hand and the various tubes and needles withdrew painlessly, punctures covering up with fresh skin, "I'm sorry about Cathy. I know you loved her."

"Since the day I met her. I still can't believe that it ended just like that. God, Lucille, it hurts. I thought that whole Jocelyn thing was bad, but this is so much worse. It's like my chest has a ragged hole in it."

"I know," she said. She leant her head against mine, "You'll get better. I know from experience."

"How'd you get over it?"

"Oh, the bad way. I dropped my pants for anyone that asked and humped the pain away," I laughed and she smiled, "Better! But I don't recommend that, you'll end up waking up one day with three complete strangers, a sore place which shouldn't be sore and a disapproving Warden glaring down at you with a dressing gown in one hand and a bag of frozen peas in the other."

I laughed again, it felt good.

"I have a Warden exactly like that."

"It was good of you to spare her what you're going through, but she feels horribly guilty for leaving you like this."

"The way you Life Mages emote, I'd have been a wreck just watching her trying not to be a wreck," I said, "I'm not exactly overburdened with intestinal fortitude, you know."

"Everyone knows that, Matty," she said, patting my arm.

"It's no fun being the littlest Archon, nobody gives you any respect."

"That's because we've seen you cry when watching Disney movies."

"I had something in my eye!" I complained.

"Sure you did," she said with an evil look, "both eyes, for an entire hour."

"You know, we're immortal, I have centuries to get you back for this sort of thing."

"Ooh, I'm so scared."

"I'll set the Pixies on you again," I threatened.

"I'll be good," she said in a tiny voice.

We smiled at each other, and I sighed, a little more relaxed.

"Thanks for this," I said, taking her hand, "making me laugh."

"You're very welcome, Little Brother," she said, "It's what family's for."

I snorted.

"Well, it's what I'm for. And I owe you for not mentioning that whole... Succubus-induced flirting thing," she said with a flush.

"What happens in Gomorrah, stays in Gomorrah."

"I really don't get you sometimes," she said, "I would imagine that I was far from the last girl who threw herself at you during that. I know you had Cathy, but as much as they would have wanted to play with you, that mark would have made you just as eager to have at them. How did you not just find an all-girls gym and ring a dinner bell? I would have, well, an Abercrombie and Fitch photo shoot, but you get my point."

"I didn't really feel any different afterwards, but then I don't think that she actually meant to mark me, she wasn't actively hunting me or anything," I said, remembering that Palmyra didn't actually know how I got musked.

"Really?" she said with a frown.

"Yep, something I should know?"

"Well, Succubae of the pureblood sort are actually rather complex entities. The way they work is to induce desire, inflame it, enhance it, and then feed off it. Over and over and over. If they are strong enough, or hungry enough, they can kill a man stone dead in a single feeding. For her to have simply taken what she needed and not leave you an over-sexed rutting animal, or a corpse, must have taken considerable self control on her part. It has to be an effort."

"We had an understanding of a sort," I said.

"You what now?" she asked, suddenly attentive.

"Without going into too much detail, because this is one of those Liaison things, the lady was in a spot of bother; she was 'dying', and she needed to be fed. I fed her."

"How?" she asked, her eyebrows raised, smirking knowingly.

"A kiss," I said with a glare.

"Oh. Boring," she said with a dismissive wave, "But still very unwise, Mathew. Don't let them in like that, it's so risky. This one may have some sense of... fair play, but most don't. You got lucky, sort of."

"I just don't think she likes to win by default," I said with a smile.

"Could be. If Demons can be relied on to have one thing, it's their pride."

We sat quietly for a bit, companionably silent.

"Can I get out of here?" I asked, "I would very much like to be elsewhere."

"The doctor will be by later, let him talk to you and discharge you. And when you get out, three meals a day, do not miss one. Snacks between. I want you loading up calories, at least four thousand a day. You're burning off huge amounts of them to replenish your Living Energy."

I nodded.

"Rest as much as possible, too. The doctor will take you through recovery, do what he says, make it as easy on your body as possible, alright?"

"Yes, Ma'am," I said, she shivered.

"Oh, I like it when you say it like that," she said with a naughty smile that belonged more properly on Tethys.

"You're a bit of a freak, aren't you?" I said.

She grinned, "Raised during a repressive age. Been making up for it."

The doctor turned up while my parents were 'talking' and gave me a once over. Told me to take exercise and gave me a list of instructions. He brought discharge papers, which I signed. I dressed in fresh clothes and stood on shaky legs.

"Wow, nothing works like it should."

"So what else is new?" Palmyra replied, "No Magic, rebuild your strength the old fashioned way."

I sighed and pulled on my shoes. I walked out the door to find my parents arguing in the corridor.

"The simple fact is that he is a Magician. We can't change that. Even if we could, I doubt he'd let us. You know what he is, it would be like blinding him!" Father said, taking my side, bless him.

"I want my children back; I just want the boys I raised, before they became a pair of... of *freaks*!" Mother replied.

"Wow, I really should have knocked or something," I said.

"It's a public corridor," Palmyra pointed out.

"Still."

My mother and father turned to look at us.

"Matty... I didn't mean... it wasn't," Mother said.

"Can you portal me to Blackhold?" I asked Palmyra.

"Sure," she said acidly, glaring at my mother.

"You know where I am if you need me," I said to them, trying to be as pleasant as possible.

They didn't say anything. I think they were too ashamed.

Oh, I knew she didn't really feel that way; she was just afraid and looking for something to blame. Father would sort her out. And in the meantime, I could go live in the house my evil predecessors built... yay.

Palmyra opened the portal and we left them behind. The lawn was freshly cut and the house was bustling with activity. I rubbed my eyes and walked towards the front door.

"It's about lunch time, you hungry?" I asked.

She gave me an arch look.

"Sorry, forgot who I was asking."

CHAPTER 26

It was less than fifteen minutes before my Mother called, desperate to apologise and begging me to come home. I said I forgave her and told her I'd be home soon. I ate with the others, already tired enough to sleep after walking ten steps and sitting down. That was Monday.

I did go home briefly, I made up with them, and promised I'd be more careful in the future, which was no word of a lie. I'd already located, practiced and perfected a poison-neutralising layer for my shields so I'd never get caught by *that* mess again. I spent time with the Pixies, caught up with Lunson and Bayano and I went back to Blackhold feeling a little better.

On Wednesday, I was sitting on a little bench in the garden at the centre of the house when Gwendolyn joined me.

"You're better," she said, "I'm glad. I was worried."

"Sorry," I said, putting the paperback I'd been reading on the bench's armrest, "How are you?"

She turned those lovely eyes on me, smiling slightly, "It hurts," she said, touching my chest, "I feel it. I can't stay too long."

"I'm sorry; here, give me a sec," I said, putting up a mental shield, "Better?"

She smiled sadly, "It's not that sort of bond, Beloved," she said, touching my face with her delicate fingers, "Evelina says that she's sorry she couldn't come. She feels it even more than I do, having known you longer. She offered to feed the concubine to her wyvern."

I smiled, "Thank you for coming."

"It's always my pleasure," she replied, "I have a gift for you, from my mother."

She stood and went to the oak tree, I followed. She pulled a golden acorn from a pocket and placed it in the owl hole. She took my hand and placed it on the trunk. There was a thump and a flash of golden light. The plants seemed to swell with life, everything was suddenly more vital. I felt familiar power flow through the whole house, mingling with its wards and enchantments.

My power, from my place of power. From Home...

"How?" I asked, in awe.

"That was an acorn taken from your favourite oak," she said, "My mother enchanted it so that your two homes could be closer. You need merely touch the tree and think of the colony, and you'll be there, or the tree there and think of here. This tree will also act as a nexus, so that you need never be apart from the people again, if you wish."

Right on cue, my Pixies flew out the hole in the oak and started buzzing around.

"Told you he had a castle!" Melody said.

"It's not a castle, it's a palace," Jewel pointed out.

"Looks like a strange place, whatever it is. Hi Matty!" Meadow said, flying down to land on my shoulder while the other two darted around looking at the square.

"Thank you," I said to Gwendolyn; suddenly Blackhold wasn't so forbidding and scary, suddenly it felt more like home. My eyes were wet.

"Our pleasure," she said, "I know that humans do things differently, but I like you, the *you* that is under my Beloved, does that make sense?"

I nodded.

"I like spending time with you, I feel safe with you. I am in no rush for anything else, and I know you will need time to grieve for your loss. So, I am content to be your friend, if you will be mine, for as long as you'll have me. Is that alright?"

I held out my hand and she placed hers in mine. I raised

it to my lips and kissed it gently, which broke her out in an adorable blush.

"Sounds wonderful to me," I said.

"Evelina's different, though, she'll be trying other things. I can't promise I won't help, some of her plans sound rather fun if they work."

"You two are getting on? That worries me."

"We are," she said with a smile, "I... I like her. We're so different, but it's like we're... I don't know how to put it."

"Two sides of the same coin?" I offered.

"Yes! That's exactly right. The same heart, but different outlooks."

"I'm glad, but where do you meet? I can't imagine your mother lets you go to Unseelie, and Adriata would spit before letting her daughter get exposed to you- you use my Grotto."

Gwendolyn smiled, "Clever boy. You don't mind?"

"Of course not, it's what it's there for. Make yourself at home."

"Careful with an invitation like that, Mathew, it means more than you think to a Sidhe," she said with a wicked smile. She kissed my cheek ever so gently and vanished.

I wish someone would teach me how to do that...

I really appreciated that nobody had said 'I told you so'. After all, the Fairies had seen this Cathy-thing coming, somehow. I imagined that it was just *killing* Adriata not to send me a gloating note.

I barely managed to warn Cassandra in time, before the various Fairies from the Grotto showed up. Even so, she was pretty startled when Kay started cantering up and down the corridors, poking into everything.

The nymphs were very put out about the lack of a water feature.

So they made one.

Lunson aided and abetted, and there was suddenly a not insignificant pond in my house garden, complete with fish transplanted from the lake in the Grotto, which gave the

Nymphs a link they could swim down.

"Mathew!" Tethys said, appearing out of nowhere, "Why did my house suddenly transform into a Disney movie?"

"Hello!" The Pixies said, flying around Tethys, who had rather a soft spot for them, and then Jewel said, "We came to visit! Princess Gwendolyn made us a place!"

Tethys sighed, "Just keep them out of the study?" she asked as Meadow landed on her head.

"Yes, Ma'am," I said with a smile as a Nymph appeared and splashed me, soaking my trousers. I turned to glare, but she was hiding in the little pond. I reached in and tickled what I found. The water exploded with bubbles as she squealed and swum away.

"Mathew!" Cassandra shouted, "They found the chocolate!"

Oh dear. I darted to my feet and headed off in the direction of her voice. It was the best I'd felt in weeks.

That Friday, Death came to see me.

Well, Killian did, anyway. He had Demise with him.

I was sitting propped up against my tree, Kandi asleep on my lap, her head resting on my thigh, snoring gently. Her back faced upwards, and I rested my arm on it while she slept.

"Good grief, Graves, are you the only male in the whole building?" Killian asked as he walked towards me, escorted by Cassandra.

I smiled and tried to rouse Kandi.

"Kandi? Wake up," I said.

"Won't, you can't make me," she said sleepily, yawning.

"Death is here," I said.

"What?" she said, suddenly awake, eyes wide before she saw Killian, "Matty! Don't scare me like that, you boob!"

"What? He's Lord Death."

"Ohh," she said, standing up and offering a curtsey, which looked a bit odd in a crop-top and jean shorts, "Sorry my lord."

"How come I never get a curtsey?" I asked.

"I sleep on you. We're a little past that, don't you think?" She flicked my ear and left us to it.

"How the hell is this Blackhold? This place used to be scary," Killian said.

"Tethys remodelled," I replied, standing to shake his hand and then Demise's.

He grinned, Demise looked even more peculiar than usual.

"What brings you two by?" I asked, leading the way to the drawing room.

"Well, it seems I have something of a staffing problem," Killian said after we were sat down. One of the valets brought in coffee for them.

"Oh," I said, a little confused.

"Indeed," he continued, "it seems you rather corrupted one of my retainers."

He gestured to Demise, who coloured slightly.

"I did what?" I asked.

"Oh yes, all sorts of strange ideas, a whole bunch of new-age hippie crap that has no place in a house of death, can't have that," he said.

Demise looked away, her expression vulnerable.

"It so happens that new-age hippy crap is rather my thing," I said, playing along, "Perhaps I might beg an introduction to the retainer in question, assuming that would be acceptable?"

"Well, if you feel that strongly about it," he said, "I was just going to retrain, but if it would please you, Lord Shadow, I'm sure I could be persuaded to part with her services."

Demise looked up at me, showing the barest flicker of a smile.

"That is a great favour, Lord Death, how might I balance the scale?" I asked.

Forms, you know, it was a pain in the neck.

"I would request a sum, but it so happens that you did

one of my retainers a good turn not so long ago, something involving Demons? I forget the specifics. I would consider this a repayment," he said with a sly smile.

"That is most generous," I said, "Assuming, of course, that the retainer in question is satisfied with the arrangement?"

"Why do you think we're here, Graves?" Demise asked sharply, apparently unable to keep to her part of the script any longer.

"Three seconds, that's all it took before she started snapping. She beat Cassandra's record of five seconds, which is impressive," I said with a smile.

Killian chuckled, "You're just the most whipped man in the country, aren't you?"

"You've seen the hands holding the whips, can you blame me?"

He laughed, startling Demise.

"Fair enough," he said, looking at his watch, "Well, I have a thing. Demise's stuff arrived ten minutes before I did, so that's all sorted."

I blinked, and started to comment, but Killian had already left.

Demise was still sitting across from me.

"So... how have you been?" I asked, not really knowing how to start.

She shook her head in exasperation.

I handed her off to Cassandra, who gave her the tour. I went back to my reading, barely able to concentrate, but glad that she was back. I'd been trying to get in touch since I came out of the hospital, but it was surprisingly difficult to get a hold of Death, and Demise didn't have a mobile.

She could be a plant, of course; that was a real possibility. But she was also my friend, my strangest friend. And I rather missed having her around, how messed up was that? I hadn't been allowed to shower alone in *months* because of her, but I'd rather grown used to it.

I fell asleep but was woken up when Demise dropped down next to me and prodded me with the edge of a chessboard.

CHAPTER 27

After another week, I was slowly beginning to recover, at least physically. That was mostly down to Kandi's relentless following of the instructions the doctor had given me. She actually made me *exercise*, for God's sake! I protested and she just made me do more. Demise 'helped' too, in her way, making sure that Kandi was obeyed. Cassandra thought this was hilarious; Tethys offered to hide me under her desk.

What was worse is that I actually took her up on it once. She giggled the whole time, nearly giving me away when Demise came looking.

I decided not to go back to Windward. I didn't need to. Leaver's Day wasn't really a thing I cared about, not now anyway, and I couldn't bear the idea of running into Cathy. Nothing short of a cataclysm was getting me back there (and even as I thought that, I knocked on every bit of wood in range and wasted an entire salt-shaker over my shoulders to avoid fate taking me up on that tempting thought).

A few days later, I was in Stonebridge, coming back from the Archive, where I'd visited Mira (the avatar of the Grimoire, my repository of forbidden knowledge). I went to see her every couple of weeks, just to make sure she was alright and keep her company. Her avatar looked a lot like Cathy, which hurt a bit, but that was hardly her fault.

I bought an ice-cream and settled down in a nearby park, enjoying the July sunshine. The space was more or less empty, and not especially big; there were a couple of trees, some well tended, very green, grass but it was quiet. I yawned and stretched as I finished the ice-cream, letting a little peace seep back into my heart after everything that had happened over the last couple of months.

"Lovely day," said a deep voice to my left.

I turned to see a man, tall and attractive, late twenties, dark hair and eyes, wearing an immaculate pinstripe suit and bespoke shoes. He carried a black cane with a silver top, carved into the shape of a snake's head, its eyes made of rubies that seemed to follow me. His complexion was healthy, his smile easy and friendly.

"That it is," I said.

"Mind if I sit?" he asked politely.

"By all means," I said, stifling a yawn, "Excuse me."

"Nice city," he said casually, which was unusual. People generally didn't make casual conversation with me. If the scars didn't put them off, the eyes did.

"That it is," I said, slightly confused.

"How does it compare with Gardenia?" he asked, his face breaking out in a smile that wasn't entirely wholesome.

I sighed and turned towards him.

"Can I help you, Sir?" I asked.

He smiled, twirling his cane with his fingers.

"Not today, Mister Graves, or would you prefer Lord Shadow?"

"Mathew's fine," I said, casting Mage Sight... and rapidly wishing I hadn't.

I'd been suspecting something along the lines of a Magician working for Sutton.

He was definitely *not* a Magician.

From the looks of him, I'd have to guess something more along the lines of... Archangel.

There was a lot more packed into that shape than there should be, a vast and powerful presence that seared my inner eyes just to look at, making me snap them shut to avoid my senses getting burned out. If Rose was a lizard, this guy was Godzilla, there was *that* much of a difference in their levels of power, and let's not forget that Rose was strong enough to bend Time, so this guy had to be... *cosmically* powerful.

And I wasn't entirely certain on this one, but I didn't think he came from Rose's side of the fence, if you know what I mean. There was something in his energy that said 'run like hell', emphasis on 'Hell'.

I swallowed hard.

"Very well, Mathew. I'm Neil," he said.

"Neil?"

"Just so."

"Alright, Neil, what can I do for you?"

"For me? Oh, nothing at all, my boy. I'm here to ask what I can do for you!" he said cheerfully.

"Sorry?" I asked, slightly taken aback. This wasn't what I was expecting, not at all.

"Well, you're practically family now, and I wanted to show my appreciation for what you did for my little Gabrielle," he said with a genuine (maybe) smile, "By the time I'd found out what was going on up here, it was all over. You saved her from a horrific fate. So I am in your debt, young man."

"I must disagree, Sir. I'd have done the same for anyone in pain."

"And therein lies the debt, don't you see? You make no distinction between a Demon and anyone else," he said with a beaming smile, "That's a very good thing."

"From who's perspective?"

Neil chuckled, "Well, mine certainly. So, what would you like? A new staff perhaps? I have weapons that could lay waste to cities. An amulet that will keep you alive even under the most mortal of wounds? Wisdom of the ages, the secret truths of human history?"

I smiled, "No, thank you, Sir," I said politely, "I don't like the idea of putting a price on what I did, not when the alternative would have been immeasurable suffering. That seems... unseemly to me."

His smile turned predatory, it was disturbing, especially bearing in mind his likely identity.

"A bargainer, good. Let's get down to the good stuff, then. Your face; I can fix that, easy as pie, really, an instant's work. I'd have to leave the eyes as they are, though; my Gabrielle is rather fond of them."

Oh, that was tempting...

Which was rather the point.

"Palmyra's working on that."

"Then how about a Succubus all of your own? To love and treasure for all time, someone who would love you unconditionally in this life and the next, you can't say better than that!"

In my current state, that was a very nice offer.

"You can't create love," I said after a hard minute's thought, "What you would do is provide a facsimile, though no doubt a pleasant one, for me. I'd think that the Succubus would feel rather tortured by the idea of being tethered to me for eternity. Oh, and I also plan on doing my level best not to end up 'downstairs', can she come into heaven?"

He laughed, a full and genuine sound, "Oh, Gabrielle was right about you, my boy. You are a sharp one. Just about everyone falls for the Succubus."

I tilted my head in acknowledgement of the complement.

Besides, I already had a Succubus (or quite possibly two). I didn't need another one.

"Alright, how about this, I'll fix your brother," he said.

I froze. He smiled slowly.

"Ah, it seems I have your attention."

Clever bugger.

I had to think about that one. Really, *really* hard.

"What's the catch?" I said finally.

"What do you mean?" he replied innocently, too innocently.

"Well, I've been thinking lately on the rules by which your two factions operate. And I'm fairly certain that you can only get involved if someone invites you to. So, the second I say 'go ahead', not only do you get your hooks into *me*, but you also have free reign inside my brother's cranium. And I'd imagine that the second you wanted something, my brother would take an instant and thoroughly unexpected 'turn for the worse', am I right?"

He coughed, his face colouring a little, "No, of course not."

I heard a tiny chuckle in my ear. Rose was around, somewhere.

"You're not used to dealing with particularly smart people, are you?" I asked dryly.

"Mostly desperate fools these days," he said sadly, "I haven't had a really good negotiation since Einstein. That man knew how to make a deal, I can tell you. Well, a fool you may not be, but that doesn't mean that you aren't desperate. Final offer, you clear my debt, I give you Cathy back."

"Just to be clear, do you mean in terms of a relationship, or do you mean that you took her and this is now a ransom?"

"The first one," he said through gritted teeth, "I'm not an animal, kidnapping little girls, what's wrong with you?"

"I'm fairly certain you're the devil, you can't pretend hurt feelings over the issue of your trustworthiness," I said.

"Really? You got Devil from merely wishing to clear a debt? That hurts."

"Well, that, and the fact that you're an Archangel from the pit with no spiritual degradation, you're talking about a Demon like she's a daughter, and I'm fairly to moderately certain that Neil is short for Sataniel, from *that* I get Devil."

He looked at me, dumbstruck.

"Shit," he said simply.

I smiled, "I get that a lot. Generally before someone tries to kill me."

"I can sympathise," he said, and after a dramatic pause, "with *them*."

I have to say, immeasurable evil aside, I quite liked the guy. He was witty, and he obviously loved his kids. That counted for a lot in my book.

"Well, you never answered my latest offer. Would you like your Cathy back?"

"Not like that," I said, "It would be a violation. Evil."

"Yes. But fun. Very, very fun," he said with a leer.

And I stopped liking the bastard. I wondered how many other people he'd made an offer like that to? How many said yes and damned themselves by enslaving the woman or man that they loved? How many people then had to love against their will for the rest of their lives?

"I think we're rather done," I said coldly.

"Wrong button, eh?" he said, "Mind if I ask why?"

"I love her. If she doesn't want to be with me, that's her choice. I'm not going to force her to be with me against her will. That would be horrific! Do I really need to explain this?"

"No, just wondering if you knew," he said, tapping his cane on the flagstones, "Alright, last chance for repayment. What do you want?"

"Nothing you can provide," I said softly, looking away.

"We'll see," he said, standing up, I did as well (manners), "Shadowborn always go bad, Mister Graves. You may need a friend in low places. Keep me in mind."

We shook hands and he vanished.

I let out a long exhale.

"Well done, Mathew," said a voice from behind me, giving me a nasty shock.

"Wah!" I shouted (and in not anything resembling a manly way, to my shame), jumping three feet into the air, before spinning mid-jump to see a familiar face, "Rose! Don't do that when the bloody Devil's wondering about the place!"

"Sorry," she said before hugging me. Unexpected... but certainly not unwelcome. Her hugs were wonderful things. It banished pains I hadn't even noticed and soothed the ache in my chest that Cathy had left.

"Dare I ask what that was all about?" I asked as she pulled away.

"You didn't believe his heart-felt tale of a debt incurred for a good deed? That's awfully cynical of you, Mathew," she said with a grin.

I rolled my eyes and sat back on my bench, she joined me. She was wearing a forest green dress that day, no shoes or socks as usual.

"We're running out of time, Mathew," she said, "The plan for Source is nearly finished."

"Wait, what?" I said, "But I thought we'd at least set them back, if not stopped them outright. How are they nearly finished?!"

"Because, just like a human, you started the job and then laid down to die half way through it," said a spine tingling voice from behind me.

"Seriously, why do you people always have to turn up right behind me?" I asked, not bothering to turn and glare as Gabrielle approached and ran her fingertips gently along the back of my neck, raising goose bumps before joining us on the bench.

"Because I like it, that's why," she replied.

I sighed, rubbing my eyes.

"Can you tell me anything?"

"Ankiala," Rose said quietly.

"What's that?"

"That's what I can tell you," Rose said, "And if you don't move on this information in the next thirty-six hours... Gardenia will die. And everyone in it."

I was a little shocked at that.

"What? The whole city? How?"

"Ankiala!" Gabrielle snapped, "Are you deaf, or something? Personally, I hope you screw up. I love it when a city burns."

"Oh, just... bollocks," I said tiredly.

"If you don't finish this task before the time limit expires... humanity suffers immeasurably. And there's nothing we can do. It will be a human choice. We can't intervene," Rose explained.

"Can you tell me anything else?" I asked.

"Work fast?" Rose suggested.

"I'd bet that's all he can manage anyway," Gabrielle muttered.

"I can literally swat you with my mind," I said. The Demon stuck out her tongue.

I stood, looking around for a convenient dark patch.

"Thanks for the warn-"

Gone again.

"I really hate it when you do that!" I said.

"We know," Gabrielle whispered from somewhere.

I grumbled and pulled my mobile, dialling as I stomped off.

"Hi Matty," Hopkins said, "What's up?"

"There may be a teeny-tiny... apocalyptic situation."

"Oh, what did you do now?" she asked.

Why do they always assume it's my fault?

Don't answer that.

I went back to Blackhold and told Tethys what was happening while preparing for trouble, which is to say changing into something I wouldn't trip over, that was about it. She darted off to call her sister and get her out of Gardenia.

Cassandra and Demise showed up, armed and armoured, while I called Price.

"My lord, it's earlier than you usually call," she said, a trace of admonishment in her tone.

"You need to get out of Gardenia, and I mean right this minute," I said.

"What do you know?" she asked, her tone suddenly serious.

"Big, very bad things happening very soon. Get off that island," I said, "Do you have a place you can go?"

"Me, yes, everyone else... not so much."

"Bring them here," I said, "Anybody you don't want to

risk in that city."

"Are you sure about that?" she asked, "That would be fifty-three vampires, lycanthropes and shape-shifters."

"Are you saying that they can't be trusted?"

"Of course not. I'm just saying that it's a lot for you to take on."

"If you don't want to come here, that's up to you. But you can't stay there."

"I wasn't refusing. It will take me time to get everyone moving, how long do I have?"

"It's what... three now? Can you be out of town by six?"

"Yes," she said.

"You know where to come?"

"I do," she said, "Good luck, my lord."

"Thank you, with any luck, you'll be home in a day and everything will be fine."

"Damn well better be, all my stuff is here. Do I need my guards?"

"Not in this house," I said, "But bring them if it will make you feel safe."

"If you say I don't need them, that's enough for us. And thank you."

"My people will take care of you when you arrive. I believe you know Tethys?"

"Of course," she said, I could hear the laugh in her voice.

"Good, then I'll see you soon. Give Crystal my best," I said.

"I think she'd much rather give you hers."

"Oh ha, ha," I said, "Don't fall in the channel on your way here."

She laughed and we said goodbye.

"So... here's the thing," I turned to say to Cassandra, who was glaring like she'd never glared before.

A little while later, Hopkins provided a portal, and I walked through with Demise and Cassandra. We appeared in the Presidential Suite of the Hemmingway Hotel. This one was much swankier than the Red Suite, huge, with gold everywhere, five bedrooms, a massive sitting room, three bathrooms, all of them highly decorated and gleaming.

Hopkins, Palmyra and Killian were standing around a table with their Wardens, a map spread out in front of them.

"It had better not be a trap, this time," Raven said icily as I walked up to them.

"Everyone's a critic," I muttered as the portal closed behind us. There had to be fifty war-mages in that room, and they all looked incredibly dangerous, enough to capture a *country*, much less a city, and these only a small portion of what the Archons could bring to a fight if they *really* took the gloves off.

Another portal opened. Kron came through, looking haggard, and very annoyed. Her armour was smoking a little bit.

"She saw me," Kron said by way of explanation.

"Who?" I asked.

Kron muttered something.

"What was that?" I said.

"Sutton!" Kron hissed, "I said Sutton, alright!"

"Really?" I said, faking incredulity, "That dear, sweet, innocent creature that nobody suspected of being a bad egg?"

Cassandra sniggered. Hopkins hit me. I probably deserved it.

Kron glared at me.

"I was wrong, are you happy, you little bastard?" Kron said.

"I'd have been happier if you could have come to that conclusion four months ago and saved me the beatings and the cold shoulder!"

Her Wardens bristled, mine stared them down, mine won. Cassandra could out-stare the gorgon and Demise was just plain *scary*.

"Alright, everybody who's not an Archon, take five, there's snacks in the reception room," Palmyra said.

The Wardens looked hesitant, but they moved out. I nodded at Cassandra and she followed Demise, who'd moved on cue.

The doors closed behind them and Palmyra moved to stand between me and Kron.

"Alright, you've both been colossal bitches about this whole thing," Palmyra said.

Kron turned to glare at the little Life Mage.

"Matty, you've been like a bull in a china shop ever since you met Sutton, and you've been stomping around like you always do when you're in a mood. You hurt me, you hurt Kron and I'm guessing Killian was slightly annoyed at some point."

Killian wiggled his hand back and forth in a non-committal gesture, grinning evilly.

"You trampled on hundreds of years worth of relationships and expected everything to just fix itself."

Kron was nodding sagely, smiling smugly.

"And you wipe that smirk off your face, Van, Matty was right all along, and you treated him like slime, in spite of him forgiving you not once but bloody *twice*! You acted horrifically to your brother. And if you'd been with us a couple of weeks ago, maybe Matty wouldn't have nearly died!" Palmyra almost shouted at Kron. She was small, and she was cute, but she could glare like nobody's business; and when she spoke, people listened, because everything she did, she did with the utmost sincerity.

"We five are a family," she continued, "It's a bond deeper than blood, deeper than mind. We rise or fall *together*. We just got our newest brother. We just became complete again. I won't have another loss. I can't bear it, not again. So you two make up, right here and now! Because we have a bloody Ancient Horror to deal with, and we will not go into this divided, understand me?"

Kron and I stood glaring at each other for quite some time before I spoke.

"I'm sorry, for what's between us," I said, "and I'm sorry

for my part in it. I never wanted... any of this to happen."

"You should be sorry," Kron muttered.

"I tried," I said, flopping down onto a convenient sofa.

"You've been an Archon for a handful of months and what have you done? Demolished buildings, made alliances with a brothel-keeper, been predated upon by vampires and started a war with the Pit. It seems everything you touch turns to crap."

I sighed unhappily. Hopkins and Palmyra glared but didn't interfere, this was our conversation.

"I can't disagree," I said, "I got people killed, I wasn't able to stop any of this Source business from happening, I fell face-first into a trap that nearly got me killed and to top it all off, the reason I bothered to even try to fix this mess told me that, by trying, I've made myself too depressing to be with. So yes, you are quite right. I don't know what else to tell you. I did what I thought was right. I've been trying my best, for all the good that's done."

Kron looked at me very intently, and her eyes softened ever so slightly.

"All we can ever do is our best, Mathew," she said, walking over so she could sit next to me, "and our lives are hard enough without dragging ourselves over the coals for our failures."

"I was doing just fine repressing the whole thing, thank you very much, you reminded me," I said, my tone taking the heat from the words.

She patted my shoulder, "I suppose that there is the very, *very* mind you, tiniest possibility that I might have, ever so slightly, overreacted. A little," she said.

I smiled, "That's as good as I'm going to get, isn't it?"

"I'd take it as a win. It's more than I've ever gotten," Killian said.

I extended a hand towards my sister, and she took it, squeezing just a little too hard, making me wince. She grinned.

"Now how about a hug?" Palmyra said.

"Don't push it," Kron replied, "it was fifty years before I'd hug *you*."

"And then under sufferance," Hopkins added.

Kron glared at them, but there was no menace in it now.

"I swear, ever since the invention of the psychiatrist, the world has become such a touchy-feely-girly place," Killian said, "sharing feelings and all this bollocks. In my day we repressed all this mess and got on with the job!"

"You want a hug, too?" Palmyra asked.

"What am I, eight?" he replied.

Palmyra hugged him anyway, Lord Death blushed.

"Are we done? Can we work now?" he said after Palmyra backed away.

"Absolutely," Kron said walking back to the table.

"Oh, what is Ankiala, by the way? Jen heard the name, dropped the phone and started panicking, so I assume it's bad?" I asked.

"I did not panic, I was surprised," Hopkins said, pinching me, "Bart, this is your area."

"Ankiala is... well, we're not entirely sure, exactly," Killian said, "We know that she's some sort of entity. In fact 'she' may not even be the right personal pronoun, but she may be anything from a kind of Demonic Elemental all the way up to an Old God."

"An Old God?" I asked, "Do I even want to know?"

"Probably not," Killian replied, "They were born of human belief in ancient times, before we could properly conceive of God. Ankiala may not even be one, she's barely mentioned in any of the old texts, which means that she was likely something nasty deliberately forgotten. And they generally only did that when the entity in question is dead."

"How are there things like *that* knocking around the place and nobody told me?" I asked, "That would seem to be one of those things I should know about!"

So I could keep far, *far* away from them!

"Jen thought you were too much of a big girl's blouse,"

Palmyra said evilly, "I was pretty sure you'd cry."

I gave her an evil look, but she ignored me.

"Okay, assuming a worst case scenario, how would you summon one of these Old Gods?" I asked, "Or bring one back, for that matter?"

Killian thought for a second.

"There was an obscure mention of something in a very old text. Damned if I know for sure. It was all very fragmentary," Killian said, "So little information survives from back then, and most of that is either untranslatable, half-metaphor or worse."

"It so happens, I have access to a book that might contain the necessary knowledge," I said.

"What?" Hopkins asked, "Oh, the Grimoire!"

"If there's information on something that dark, she'd probably have it," I said.

"Okay," Kron said, "Killian, you take Graves and consult the book. We'll continue preparations here. Sutton's fortified the central quarter and the Council Buildings, there's a fortress shield and it's powered by something very strong. I need time to break through it. I taught the brat too well."

"*Time*, you say?" I asked.

Four heads swivelled to glare at me.

"Sorry. Had to."

CHAPTER 28

Killian came with me; he brought Raven, I brought Cassandra, who told Demise to keep an eye on the planning. She'd be able to dumb it down for me later. Killian didn't open a portal. I felt a flex of Space Magic, and we were suddenly standing outside an entrance to the Archive I didn't recognise. There was one in every major city; I thought that this one might be in Cambridge, but I couldn't be sure.

I checked my watch and saw that it was just after six in the evening. I hoped that Price had gotten out alright; things were likely to go south *fast*, now that five Archons were turning their complete attention to that city.

Killian led the way inside. Cassandra fell in next to me and we followed. We walked down a short corridor, which contained the entry portal, and into a wide foyer containing the reception desk, behind which was the familiar figure of the Archivist, a snarky, middle aged man with greying hair, wearing a threadbare cardigan.

"My lord!" he said, darting to his feet as Killian approached.

"I never get a reception like that," I whispered to Cassandra, "The best I ever get is a hefty gulp and hasty retreat."

My Warden snorted, "If only people could know you like I do, then you'd get a lot less terror and lot more pointing and laughing," she said nastily.

My position as Lord Shadow remained largely unknown to just about everyone. To all but a few people outside my inner circle, I was simply Mathew Graves, Shadowborn Sorcerer and imminent genocidal maniac. I was not well liked.

The Archivist (essentially a glorified librarian) was definitely not a fan of mine. But I had every right to be in that Archive, so he had to be civil, if not cordial.

The building was comprised of thirteen floors, descending from one at the top to thirteen at the bottom, with each lower level being restricted to those with certain qualifications. The only exception was the book they kept on the thirteenth floor, nobody but an Archon could get onto thirteen, not that I needed to be next to her to speak to Mira.

"I need access to the Grimoire," Killian said, walking straight past the receptionist.

"With that thing, Milord?" he said, gesturing at me.

Cassandra glared hard at him, but he either didn't notice, or didn't care.

"Treat Mister Graves with respect, Archivist," Killian said coldly, "or I'll want to know the reason why."

"Milord," the man said, bowing and walking backwards out of Killian's way.

I followed Killian to the lift.

Wait. Lift? Where the hell was that before?

"Has this always been here? Have I been walking up and down thirteen flights of stairs for no good reason?"

"Old bugger keeps it hidden," Cassandra said with a grin.

"You could have told me!"

"It's more or less the only exercise you get that doesn't involve Nymphs, you randy sod," Cassandra retorted.

Killian and Raven turned to give me a look.

"Not what it sounds like, folks," I said.

"Which part?" Killian said with a grin.

"The randy sod part, I just swim with them," I explained.

"For many Nymphs, that would be considered part of a mating ritual," Raven said.

"Not these ones," I said firmly.

Cassandra sniggered.

The lowest level was the smallest, but it was still pretty

big. It was made up of a massive circular platform suspended over a chasm. The other twelve floors were suspended above the thirteenth, in an inverted conical arrangement so that you couldn't fall from an upper level and land on a lower one. The Grimoire rested on a mahogany pedestal. The book was large and black, half a metre tall, bound in leather (that may or may not have come from a sentient source, I didn't want to know for sure). There was a large red circle on the front containing a smaller black circle inside, like my eyes.

Killian pressed his signet to the door and it slid open; a black bridge extended from the viewing gallery to join to the platform.

"Oh, that would have been so useful," I said.

"Finally going to admit that was you?" Cassandra asked slyly, referencing the day I'd broken into that very room (and got away with it, too).

"No, you've been saving an extra-hard smack for the day that I do, I can feel it."

"Hm, maybe you aren't as dumb as I think you are," Cassandra replied.

"You know, you don't see Killian's Wardens calling him names."

"If I stopped calling you names and hitting you, how would you know I cared?"

"Fair enough."

We crossed the bridge and Mira appeared next to the book.

"Good evening, Master," she said cheerfully.

Mira's body and face were Cathy's. She wore a slightly less conservative Windward uniform than I was used to, tight around the (slightly larger) chest and with a shorter skirt. Her hair was jet-black, like Tethys', and her eyes were mine. The whole look was a little bit sexy.

"Hi, Mira," I said with a smile.

She wasn't Cathy, I knew that, but it was still a little painful.

"You know," she said, "I'm not sure I like that little wrench when you look at me. Time for a change, I think."

Her image flickered, and suddenly she looked *very* different.

Much more like Tethys, actually, in her body and her facial structure; but with a trace of Hopkins in the nose, Cassandra's lips, Crystal's hair and Kandi's freckles. She wore Gabrielle's tight black clothes. Tiny familiar pieces in a brand new whole.

"You like?" Mira said with a twirl, "I think I'll call this look 'Sinful Sister'."

"Oh my," I said, trying not to drool.

Mira smiled.

"Hey, pervert, we're in the middle of something, here," Cassandra said, elbowing me.

"Right, right," I said. Killian was sniggering off to one side, "We're in something of a pickle," I said to the Avatar of the Grimoire.

"Well, you brought Death with you, I didn't assume you were planning a picnic," she said sardonically, moving over to stand next to me. I'd only seen her a few hours ago, but she was looking at me like she hadn't seen me in years.

"Would you happen to know anything about an entity called 'Ankiala'?" I asked.

I didn't think it was possible for her to pale, but she pulled it off.

"Where did you hear that name?" she asked.

"Tell you later, what does it mean?"

"Ankiala was what modern Magicians refer to as an 'Elder Goddess', which is actually something of a misnomer, being as she was by no means a 'God' by any stretch of the imagination. Entities like her were born out of human emotional response in a time when you were essentially food, being hunted by everything from mortal predators to immortal monsters. She was merely one of dozens of such forms, some of whom were benign, like the ones associated with healing and the home. The 'good' ones actually helped mankind to thrive and drive back the darkness and barbarity of pre-civilisation.

"Ankiala was *not* one of those good ones. She was the manifestation of early man's fear of the dark. She was, in effect, the think hiding under the bed of every early human being. She was worshipped by some, who sacrificed to her for freedom from nightmares and death in the night," Mira said.

"Well, that's not good," I said, now *very* worried.

"You don't chuckle! However, and my records are a little fragmentary, she was supposedly destroyed by a group of Elder Gods who would eventually evolve into what we'd recognise as the Greco-Roman pantheon... before they themselves eventually got eaten by the Scourge in about six-fifty b.c.. Light was her weakness, which makes sense. She was, in effect, the Goddess of Shadows."

"Wait, what's that about a Scourge?" I asked, getting steadily more overwhelmed as time went on as I learned more about this new and exciting realm of world-ending horrors.

"Don't worry, an Archangel smote it," Mira said brightly.

I rubbed my now aching head, "But Ankiala's dead?" I asked, to clarify.

"Well, there's dead, and then there's *dead*," Mira explained.

"Which one is Ankiala?"

"The bad one," Mira said with a sigh.

"Meaning?"

"That given sufficient power and skill... it might be possible to bring her back."

"How much power?" I asked.

"Well, a combination of Magical Energy and Life Force... far more than a Sorcerer could come up with, or even ten, for that matter, closer to thirty, I'd say, and they'd all have to be top end. But such a ritual would kill them all stone dead; drain them down to husks. Bearing in mind the current mage population, I doubt that there are enough Sorcerers of sufficient power stupid enough to go along with any such spell."

I thought about that, and sighed, it looked like we were safe...

Wait...

My eyes went wide, "Oh no."

"What?" Killian asked.

"Source," I said, smacking my leg in frustration, "One of the people I met while doing something stupid told me that Source carves off a piece of the user and sends it somewhere. Some sort of energy."

"Demon-essence, distilled and focussed, crystallised. Checking," Mira said, tapping her lip, "Yes, that could do it. It's rather technical, but Demon essence can affect the soul. It's conceivable that it could cleave a piece off. Souls re-grow, so the victim could be repeatedly tapped. Enough energy... how many doses of Source have been consumed?"

"Thousands," Killian said, "Hundreds of thousands."

"Oh dear," Mira said, "That might well do it."

"Damn," Killian said, "What else can you tell us?"

"If one of the Old Gods isn't destroyed, and generally that means obliterated, then generally 'dead' means that they are simply too damaged to affect the Newtonian World. Some are awake, minds trapped in wrecked 'bodies' or the equivalent, others mangled into a metaphysical coma. Without knowing which category Ankiala falls into, we can't be certain what the procedure is. There are a number of ways to bring back an Old one. The easiest would be to repair the damage, make it whole again. Or, you could provide a new body for it, offer one up for possession, but that generally ends in an exploded body; there's transfusion, but that needs another Elder God. I think repair is the most likely option."

"What's the minimum Sutton would need?" I asked, "Other than lots and lots of power."

"Ankiala's grave, for one... and that's about it. I can see from your memories that you've already found it, or she has anyway, my records can confirm that much. No wonder that city's such a mess; it's built right on top of one of mankind's ancient terrors. Any idea about a time frame?"

"No more than thirty-ish hours or so," I said, "Probably less now that she knows we've found her."

"Then you need to find the focus of the resurrection, the grave, the caster, whatever it is and break it. If you should fail, concentrated Light Magic on as much of the creature as you can reach, but I strongly advise against letting it get that far. Even Archons should worry about battling an Old One."

We nodded.

"Anything else?" Killian asked.

"The second after the creature is resurrected, it will begin to get stronger. The sooner you get to it, the better your chances will be, so quicker would be better," she said.

"Can't argue with that," I said. Killian turned and walked away with Raven.

"I'll be right with you," I said.

Cassandra followed them out, and I turned to Mira.

"Now seems as good a time as any," I said quietly.

"Agreed, two steps to the left, please," she said with a smile. I obeyed.

"Perfect," she said.

She closed her eyes for a second. There as a dim pulse of Magic (more or less impossible for anyone but an Archon or *her* in that place), and the book looked like it had dropped to the pedestal. Mira vanished, and I followed the party out.

Yes, I stole my book.

No, I probably shouldn't have.

Yes, Cassandra was going to be pissed.

I waited until we were outside, so she'd be less inclined to make me take Mira back.

"Cassie?" I asked nonchalantly, "Would you mind holding onto this for me until we get home?"

"Sure Matty, what is i- oh you son of a bitch!" she said as I handed the (now two inches tall) Grimoire to her.

Killian turned and saw, rolling his eyes, "Can't take our eyes off you for a second, can we?"

"She's my friend," I said, "She gets lonely."

"It's true, I do," Mira said, popping out of nowhere like she usually did.

"Matty, you can *not* just take the Grimoire!" Cassandra said, holding it up in her palm.

"Easy," Mira complained, "I'm not some train station paperback!"

"Sorry," Cassandra said, "but this is such a bad idea!"

"Why?" I asked.

"Because it's evil!" Cassandra almost wailed.

"It's part of me Cassie. It's only evil if I am," I pointed out.

"Don't you give me that double talk!"

"Warden," Mira said, moving towards her, "Mathew is my master. My heart is built on his. I am a tool, nothing more. If he chooses the Black, that's up to him. If he chooses something else, that's also up to him. I'm his help, not his corruptor. And I don't like it down there. If there was any danger, would I be in your hand right now? I could have produced an illusion, I didn't. He trusts you, so I do. Please don't put me back in that place."

Cassandra looked *really* miffed.

"Bugger!" she said, stuffing the book in her pocket, before glaring at me, "You are in so much trouble!"

"I won't be any trouble, won't even make a peep, I promise," Mira said.

"Miserable guilt tripping book," Cassandra muttered, and then louder, "If this goes wrong, I'm going to silent treatment you into your grave!"

"Alright, if you tell me, right here and now to put her back, I will, until you are ready for me to bring her home," I said.

"Don't be so reasonable, it's harder to be mad at you!" Cassandra said, "Do you have any idea how many years I spend guarding this cursed book?! And you just walk out with it?!"

She dragged Mira out her pocket and flapped her in my face, causing the Avatar to wince at the mistreatment.

"In your defence, you weren't guarding it when I took it," I said.

Okay, I probably deserved to get hit for that one.

"Ow," I said rubbing my latest arm-bruise, "Look, it's going to be even safer at Blackhold, which is rather conveniently guarded by your hand-picked Wardens, and all but impregnable to outside attack, even more so if Mira's there and helping."

"True," Mira said, "I'd be perfectly safe there."

Cassandra muttered under her breath, cradling the book.

"Fine," she said, placing the book back in her pocket, "I'm still mad at you."

"You can hit me some more, if that'll help," I offered.

She glared and fell in beside me. Killian did his thing again and we reappeared in the Hemmingway.

"Literally the first chance you got, you bastard," Cassandra grumbled.

"And the first thing I did was give her to you," I replied.

"I hate your manipulative guts so much right now..." she said, but she was smiling just a little bit.

"Took the book?" Hopkins asked.

"Took the book," Killian confirmed.

"Ha, I win the pool!" Palmyra said.

"Do you lot have nothing else to do but bet on when I'm going to do stupid things?" I asked.

"In our defence, Matty, you do provide quite a bit of fodder for betting," Hopkins said, "just throwing it out there, any inclinations towards creating a familiar yet?"

"Hey! That's cheating!" Palmyra said, swatting her sister's arm.

"I have Burglar, does he count?" I asked.

"No dogs!" Hopkins said, "Especially not that one, he's afraid of Magic. And he sheds. And he steals people's food."

Kron looked like she was ready to start banging her head on the table.

"Did you get the information?" Kron asked.

Killian explained what we'd learned. Kron didn't look happy.

"I can bring down the shield," Kron said, "but I don't know if I can do it in time, not if it's powered by the stolen Source energy. It's a near-impregnable shield. Portals and Space Magic can't breach it; it has to be brought down the hard way."

"What if we could get someone inside?" I offered stupidly.

"Shut up, Mathew," Cassandra said, dragging me down to sit next to her.

"What do you mean, Graves?" Kron asked.

Cassandra stomped on my foot. I winced.

"Just spit it out," Hopkins said.

"I can Shadow-Walk," I said, "I can get past the shield."

"Can you take us with you?" Killian asked.

"I've taken one with me before, Demise, I don't know if I could take more than one, and now might not be the best time for experimentation. Not if there's a Goddess of Shadow trying to wake up. And I'd be playing around quite a bit with the Shadows, I'd better go alone."

"Fair points," Killian said.

"Leaves you rather out on a limb," Palmyra pointed out.

"Horribly out on a limb," Hopkins said.

"Good, terrible plan put forward, terrible plan rejected," Cassandra said.

"Hey, hey, let's not be hasty," Kron said.

"Absolutely not, I forbid it!" Cassandra said.

"You what, Warden?" Killian said politely, but with a note of danger in his voice.

"Cassie, let's have a word?"

I stood and she harrumphed, but followed me out into the corridor, which was guarded.

"What?" she asked.

"Gotta go," I said simply, "it's a Pineapple thing."

"I won't let you," she said, calling power, "You'll die, you idiot!"

"No I won't," I said confidently, "I'm ready this time."

"It's an Elder God, how can you be ready for that?" she asked, grabbing my shirt and shaking me.

"Blatant sneakery and backstabbing, of course," I said, putting my hands over her clenched fists, "It's going to be fine. What are the chances I'd screw up twice in so short a period?"

"It's you, so middling to damn near certain, I should think," she said quietly.

"It'll be fine, I promise."

"You can't make that promise!"

"Sure I can. I just did."

Her eyes were wet.

"Seriously? That little confidence in the First Shadow?"

She punched my arm, not too hard this time.

"If you get hurt, I do twice as bad when you get back, understand me?" she said.

I nodded.

She opened her jacket and pulled out the revolver I'd given her, "Just in case."

"I don't think I should have a gun, I'm far more likely to shoot myself by accident."

"Better to have it and not need it than need it and not have it," she said, shoving it into my pocket.

"Don't you need it?" I asked.

"I have three other guns on my person."

I looked her up and down; there was nowhere to hide that many guns.

"Where?" I asked, not really sure I wanted to know.

"Hope you never find out," she said, leading me back into the meeting room.

"Lover's tiff over with?" Killian said.

Cassandra glared at him.

"Alright, here's the strategy," Kron said, "We'll advance on the shield and bring it down, Graves will make his way inside and distract Sutton's forces until we can get in and finish her off. Any quest-"

Before she could finish, there was a deep almost subsonic *roar* of power. It washed over us, scratching at our minds. I felt the wave flow over the city, spreading all around us.

"What was that?" I asked.

"Unless I'm very much mistaken, the starting gun on the end of days," Mira said, appearing again, "Awakening Spell. Greater Class. City wide area of effect. This city is now a hostile environment to anything human."

"Are you sure?" Killian asked, his face going pale (not easy on a man who cultivated 'corpse-grey' as his skin tone of choice).

Mira nodded, "There's no doubt."

She vanished again. Kron picked up her phone, dialling quickly, "Code Black, Gardenia," she said, "Yes, I'm sure. No, this isn't a drill. Good."

"What's an Awakening Spell?" I asked.

"It tears civilisation from monsters; sentience, minds. Any non-human predator within the city has been rendered little more than an animal, driven mad with hunger and rage, directed by the caster," Mira reported dispassionately, "it shouldn't be possible. It would take Black Magic of horrific proportions, and I didn't feel any."

"All of them?" I asked with a shudder, "That could be thousands!"

"Time to go!" Kron said before I had the chance to ask any more, "We're out of options, everybody execute the plan!"

The Archons and their Wardens disappeared, leaving me with mine. It was very instant. Hopkins left a portal for us to follow, though.

"You two do me a favour? Watch out for each other?" I said to Cassandra and Demise.

"Of course," Cassandra said with a small smile.

"I'll protect her. Here, my lord, take this," Demise said.

She drew her sword, which shimmered and condensed into a rod about thirty centimetres long.

"I can't disarm you," I said.

"I'm more heavily armed than your Cassandra," she said, placing it in my hand. It was cold and heavy, like the grave; packed with Death Magic, "Just bring it back in one piece."

"Of course," I said, "thank you both. I'll be back as soon as I can. Don't lose Mira, and stay near Hopkins, just in case, alright?"

"No stupid risks, okay?" Cassandra said, pulling me into a hug and squeezing me tightly enough to bruise.

"Naturally," I said.

Demise looked at me very intently and then leant forward to plant a little kiss on my cheek.

"Keeps Death away," she explained.

We walked through the portal... and into a war zone.

CHAPTER 29

My little party was standing inside a circle of Magicians, the four Archons were facing towards a clutch of high rise buildings, all of equal height, but different colour, red, black, gold and blue, overlooking a massive central plaza containing what looked like an ancient church. The high rises were surrounded by a massive Fortress Shield, my brother and sisters were trying to tear it down, and weren't making immense progress.

Behind them, a battle raged. About a hundred War Mages were fighting every abomination and horror the city had to offer, Ghouls, Vampires, Succubae (mortal variety), Incubae, Lycanthropes, Ogres, and a few things I'd never seen before all swept forwards in a mad rush, many slashing at their fellow monsters as they charged.

The Wardens closed up around their Archons and engaged the enemy.

It was a once in a generation sight. Magic and gunfire blazed in the darkened city, lightning and fire, frost and air, death and space, it all lashed out and monsters died in their hundreds. Most ran to seek easier prey, but so many were left. Demise and Cassandra moved into the line, and their Magic joined the others.

I wanted to help, but I had my own job to do. I walked to a nearby patch of Shadow, opened a Gate and walked into the Shadow Realm.

I immediately discovered that it was a good thing that I hadn't brought someone with me. If I had, they would have been thrown out of the Realm, or worse. The Shadows felt... almost afraid, though that wasn't the word. It was like they were tensed against a wound, they way you flinch when someone throws a ball at your head (my memories of school sports were not the happiest). I instinctively knew that they would have ejected anyone or anything other than me, which was a pain. I'd been counting on being able to go for help if I couldn't handle what I found.

Well, onwards and upwards as they say. It was either that or find a new reality to live in.

I looked towards the plaza, which was the centre of the Fortress Shield, and had absolutely no trouble figuring out where I needed to go.

The Church was merely the cap on a warren of caverns, catacombs and chambers that wormed their way under ground, miles and miles of them, getting rougher as they went deeper.

And at the very bottom, a hundred metres below the surface, there was a circular space surrounded by corridors and antechambers. And there was... *something* in there, not quite here and not quite there. Something scrunched and under great pressure. I moved there with a thought, and it wasn't as easy as Shadow-walking should be; almost like diving through thick treacle.

I stood in the Shadow counterpart of that big room, taking in the details in safety before I acted. There were two sets of thick columns around the room, a smaller circle inside a larger. The columns were carved with pictures that made my head hurt, depicting things that shouldn't exist. There were stairs leading up to a gallery, wide and heavy. The room was otherwise empty but for a raised platform at the centre, covered in ancient writing and more of those dreadful images.

I made my way to the edge of the room and found a convenient patch of Shadow, listening in carefully. I heard wails and moans, the sounds of people in fear and pain, and above it all, the voice of Namia Sutton.

"Get the last of them in place, there's no more time! The

Archons are at the gates, and there's no telling how long the creatures can hold them!"

"Yes, Milady," said an obsequious tone.

I opened a Gate and slid out carefully behind a column. I took a peek, and it wasn't good.

As you know, certain things couldn't be seen from inside the Shadow Realm; people, for example, of which there were quite a few. Well, not people, per se, it was the Hyde, about a dozen of the smaller ones in addition to Sutton and her followers.

But there was also a colossal glowing object directly above the platform. It swirled, white, black and grey light shifting and flowing. There were about a dozen men and women, tied hand and foot with Spelleater Manacles to the platform. All but one of them was dead, their throats cut, and the last was about to follow them to a similar end. I nearly gagged at the sight of so much blood and death, but that would have been fatal.

I cast Mage Sight and saw that the last man was Dirk Wallace, the Mage I'd met at Michelangelo's.

Wallace's head was held in the hand of a huge Hyde, almost seven feet tall and broad with it, his skin marked by metal staples and green with rot. He wore a loin cloth and his body was soaked in blood, his head a grotesque amalgam of cyclops and ogre that made me queasy.

Sutton was on the upper level, walking away from the chamber, only to halt and raise a hand towards the Hyde executioner. It stopped, looking towards her. She stood for a long moment, concentrating hard; I felt Magic flow and what looked almost like a ghost appeared in front of her, vaguely male, wrapped in long robes that concealed his face. He held a staff in one hand and a glowing sphere in the other.

"My Lord," Sutton said, bowing low to the figure.

"Namia, what have you done?" the ghost rasped, "You've unshackled the entire city!"

"I had to! The Archons are here, they were going to stop

me!"

"Do you have any idea how important Gardenia was to me? How crucial it was to my return? That's ruined, now! The city will be nothing but ash by the end of the day! The Five ignored it because it didn't draw attention; now they'll raze it to the ground!"

"Not with Ankiala roaming around; they won't have time," she said, her expression distinctly worried.

"Foolish girl! Ankiala is a means to an end, nothing more! It *can't* be allowed to 'roam', it's an Elder God!"

"Then... why am I doing all this?" she asked, her face creased with confusion and just a trace of her usual anger.

"Because Ankiala's soul being in the Newtonian World weakens specific parts of my prison, that's why! Just enough for me to break them and bring me a little closer to my return! I told you all this, weren't you paying attention?!"

Alright, who the hell was this prick? From the sounds of it, he'd orchestrated this whole mess!

"I thought... I thought you were being coy."

"Coy?! Who the hell do you think you're talking to?!" he barked, making her cringe, but then she stopped, standing up straight to glare at the figure.

Sutton's eyes blazed with sudden rage, "I think you're a trapped old man with no power other than what *I* give you. This is my organisation, my power and my plan. You'll get your precious resurrection, but Ankiala is *mine*. I will bring her back, I will use her and I will take what I deserve, what I've *always* deserved!"

"You stupid girl," the apparition said, sighing, "Don't say I didn't warn you."

He vanished, leaving Sutton swearing like a sailor. She snapped a command at the executioner, and left the room, leaving me with no time to contemplate the appearance of this new player, as Wallace's eyes had widened in terror. The Hyde holding Wallace raised a bloody knife, his mismatched eyes on his victim's exposed neck. I threw a quick Illusion around the platform and dropped the Hyde with a blast of concentrated Force that blew his monstrous head off and dropped the rest of the corpse to the ground. I darted out from behind cover and snapped Wallace's manacles away with an effort of Will before helping him up.

The other Hyde hadn't even noticed, yet. It was nice to know that Illusions worked on Reanimates.

Wallace yanked the gag out of his mouth.

"Thank you, thank you!" he said, "She's gone insane! She's killed almost everyone!"

"What can you tell me?" I asked.

"I didn't know about all this when we last spoke, I swear, but she's trying to resurrect an Old God!"

"I know that bit, tell me how," I said, a little impatiently.

He was breathing hard, barely this side of running away in a panic, "That glowing thing up there is the collector, storing all the Source energy. The bodies are Magicians she used to open the gateway in that platform, it leads to her grave. The gate opens, the collector releases the life force, and Ankiala is reborn."

"What can I do to stop it?" I asked.

"Nothing, 'My Lord'," Sutton suddenly said from above us.

She had six Mages with her, all Wizard-Class, nobody I couldn't handle. I figured this was probably as close to the end as we were going to get. If I couldn't use Magic on her now, I never would...

Not yet! Rose's voice in my head.

Bollocks.

"It's already set in motion. Lives added to the gateway only speed it along. Not even the Great One himself could stop me, much less a nothing Shadowborn like you."

I backed us up to the wall, Wallace at my side. I was about as ready for a fight as I could be. I had my borrowed stave in my hand, and magic ready to go. Wallace put up some shields, sensible fellow.

"Charming as always," I said confidently. I was preparing to talk my way out of this, to buy time if nothing else.

Wallace had other ideas... the idiot.

He called Will and Chemical energy and hurled it at the wizards, all of whom were standing on the sacrificial platform over Ankiala's tomb.

"I'll protect you, Brothers!" Sutton said, calling her light and throwing up a great, glittering barrier. The Wizards with her called their powers, too, preparing combat spells.

Wallace's attacks fizzled out on Sutton's barrier, and what few defences the Wizards were preparing were recycled into attack spells. They must have felt that Sutton's defences would be enough. Wallace screamed in rage, and in spite of my yelling at him to stop before he got us both killed, he cast another great array of attack spells at the other Mages, all of whom were quite safe behind Sutton's shields.

Or so they thought.

At the last instant, Sutton darted away from them, pulling the shields she'd put in front of them back around herself. Wallace's attacks hit home, and Sutton's Mages died screaming before I could do anything to help them. Their life's blood and death's suffering struck the platform, as Namia Sutton threw her head back and laughed like a lunatic, screaming her joy into the chamber.

The platform... fell away, taking the bodies with it. The collector powered up, and released its energy straight down into the grave of Ankiala.

For a long moment, nothing happened. And then I felt her stir, deep, deep down, further than the planet's volume should even permit. Her presence scraped at the edge of my senses, like an awful itch I couldn't scratch. She was definitely a thing of the Shadows themselves, vast and powerful, and she was coming towards me.

With all my might, I slammed a barrier of Will over the hole.

"Distract her if you can!" I shouted, putting more power

into the construct, which probably wouldn't work, but I had to try. If nothing else, I'd force the entity to weaken herself battering through it.

"Yes my lord," Wallace said, steel in his tone as he threw Chemical lances at Sutton and the Hyde around her, which had finally woken up to the situation, only to melt and rot under the power of Wallace's attacks.

Ankiala slammed into my Will while I was distracted, hitting monstrously, *enormously* hard. My cover bent under the strain.

"Bloody hell!" I shouted, pressing down harder, gritting my teeth against the pressure.

The Goddess was laughing; I could hear her, a sound reverberating down my link to the Shadows. She didn't think much of what I was doing. My Well was draining fast, Magic being pulled into a barrier that wasn't going to hold much longer.

I used some of my dwindling power to call Light and conjured a great ball of it above the hole. The Goddess recoiled, dropping back into the darkness.

Sutton counter-attacked and Wallace fell back with a burning hole through his head. He slammed into a column and fell to the ground, dead instantly. I turned and caught her next attack on my shields, but it drove me back from the hole.

Ankiala was rallying, and I was flagging. Sutton was firing more and more light at me, and I couldn't stop them both. I lost concentration.

The Old God shattered my Will cap and I staggered back as she pushed herself the rest of the way up from her grave.

Sutton laughed, pausing in her attack to gloat (like an idiot).

"Ha, look at you now, Graves!" Sutton shrieked, "Where's your snide threats now? When the scores are finally tallied, it turns out you're just another weak, pathetic- urk!"

Simply put, Ankiala killed her on the spot, and there wasn't a damned thing I could do to stop it, it happened so fast.

The tiniest part of the Old God poked over the edge of the pit, a coiling mass of rotten, semi-ephemeral meat streaked with grey and mottled white. A tendril emerged, faster than a snake, the tip harder than diamond.

At that moment I realised why I hadn't been allowed to use any Magic on Sutton.

Whatever process Sutton had used to resurrect the creature had imprinted the essence of her power signature into the fabric of that ancient entity; an imprint that let Ankiala's tendril slide effortlessly through the Sorceress' shields and punch into that poor woman's skull like a spoon through pudding.

I felt the light of Sutton's soul vanish as the Old God fed on her essence; and then there were more Magical signatures in the creature's Aura; Wallace's, Kron's, Killian's, a hundred others, more, even. Every person who'd used Magic on Namia Sutton over the course of her long life, in practice or anger. Each and every one of them was now vulnerable to Ankiala.

And so was I. I felt my own signature in there, too, goodness knew where she'd picked it up, I'd been so careful. I did notice that my signature was muted... different than I felt at that moment. Different enough to make the difference? I hoped so, or I was so screwed...

Two smaller tendrils joined the first in Sutton's head, each a massively dense piece of Shadow fused with immortal flesh, that hit with a wet crunch (the sound alone nearly enough to cost me my lunch). I felt them shove the last few shreds of Sutton out, and begin to replace them with something that really had no right to be in there; it was simply too *big*. The transfer was slowing, now to a crawl, but it was still happening, Sutton's empty shell was slowly filling up with the ancient mind of one of mankind's first monsters.

Ankiala turned towards me, her eyes black like a Shadowborn's.

"Well met, Lord Shadow," she said, her voice was resonant, like several different tones overlapping at once, "I've been waiting for you, I'm glad you could be here for my return."

Alright, thinking *very* quickly. Ankiala's 'body' was dead; I could practically feel the lack of life oozing from the thing. That meant that the Source-power had merely revitalised her slumbering mind and given it enough energy to overcome its death, but likely only for a short time.

Therefore, Ankiala needed a new body; her 'divine' one was just unable to support her, anymore. That meant that she was now in the process of compacting a multi-planar creature's consciousness and power into a human being. That would be impossible, except that Namia Sutton was a Sorceress, and a very powerful one, and therein laid the key. If I'd had to guess, I'd have said that the Old God was shovelling itself into the remains of Namia Sutton's *Well*. That was so disturbing because Wells were supposed to be tied to our souls, and I was sure I'd felt Suttons depart.

Anyway, making those sorts of alterations to a creature, changes that would allow a human body to support an entity of Ankiala's power, would take time; time where she wouldn't be at full strength.

Time enough for me to act? But how? I'd used up a *lot* of power just trying to hold her back and failed dismally.

"I find that unlikely," I said, trying to buy time while I thought this one through.

I did have one idea; it was desperate, but it was the best chance I had, so I started moving slowly in the direction of the platform.

The body may have been dead, but it was still the seat of most of Ankiala's mind and power; if I could find a way to interrupt the flow, I might be able to stop all this. I cringed as I watched Sutton's skull flex outwards before resuming its previous shape, another wet crunch accompanying the dreadful changes. I could have gone my whole life without seeing that happen. I'd never be able to eat lobster again; it was the same sort of sound that came from cracking a claw open.

"And why's that?" Ankiala said, "I'm not Sutton. I have no quarrel with you or your fellow Magicians; especially not you. You and I are of a kind, born to the dark, part of it."

"I'm nothing like you. Look what you did to that girl! You murdered her!" I said, facing her side on, getting Demise's staff ready.

Ankiala laughed, it wasn't a pleasant sound.

"This creature?" she asked, "When I ate her up, I learned almost everything she knew. This 'girl' as you call her orchestrated some of the greatest atrocities of the last five hundred years and nobody even knew about it."

Are you there? I sent to my Shadows as she talked.

Always, came the speedy reply.

That was good to know. If everything went wrong, then the Elementals were my one chance to survive this mess, and that was a *slim* chance.

"She had plans for you. Though even she wasn't completely sure what she was going to do when she had you in her grasp. She loved you in her own rather twisted way, did you know that? You were the first person to ever really see her as an adversary rather than a victim. She loved that feeling even as she plotted to defeat you, to *mutilate* you. That was to be my first task after she'd 'freed' me, you know, bring you to her. Stupid girl."

"She still didn't deserve to die like that," I said.

Nearly ready...

"Why?" Ankiala asked, seeming to be genuinely curious.

"Because life is a precious thing, even hers."

"People are transitory things. One hundred years or one thousand, makes no difference, dead is dead."

"Everything dies," I agreed.

I drew Cassandra's gun, pointed it at the monster, and pulled the trigger.

Ankiala deflected the dispel-coated bullet with an easy wave of her hand as I raised the staff and poured Magic through it, aiming carefully. I wasn't aiming at her; the bullet had just been a distraction. My true target was the tendrils connecting the Old God to her new host.

Demise's staff was a Death Magic converter. It took any Magic applied to it and coiled it in Death before passing it out again, a very dangerous, very powerful weapon. I used Light, which erupted from the other end of the staff as a light grey beam, the energy fundamentally altered under the influence of pure death.

Light and Death were a potent combination, especially against something of the Shadow Realm. My power slashed into those tendrils, and for an awful moment I thought I'd failed as my energy signature, captured by the Old God, rose to meet my attack.

But it wasn't the same as what I cast against it, and in that instant, which seemed to last forever, I understood the difference. It was my connection to the Fairies that made the change possible, I knew that instantly. That was a power that Ankiala couldn't understand, couldn't internalise; she was of *this* world, the Newtonian World, where Magic and science intertwined in their own bizarre way. The Sidhe's power was different, and my connection to them had only grown in the months since I'd first met Sutton in the Conclave, which was the only chance she'd have had to get a real taste of me.

It was almost enough to make one believe in destiny. Was there any other living human being who could have been in that place, at that time, with the powers and advantages necessary to make that *one* attack in that manner?

Without Evelina and Gwendolyn *both*, I would have failed. Without Cassandra's gun, I'd have failed, the same with Demise's staff, Price's information, which had come through Tethys... The most important people in my life each played a pivotal role in helping me be in the right place at the right time, able to do what was necessary.

That thought was simply terrifying. What if I'd made different choices?!

What if I hadn't gone to that conference with the Fairies? What if Demise hadn't wanted to become one of my Wardens?! It could all have been so different!

Those thoughts nearly made me lose my concentration, which would have killed me, so I pushed them aside and focussed, though I needn't have worried so much. My powers *were* different enough, not a huge amount, but just enough to make Ankiala's greatest defence fail, and my attack strike home in Shadowborn flesh.

My Lance tore those tendrils apart, reducing them to ash, and Ankiala screamed as her dead body fell back into the deep places of the world. Sutton's body fell to the ground, like a puppet with its strings cut, falling out of sight behind the platform. The doorway slammed shut, sealing the Elder God' corpse away forever.

I couldn't believe it. For a long moment, I just stood there like an idiot, not quite able to take it in.

I'd done it! I actually managed to double talk and trick one of the ancient terrors of the worl- wait a minute, why was Sutton still moving?

No. Not Sutton.

Ankiala stood under her own power, her eyes blazing with rage. It would appear that things hadn't gone *precisely* according to the plan.

I checked my shields, which had recharged and were as ready to go as could reasonably be expected. I had a Plan B. It was really more of a cleanup plan, but needs must.

"I'm going to spend a long, *long* time making you pay for that," she growled.

She raised her hand and Shadows came for me.

My constructs were generally shaped like the elements; flowing waves of dark water, or sharp and flickering tongues of black flame when I was annoyed. Hers were more organic, taking on the shapes of animals and monsters from the deep depths of time in which she'd been 'born'.

They came for me in a flood, shaped from terror and ugliness...

And stopped five feet short of me, changing and smoothing out as they hit my aura; becoming my recognised forms, linking to my own Shadows and pulling away from her to surround me.

I smiled.

Ankiala's face widened in horror and shock.

"No... that's impossible! How are you doing that?!"

"The Shadows are mine," I said coldly, "They've forgotten you."

She screamed in rage and pure hatred.

"Maybe, but you can't command them if you're dead, and Namia Sutton knew more than enough to tear you apart!"

She called Light.

I called something else entirely, even as I was diving out of the way.

Bring this place down! I commanded down my link before calling my Shadows to pull me around and away from her attacks. I returned fire with Demise's Staff, but Ankiala had Sutton's memories; she knew how to duel and caught my blast on a Will shield.

I felt most of the energy I had left pour into the Shadow Realm, and *dozens* of Elementals sprang forth throughout the warren. There was nobody living left to protect, Sutton had killed everyone who wasn't a Hyde monstrosity and so my creatures started tearing it to pieces with wild abandon. The whole place began to shake as centuries-old caverns and chambers were torn apart.

"NO!" Ankiala screamed as dark shapes appeared and tore into the columns keeping the chamber upright. There was a great thunder above; the roof trembled, shedding decades of dust that made me sneeze. Ankiala lashed out at the Elementals, Light attacks that forced them to retreat, but the damage was done. I saw the church far above collapse onto the level below, the impact brought that floor down too, and then the next.

"This isn't over, Shadowborn!" Ankiala screamed as I opened a Gate behind a column and leapt through it, "I hate you! I'll hate you forever! You'll never be safe from me!"

The gate slammed shut as the descending tide of rock struck the chamber, and I was plunged into safe darkness. I watched the Shadow Realm change to reflect the real world. Ankiala's grave was quickly buried under thousands of tons of rock.

The Elementals returned to the Realm, swimming gently through the darkness, surrounding me.

"Thank you," I said, "you saved my life."

Honour for the One.

Always, we are here.

I expressed my thanks again and let myself relax a little as I Shadow-Walked back in the direction of the plaza where I'd left the others.

Naturally, I picked the wrong moment to emerge and nearly died by friendly fire.

Again.

CHAPTER 30

I emerged back into the real world in the shadow of a tree inside the circle of Wardens. The stench of death was all around us, and there were piles of dead monsters everywhere.

One of the Wardens closest to me turned and launched a Lightning Bolt at my face, letting out a startled "Danger!"

Thankfully I was still shielded, or I'd have died. As it was, my defences took a hard hit, losing the outer layer; I turned to glare at the idiot.

"What is it with everybody's Wardens trying to do me in!" I barked loudly, turning every head towards me.

"God, Matty!" Cassandra said, darting towards me. I dropped my shields and was subjected to a thorough going over for injuries before a crushing hug, "Was that you? Did you knock over a *church*?"

"Technically, the Shadow Elementals I summoned did, so... no? -ish?" I offered as Demise came over and did much the same thing as Cassandra did, only with an even tighter hug at the end.

"You two saved my life tonight," I said, handing their weapons back to them, "I'd have been so thoroughly screwed."

They smiled.

"What happened?" Kron said, storming towards us, Killian, Palmyra and Hopkins on her tail.

I laid out what had happened, while looking for a place to sit down, I was knackered.

"So, she's dead?" Kron asked sadly.

"Hardly," Ankiala said from right behind me.

Always... *always* from bloody right behind me!

We all turned, lightning-fast towards the danger, every-one readying Magic. But Ankiala had her hands raised, and wasn't using Magic at all; she just stood there, calmly.

"Peace, Archons, I mean no harm. I'm here to surrender."

"What?" I asked.

"Surrender, Lord Shadow," she said, "I offer it. I'm as much the victim of Namia Sutton's schemes as anyone else, I merely wish the chance to prove it."

"Oh, this stinks," I said.

"You murdered that girl," Kron said, readying her Magic.

"I only acted in self-defence!" Ankiala said desperately, "She meant to enslave me! Use me as a weapon, how could I not act to free myself?"

Killian walked forwards, "Easy, Van, hear her out."

Bad idea, bad, bad idea...

"I can tell you everything she knew about her Legion's criminal enterprises. I can tell you every evil thing she ever did, and I'll do it willingly. All I ask is that you listen, and judge me fairly. Lord Shadow saw everything that happened. My... nature allowed me to watch the world outside my prison, at least a little, I've been watching him; he's a man of honour. Tell them what role I had in my resurrection, my lord."

I coughed, vastly annoyed, because she had a point. Whatever she *intended* to do, she hadn't *actually* done any-thing except free herself from probable, no, *certain* enslave-ment...

"Nothing that I saw," I admitted, "which doesn't mean that she hadn't been working behind the scenes somehow."

"How could I? I was dead," Ankiala pointed out.

Oh, I hate it when the bad guys make good points!

We were all looking rather shifty at this point, itching to blast her, but without any actual reason to do so. It was making me twitchy.

"And you're willing to come quietly?" Kron asked.

"Of course," Ankiala said, "I have to live in this world. I can't afford to make enemies of you. Accept my surrender, hear what I have to say, and I'll accept your fair judgement."

"We're listening," Kron said.

"I would point out that the last words you said to me before the church came down were, 'I'll hate you forever, you'll never be safe from me'," I said.

"I've mellowed," she countered.

"In the last half-hour?"

"I'm not like you, Shadow," the monster said, "I think faster than your kind."

"Doubt you think faster than me," I replied, glaring.

I had, after all, just out-thought her quite handily... I'm still quite proud of that.

"Oh, I know you think you're clever. Tell me, how ever were you in two places at once? You took that whore from one of my- *her* laboratories just as you were bringing down another."

"Call her a whore," I said coldly, "One more time."

The look in my eye made her gulp and step back.

"My apologies, Shadow," she said, "I didn't know you were so... attached to the creature."

"I'm beginning to get quite annoyed with you," I said; the world started to get that little bit darker.

"What's this, Graves?" Kron asked.

"Liaison issue," I replied.

"Right, say no more," Kron said, turning her stare back to Ankiala.

"Really?" the Fallen Goddess asked, "Just like that, you trust him? He broke his promise, after all, he wasn't watched by Demise while he was rescuing his demon."

Apparently an Elder God that lost the majority of their powers or which was reduced to some sort of mortal or semi-mortal state was called a Fallen God; the terminology could drive you insane. I was brought up in a house where only one God got a capital letter, for heaven's sake, this was just maddening.

"Technically speaking, my timeline was altered, and I

was never actually gone. Technically," I said.

"Barracks room lawyer," Kron muttered, but she smiled, just a tiny little bit, like a hair-crack in a granite cliff.

I shrugged.

"And also a corruptor. Look what he did to your loyal retainer, Lord Death. And the secret she carries, oh my..." Ankiala said, "You'd all kill her right here if you knew what she'd done. She betrayed you all."

There was a rasp of steel and the sound of guns being cocked as Cassandra and Demise pointed weapons at her.

"Shut your mouth," Demise snarled, her blade glowing black with Entropy.

"Really? After what you did to your new 'lord', *now* you act righteous?" Ankiala said smugly.

"I really think that's quite enough out of you," I said; my Shadows came at my call.

I didn't believe a word of it. This bitch was trying to play a mind-game on us.

"Lord Shadow, that's enough!" Killian said.

I grunted, but obeyed, pushing my Shadows away.

"Demise, what's she talking about?" Killian asked.

"My lord," Demise said, "It's... I..."

"She violated his mind," Ankiala said smiling in a manner I found deeply offensive, to the point where I almost wiped it off her face.

"What?" Hopkins, Palmyra, Killian, Kron and I all said at once.

"Still think you're smart, Shadow?" she said, "The vampire bit him, formed the bond with him, which he *liked*, by the way, let her mistress do the same... and then they helped precious Demise invade his mind. All for his own good of course; the things she told those pathetic creatures to get them to cooperate... I'm an ancient terror from the depths of time, and even I was impressed."

Alright, I must admit, I didn't see *that* one coming. I figured Demise's secret shame involved her getting a little handsy with Crystal or something, not... this.

Demise looked like she was going to be sick. Her sword was shaking in her grip. I put my hand over the one that was holding it.

Don't get me wrong, I was pretty pissed off for a second there; but all I had to do was give it even the tiniest bit of thought, and that quickly turned to something else entirely.

"Not your fault, Dee," I said softly, "I was dosed with Succubus stench. Nobody's actions that night were their own. I know that you had a good reason for what you did, hell, I could *list* them right now."

And I could, too. She was the one sent to watch me, she had a prime opportunity to look in my head and *really* see what kind of man I was, to learn how to defeat me if it came to that, and she'd taken it. It also wasn't lost on me that it was after that intrusion that we'd really started to grow close. She taken a look at the real me... and decided that she liked me after all. She hadn't even told the others about the Time Sling, and she had to have known. How could I hate her for *any* of that?

"I could list the *other* reasons, if you like?" Ankiala chimed in.

I hit her with a Coma Hex and she dropped like a landed tuna.

Everyone looked over at me.

"What?" I asked, "It was the very least evil thing I could have done. Also, it's reassuring that her brain still works like a human's."

"How can we interrogate her with one of your un-un-tangleable Hexes in her head?" Kron asked.

"I think that's the nicest thing you've ever said to me, did it hurt?" I asked sweetly.

"You want another beating?" she asked.

"I'm actually starting to enjoy the rough treatment."

"And you say I'm a freak," Palmyra said with a grin.

Demise was still shaking, and I put a hand on her shoulder. She was looking down.

"Give us a sec?" I asked. They nodded and backed off a bit, dragging Ankiala along by Will, her head juddering along the ground.

"Look at me," I said gently.

She shook her head.

"Please?"

It took a minute, but she did what I'd asked.

"You've got nothing to be ashamed of," I said, quietly, "You are my friend. Nothing else matters to me than that. If you are feeling bad, don't. There's no tether for it in me."

"You don't understand, Mathew," she said, "You trusted me, you saved me, and I still mistrusted you enough to do what I did... and then I saw you, really saw you, and I couldn't bear it. I'm so ashamed."

"Dee, I can count on one hand the number of people who really know me, and the number of people who know me and still want to be around me is even smaller than that! You know me now, and you're still here. That's a gift, my friend. Am I thrilled that you went poking into my private places? No, of course not, but I'm happy about how it turned out, really I am. If anything, I trust you *more* now, not less. I trust you, my Warden. You keep me safe. That's what matters."

She looked in my eyes, searching for the lie, I think, but she wouldn't find one there.

"How can you forgive what I did?" she asked.

"One, and I hope I'm saying this for the last time, not your fault; two, you were doing your job; and three, you kept my secrets, not that I had too many of them."

That raised a smile from her. I cupped her face, and she leant into the touch.

"And four, most importantly, you meant me no harm, and would never do me any, because you are my friend and my guardian, even then, especially now. I want this to be the last time you let this hurt you, understand?"

"Yes my lord," she said with a smile.

"Good. Now, let's go get a couple of quiet kicks in at

Ankiala while she's passed out," I said.

Demise laughed.

We rejoined Cassandra while Palmyra sidled up to Demise.

"I will pay you so much money for any details I can tease him with later," she stage-whispered.

"Pixie attacks, all aimed at you," I said over my shoulder.

"Spoilsport," Palmyra said.

"The vampire said she recorded everything," Demise said.

"What?" I asked, turning around.

Demise clapped her hands over her mouth.

"I don't know why I said that!" she said, mortified.

"Lucille!" I said with a glare.

"What? I have a trustworthy face," she said, all innocence.

Hopkins was shaking with suppressed laughter. Killian was looking away, grinning evilly. Kron looked disgusted.

We went back to the Hotel, and they had me dismantle my Coma Hex, but not until they'd slapped Spelleater Manacles on Ankiala.

"Well, that was undignified," the Fallen Goddess said after she'd awoken.

"Don't annoy the First Shadow, it's a lesson we all learn in time," Hopkins said, "He can be a little touchy and holds a grudge."

I was sitting at the side of the room on a sofa next to Cassandra, Demise standing next to me. Ankiala was in an armchair, Killian sat in front of the prisoner, Palmyra and Hopkins nearby, on sofas. Various Wardens were close, Spells ready to go if she proved problematic.

"You're telling me? He decapitated me for all intents and purposes," Ankiala replied.

"Oh dear, how sad, never mind," I said in a dark mutter,

quoting one of my father's favourite TV shows.

"Explain that," Killian said.

"I took this body and all it contained," Ankiala said, "For all intents and purposes, in that instant, I became Namia Sutton, just with a little extra... 'me' thrown in. I then began to hollow her out so I could get the rest of me in; widen her, what do you call it... Well? I managed to get the core of my personality and memories in, at which point your intrepid fifth cut me off! Which should have been impossible. I underestimated you, Shadow."

"You wouldn't be the first, and God willing, you won't be the last," I said.

Ankiala snorted, "Anyway, I barely got a tenth of myself into this shell, and that is diminished further by the alien nature of this body. I'll not be up to whatever my full strength is now for months, maybe years, and the Shadows don't truly obey me anymore," that last said with a venomous look my direction.

I grinned evilly.

"My point is that you have little to fear from me. I want to live. I want to grow rich and strong and decadent. I have no choice but to live peacefully and as well as I can. I will not go back to that endless, awful cold," she said, rubbing her stolen arms for warmth.

"And getting into a war with you... and him," she continued, glaring at me at that last bit, "is badly counter to that goal. I just want to get as far away from this place as I can, go someplace beautiful and dark for a while. Get used to this... three dimensional flesh."

"And what guarantees do you offer that you won't turn on us one day?" Kron asked.

"Isn't that really your department, Lady Time?" Ankiala answered.

"Too many possible futures, some good, some bad, some middling. No certainty," Kron said.

"Isn't that true of everyone?" Ankiala asked.

Kron grumbled, but nodded.

"Are we forgetting the whole mortal terror, certain horror thing?" I asked.

"May not apply anymore," Kron said thoughtfully, "I hope. She isn't Namia Sutton anymore."

I slumped back on the sofa.

"So, what do you think?" Ankiala said, "Are you going to condemn me for saving myself? Will you accept the information I have on Sutton's little empire in exchange for my life?"

Kron and Killian looked at each other and then at Hopkins and Palmyra.

"We need that information," Kron said.

"Couldn't she give it to us from safely inside the Farm?" I asked.

"Freedom or nothing," Ankiala said, "I won't be confined again."

Kron led us into an adjoining room. I knew where this was going, and I hated it. I wanted that creature safely locked away where she couldn't do something unpleasant to me in the future.

They discussed it, but they already had a consensus.

"Matty, you've been uncharacteristically quiet; it's bothering me," Hopkins said.

I sighed, rubbing my eyes, "Fine, let her go, just don't say I didn't warn you if she turns up one day with my head on a pike."

"Such a drama queen," Palmyra said.

I muttered under my breath, but the matter was resolved. And I think that it was almost certainly down to one factor: Ankiala was the occupant of Namia Sutton's body. My brother and sisters were hoping (somewhat desperately in my opinion) that Namia was still in there somewhere. I could empathise with that train of thought, the only problem was that they didn't really *know* Namia Sutton, they only knew the mask she presented to them.

The *real* problem was that Sutton probably *was* in there

somewhere, and she was all mixed up with an ancient horror, neither of whom liked me very much. I couldn't see a way those two ingredients could come up with something that wouldn't poison me at some point down the road.

They finalised the deal, which I thought was vastly skewed towards Ankiala, but nobody asked for my input. She would sit down with someone from the SCA and tell them everything she could remember, at which point she would be released and could lead whatever life she saw fit, as long as she didn't break any laws (I almost choked at the idea of a law-abiding Elder God, and got the Kron stink-eye for my trouble).

Ankiala was placed securely in one of the bedrooms with a couple of Wardens while the rest of us went out and did what we could to clean up some of the mess, not that there was much left; the SCA had been very effective in their efforts while we were dealing with Ankiala.

I spent most of my time healing injuries with Palmyra, barely managing to heal one person to her five or six, but it helped, and it felt... good, like the way Magic should be used. Human casualties had been relatively low, a few dozen people dead, a couple of thousand injured. After all, this was Gardenia; people who didn't know when to get under cover didn't tend to last long.

The non-human casualties, though...

They'd been horrific.

There was no healing the damage to their brains, that spell had been ugly, effective and irreversible. What remained, the ravenous bodies, had needed to be put down the hard way.

Thousands were dead.

Many had been true monsters *before* the spell was cast, but many weren't. Thank God the children weren't affected. I was informed later that they were re-homed successfully with other packs and groups around the country, but what a mess...

Afterwards, Killian took charge of Ankiala and secured her in his... I'm guessing 'lair' is the correct term, until she could be interviewed.

I hoped I wouldn't be seeing her again in a hurry.

Three *long* days after we'd turned up to sort out that wretched mess, I staggered back onto the Blackhold grounds through a portal Palmyra had opened for me, along with Demise and Cassandra. They'd been just as active as I had, and yet, they looked fresh as daisies, while I could have auditioned for an extra in a zombie movie without bothering with makeup. I was still far from recovered from the Life Siphon and I was badly weak after my poisoning, so the last few days had been immensely taxing, and I desperately needed to sleep for about a week.

It was after eleven at night on a Friday, warm and humid. I yawned heavily as we walked up the stairs. I said hello to the guards on the front door, who looked tired as well, and walked into my reception room, I was heading for Tethys' office to check in before falling into bed.

I asked Cassandra to put Mira in my Library for me; she'd been very useful the last few days, offering pertinent and useful advice. I was glad I'd pinched her.

"There you are, you bastard!" Tethys said before I'd made it three steps, "You drop half a hundred vampires and other assorted creatures on me and just bugger off for three days?!"

"I was busy?" I offered lamely.

She pulled me into a hug and looked me over with a grimace.

"You look like crap, have you been eating right? Sleeping enough?" she said, stroking my cheeks.

"God no," I said with another stifled yawn.

"Idiot," she admonished, "And you two were supposed to be taking care of him!"

"What were we supposed to do? He's an Archon and he's tricky," Cassandra said with a glower.

"That's why we normally leave him with Kandi," Tethys said, "She can handle him."

"Hey," I complained half-heartedly, "And where is Kandi?"

"Oh, she went into the East Wing to 'visit with the pretty vampires', I haven't seen her since, except to briefly emerge for food, with shaky legs."

"Oh crap," I said, walking in that direction, "If she's been dosed with venom, I'm going to burn someone."

"She's fine," Tethys said, "I'm keeping an eye on her, and ensured that wouldn't happen. I believe your Crystal's been doing a bang-up job of keeping her intact, so to speak."

I sighed, rubbing my eyes.

"Okay," I said, "Karina get out alright?"

"Oh yes, she's in the East Wing, too," Tethys said with a grin.

"Dare I ask what *you've* been doing?" I said.

Tethys smiled naughtily.

"That's what I thought," I said with a smile, "I'm going to take the world's longest shower, and then I'm going to sleep."

I walked towards the stairs, Tethys in tow. I told her what had happened as we walked. I changed and showered, still talking while she waited outside the bathroom, before dropping into bed.

She hopped in with me and curled up against my side, her arm around me.

"The next time those bothersome Liaisons show up, let's refer them to another Archon," Tethys said.

I held her close and relaxed.

"Agreed," I said, "This whole 'doing good' thing is a pain in the arse. I want to go back to selfish, mean-spirited sneakery. It's easier."

"Maybe, but there are fifty-four people in this house and countless others in Gardenia who would be dead if not for what you did."

"What *we* did," I said, "All of us; team effort, all around. You being the team, I being the effort."

She snorted and tweaked my nose.

"So, these vampires..."

"Yes?"

"Can I keep them?" Tethys asked.

I groaned.

CHAPTER 31

And you'd think that would be the end of it, wouldn't you?

But nooo. That wretched Demon had to come back and have a good gloat.

I must admit, though, I did like the way she'd taken to waking me up; that soft, building movement that culminates in a fantastic kiss. Naturally it all happened while I was too groggy to really appreciate it. There was something softer in her gestures this time, though, something just a little more indirect and teasing than before.

I woke up and Gabrielle pulled away to sit straddling me, her hands on my chest. Rose was perched on the bed next to us, and Tethys was fast asleep next to me.

"Still don't know how to use a phone, I see?" I said, rubbing my eyes.

"I can use other things," the Demon said, moving her hips just a little.

"Haven't we done this dance before?" I asked.

"Oh yes," she replied, leaning down again, "We both know all the steps now. And we both know how this ends."

"Rose, can you control your friend?" I asked.

"Would if I could," she said, "But she's your business, now."

"How does that compute?" I asked, a little exasperated.

"You... opened a loophole in the rules when you fed her," Rose said, "Willingly at that. I'd be able to stop her if it was involuntary, but alas..."

"Do I have to Shadow you or something? I'm knackered

and I can't promise precision," I said to Gabrielle.

"If you are so determined for me to get off you, then why are your hands on my bottom?" she whispered.

I pulled my hands away and the Demon laughed as I blushed.

"What can I do for you two?" I asked with as much dignity as I could manage.

"This is your debriefing," Gabrielle said, her eyes dancing with mischief, "so to speak."

"A double entendre from a single track mind, how interesting," I said deadpan.

"Careful, Magician," Gabrielle said, "You'd be amazed at how easily I can take offence."

"You can imagine my terror," I said.

"Keep talking," Gabrielle said, "I enjoy your defiance in the face of defeat."

"I swear, everyone I meet these days is so dramatic," I said, "they can never just say hello or show up with a cake. It's always, 'you're facing defeat', and 'here's this bucket of drugs you have to deal with'."

Rose chuckled. Gabrielle rolled her eyes and made a disgusted sound. That's me, exasperating even creatures bred to exasperate.

"Can I ask a question now that I have you here?" I asked.

"You can always *ask*," Rose said, "But that doesn't necessarily mean we'll answer."

I rolled my eyes; see what I mean about the 'dramatic' thing?

"Well, I was thinking, a great many things had to go right for all of this to turn out without the world ending, and I was wondering... how much was... well..."

"Divine intervention?" Rose asked.

"Essentially."

"That's a complicated question," Rose replied.

What a surprise.

Rose scrunched her pretty nose, thinking.

"There's no such thing as fate, or destiny, Vanessa Kron would tell you that. Time is a colossal web of infinite potential futures, some of which are more likely than others. The number of potential futures where Sutton and Ankiala didn't cause an apocalypse were... few, to say the least. Most of *those* ended with you dead and the next apocalyptic event largely unopposed."

The *next* one?! I barely survived this one!

"In a situation like that, where the human race faces its end, and *only* in such a situation, we are allowed to prod, just a little, enough to get the right people into the right place. Whether or not they do the right *thing* must always be up to them. To you."

I let out a puff of air.

"So, I did the right thing, then?" I asked, hesitantly; there sure were a lot of dead non-humans in Gardenia, if that was the case.

"You did very well, Mathew," Rose said, "Far better than we anticipated."

"Are you sure? I'm not sure I *could* have made a bigger mess of that," I replied, "aside from the whole... no-end-of-the-world bit."

Tethys was still asleep by the way; they must have enchanted her, or be doing something with Time again.

"Are you sure? Think it through, you destroyed the labs, which forced Sutton into a precipitous action *months* before she was ready with either the correct enchantments, research or a proper host body for Ankiala," Rose said, "You made ultimate success possible, and acted in accordance with your conscience; in effect, the right way, in the right time. Things shouldn't have worked out this well. Not even slightly. It was expected that you would be more... conservative in your actions."

"You mean cowardly," I said, "It's alright; I understand why you'd think that."

"I like cowards," Gabrielle purred, "So much easier to

manipulate."

"I never thought you were a coward, Mathew," Rose said, "I just thought you were too... innocent for things to turn out this way."

Gabrielle snorted, "Not that innocent. He fed us some lovely drug-makers after all," she said nastily.

"Nobody's ever letting that go, are they?" I asked.

"Embrace your dark side, Archon. Admit that you enjoyed feeding those people to demons; go on, I won't tell anyone," she whispered in my ear.

"I'm finding you less attractive the more time I spend with in your presence."

She stuck out her tongue. It was almost cute. Almost.

"Anyway, you have the thanks of our masters for maintaining the balance, and preventing any further atrocities," Rose said, "We look forward to a long and productive relationship."

"This last little job of yours cost me in ways I can barely calculate," I said, "Please don't make it too often."

"I'm sorry for what it cost you, Mathew," Rose said, "I would end that pain for you if I could. But you sacrificed so that others could be safe. Cathy would have given her life for that, if that helps."

"It doesn't," I said quietly.

"Well, you know what they say... nothing gets you over the last one like the next one," Gabrielle said.

I raised an eyebrow at her and she sighed before hopping off me, "I'll get you."

"Why?" I asked, "You can't seriously believe I'm worth it on any level? Is it a 'notch' thing, just to say you have?"

"Must you make it sound so tawdry?" she asked, "So clinical?"

"So it's a corruption thing?" I asked slyly.

She snorted irately.

I rolled my eyes and sat up so I could rub them.

"I'm not interested in that sort of relationship," I said,

"But you knew that. You are tempting beyond all reason, and one of the most attractive creatures I've ever laid eyes on, which is precisely why you can't get to me. I have no interest in being with someone who isn't really interested in me. And you may be attracted to the challenge, but you're not attracted to me. Am I wrong?"

"Very," she said, turning those red eyes on me, "Once correct. Now very, very wrong."

"Well, you would say that," I said, flopping back onto my pillow.

Rose laughed; a high, lovely sound that startled the Demon and made her scowl.

"We'll see you around, Mathew," the Angel said. She leant in and kissed my cheek and then they were gone.

Tethys stirred and wrapped herself back around me. I smiled, held her, and drifted back off to sleep.

The door creaked open at about three in the morning as Kandi staggered in, none too quietly. Thankfully Tethys slept like a log, because she did *not* enjoy being woken up. Kandi flopped onto the bed on my other side, quite exhausted.

"Shame on you for bringing those vampires in here, Matty. Do you have any idea what they know how to do? All I had to say was, 'Matty's a friend of mine', and my legs haven't worked right since."

I pulled the duvet out from under her and tucked it around her, pulling her in to me.

"You smell awful," I said.

She snorted and nuzzled my neck.

"Glad you're home," she whispered.

"Me too."

I slept for fifteen hours after that. I woke up feeling slightly better; Kandi sitting next to me with a bag of frozen peas between her legs, playing with my phone again.

"What happened to you?" I asked.

"I don't want to talk about it," she said with a blush.

"Want me to fix it?" I asked.

"God, would you? I can't sit down on anything other than this bed!"

"When did you even do this?" I asked, casting Mage Sight and adjusting it so I could look at her physiology.

"After breakfast," she said, "I was eager to get back, so I rushed things, and now my bits hurt."

"Ohhh," I said as I looked her over, "Kandi, you have to slow down. I'm seeing more than a dozen pulled muscles, three sprains and some pretty badly wrenched ligaments, and that's in addition to the... downstairs damage."

"I know, I know, I've learned my lesson, take it easy with the supernatural creatures. I suggested that they just slip me a little blood, but they refused to do that under your roof, the pansies."

I went to work repairing her self-inflicted injuries one by one until she slumped back against the headboard and tossed the peas onto the floor.

She kissed my cheek and leant against me, "Oh, thank you. I was not in a good way."

"Nitwit," I said, kissing the side of her head, "What would I ever do if you did yourself a mischief I couldn't fix?"

"You're Mathew Graves, you can fix anything," she said, taking my hand.

"Silly girl," I said, "I can't tell you how much I wish that were true."

"You can't call me a silly girl, I'm older that you!" she protested.

"By fifteen minutes-"

"Eight months," she interrupted.

"There's a difference between age and maturity, you know," I replied.

"If you hadn't just put out the fire in my ladybits, I'd be kicking your arse right now," she replied with a glare, ruined by the grin peeking its way out.

"Damn, I'm used to freezing ladybits on sight, but now I

went and did it on purpose?" I said with a long-suffering sigh.

Kandi squeaked and clubbed me in the side.

"Arse!" she said, having wrestled me onto my back.

"Hey, I'm not well; the doctor said no rough stuff!" I complained.

"You're objecting to a spicy redhead lying on you?" she asked softly, brushing her nose against mine.

"God no, not when it's you, certainly," I said, tucking a lock of hair behind her ear.

"Careful you, my bits may have broken down from slight overuse, but keep up that kind of look and I'll crank them right back up again," she said.

I laughed and hugged her.

"You know, sometimes, I truly despair at the horrible things people can do to each other, but then I come here and I spend time with you and Tethys and the others... and I'm hopeful again. I just wanted you to know that."

"You're such a big girl," she said, smiling down at me.

"It's been said."

"It's okay, you know I can make do with that."

I laughed again and she looked in my eyes. She stroked my cheek gently...

And the door opened, killing the moment stone dead.

Kandi let out a frustrated sound as she looked at the figure in the doorway, which turned out to be Tethys.

"Matty," she said softly, "You have a visitor."

"Dare I ask?"

"Cathy, Matty. It's Cathy," Tethys said.

"Okay," I said, sitting up, "Is it too late to get rid of her?"

"What do you think?" Tethys said wryly.

"Kandi, upsie, I need to hide in the- I mean get dressed," I said.

"We'll give you a minute to *get dressed*," Tethys said pointedly, all but commanding me not to hide, "Come on Kandi."

Kandi stood and followed Tethys.

"I was *this* close!" she said after they were out of sight.

"Really? Damn it, that girl has been a pain in my arse since he started dating her," Tethys replied.

"I can hear you!" I said.

"Stop eavesdropping!" Tethys barked, making me smile for a moment.

Okay.

Okay.

Alright.

It's fine... I could do this. I'd just faced down an immeasurable horror, I could meet my ex-girlfriend.

I pulled fresh clothes on and marched firmly towards the door. I had my hand on the handle, I was determined!

For about a second.

Nope.

Couldn't do it.

I shut the curtains and moved to switch off the light.

The door opened, it was Crystal.

"You were taking too long, Tethys sent me to check on you. Your ex is waiting in the drawing roo-"

She saw where my hand was poised and immediately twigged that I was planning to escape through the Shadow Realm.

"Really?" she asked, raising her pretty eyebrow.

"Oh yes," I said, reaching forward again.

She captured my hand in one of hers and very elegantly pulled it to the small of her back, sliding up against me.

"You run, she wins," Crystal said.

"She broke my heart, Crystal."

"What's the worst she could do after that?" she asked, stroking my face.

"I don't know, and I'm not over-eager to find out!"

"She may be here to win you back, you don't know."

"I am not a toy to be picked up and put down at her whim!" I said, a little harshly, "I may not be much, but I'm worth more than that! And no, she was very clear on that point."

"Mathew, trust someone who found out the hard way, knowing is far better than speculating. If you hide instead of facing her, that's a decision that will haunt you," she said gently.

I scowled. She smiled at me and pulled away, leading me by the hand.

"Want to make out a little in front of her?" she asked coquettishly, "Make her a bit jealous?"

"Maybe next time."

She giggled, "And I don't like her at all, so you know. Far too prim and prissy for you," she said as we walked down the stairs and left towards the drawing room. Crystal opened the door for me.

Tethys had redecorated again. The wide room was now filled with comfortable sofas and armchairs, coffee tables strategically dotted about the place.

Cathy was wearing casual clothes; skirt, cotton shirt and jacket with thick socks, stockings and polished shoes. She was beautiful, her hair pulled back into a bun, her glasses slightly slipped down her nose.

Tethys was there, glaring slightly at my ex-girlfriend. The very sight of her sent a lance of pain through my chest. She stood as I approached and winced as she saw me. Well, I couldn't blame her for that; between the Siphon and the poison, I was a horror show, paler than I'd ever been, slightly more gaunt in some places and saggy in others, it wasn't pretty.

I walked over to the sofa opposite hers, bypassing any awkwardness over any sort of hug-type situation. She was watching me like a mouse in the presence of a snake, very intent and careful, like even the slightest movement would set me off, or something.

I sat and she followed suit, Tethys slid out discreetly.

Cathy's eyes looked around the room while I waited, almost entirely disinclined towards helping her out of the silence.

"The place looks good," she finally said.

"Thank you," I said as politely as I could.

"I imagine Tethys is owed the compliment far more than you, though," she said with a small smile.

"Why are you here, Cathy?" I asked in a voice that sounded tired even to me.

"I... I didn't like how we left things."

"How... *we* left things, you say?"

"How I left things," she replied, looking down.

"How would you have preferred to have left things?" I asked, falling back on my tried and tested verbal nonsense that covers up my insecurity and hurt feelings.

"Not like that," she said, "I... you are my best friend, Matty. I hate that we haven't talked. I hate that I had to hurt you like that. I miss you."

"How's Bill?" I asked.

She started, "He's fine," she said, her voice a little shaky.

"Funny, he hasn't called, picked up or answered a text in almost as long as you," I said slowly.

I stared her down.

"It's not what you think, I swear."

"Hardly matters, does it? You made it quite clear that I have no further say in your... affairs."

"He made a pass. I said no, alright? Is that what you want to hear?"

It very definitely was *not* what I wanted to hear. That hurt quite a bit; maybe Bill hadn't managed to escape the effects of Source, after all. I couldn't imagine the Bill I knew doing something like that.

"Again, you made it perfectly clear that what I want doesn't make the slightest difference to you," I said, pushing past it, "I nearly died. And you just left me in that hospital. After that day, I got even sicker, and that moment was the source of quite a few delirium nightmares. You took away my hope in that moment, do you understand that?"

"Yes! Of course I understand, Matty, and I'm so sorry! I came here to say I was sorry! I'm so sorry!"

I sat there sadly.

"Do you want me back?" I asked, half-hopefully, "Is that why you're here?"

She looked away. No, she didn't. God, I wish she hadn't come, this was agony.

"No, I don't, not like that. I want my friend back," she said, tears in her eyes, "I miss you so much!"

"So you're willing to have me as a friend, knowing what I do, but not a boyfriend? Interesting," I said.

"Don't be like that, Matty, don't you understand that I can't be with you like that if there's a chance you won't be there in the future?" she said, slightly desperately.

I sighed and rubbed my face, "Yes, I can understand," I said sadly, "but what are you hoping to get out of this? You aren't coming to Stonebridge University. We won't even see each other."

"I want to be there for you, and I don't want to lose touch with you, not after everything we've been through. I want to talk to you, to know that I can call and you'll pick up."

"Okay," I said, "We'll do that, I guess."

She nodded, and the silence came back with a vengeance.

"Call me then?" she said, standing up, eager to get out of there, I thought.

"Yeah," I said. I opened the door to the drawing room and found Kandi with her ear to the keyhole.

"Really?" I asked.

"I was just checking the fixtures for... holes and wood-worms and stuff," she said sheepishly.

"Why don't you go check the fixtures upstairs?" I suggested with a glare. She grinned and darted away.

I walked Cathy through a deserted house and out to the front gate.

"Bye Matty," she said softly.

"Bye Cath," I said, barely preventing my voice from trembling. She got in a cab and left. I walked back inside, where Demise, Cassandra and Tethys were waiting.

"The traitor, Hedrin," Demise whispered, "It would be my pleasure to kill him for you, my Lord."

She was perfectly serious. She'd do it and not sweat at all.

I almost said yes.

And in that moment, something nasty woke up inside me.

It wasn't anything really, barely a worm at the bottom of my Well, very definitely part of me, something that had always been there, dormant and quiet, something that perked up its evil little head and said *'You called?'*

No, no I didn't.

'Ha, too late, you looked at me, and now I'm awake!'

Evil.

My own personal Evil; that black kernel at the heart of every man, just waiting for the right chance to make itself known. In a Shadowborn, that was the part that used the Black.

I didn't really have a conversation with it, it wasn't a separate part of me, it was just... me. The ugly part of me that I'd been suppressing for so long. The part I'd stomped down when I met Hopkins and she taught me the error of my ways. This was the part of me that was petty and vindictive and cruel. It had always been tempered by a sense of justice and decency, but right then, it was at its strongest, glutted on pain and sadistic satisfaction over the destruction of all the evil creatures of Gardenia. And I was so sore...

I dared not look too closely at it. In my heart, I knew what was underneath it, feeding it, and I dared not admit that to myself. Not then, not ever. Not if I wanted to keep my soul.

But just in that moment... I almost lost Mathew Graves to my hate, my loss and my grief.

"No," I said after a struggle, "Thanks, though."

"Of course, my lord," she said, patting my shoulder, smiling grimly.

"I won't kill him, but I'll happily track him down and kick him square in the balls for you," Cassandra said.

"Go forth, Warden, as my emissary, and with my blessing," I said with a smile.

Cassandra smiled back and kissed my cheek before leading Demise away and leaving me with Tethys.

"Want I should arrange for a Warlock of my acquaintance to curse him with a limp doodle?" Tethys asked.

I smiled sadly and she wrapped her arms around me again.

"It's alright, Matty," she said, "It's all going to be alright."

Afterword

Thanks for reading *Shadowborn's Terror*! I hope you had as much fun reading it as I did writing it. I would like to offer a special thank-you to all my readers, and especially those who wrote to me with questions, comments and feedback; you've been a real inspiration and help to me, so thank you!

If you enjoyed the book, and you have some spare time, I would greatly appreciate a review, and any comments or questions can be sent to me directly at hdaroberts@gmail.com.

Mathew will return in *Heart's Darkness*, coming (relatively) soon.